To Everything
A Season

Also by Judith Glover

The Stallion Man
Sisters and Brothers

To Everything
A Season

Judith Glover

HODDER AND STOUGHTON
LONDON SYDNEY AUCKLAND TORONTO

British Library Cataloguing in Publication Data
Glover, Judith
 To everything a season.
 I. Title
 823′.914[F]   PR6057.L6/

 ISBN 0 340 38258 9

Hodder and Stoughton Editorial Office: 47 Bedford Square, London WC1B 3DP.

To Everything
A Season

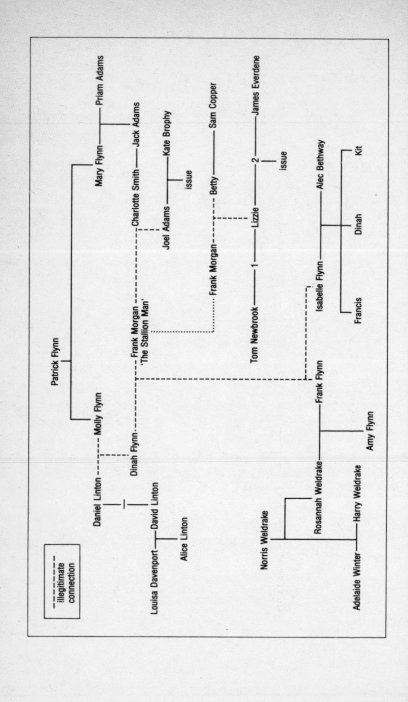

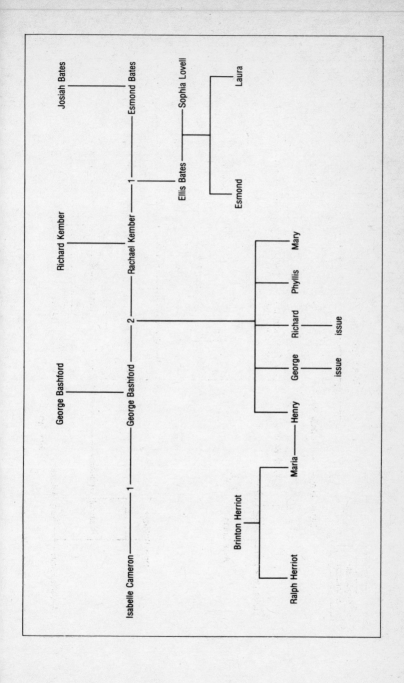

"*To everything there is a season, and a time to every purpose under the heaven: a time to be born, and a time to die . . . a time to kill, and a time to heal . . . a time to weep, and a time to laugh . . . a time to embrace, and a time to refrain from embracing . . . a time to keep, and a time to cast away . . . a time to keep silence, and a time to speak . . . a time of love, and a time of hatred . . .*"

Ecclesiastes 3:1–8

1

Amy woke with a start.

In the echoing stillness of the night the hall clock downstairs was striking three; but that was not what had disturbed her.

Then it came again. A child's scream.

She dragged herself up in bed, clumsy still with sleep as she fumbled about in the dark for the box of vesta matches to light her candle. Her wrap was lying where she had thrown it across the brass bedrail little more than two hours ago. Wearily she reached for it as she got up, pushing back the heavy waves of hair that fell round her face; then, taking the candle, opened the door and went out barefoot on to the half-landing.

The house was silent again, the stilly hush broken only by the ponderous tick of the mahogany longcase clock in the entrance hall. The young woman stood, uncertain. She hated this place with its dark panelled walls, its ugly furniture and oppressive atmosphere. She would never have agreed to come had she not been driven to leave her own home by her uncle Harry Weldrake's latest "housekeeper", a vulgar loud-voiced creature whom Amy had loathed on sight and lost no opportunity to provoke into stormy rages.

The child's scream, when it came again, made her jump violently. Shielding the guttering candleflame with a hand, she hastened down the short flight of stairs to the main landing, which ran as an open gallery almost the width of the house and overlooked the hall below. The nursery wing, occupied by little Laura Bates and her brother Esmond, lay at the far end.

"What is it? What's wrong?"

A door on the left swung open as Amy went past and the children's father, Ellis Bates, came out holding up an oil

11

lamp before him. Despite the lateness of the hour he had still not changed out of the formal dress suit worn last evening to a meeting of the board of schools inspectors.

"What's wrong?" he repeated.

"It's Laura." Amy paused and turned back to answer. "She's having another nightmare, I shouldn't wonder. What happened yesterday was enough to frighten the wits from anyone, let alone a four-year-old baby."

"She has a nervous disposition. Like her mother." Ellis Bates's voice was toneless. "Don't fuss the child, or she'll be spoiled."

"But listen to her!"

From the darkened end of the landing, beyond the closed nursery door, a low plaintive sobbing was now clearly audible.

"I've a strong stomach for most things," Amy went on heatedly, "but even I was sufficiently unsettled by that crypt to lose my sleep tonight. The stench in the place . . . half-rotten coffins stacked about the walls. Thank God the light was so dim, or we might have seen things to unquieten our minds even more . . . things best decently buried, not kept down in the cellars to be visited after tea of a Sunday—"

"I've already had your views, thank you," he interrupted tiredly. In the brightness of the lamp, the lines of weariness on his handsome features were cast into sharp relief. "Have I not promised to ensure that any future such—visit is forbidden when the children are at Heydon House?"

He had said as much before he left for the board meeting, when Amy, returning with the two little ones from spending a few days with their great-aunt, had burst into the study to protest indignantly at the horror they'd been forced to experience in her house.

It was no new thing for Laura and Esmond, that macabre descent to the family vault to pay their respects to the departed. Since the tragic death of their mother in a carriage accident two years ago in 1889, the ritual had been observed on each of their periodic visits to the great-aunt, their only surviving maternal relative, who resided alone in decaying grandeur high on the Sussex Downs, passing what remained

12

of her days in communion with the family dead interred in a private crypt in the cellars of the old house.

The visit just made had been Amy Flynn's first taste of this grisly custom. As temporary governess, she had been looking after Ellis Bates's children for less than three weeks and had been quite unprepared for the ceremony which invariably followed Sunday high tea at Heydon House. True, seven-year-old Esmond had hinted in his odd little way at something sinister; but the new governess had dismissed his words as the embroidery of a vivid imagination, being more concerned for his sister's clinging tearfulness and nightly terrors.

"Don't fuss the child," Ellis Bates repeated as she made to turn again towards the nursery. "Leave her be. She has Esmond with her for company."

"How can you be so heartless?" Amy flung back at him. "Have you never learned that children need comforting for their fears? Or has working in board schools taught you only the need for obedience and self-discipline?"

His face tightened at once.

"That will be enough. Remember you are only here in my house at the request of my mother. It was not my wish to have you."

"And it was not my wish to come. But for Laura and Esmond I'd rather have found myself lodgings elsewhere in Lewes."

She faced him across the width of the landing, and though her expression was half-hidden by the shadows of candlelight, Ellis Bates caught the note of defiance in her voice.

He could remember Amy Flynn when she had run the streets as wild as any gutter urchin. His years as a student at university, and later as a master and then inspector of schools, had removed her for long periods from his life; but he had watched her in his mind's eye mature from a child into a spirited young beauty whose nature, knowing neither fear nor falsity, exhibited warmth and directness with a strong-willed independence.

Despite the stigma of her paternity and background, she was the only woman ever to arouse in Ellis Bates the power of emotion; but he would rather have died than admit as much to anyone.

"I came here because I was needed," Amy continued, "and because Aunt Bashford asked it of me."

"My mother only made the suggestion since you required somewhere to stay, having put yourself out of home—"

"Was I then expected to stop at Tea Garden Lane as skivvy to some music-hall drab?"

"No, of course not. You know well enough my opinion of Mr Weldrake and the fashion in which he chooses to run his household. But while you are lodged beneath *my* roof, I must ask you to respect the discipline I exercise with my children. You undermine my authority and make the task of correction the more difficult by coddling Esmond and Laura with too much attention."

Amy made a half-gesture of the hand.

"At least let me go in and settle her," she said; and without waiting for further response swung round and walked from him, her bare feet moving soundlessly across the Turkey-carpeted floor.

He watched her enter the nursery, heard the gentle murmur of her voice quietening his child's sobs. Lips compressed into a bloodless line, he turned back into his own room and shut the door.

"There, there now, Laura. Hush, it's all right. There now."

Amy drew aside the bedclothes and lifted the quivering little body on to her lap, smoothing back the curls from the wet face.

"Hush, now . . . hush."

She glanced over her shoulder towards the window. Framed in its oblong, the gleam of his fair hair reflected palely against the panes, young Esmond stood staring out into the moonlit garden.

"Why is the blind up, Esmond? What are you doing there when you should be abed?"

The boy's response was curiously matter-of-fact.

"I'm looking for Mama."

"Now don't be silly," Amy said sharply. "Draw the blind at once and come away."

He obeyed reluctantly.

"But she *is* there," he insisted when the lamp on the chest

14

of drawers had been lit and the night shut out. "I saw her beneath the trees looking up at me."

"No . . ." wailed Laura, her arms tight about Amy's neck. "No, 'Smond."

"What a naughty, wicked boy you are to frighten your sister so! I shall box your ears if I hear you repeat such nonsense. Your poor Mama is dead—"

"But I did see her," he protested. "And I heard her calling to me, too, just as she does at Great-Aunt Lovell's."

Amy let out a loud sigh of exasperation. Esmond's easily stimulated mind was being fed the most unhealthy diet by these visits to Heydon House. It was a place full of horrors . . . old Mrs Lovell tapping with her stick along gloomy cellar passages . . . the echoing drip of water . . . the fetid smell of mouldering decay . . . and, worst of all, that sinister chamber of the dead shrouded in darkness behind its rusted grille. What sensitive child could possibly remain unaffected?

Yet this was an age when the ever-present reality of death was held up as a constant reminder of the transience of life and the fate awaiting every mortal soul; an age when the grave was regarded as but a prelude to the after-life, and its grisly spectre dangled before young children to frighten them into good behaviour.

"Mama is not really out there?" Laura whispered against Amy's shoulder.

"Of course not, my pet. What Esmond heard was only a little owl hunting for its supper in the garden."

"Your Mama is dead too, is she not?" Esmond came and seated himself on the bed beside them, tucking up his knees beneath his nightshirt to rest his chin.

Amy made no answer.

He turned his head sideways and looked up at her, waiting.

It would be an untruth to say yes; though for all the life Rosannah Flynn had, shut away inside an institution for the insane, she might indeed as well be in her grave.

"I have no father," Amy said finally, evasively. "He passed away when I was very small."

"How fortunate for you."

"Esmond!"

"Oh, pray don't be offended," he cried in his strange little adult fashion. "I merely meant I would've preferred it if *my* Papa had died instead. We would not have missed him quite as much as Mama, would we, Laura?"

There was a pause, then a shake of the small head beneath its tangle of brown curls.

Looking from one to the other and seeing their pale, closed faces, Amy felt the same quick pity which had first prompted her to come to this house, despite being always so ill at ease in Ellis Bates's company.

"You should not say such things of your father," she chided gently. "It is not his way to show you love as your Mama did, but you mustn't think he cares any the less for you both, even so. Be good, now, and love him as you did Mama."

Laura's arms tightened their grip and the sobs began afresh.

Since the death of Sophia Bates there had been no one to give these two much affection. Their father was coldly reserved, incapable of demonstrating his emotions openly. He provided for his children as handsomely as any other professional man of good income, with dancing and music classes, a pony for Esmond, nursery toys for Laura; yet there was never any warmth in his giving, never any spontaneous gesture of kindliness, no playful relaxation in their company, or sharing of pleasure in their interests.

Their young lives, bound by a regimen of lessons and loneliness, had grown bleakly austere without the softening presence of their mother. Little wonder they still missed her so.

Amy Flynn knew all too well what it was to hunger for a parent's love. She had never known her father—nor, indeed, her mother. For the first twelve months of life she had been fostered out with a wet nurse, and taken in by her Uncle Harry Weldrake's childless wife to be raised as their own.

Within a few years more that marriage had ended amid a blaze of public acrimony in the divorce division of the High Court of Justice. Thereafter Weldrake, though Amy's legal guardian, had lost all interest in his small niece, and until being removed to the south coast by another relative, she

16

had been left to roam the Lewes streets, dirty, unwanted, and often hungry. It was a bitter schooling and its lessons hard learned; but an inborn resilience had inured the child to need and the marks of neglect were never deep enough to scar her.

From this guttersnipe existence she was plucked at the age of seven by her father's sister Isabelle, a clergyman's wife, and taken off to the very different world of a quiet Eastbourne parish. These next few years were to prove the only settled period of Amy's childhood. Too soon, alas, they had to end: Rosannah Flynn, judged sufficiently sound of mind to leave the Bethlehem Hospital at Heathbury, was released into Harry Weldrake's keeping and her young daughter uprooted and brought back to Lewes.

Their reunion failed completely. Rosannah hysterically refused to communicate in anything other than French, and since Amy spoke none, her efforts to understand this frightening stranger produced only tears and frustration. Within two months of the release Madame de Retz—as her mother insisted on being called—had tried to burn down the house, and was hastily returned to detention in bedlam.

It had been a nightmare interlude, and the child quite naturally wanted to go back to her Aunt Belle. For some reason Weldrake would not allow it. Instead, she was made to remain at Tea Garden Lane as a drudge to the women he brought there; and though she repeatedly ran away, the Law, being on the side of the guardian, had repeatedly returned her.

"Why are you sighing so?" Esmond asked, curious.

His voice, breaking the silence now that Laura had at last been lulled to sleep in Amy's arms, made the young woman jump a little.

"Oh, was I sighing? Perhaps I'm tired. It's time we should all of us be abed."

"No—do stay a while longer," he pressed her. "You haven't said about visiting Grandmama at Bonningale. Will Papa let us go, do you think?"

"Ssh . . ." Amy put a finger to her lips. "Not so loud."

Moving quietly, she placed the sleeping child down and covered her with bedclothes; then, reaching out, took Esmond by the hand and led him to his own room next door.

17

There was only a night-light burning here and its feeble rays edged in dark relief the treasures of his young world: a case of mounted butterflies, a hobby horse, a wooden fort with painted lead soldiers, birds' eggs, books; and on the wall above his bed, a pastel portrait of Sophia Bates before her marriage.

Amy tucked him in and bent to kiss him goodnight. For a moment the boy's arms were flung about her neck and his cheek pressed to hers.

"Will he, Amy? Will he let us go to Grandmama's? You did ask him?"

"Yes."

"And what did he say?"

"That he would think about it."

Esmond released her and fell back against the pillows, his mouth turned down. Amy was leaving at the week's end on a visit to his Grandmother Bashford, who lived on the far side of the country. The family were celebrating the engagement of the youngest son, Henry Bashford, to a wealthy land-owner's daughter; and since the occasion fell within the week or so before a new governess arrived to take over Amy's responsibilities here in Lewes, she had suggested that the children go with her.

"It's always such fun at Bonningale," Esmond said wistfully from the shadows as she closed his door. "I *do* hope Papa will give his permission."

Returning towards her own room, Amy noticed at once a light shining out from it. She hastened up to the half-landing, and was astonished to find Ellis Bates there. He had changed now into a crimson quilted bed-robe and was standing at her table holding in his hand the opened pages of a letter.

"What are you doing—? How dare you read that!"

She made a swift grab for it, but he held it away at arm's length, and there was responding anger in his own voice as he snapped back, "How dare *you* invite such correspondence in my house. I have warned you before, I will not permit you to receive this man's letters."

"What business is it of yours whose letters I receive? You have no right to come prying. I suppose you saw the

18

envelope lying in the hall yesterday and let curiosity get the better of your manners."

She made another lunge. "Give me that!"

For reply Ellis Bates sent the closely-written pages fluttering to the floor. As the young woman swooped to retrieve them, he caught her by the arm and pulled her against him.

"What are you doing?" she cried out again, beating at him with her fists. "Let go of me!"

The wrap fell away in the struggle, leaving her in nothing more than her linen night-shift. For one awful moment she thought he meant to strike her; but instead, he shoved her violently aside and turned away.

After a few tense seconds he asked bitterly, "Why must you persist in encouraging Linton's attentions?"

"What attentions?"

Amy snatched up the scattered pages and thrust them out at him. "Look—you've just read for yourself what David wrote. News of Weatherfield. The village fête . . . his wife's health . . . In God's name, where is the wrong in that?"

Ellis Bates straightened the cord of his bed-robe. Already, he very much regretted inviting this scene, regretted the suspicions which had driven him against all logical reason to seek in David Linton's letter the proof of a relationship more than friendship between these two.

"You know where the wrong lies."

He had no doubt that the respectable Doctor Linton, married to an ailing, demanding wife, was more than a little in love with Amy Flynn; and however hard he fought to suppress such feelings, this had stirred up a raw and corrosive resentment. Unable to rest since he had seen that envelope on the entrance hall tray, with its tell-tale Weatherfield postmark and firm, clear hand, Ellis had given in to the darker promptings of temptation and stolen up here to Amy's room to search for it while she was tending his children in the nursery.

Slowly he looked across at her again. The net curtain at the dormer window had been looped aside, and above the treetops the pearly greyness of a summer's dawn breaking on the rim of the Downs lent a ghostly outline to her slim figure.

His eyes moved coldly over her face, that face of defiant

19

beauty, straight dark brows contrasting with the corn-gold fairness of her hair. The touch of her warm skin just now, so invitingly soft, had both roused and repulsed him. As ever, her very nearness threw him into a turmoil: he seemed always to be in two minds about her, hating her with his head, as it were, while feeling something quite other for her in his heart.

Harshly he said, "It was wrong to have you to live here. I should have known. Should have known better than invite you beneath my roof. You create nothing but trouble wherever you go."

"*I* create trouble?" came the spirited retort. "What have I done? I respect your wishes. I keep out of your way. I see after the well-being of your children—"

"You have always brought trouble. You were born to it. Born with the taint of incest and murder. A mad woman for mother . . . a father hanged for the killing of his mistress's husband . . ."

"My father was not hanged—"Amy began; and Ellis Bates saw by her suddenly stricken expression that he had trespassed far enough.

He could not restrain himself. "Oh, let us not split hairs. He choked himself to death by his own hand rather than live locked up with his guilt. There is the same bad blood in you as there was in him, and doubtless it will lead you to the same bad end."

He swung away towards the door, and still the words of hurt came spilling out.

"There will be no visit to Bonningale for Laura and Esmond. You are no fit person to care for my children. Mine or anyone's. The sooner you are gone from my house, the better."

20

2

The first time David Linton and Amy had set eyes on each other, she was seventeen years old and sitting in tears in the garden of the alehouse in Weatherfield.

This ancient hostelry had belonged to the Flynns since the 1830s, and situated as it was within a few hours' travel of Lewes, Amy had sought refuge here on several occasions from her guardian's harsh authority. Its present licensee was her father's half-brother, Joel Adams, a stolid individual whose red-haired Irish wife had given him a family of eight children.

It was on account of the smallest of this brood that David Linton had called that September evening in 1888.

He had spent much of the day visiting outlying hamlets on the edge of the Ashdown Forest, something he generally did twice a month to attend the sick and elderly and those others unable to make the journey to his surgery in the small market town of Weatherfield. Though dusk was starting to fall, the air was still very close and the young doctor had been glad to accept a tankard of ale from Joel Adams to slake his thirst before continuing his way home.

Taking it into the garden, he was enjoying a rare moment of solitary peace when he became aware of somebody sobbing quietly within the concealment of a rose arbour; and going over to see what was amiss, had discovered Amy Flynn.

"I do beg your pardon," he said at once as she raised a tear-stained face from her hands at the interruption. "I didn't mean to intrude. But you seemed troubled. Can I help you in any way?"

Amy's appearance at this time was still gawkily immature, and the hardships of her young life had caused an unfortunate abruptness of manner to develop. Her only answer to the

21

doctor's solicitous enquiry was to thrust out her lower lip
and stare resentfully ahead of her.

He was a patient man, and not in the least deterred by this
ungracious response. Putting down his tankard on the rough
wooden table, he removed his curly-brimmed bowler and
took a seat beside her in the shade of the arbour.

"You're a stranger to these parts, surely?" he began con-
versationally. "I don't believe I've seen you before. Linton
is my name. David Linton. May I know yours?"

Amy shifted herself to the further end of the bench and
sniffed. Wiping the tears from her cheeks with the back of a
hand, she said sullenly, "It's Flynn."

"Flynn? Not one of the Weatherfield Flynns?"

There was a terse nod.

The doctor regarded the young girl with fresh interest.
"Then you must be—let me think. You must be one of
Dinah Flynn's grandchildren?"

A pause. Then another nod.

His pleasant face grew suddenly grave and he said slowly,
"You're Frank's daughter."

This time there was no answer.

"I'm sorry," he went on after a moment, "but I can't for
the life of me recall your given name. I ought to, I know.
We're family almost. I met your Aunt Isabelle and Mr
Bethway when they came to visit—"

"Oh, you know them?" Amy's expression brightened
a little at this mention. "You know Aunt Belle and her
husband?"

"It was only the briefest introduction through our rector,
I'm afraid. After evensong one Sunday. He's writing a paper
for the local history society on families in the parish and had
somewhere uncovered the fact that the Lintons and Flynns
are distantly connected."

The girl pulled out a handkerchief from her jacket sleeve
and blew her nose. He was pleased to see that she had
stopped crying, at least. She made such a sorry little picture;
and her woebegone appearance only added to the general
unkempt look about her—clothing rather shabby, skirt hem
fraying, elasticated boots scuffed and down at heel.

"Please tell me your name," he pressed again gently.

"It's Amy, sir. I was christened Aimée—" she spelled the

name out for him—"on a whim of my mother's. It's French, you know. But no one's ever called me anything but plain Amy. Who . . . who did you say you were?"

More animated now, she twisted round on the bench and looked directly at him as she put her question. He had nice eyes, she decided at once: a warm hazel brown and full of good humour. She had always noticed people's eyes before anything else about them. The face was pleasing, too, an honest and kindly face, clean-shaven but for thick side-whiskers which gave him an old-fashioned rural appearance: whiskers, beards and suchlike facial adornment were going out of style now in Lewes.

"My name is David Linton," he told her once more, smiling a little at this earnest scrutiny.

"And do you live in Weatherfield?"

"Yes. I have a medical practice here."

"Oh. You're a doctor?"

He took up his tankard of ale and drank from it, then nodded.

Amy examined him further. She had been crying because Irish Kate Adams disliked her so, and had flown into a temper that afternoon saying Amy was insolent and lazy and gave herself airs, swanning about the alehouse as though she owned the place, when everyone for miles around knew what shameful bad deeds her father had done to lose it.

"Your family comes from these parts, did you say, sir?"

"My father's people, yes. From Shatterford. But my wife . . . my wife Louisa, she's a Londoner. I met her while doing my training at the London Hospital in Whitechapel."

He set down the emptied tankard. At one end of the garden a small apple orchard had been planted. Someone had told him there used to be a ratting pit there years ago, and that the body of a murdered man—killed by this girl's father in a fight—had been hidden nearby. It was hard to imagine that kind of violence amid the setting of such a peaceful scene. The apple boughs were heavy with ripening fruit, the evening air filled with the scent of roses trailing over the arbour, and from the distant fields came the faint "come-up, come-up" of a dairyman calling in his cattle from pasture.

23

"And what of you, Amy?" he had asked. "Won't you tell me about yourself? Where you live, what you do?"

There was something so patently genuine in this stranger's interest that the girl had found herself, almost for the first time in her young life, able to answer such questioning without feeling at once resentful and hostile. She started hesitantly, not looking at him now but fidgeting with the handkerchief in her lap; then, encouraged, found her confidence growing.

Listening to her story, David Linton had been moved. Child neglect was common enough in these times: workhouses and orphanages were filled with its result, and the sights of London's East End had acquainted him early in his medical career with poverty, abuse and the loss of innocence among even the smallest of children.

He was glad for this young creature that at least she had been spared physical mistreatment, and that she should harbour nothing worse than a healthy contempt for her guardian-uncle, Harry Weldrake.

"Uncle Harry? He's a fool—a fool to himself and all others," she answered dismissively when asked at the end of her tale. "A selfish, mean, grasping old fool. Money is his god. If he didn't buy friendship, I swear there'd not be a soul in the world to give him a decent name."

It was at this point in the conversation that their quiet privacy had been disturbed by the noisy arrival in the garden of a party of people, whose horse-brake had been heard a short while earlier drawing up at the front of the alehouse.

Seeing one of his own patients among their number, and remembering that the lady had a tendency towards garrulous hypochondria, David Linton thought it politic to slip out by the side gate before he was noticed; but not before insisting Amy sent him news of herself from Lewes.

"Promise you won't neglect to write," he had urged. "I should be sorry to lose touch after learning so much about you."

His open manner had won the girl's trust; and over the following months a lively correspondence had sprung up between them, leading in time to a warm friendship—a friendship which others, including Doctor Linton's wife, suspected concealed a much deeper attachment.

*

24

The Lintons lived in a large house which had been built only a short while before they came to live in Weatherfield five years ago, in 1886. It stood in its own spacious grounds not far from St Anne's church and the rectory, in the old unspoilt part of the original village, shielded by the green and the high street from new urban developments of red-brick terraces and small manufactories which had appeared in the last decade or so along the Shatterford road.

Their relationship had been a happy one, blessed by the birth of a daughter, Alice; but not long after her husband first met Amy Flynn, Louisa Linton had miscarried of a second pregnancy and this sad event had had a most distressing effect upon the couple's marriage.

As a child, Mrs Linton had been indulged by over-fond parents and was perhaps rather too used to being allowed her own way in everything. As a grown woman, she had retained a marked childishness in her behaviour, loving to be given presents and other marks of attention, sulking violently if she thought she was being ignored, and indulging in little fits of temper when thwarted of something she wanted. Even in appearance she seemed very young still, with her large china-blue eyes and pale blonde hair worn in long ringlets tied up with ribbons.

David Linton, who had a great fondness for the works of Charles Dickens, had often used to call her his "own dearest Dora", a reference to David Copperfield's child-wife who "had the most delightful little voice, the gayest little laugh, the pleasantest and most fascinating little ways, that ever led a lost youth into hopeless slavery."

Perhaps it was not the kindest of comparisons, however lovingly meant, for the novel portrayed Dora Copperfield as a naive and immature character and had had her expire most touchingly in chapter fifty-three from the lingering effects of a miscarriage.

After the failure of Louisa's second pregnancy, her husband never called her by that name again: in her case, too, there had arisen complications, causing an illness from which she never seemed entirely to recover, so that her life was now that of a semi-invalid. Unlike the fictitious Dora, however, Louisa did not suffer this loss of health and strength with patient forbearance. On the contrary, it seemed to exacerbate the petulance of her nature so that she was for ever fretfully complaining of something or other, or else weeping that her husband no longer loved her as he once did.

It seemed useless his pointing out how little opportunity he had to demonstrate his affection, since she consistently denied him her bed.

"You know very well why, David," she answered plaintively when he remonstrated with her over this coldness. "*Must* you trouble me yet again with your . . . approaches?"

"But, sweetest heart, it has been so long—"

"And is that my fault? Am I to blame for falling ill? Oh, how cruelly you misuse me . . . was ever a poor creature more wretched than I to have such a husband . . ."

As always, the tears began, squeezed out on purpose to fill him with guilt for his selfishness.

Had he been some other type of man, doubtless he would have troubled his wife no further but sought a woman in one of the towns to satisfy his need. David Linton, however, had too high a sense of moral integrity to soil his marriage vows by resorting to cheap adultery in the arms of some drab. He was no prude—as a medical student there had been many occasions when he had shared his fellows' enjoyment of ladies of the night in the music halls and taverns of the East End—but now that he was husband and father, a respected and respectable member of the community with a position of authority to uphold, those days of drunken sprees and wild oats had long since faded in his memory.

"There is no need to weep, Louisa dearest," he told her, leaning forward to press her hand. "I am at fault for having upset you, and I beg your pardon."

They were together in the drawing room of their house in Church Lane. The August day had been a hot one, but even so, at Louisa's insistence a small fire had been lit for the evening. She lay beside it now on the chaise longue, a light blanket covering her limbs, gazing into the flames; and though the few tears had soon dried, a peevish expression of discontent marred the faded prettiness of her face.

To distract her, her husband began admiring the flowers she had earlier arranged about the place. Gardening and needlework were Louisa Linton's favourite pastimes and the

26

elegant room reflected both, bowls of roses, pinks, irises and china asters complementing the rich colours of the silks embroidered into wall hangings, cushions and screens.

Her features softened a little in response to his compliment.

"Yes, the roses have been especially lovely this year. *Boule de Neige* has done wonderfully since I had Albert move it into the new bed by the summerhouse—" she turned on the chaise longue to indicate a vase of fragrant creamy white blooms on a flower stand near the piano. "Though perhaps we should have left *Reine des Violettes* in the shelter of the wall as before—" this of an arrangement of velvet crimson roses on the pembroke table behind her husband's armchair. "Last week's rain has battered the poor things about so dreadfully."

"Did little Alice help you in the garden today?"

"This morning, for a while. But when the sun grew too hot I told Lily to bring her indoors."

"She could have taken her nap in the summerhouse, surely? You keep the child too much inside, Louisa. Clean air and sunshine, that is what she needs if she is to lose the weakness in her lungs. Look how well she was last summer when Amy was here to take her for long walks in the countryside—"

No sooner had Amy Flynn's name passed his lips than David Linton knew he had said the wrong thing. His wife's face had in an instant become a tight little mask of dislike.

Doggedly he finished his sentence. "And those few days spent with the Bethways at Eastbourne. The sea air did the child a world of good. Why, my dear, you yourself remarked as much."

Louisa gave a little shrug of the shoulder. All the animation she had shown for her roses seemed suddenly to have drained away again.

After several moments' silence she said, "Would you put a few fresh coals on the fire?" And when he had done so and replaced the tongs in the hearth, went on—"I hope, David, you are not thinking of inviting Miss Flynn to stay again? When you read out her letter at breakfast this morning, it sounded quite as though she were asking to come back here."

"Did it?" The doctor re-seated himself. "No, surely not, Louisa. As I recall, Amy wrote that she'd left Spences Lane sooner than intended—"

"Yes, because Mr Bates didn't find her suitable for governess."

"She was perfectly well suited. No one has a better way with children. If she had left his house, it's for good reason of her own, and I believe I can guess what that is. Ellis Bates is a queer fish."

Louisa's tone grew irritable. "How can you say that when you've scarce even met the man?"

"First impressions tend to be sound ones. I've learned enough from the few conversations I've had with him when he's been here to Weatherfield."

"You have allowed your judgement to be coloured, I think. Few others would trouble to visit a father's grave as dutifully as he does."

"That may be so, my dear." David Linton reached to the smoker's companion, a circular stand beside his chair, and selected a pipe from among several on a wooden rack.

"I hope you are not going to smoke here," his wife said petulantly as he tapped the bowl against the palm of his hand. "You know how the smell of burning tobacco makes my poor head ache so."

"In that case, I shall take a walk in the garden."

He began filling the pipe from an oilskin pouch, pressing down the thick dark strands of tobacco with his thumb.

"As for Amy," he went on when he was finished and the pouch replaced in its airtight jar on the companion, "I was intending that we should invite her for a week or two when she returns from her friends at Bonningale."

"No!" Louisa's reaction was typically childish. Beating both her fists together upon the blanket, she cried out, "No, David!"

Her husband stared at her. "But, why not?"

"I—I don't like her in the house."

"What nonsense. Amy's like a breath of fresh air about the place. Even the servants are pleased to see her. Why, only the other day Lily was asking when she might come to visit again."

28

The corners of Louisa's mouth were turned down in an ugly expression.

"Why do you need to concern yourself so much on her behalf? She is nothing to us . . . a stranger, almost. I wish you would not encourage her as you do."

"But Amy is a relation of ours—"

"A very distant one."

Patiently he tried to explain. "Her great-grandfather was Daniel Linton—my grandfather. The rector has uncovered proof of that fact in parish records. Old Daniel's illegitimate daughter was Dinah Flynn, who was Amy's grandmother."

"If *I* had discovered some . . . illegitimate relative in the family closet, I should be far too ashamed to acknowledge them," came the sulky response. "It's so terribly demeaning, David, to have you flaunt this kinship with the Flynns as though it was something to be proud of. They were a very common family, I believe. Tavern keepers and prize fighters and horse dealers . . . people of that sort. There is even gipsy blood somewhere. No doubt that would account for Amy Flynn being such a fearfully ill-bred type of creature."

"She is not ill-bred in the least. High spirited and impetuous, perhaps. But then, that is her temperament."

"She has had scant education—" Louisa began again.

"Oh, come now, sweetest, that is hardly her fault. The Reverend Bethway did what he could to remedy the lack of schooling while she lived as a member of his family. She has a quick and lively mind and a readiness to learn which I admire—"

"You admire! Oh yes, David, you make it perfectly plain how much you do admire everything about Miss Flynn. She is a very paragon of virtue in your eyes."

"Dear heart, that is not true," he protested.

The protest was ignored.

"It amuses you, I suppose, to have her here so that your wife may be made an object of scorn and ridicule?"

"Now you are talking nonsense again. When have you ever been scorned or ridiculed by Amy's presence in this house?"

"The servants make comparisons . . . she is so familiar with them. And Alice prefers her company to mine because I'm unable to romp and play. Even you—you, my own husband . . ." The tears began to well again in the large blue eyes. "I have watched you looking at her . . . seen the silly doglike way you follow her about . . . and at times I sit all alone and think that no one wants me, I am nothing but an encumbrance, how much better it would be if I were dead . . ."

Louisa's head fell forward into her hands and she started up a noisy weeping.

David Linton closed his eyes. This scene, or variations of it, had been played so many times between them in the past few years; and there were moments, as now, when he felt so utterly wearied by their repetition that his natural good nature deserted him.

Opening his eyes again he got to his feet and picked up a box of vesta matches from the smoker's companion.

"Where are you going?" his wife demanded to know between her sobs.

"I am going into the garden to smoke a pipe of tobacco," he answered tonelessly. "So I will bid you goodnight, Louisa."

There was a pause as he went across the room to the door; then—"Please do make an effort to be more charitable in your attitude towards Amy. I am sorry that you don't wish her to come here again, but I'm afraid your objection is a little too late. I have already posted my letter inviting her to stay with us next month."

3

"Ah, a partner in exile! So you, too, have sought escape from the madding crowd's ignoble strife."

Amy Flynn looked round, startled for a moment by the unexpectedness of the voice. Then, seeing who it was there in the lane behind her, she jumped down from the five-bar gate from which she had been admiring the distant view, and smiled.

"What did you say, Mr Herriot? What was that about crowds?"

Ralph Herriot smiled back. "'Far from the madding crowd's ignoble strife their sober wishes never learned to stray . . .' It's a quotation from Gray's *Elegy*."

"Oh."

"Used by my friend Mr Thomas Hardy for the title of what many consider his finest novel to date."

"Ah."

"You've read it, of course? The novel?"

Amy gave a slight shake of the head. It annoyed her when people asked questions about books since she seldom had any inclination to read one and was made to feel ignorant as a result.

"You have not? Then I shall insist upon providing you with a copy before I leave Bonningale," said Ralph. "No person of any sensitivity should deny themselves the pleasure of savouring Mr Hardy's work."

"What makes you think I'm a person of sensitivity?"

"My dear Miss Flynn, would you otherwise be here, preferring the solitude of a quiet lane to the hurly-burly of my sister's betrothment? Would you otherwise be leaning upon a gate to admire the beauty of the evening landscape, so lost in your appreciation that you failed to hear an intruder until he was upon you?"

31

This was uttered in such a droll manner that Amy could not resist laughing aloud.

"But it *is* beautiful," she declared, waving an arm towards the distant view. A soft dusky haze was falling upon the nearer fields, deepening the shadow patterns of wind ripples on the surface of the ripened corn; but further off, the land was bright still with sunset, rising away gradually in tier upon tier of wooded hills to merge on the skyline with the green swelling smoothness of the Downs.

"Don't you agree, our scenery's worth admiring, Mr Herriot?" she went on, glancing back at him over her shoulder. "Or do you prefer your own bit of the country? Dorsetshire, isn't it?"

The young man nodded. "Aye, Dorset it is. And aye again, I prefer it to any other part of England—though I'll admit Sussex runs it a close second. Perhaps now that my sister Maria is marrying into your family, she'll bring you to visit us at Sutton Bassett and you can judge for yourself."

"That'd be very pleasant. Thank you. But we're not really family, you know." Amy moved away from the gate and stepped across the track ruts to reach the grassy verge of the lane. Ralph held out a hand to assist her, but she refused it with a little smile and a shake of the head.

There was a piece of bramble caught on a flounce of her dark blue skirt, and she bent to pull it free before continuing, "Mrs Bashford is godmother to my Aunt Belle. Her first husband—Mrs Bashford's, that is—he was rector of Weatherfield once upon a time, you see, and that was how she came to know our family so well."

"The connection goes back a long way, then?"

There was a nod.

Seeing her look past him along the lane, the young man asked, "Are you going back to the house now?"

Another nod.

He offered an arm. "Will you let me escort you?"

Amy hesitated. Their acquaintance with one another was rather too brief for such familiar courtesy. The gesture had been made, however, and not wanting to seem ill-bred by rejecting it, she placed a hand in the crook of his elbow and fell into step beside him.

Only two days ago, Ralph Herriot had been a perfect

stranger. She knew his name, his rank of gentleman farmer, the reason for his being at Bonningale; and nothing more. His sister Maria she had liked at once, but Ralph himself invited a more cautious response. Whenever he was among their fellow guests, Amy had noticed that while he appeared to give his full attention to whoever was speaking, his eyes would be on some other part of the room studying someone else.

This was a practice she herself frequently indulged in, loving to watch people when they thought they were un-observed; but now she was made to realise the discomfort of being the object of such scrutiny, for several times in com-pany she had looked round to find those grey eyes fixed upon her in precisely the same speculative fashion.

Though there had been little chance, beyond sociable conversation, to form a judgement of young Mr Herriot, Amy suspected that he concealed a good deal of himself behind a facade, and that the agreeable affability of his manner hid a deeper, very different type of character.

As they strolled together along the winding lane, admir-ing this and that of the countryside about them, she said casually, "Fancy Mr Thomas Hardy being a friend of yours. I didn't realise."

There was a note of regret in the reply. "To be quite truthful, Miss Flynn, it's my father who is the friend. I'm more by way of being an acquaintance."

"Oh. I see."

"Now you're disappointed."

"No."

"I only said it to impress you, you know."

She gave her companion a sidelong glance. "And why should you want to impress me, sir?"

He returned the glance with a grin. "You shall have the answer to that when I've known you a little longer."

"You're very bold. I'm not sure I should be wise to believe anything you tell me."

"Why, because I laid claim to Mr Hardy's friendship? That was no more than an exaggeration of fact. I tell no lie when I say he's dined with us on occasion, and returned the compliment with invitations to Max Gate."

"Max Gate? That's a place, is it?"

Ralph nodded. "Hardy's house. On the outskirts of

Dorchester. He designed it himself, I believe—one of those large red-brick piles. I don't care for it myself. There's something about our present-day architecture—"

"Oh! Look, there's my cousin Francis!" Amy interrupted to exclaim, pointing.

Through a gap in the hedge, a view of the lane further down revealed a dark-haired youth moving steadily in their direction.

A little slyly she continued, "It's him you should be impressing with your friends, Mr Herriot. I recall he's reading something or other in the *Graphic* newspaper, about a country girl who thinks her family's descended from nobility and—"

"Oh, that will be *Tess*," her companion interrupted in turn, choosing to ignore the gentle mockery. "*Tess of the d'Urbervilles*. Yes, the *Graphic* has been printing the work in periodic episodes. I believe Mr Hardy intends it shall be published as a book towards the end of the year."

"You seem to know a good deal."

"Well, my people have a personal interest, you see."

"So they should, hobnobbing at Max Gate."

Ralph gave a silent smile. "I mean, there's a farm in the story—Talbothays, I think it's called—it was modelled upon our own at Sutton Bassett."

"Now you're trying to impress me again."

"No, no. My father told me as much. It's the very same, though set in some place described as the Valley of the Great Dairies, instead of the Froom."

By this time the pair had rounded a wide bend in the lane and could see Amy's cousin ahead coming towards them. The rays of the setting sun now slanting low across the hedge-tops cast a fiery tinge upon everything around, and the ruddy light caught the surliness of the youth's expression as he beheld the approaching couple arm-in-arm together.

Francis was the cuckoo in the Bethway family nest. His sister Dinah and brother Christopher, known as Kit, tended to favour their parson father in their quiet, industrious nature, and their mother in the colouring of their auburn hair and grey-green eyes. Francis, however, had been formed in the flawed mould of a more distant heredity, for in him ran the wild dark blood of his grandfather, the stallion

34

man Frank Morgan, and that affinity showed plainly in the thick black curling hair and strong muscular build.

He was no more than seventeen years old, yet was already becoming the despair of his parents and the bane of a rapid succession of maids who came and soon went again at the Eastbourne parsonage.

Amy released Ralph Herriot's arm and ran in front to meet her young cousin.

"They've sent me after you," he called truculently, halting in his tracks. "I've to fetch you back to the house."

"Why? What's wrong? Has anything happened?"

Francis shrugged. Then, instead of an answer—"I might've known he'd be with you." This was said with a thrust of the chin towards Ralph, who had now caught up with them.

Amy bridled. "What's it to you who's with me? I'll keep company as I like, and don't need permission from you, Francis Bethway. Now what's this about? Why've you been sent to find me?"

Again he ignored her questions. Addressing himself to her companion he said churlishly, "You leave our Amy alone. She doesn't want strangers following her about—"

"Oh, take no heed of him, Mr Herriot!" the young woman broke in, vexed by this rudeness. "He fancies he's the only one should speak to me, even, that's what it is. I wish to heaven he'd hurry and grow up, and not keep behaving like some silly child."

Turning on her cousin, she seized him by both shoulders and gave him a hard shake. Though shorter by an inch or two, Amy's slender build belied her strength and the youth's head was jolted back and forth.

"Now stop your nonsense, will you!" she told him sharply. "You make me ashamed, you do, the way you act. I don't want you tagging along at my heels all the while—"

"I don't tag along at your heels. I said I'd walk with you if you wanted company, and you told me you didn't." Francis Bethway's features were contorted into a scowl as he pulled away. "Yet here you are letting somebody else attend on you, strolling along arm-in-arm—"

"I think that's enough, don't you?" Ralph Herriot's tone was friendly, but there was an explicit undernote of warning. "If I considered it any business of yours, my boy, I'd have

35

manners enough to explain how it is you find Miss Flynn and me together. But since it concerns no one but our two selves, plainly we owe you neither explanation nor excuse. Now, I suggest you do as you're bid, like a good fellow, and tell your cousin why she's needed at the house."

The rebuke had its effect, and not even the flush of sunset could mask the dull reddening of the other's face.

"There's a message come," the youth said sullenly, looking down at the ground. He aimed a kick at a stone. "A message from Lewes about Amy's uncle. The old devil's been taken bad and seems like to die."

In his younger days, Harry Weldrake had been considered a handsome man. Very little remained of those good looks now, though. The stroke he'd suffered had paralysed the left side of his face, so that his one eye was dragged down like a bloodhound's and his mouth gaped slackly in a dribbling parody of a leer.

He was not yet fifty years of age, but drink and debauchery had together taken their toll of his body and anyone seeing him now for the first time, a trembling, helpless wreck of man lying on a soiled bed, would have been excused for thinking him full twenty years older.

Amy left Bonningale immediately she knew the details of her uncle's illness, and was at the house in Tea Garden Lane before noon the next day.

Receiving no answer to her ringing of the front porch bell, she walked round to the stable yard at the rear, and finding the back door to be open, went in. There was an ominous silence everywhere. The familiar smell of stale cigar smoke, cheap scent and mustiness seemed stronger than she remembered and unpleasantly tainted with an underlying odour of stale food, most noticeable at the head of the scullery stairs.

Used as she was to the general untidiness of the place, Amy was quite unprepared for the chaos she came upon in the entrance hall: dining chairs on top of side tables, pictures and clothing heaped together, vases, mantel clocks, candlesticks stacked higgledy-piggledy on a chaise longue, and a canteen of cutlery spilling its silver contents across the floor.

"Hello?" she called loudly. "Is there anyone there?"

Hearing a sound from somewhere above, she began picking a way through the jumble towards the staircase.

"Hello?" she called again.

There was silence for a minute or two; then a clatter of heels on the uncarpeted landing was followed by a face appearing over the balustrade. From the frizzed dyed hair and crayoned eyebrows Amy recognised Gertie Jukes, the latest of Harry Weldrake's kept women.

"Oh, Lor'." The "housekeeper" clapped a hand to her mouth. "What you doing back here?"

"What do you think? I've come to see Uncle Harry."

Amy stepped over a pile of what looked to be bed curtains to reach the foot of the stairs.

"You can't come up here," Gertie called down nervously.

She scurried to the stair head as if meaning to bar the way, but in her agitation tripped over something; and as her hand flew out towards the banister rail, she let drop whatever it was she'd been holding. It bounced down the stairs towards Amy and struck the newel post in a splintering crash of blue and white china fragments.

"Oh, Lor'." Gertie cried again. Her thin, young-old face took on a stricken look beneath its coating of greasy powder.

"What the devil do you think you're playing at?" Amy demanded angrily. "What's going on here? Who said you could shift my uncle's belongings?"

"We're having a clearing out, that's all," the other responded shrilly. "For the rag-and-bone man. I told Harry we'd get rid o' the rubbish, me and our Fred."

"Rubbish? You call this rubbish?" The blue eyes flashed. "I'm no fool—I can see what you're up to. Helping yourselves, that's what. Grabbing all you can while there's time, like rats on a sinking ship."

"Here, who you calling rats—"

"You and your brother Fred. A couple of scavengers, the pair of you. I suppose it's Fred who's the rag-and-bone man?"

Avoiding the shattered ornament, Amy hoisted her skirts and went nimbly up the stairs.

"I might've known you wouldn't be too proud to pilfer from a dying man," she went on heatedly, reaching the top. "Lord knows, you've thieved enough already from under his drunken nose. Oh, get out of my way!"

She pushed the other aside; and as Gertie Jukes, protesting weakly, retreated along the landing, threw after her—"You can make a start tidying some of the mess you've caused. And mind, if there's so much as a teaspoon missing, I'll have the Law on your heels, you watch if I don't."

Leaving Gertie open-mouthed, Amy spun round and ran along the landing corridor past the open doors of dining and drawing rooms to a second flight of stairs leading up to the bedrooms.

There was dust and grime everywhere, as though no one had taken a broom to the place for weeks; and outside her uncle's room the kitchen cat was crouched amid a pile of dirty dishes gnawing at the remains of a fish head.

"Shoo! Go on, shoo!" The young woman clapped her hands and the animal turned and fled, taking its meal with it.

She pushed the door ajar.

"Uncle Harry?"

The mephitic stench in the darkened room made her nose wrinkle. Going quickly to the window, she drew back the half-closed curtains and threw open the bottom sash, letting in the sweetness of fresh air and birdsong; then looked across at the figure in the bed. The stroke-ravaged face was turned towards her.

"Oh God . . ." she said.

Harry Weldrake raised a trembling hand from the coverlet and mumbled her name.

Mastering her revulsion, Amy went to the bedside and knelt down. "Is there anything I can do for you? Anything you need?"

With obvious difficulty her uncle made an effort to raise himself on one elbow. His nightshirt had been left unbuttoned and the skin of his throat hung in loose mottled folds. He had obviously not been shaven for some days for his moustache, always kept neatly clipped, had grown untrimmed and there was a shadow of grey stubble on his cheeks and jaw.

"Is there something I can get you?" Amy asked again.

Weldrake motioned towards a bureau by the door. Thickly he said, "Lef' . . . lef' drawer . . . papers."

"You want me to fetch them?"

A nod.

38

The drawer was crammed with material of every description—letters, invoices, unpaid bills, receipts. At a loss to know which he wanted, she caught up a handful and brought them back to the bed.

"These?"

For a moment there was a glint of the old impatience, the old dislike, in the look he turned upon her from his one good eye.

"Pa'et . . ." he mumbled. "Pa'et."

"Packet?"

Another nod.

At the very back of the drawer her hand felt a bundle of papers tied with string. This seemed to be what her uncle wanted, for he gestured to her to undo them; and when she had spread them out on the bed, he feebly reached out and touched a sealed buff envelope.

"'S f' you . . ."

"This? For me?"

"Mmm."

"You wish me to open it?"

"Mmm."

She did so, and drew out a single sheet of foolscap. It proved to be a codicil, or schedule, to Harry Weldrake's Will.

He motioned his niece to read it.

"Be it known unto all men by these presents, that I, Henry Norris Weldrake, of the parish of All Souls, Lewes, in the county of Sussex, gentleman, have made and declared my last will and testament, bearing date the twelfth day of April, one thousand eight hundred and eighty-one: I, the said Henry Weldrake, by this present codicil, do ratify and confirm my said last will and testament, and do give and bequeath unto my living niece, Aimée Weldrake Flynn, the sum of five hundred pounds, to be paid to her within one month of my decease, together with my house, all my household goods, debts and moveable effects; and my will and meaning is, that this codicil be adjudged to be a part of my late will and testament; and that all things therein mentioned and contained be fully and amply performed in every respect, as if the same were so delivered and set down in my said last will and testament.

"Witness my hand, this third day of October, one thousand eight hundred and ninety. Henry Norris Weldrake."

The codicil had been duly signed and sealed in the presence of three witnesses, whose signatures were appended at the foot.

Amy laid the copy slowly down and looked at her uncle. A thread of saliva hung from one side of the slack mouth. She leaned forward to wipe it away with a corner of the bedsheet, and said in a tone of puzzlement, "You're leaving me all this? The house, the furniture? Everything?"

"Mm."

"But—why? You've always hated the sight of me. Ever since I can remember, you've tried to disown me, blamed me because of my father, because he got my mother pregnant before they married . . . blamed me for the shame he brought on the family . . . blamed me even for my mother being lodged in a bedlam. Often and often you've said how you wished I'd died at birth, like my twin brother. So why? Why give me anything? Why not leave it all to somebody else?"

Harry Weldrake lay back among the mound of soiled pillows and that side of his face that had not been paralysed by the stroke wrinkled into a mesh of lines, as though he were grinning.

When he spoke, the words seemed to come a little more distinctly.

"All yours anyhow . . . this. Was your mother's house . . . not mine. 'S all legally yours."

"What? You mean—you mean this place has never belonged to you? All the years you've lived here, yet you've never owned it?" Amy stared at those flaccid, wrinkled features.

Weldrake's good eye closed in what might have been a wink.

"You old devil!" she said. "You cunning old devil. This paper's nothing more than a ruse to cover your tracks, isn't it? All you've done is give me back what's always been rightfully my own. You stole my inheritance to pay for your gambling and your drinking and your painted women . . . you robbed me of a happy childhood . . . and now you want to make your peace with your conscience before you die. Well, damn you, Harry Weldrake. Damn you!"

4

"You know, Mother . . . I have always believed that my father was . . . murdered."

Ellis Bates had to force himself to say the words out loud; and, with almost as much difficulty, look his mother directly in the face as he did so.

He and Rachael Bashford were alone together in the parlour of the farmhouse at Bonningale. His half-brother George, who had taken over the farm at the death of Rachael's second husband some three years earlier, was out with the men harvesting the top field; and his two children had gone with George's young family on a visit to Arundel.

Ellis did not come to visit his mother often. Once or twice a year, perhaps, no more. The two of them had never been close. Nor was there much love lost between him and his Bashford half-brothers and sisters: all his life he had been made to feel the outsider, the intruder, a Joseph despised by his brethren. Before he grew old enough to curb such emotions, he had yearned for a share of his mother's affection, and her deliberate negligence had left scars that cut all the deeper for being kept so long unseen and unexpressed.

It had not, therefore, been easy for him to come here to Bonningale to ask the questions he had never had courage to raise before; and it showed the length he was prepared now to go to in order to keep his feelings toward Amy Flynn in proper proportion.

The news of her suddenly acquired respectability had come as quite a jolt to Ellis Bates. When he had learned of Harry Weldrake's death, in the last week of July, he had wondered who would be the beneficiary of the estate—if, indeed, there was anything left worth calling an estate—and was all the more perplexed, in view of the old reprobate's lifelong antipathy to his young niece, to learn that the sole beneficiary was Amy herself.

This unlooked-for elevation to the ranks of the middle classes and status of householder served to cast her in a very different light. While she had been, so to speak, little more than a waif and stray wandering from one place to another, she was a social inferior; and the curious emotional dichotomy of like and loathing which Ellis Bates harboured for her was held in check by the barriers of rank.

Now, however, those barriers had been swept aside by Weldrake's Will, and the restraint so rigorously exercised could no longer, it seemed, be justified by class division. As Ellis saw it, he must now turn to some other form of self-defence to protect himself from the folly of his own weakness. And that defence was to keep open the wound of the past . . . to seek to hide himself within the shadow of old tragedy . . . a shadow reaching back over two generations to a day in 1852 when a church minister and a stallion leader had died together in bizarre and bloody circumstances which had never been satisfactorily explained.

"I've always believed that my father was murdered."

The pale blue eyes held his mother's darker ones in a troubled gaze.

"I think it is time I was told the truth, don't you?"

Rachael Bashford had aged noticeably since the death of her beloved second husband. The hair beneath its lace-edged widow's cap was iron grey and the once smooth flesh of her face had wrinkled into a tracery of lines.

"Why now, Ellis?" she responded calmly. "Why, after so long?"

"I should have asked you years ago." He sat forward in his chair, elbows resting on the padded arms, hands locked together in front of him. "I was always curious, yet always too afraid to broach the matter. My father was never mentioned in this house."

"And with good cause. Your stepfather and I were agreed that the memory of Esmond Bates was better buried with him."

"Was it then so very painful to you, that memory?"

"It was."

"For what reason?"

42

Rachael Bashford bowed her head, and for a moment he thought she was going to refuse him an answer.

Then, slowly and without looking up, she said, "It does not become us to speak ill of the dead. But since you wish for the truth . . . so be it. Your father was a sick man, Ellis. Not sick in body, but in his mind. He was not like other men. He . . . he could not accept the natural concourse between husband and wife. Purity—oh, how many times did I hear him use that word—purity was an obsession with him. Purity of body, of heart, of spirit. Everything else was defilement, even love itself."

"Yet the marriage *was* consummated—"

"Yes, the marriage was consummated! Consummated by an act of rape. And you, Ellis, you were its fruit . . . conceived in violence and shame."

She closed her eyes. It had happened so long ago. In another lifetime, it seemed, and to another woman; an unhappy young creature married to a man she feared, a stranger whose coldness she could not even begin to understand.

A little sadly she went on, "Why seek to rake up these dead embers?"

Her son's lips, compressed in a bloodless line, were as white almost as the knuckles of his clenched hands.

"What happened?" he demanded harshly. "Tell me."

Rachael shook her head.

"What happened?" he asked again, his voice rising. "I have a right to know. A birth-right, if you like."

"Isn't what I have said enough? What more do you want?"

"The truth!"

"Very well. You shall have it." Rachael's head snapped up and there was anger as well as pain in the look she turned upon her son.

"Your father was determined to believe I had been unfaithful. It was a nonsense, of course, but he had convinced himself that it was so. Any pretext for suspicion, however far-fetched, was enough for his twisted mind to work up into something fantastical. On the night—that last night—he was roused to such a pitch of insane rage I thought he might kill me . . . he had never touched me before."

43

She stopped, agitatedly twisting the heavy gold band on her wedding finger.

"Afterwards, he went out from the bedroom. I didn't see him alive again."

"And that was the night he died?" her son said.

"It happened the next morning, I believe."

A silence fell between them. Beyond the mullioned windows, small birds fluttered in and out of the laden branches of wistaria, and further off, above the home meadow, the cadenced notes of a lark sounded from a cloudless sky.

Ellis Bates cleared his throat.

"There was a man found dead with my father in that barn, a stallion leader—"

"Frank Morgan."

"Yes, Frank Morgan. Amy Flynn's grandfather. Was it he who was suspected of being your . . ."

A slight gesture of the hand sufficed tactfully to complete the question.

Rachael nodded.

"But there was no truth in it?"

"No!"

He frowned a little at the vehemence of her denial.

"As I've said," he went on after a pause, "I am of the opinion my father's death was no accident. I believe he was struck down in cold blood, and that Morgan was his killer."

"You truly believe that, Ellis?"

"I do."

"Where is your proof? How can you be so certain?"

"I feel it here." He tapped a finger against the breast of his high-buttoned waistcoat.

"But the finding of the court was death by misadventure."

"Courts can be wrong."

The perverse obstinacy of her son's argument irritated Rachael, and there was some heat in her words as she said, "Frank Morgan had neither reason nor motive to kill Esmond. The truth is more like to be the other way—that it was your father in his madness who struck first. God knows, he had used me violently enough! If he could abuse a mere woman in such manner, what might he not be capable of doing against a man—and one for whom he held nothing but prejudice? I am entitled to my opinion, Ellis, just as you are to yours, and it has long been my firm conviction that Esmond deliberately followed Frank Morgan to that barn, and there made a frenzied assault upon him—an assault which drove Morgan's stallion in a panic to trample them both underfoot."

"This is ridiculous." Ellis rose angrily from his chair. "My father was a man of God—"

"Your father was a hypocrite . . a sham. If there was an ounce of Christian love anywhere in him, he kept it well hidden for I never saw sign of it. He treated his parishioners at Weatherfield as though they were dirt beneath his feet."

"Doubtless he had good reason. There are clods aplenty to be found there still. It must have galled a man of his intelligence to have to waste himself in such useless ministry."

"Oh, how like him you are! Contemptuous, mean-hearted—"

"Mean-hearted? Is it not rather you yourself, Mother, who has the meanness of heart? All my life I have been made to feel guilty for my birth. There was never a moment in my childhood that I was not passed over by you in favour of the others, held to blame for being my father's son, used as a scapegoat for whatever brief unhappiness you may have suffered—"

He broke off, biting his lip; and after a few moments re-seated himself and in a curiously flat voice continued, "I am sorry you feel the need still to vilify my father's memory. To suggest that he was the aggressor and not the victim demonstrates your own lack of Christian spirit."

Rachael Bashford listened to this indictment of herself without any visible emotion.

"You have inherited more of his traits than I realised," she said calmly. "Perhaps that may explain the obsession you've always had with the manner of his death. A pity in a way that George had to tell you about it."

"It was George Bashford's duty as stepfather to do so."

She ignored this. Almost to herself she went on, "Then there was the curious attachment you formed for Lizzie Newbrook when she was found to be Frank Morgan's natural daughter. Was that, too, a part of your obsession, I wonder? She told me about it, you know, how you pestered her on that account. How fortunate she had the good sense to marry her neighbour Mr Everdene and put an end to your pursuit."

Ellis Bates's face flushed a dark red.

"I was eighteen years old—" he began.

"And now you are thirty-eight, and still obsessed," his mother answered tartly. "Only this time it is Amy Flynn who occupies your unhealthy fancies."

A sudden disturbance from outside on the drive—the shrill pipe of children's voices above the grate of metal cart-tyres on gravel—caused her to pause a moment and glance at the clock on the red lacquer Chinese cabinet.

"There, that will be the little ones home already from Arundel."

On the same note still, she turned back to her son and continued, "I think, however, you will find that Amy has moved beyond the sphere of your influence. She has found herself a very warm admirer in Henry's brother-to-be, Ralph Herriot."

And as the door flew open to admit some half a dozen lively, noisy grandchildren into the parlour—"Well, I suppose you must be leaving us again, Ellis? A day seems barely long enough. Thank you, though, for bringing Laura and Esmond to visit. It will be such a pleasure having them and the new governess to stay the whole week."

Megwynn Evans stood back from the looking-glass and twisted around to see if the ribbons on the thick brown plait were tied to her satisfaction. It was stiflingly warm up here in the little garret, and whisps of hair that had come loose were stuck to the dampness pearling her forehead and the nape of her neck. She tucked the stray pieces into place, then moved the looking-glass aside on the low chest of drawers and leaned forward to push the dormer window further open.

There was something about the green swell of the downland landscape that reminded her a little of the country about her home at Bettws-y-Crwyn in the Forest of Clun. What a shame they were not to remain longer here at Bonningale. She liked it so much better than that gloomy house of Mr Bates's in Lewes where she'd been engaged since midsummer as governess to his two children.

46

Still, she should count herself fortunate to be with such a genteel household. Her first position, as nurserymaid to a family in Ludlow when she was no more than fourteen, had been a deal of hard work for very small return; and the second, with a lady who'd removed to live with relatives in London, proved quite as bad, for Megwynn had hated the dirty, crowded, fog-fumed city only little worse than she hated the leering, foul-breathed familiarity of her mistress's old father-in-law.

Being an intelligent and practical young person, she had spent her free evenings at an adult educational institute to fit herself with the necessary qualifications to become a governess, and after two years in London had found her first such post through a domestic agency. She was now twenty years of age, a round-faced, freckle-skinned young woman with the attractive lilt of the Welsh border country in her speech still; unattached, but content to be so, and happier than she could say to have shaken the dust of the city streets from her skirts at last.

Bending forward to rest her arms on the ledge, she drew in a deep breath of sweet-scented air from the open window; then, her attention caught by a movement below, put out her head and saw that it was Mary Bashford, the remaining unmarried daughter of the family, waving to her from beside the pony trap.

"We're taking the coager up to the field," the girl called. "Are you coming along?"

"Yes—yes, wait for me! I'll be down directly."

Seizing up her pleated sun bonnet from the chest, Megwynn hastened from the garret. At harvest time, everyone—no matter who—was required to give a hand; and though a governess would not be expected to do labourer's work, she could help to carry the "coager" or midday meal out to the fields, and stay to keep a watch on the children to see they came to no harm with the unattended scythes.

The back of the trap had already been loaded with wicker baskets, each covered with a clean white cloth and holding a generous supply of baked meat pasties, hard cheeses and apples, cans of cold tea and stone bottles filled with lemonade or mild beer. Besides the Bashford men and their farmworkers to feed, there were the two Bethway brothers,

Francis and Kit, as well as several Irish labourers hired for the season from the itinerant harvest gangs who came over to England each summer.

The drive through the quiet lanes was not a long one—they were harvesting the last of the home fields now—and Megwynn was pleased to find Esmond and little Laura cheerfully occupied with their cousins in plaiting bonds of hay to be tied round the sheaves. Three-quarters of the corn had already been cut and bound, leaving a standing square in the middle; but that, too, would be down by evening, and as the last section fell, there would be shotguns at the ready to bring down the rabbits bolting from cover.

"D'you want that bottle stringing up anywhere?"

Megwynn had not heard anyone approach. She looked up, a little startled, and tilted back the wide brim of her sun bonnet. One of the young brothers staying at the farmhouse had walked over to where she was sitting to take her meal in the shade of the hedge.

He indicated the stone bottle with a jerk of the head, and said again, "D'you want it stringing up for you?"

She had had to prop the children's lemonade among the roots of a nearby tree, being not quite tall enough to reach up and attach the bottle by its neck-string to a branch where the light breeze would have kept it nicely chilled inside its cover of damp sacking.

"Well, thank you . . . ." He was too much her equal to be called sir, and she was not sure she could recall his name aright. "Thank you, yes, that would be kind."

"Stay where you are—" he said gruffly as she made to get up. "I'll see to it."

Megwynn could not resist a smile to herself at this self-conscious manner. She followed him with her eyes, watching as he jumped up to grasp the end of a branch and with an unnecessary show of force bend it towards him.

Bethway. Of course—she had the name now. Francis Bethway.

He was clad like the rest of the men in a collarless shirt worn unbuttoned at the neck, and cord trousers secured with a leather belt and tied under the knees with straps called "eightses". Didn't Mary Bashford tell her that his father was a clergyman? No one would guess it from the rough way he spoke.

"There."

The youth came back to where she was sitting and stood against the hedge, hands thrust into pockets.

She smiled up at him over her shoulder. "You've had something to drink yourself, have you?"

"Aye."

There was a wedge of cheese and some apples that the children had left from their meal.

"Then would you care for these?"

Francis sucked in his lip. He'd already had his share of food and beer; but her invitation gave him the excuse he wanted to sit beside the young governess and talk to her. He'd thought about doing so ever since she'd come to Bonningale last Sunday. There had been no earlier opportunity, though, for he was up at dawn with the others each day to start work in the fields, and this was the first time she'd given Mary a hand with the coager.

"Mebbe somebody else might want it," he said, his eyes on the plump swell of her breast under the white tuckered blouse.

"Oh, no. The children have eaten their fill, and so have I. You finish it for yourself."

He pulled a clasp-knife from his belt and knelt down at her side; and after slicing himself a piece of the cheese, said awkwardly, "I don't know your name, do I. Your given name."

"It's Megwynn. Megwynn Evans."

"Megwynn. That's pretty. I like that."

Emboldened by her friendliness he leaned across to take one of the apples, and cutting it into quarters, offered one to her.

"You're not from these parts, are you?"

"No." She accepted the piece of fruit with a smile. "My home's up in Clun."

"Clun?"

"Yes, at Bettws-y-Crwyn."

The youth shook his head. "I'm none the wiser still."

"It's in the Welsh marches, beyond Shropshire. Its name means 'chapel of the fleeces'."

49

"That's a rum thing to call a place."

"Well, the village is on one of the drovers' roads into England, see, and in the olden days shepherds used to bring their fleeces to be blessed at our church. Mind, this is going back a bit. When tithes were paid in wool to Chirbury Priory."

Francis chewed stolidly, giving her all his attention.

"So St Mary's church came to be known as *bettws-y-crwyn*, and in time gave that name to the whole village."

"Ah."

He helped himself to another wedge of cheese.

"My father has a farm in the hills above," Megwynn went on. "At Gaudy Hall. He works it with my uncle—oh!"

Her hand flew to her throat. She had not been watching the children while she talked, so had failed to notice young Esmond go over and start playing with one of the scythes left against the stack of sheaves. He now had the handle gripped in both hands and was hacking clumsily at the stubble.

Leaping to her feet, she cried out his name—but too late to prevent the boy from swinging the curved blade against his legs. There was a high-pitched scream of pain as the razor-sharp edge carved into the bare flesh.

"Oh, *Duw*, God—"

Megwynn picked up her skirts and rushed across to him. Blood was already pouring from the deep gash and she looked round in panic for something to staunch the flow.

"Here—" Francis was with her, tearing off his shirt. "Use this!"

One of the Bashford men, taking in the situation at a glance, ran down the field to get the trap to carry Esmond back to the house. The others were already gathering round the stricken boy, shaking their heads and commenting among themselves as they watched the young governess bind his leg.

Most of the children had huddled together into a little group and stood looking on in silence, except for Laura whose tearful wails added to the noise her brother was making.

"That's a bad wound he's give hisself," one of the men observed. "Cut through to the bone. He'll be lucky to be walking on that leg again afore the end o' summer."

"Aye," his neighbour agreed glumly. "It'll need stitching, I'll be bound. Careless pup—that'll learn him to go playing wi' scythes. He'll be abed a good week or more till his flesh knits sweet enough for movement."

A week or more . . .

Francis Bethway looked down at Esmond's young face screwed up in anguish. He grinned to himself. A week or more before they could leave to go back to Lewes. His dark eyes moved to rest upon Megwynn Evans, and the grin broadened.

5

"I've been so busy with the practice," said David Linton, "I've scarcely had time to notice how long it's been since last we met."

That was the second untruth he had uttered since arriving at the house in Tea Garden Lane.

The first was in his answer to Amy Flynn, when she asked after his wife and he'd replied saying, "You really should have come to see us when you promised, you know. Louisa was as disappointed as I that you put off making your visit."

On the contrary, far from being disappointed, Louisa Linton had expressed the greatest satisfaction at the postponement; and far from his scarcely having time to notice Amy's absence, the doctor had missed her company to the detriment of his own peace of mind.

A single letter to Weatherfield in the summer had informed them of her inheritance of the Weldrake property, that there was a great deal needing to be done, but that they must come to stay in due course. Since then, not a word.

Taking advantage of his attendance at a symposium in Brighton to discuss the effects of sea water upon certain types of skin disorders, David left the coast a day early with the intention of breaking his return journey in order to call upon Amy in Lewes.

He had never been to the house before, and its appearance came as something of a surprise. He had always imagined Harry Weldrake as living in one of the poky, narrow streets which criss-crossed the town centre. Instead, he discovered Tea Garden Lane to be a quiet, almost rural by-way winding sedately uphill towards the Downs; and the house itself a most elegant example of early Georgian architecture.

Climbing the steps to the front porch, it occurred to him to wonder whether the new occupant might not herself have been transformed to match these fine surroundings; and was somewhat taken aback when she answered the bell in person, shabbily dressed in an old pinafore and her hair tucked up out of sight beneath a man's cap.

"Heavens!" she cried, seeing who it was standing there. Then, laughing, "Oh, come inside, do, before the wind changes and fixes your face in that expression. I'm sorry you find me looking like this—" closing the door behind him—"but Minnie and me, we're up to our eyes cleaning the back stairs."

She ushered her visitor into the entrance hall, delighted to be seeing him again, apologising for the untidiness everywhere, exclaiming how well he looked, and asking after Louisa and little Alice.

"I came by hackney carriage from the station," he said in reply to her next question; and—"Yes, thank you, Amy, a cup of tea would be most welcome."

She called down the scullery stairs to the unseen Minnie below.

"There's only her and her husband Ted," she explained, leading the way up to the drawing room on the first floor. "Minnie used to work in this house as a girl, you know. She was here when my parents married. She remembers me being born, even. Now—" dramatically throwing open a door into a large, airy room—"what do you think?"

Used as he was to heavy pieces of furniture, overcrowded walls and cluttered surfaces, David was pleasantly impressed by the effect of light and space which had been created here. Instead of the usual dark flocked paper, the walls had been decorated a pale eau de nil, repeated in the background colour of the carpet underfoot; and apart from a circular table at the centre of the room, bearing a large blue and white china bowl of chrysanthemums, the only other furnishings were several smaller side-tables, a cushion-strewn chesterfield, and a pair of deep armchairs on either side of the marble fireplace.

He walked across to the window. The shutters had been folded back and there were no fussy drapes to obscure the view beyond the stable roof of a clump of trees, ablaze with the sunset hues of autumn. A bonfire had been lit somewhere in the garden, its plume of blue-grey smoke blowing sideways in the light wind, and the room was faintly perfumed with an aroma of burning applewood.

"Well?" Amy asked impatiently. "Do you like it?"

"Very much. Very much indeed."

"This is the only room we've managed to finish so far. Ted Brocklebank did all the work for me. He's a marvel."

"But the credit must go to you, my dear Amy, for your taste in colour and arrangement."

David Linton turned from the window to face her. She had taken off the incongruous cap and shaken out her hair so that it fell in heavy golden waves across her shoulders. She *had* changed—he could see it now. Her beauty had acquired a glow of loveliness, a lustre almost; and the eyes beneath the straight dark brows had lost their old expression of mistrust and were full of confidence.

"David? What is it? Why are you staring at me in that way?"

"Oh, was I? I'm sorry. It's that I haven't seen you . . ." He swallowed hard to clear his throat of a sudden huskiness. "I've been so busy with the practice, I've scarcely had time to notice how long it's been since last we met. You've altered, Amy."

"I have?"

"Yes, you've grown more . . . mature."

She smiled. "It's a wonder I haven't grown positively ancient, the worry and work this place has brought with it. Oh, there—" turning her head at a sound beyond the door—"that'll be Minnie with the tea."

Nothing about this singular young woman should surprise him, David Linton mused, leaning back a while later, refreshed, against the chesterfield cushions.

"Our first task, of course, was to give the house a thorough good cleaning," Amy was telling him. "There were corners that hadn't seen brush nor broom for years, I swear. You'll take another cup of tea?"

She laid her own cup and saucer aside on the tray.

"And the kitchen! Dear Lord, how Minnie and I worked. As for the attics—you should have seen what we fetched down. Everything from boots and books and mouse nests to a box of underpinnings and a wig stand. And such clouds of dust, you'd think the place was afire!"

"But why d'you take so much upon yourself?" David asked. "Surely it would be less trouble to employ others to do the labour?"

"There's Ted and Minnie—"

"I meant professionally."

"What, and pay the earth? Oh, I'd far rather see to it myself, and have the satisfaction. Besides, my uncle bequeathed me his bills as well as the house, you know. After honouring those, I'm almost down to my last penny-piece—"

"You're not short of money? Can I help? You know you may count upon me for anything—you've only to ask."

Amy shook her head. "You're very kind, David. But no. I can shift well enough with what's left. I suppose I must seem a stubborn creature, mustn't I, wanting to do it all for myself. But—oh!—"

She jumped to her feet and turned round, arms spread as if to embrace the room.

"You can't imagine how it feels to have something of my very own at last. I never had a thing before, not even a dog. And now—all this to look after . . . a home to live in. Even the simplest thing, like bolting the doors at dusk and knowing I'm safe for the night, gives me more pleasure than I ever dreamed possible."

She sat down again, her face flushed with happiness, and after a moment began to laugh.

"You must think me quite absurd, going on in such a fashion."

"No. Not at all. I understand."

"Do you, I wonder?"

David nodded. He was glad for her, glad for her security; and yet growing inside like a shadow on his heart was the fear that he was about to lose her. This sure-minded, un-afraid young woman who had so often in time past turned to him for counselling, for consolation . . . what part would there be left him to play in her life?

A sudden feeling of despondency crept over him. It was as though their roles were being reversed. Amy was her own mistress now, needing no master; and as her strength grew, somehow his own was being sapped. The less she needed him, the more he found himself desperately needing her.

When she was younger, a child still in so many ways, her affection had been a spontaneous, open thing, innocently given; and he had responded in like manner, as a fond relation does. Now that she had become a woman, he found the corresponding change in his own feelings confusing, knowing he had no right to love her as a man.

"You're very quiet of a sudden," Amy said, interrupting these thoughts. "Is there something wrong?"

He passed a hand over his face and drew a deep breath; then looked at her and smiled.

"I'm a little tired, nothing more."

"You do too much. It's *you* who should be getting the assistance, not me."

"Perhaps. Amy . . ." He paused, uncertain what it was he needed to say to her.

"Amy . . . promise me something."

"Of course."

"Promise you won't allow our friendship to die. Promise you won't become so detached by your change of fortune that you'll forget what it's meant to us."

"Forget—? Oh, David, how can you think such a thing?"

The cry was full of reproach.

"Circumstances have not been kind," he went on doggedly. "I can appreciate how you must want to put the past behind you now, blot out all memory of those years. It's natural enough, heaven knows. But don't sever yourself completely, my dear. Not everything needs be discarded from your old life, surely? Don't reject those you once turned to—"

"You think I've rejected you, and all because we haven't seen one another these few months? You take my silence as a sign I've grown uncaring? But you can see how occupied I am here! There's been no time for anything else. And you, David—you owned just now yourself, you've been so busy it scarce seems five minutes since we last met."

In a low voice he said, "That wasn't the truth. I've missed you more than I can say. We both have, Louisa and I—" Then abruptly checked himself; and after a moment or two, in a kind of bewildered anger went on, "Damn it, why do I keep up this pretence! It's *me* that's missed you, *me* that's talked of you, *me* that's looked forward always to your company. Louisa's too riddled with self-pity to care much

56

whether she sees you again or no. But I care . . . oh God, Amy, what am I to do?"

He got hastily to his feet, his features working.

"I'm sorry, I shouldn't be talking to you in this way. It isn't fitting. Perhaps it's best I went now."

"No. Please—" Amy reached out a hand. "There's no need for you to go. You've said nothing wrong."

Slowly he turned his head and looked down at her, and there was an expression of such anguish in his eyes that she said again, more urgently, not understanding, "Please, David—don't go. Sit down, won't you?"

He did as she asked, and leaning forward buried his face in his hands.

"Oh, my dear, what must you think of me," he said awkwardly. "To forget myself in such a manner. I feel ashamed."

"I'm not offended. I've sensed for some while that Louisa doesn't like me. She's never understood, I don't think. It's as though she's afraid our friendship in some way harms her own happiness."

"Yes, that is what she seems to fear. But why?"

"Perhaps because she thinks you have a greater regard for me."

David shook his head. "Louisa is my wife. I love her. I've never once done anything to make her believe otherwise. Whatever she wants I provide for her. She has a comfortable home, a little daughter beloved of us both. What more can I give her—what more can I do–to reassure her of my devotion?"

Amy looked down at her hands, clasped together in the lap of her shabby apron. The insecurities of childhood had caused her always to shy away from the involvement of close relationships, not trusting herself in love with any man for fear of rejection. Apart from Alec Bethway, her aunt's husband, the only man she had ever had faith in was David Linton; and he held a special place in her affection, always so considerate of her needs, so compassionate in her times of despair, so caring of her happiness.

"Louisa has greatly altered," the young doctor went on miserably. "Since losing our second child she's become fretful . . . complaining. I know her health is not good, but to be

57

honest I do wonder at times how much should be attributed to her state of mind, rather than her state of body."

Straightening himself up on the chesterfield, he turned towards Amy and reached hesitantly to place a hand on top of hers.

"It's seemed to me of late that Louisa's resentment of our closeness stems from jealousy. Jealousy of you, Amy—of your beauty, your vitality, your ease of manner, your ability to rise above life's trials—everything, in fact, which she feels lacking in herself. But then, that's your nature. That's why you are uniquely your own self. And it's why I . . . why I'm so very fond of you. No—" Again he stopped deliberately to correct himself. "This is a day for truthfulness. It's why I love you."

His fingers tightened their warm clasp.

"There, now it's said. I love you, Amy."

She bit her lip, not sure how to answer such a serious confession.

"Ah, now I *have* offended you, my dear," he said sadly, watching her downcast profile, half-hidden by a curving wing of corn-coloured hair.

She gave a slight shake of the head, and without looking up replied, "No, truly . . . But you're not to say these things, David. You haven't the right."

"Haven't I? No right at all?"

"You're a married man—"

"I need no reminder of that fact. Being married to Louisa, however, does not set barriers upon my ability to feel affection for another."

"I think we're talking about something more than affection, you and me." This time Amy did glance up at him as she spoke, her eyes flickering quickly over his face. "You say you love me. Love's a word with many meanings to it. *I* love *you*, David—but not, I think, in the same way as you do me. I love you because you're my friend—like a brother to me, almost."

"And how d'you imagine I feel for you?" he asked her. "As a sister? No, don't pull your hands away, Amy. Please don't. May I not hold them—if only as a brother would?"

Drooping her head again, she acquiesced; and for several minutes they sat together in silence. The scent of applewood

58

burning on the garden bonfire had grown a little stronger within the room, and David thought poignantly that he would never again smell its odour without recalling the bitter-sweetness of this scene.

At length he was the first to break the stillness, saying quietly, "Will you want to see me again?"

"Of course. Why not?"

"Why? Well . . . because of my lapse from grace, my trespass into the forbidden . . . my falling in love with you."

Now Amy did pull her hands away. Clasping them to her breast, she half-turned from him, experiencing a strange, momentary feeling of betrayal, almost; as though the words he'd just uttered despoiled the trust she had in him.

When she spoke, however, her voice was perfectly controlled. "I hope we shall continue to meet as friends. I can't be a guest in your house again, of course. Not now you've made it plain Louisa doesn't welcome me. I wouldn't for the life of me do anything to hurt her, David—"

"No. Nor would I."

"Perhaps, so that it won't seem odd—my not visiting, I mean—I'll call upon her briefly when I'm next in Weatherfield. I shall be going there within the month."

"Oh?"

"Yes. I'm taking someone to see the place."

"May I know who?"

"His name is Ralph Herriot. I made his acquaintance at Bonningale. His sister is to marry Henry Bashford."

"Is that so." The young doctor's voice had grown suddenly dull.

Amy rose to her feet and moved away from the chesterfield towards the table at the centre of the room. One of the purple chrysanthemum heads had shed a few of its petals on the polished wood surface. She began slowly to pick them up, one by one; and without turning round, said, "I think you should know that Mr Herriot has been corresponding regularly with me since our meeting. He's a very presentable young man. From the warmth of his tone, I think he's formed quite an attachment for me. And I intend to encourage him, David. So you see, there's no use you being in love with me, no use at all."

6

A short way along the lane that led away from Weatherfield
into the countryside around Snow Hill, a pair of cottages
stood back behind a patch of ground.

Someone had once made an attempt to turn the patch into
a garden; but that was obviously some time ago, for banks of
nettles now blurred the outline of flowerbeds, and although
nasturtiums still thrived, splashing the lichen-crusted wall
with their bright orange, the only other flowers were self-
sown ragged robin and purple loosestrife.

The right-hand cottage housed the family of a labourer,
whose chickens had made a dusty desolation of what had
formerly been a square of lawn. Its partner on the left was in
a poor state of repair, its window frames bleached and
roughened by the weather, the pointing crumbling away
between the brickwork, the thatched roof sagging inward
like dried flesh upon the skeletal frame of the rafters.

For the past forty-odd years its small dark rooms had
housed only one tenant, a farmworker named Robert Lambe.
Throughout those years he had risen each morning at half-
past four, laved himself at the shared pump in the back-
yard—rather more quickly in winter than in summer—and
broken his fast on cold bacon and beer.

If it were a weekday he would prepare his noon meal and
be up at Bostall Farm on the flanks of Snow Hill by six
o'clock to get the team of oxen ready for the day's work. If it
were a Sabbath, he would sweep out the cottage, turn his
straw mattress, lard his boots against wet weather, and dig in
his garden.

For six evenings a week he enjoyed the company of his
neighbours, with his pipe and his "husser and squencher",
which was a pot of beer with a dash of gin. On the seventh he
went to evensong at St Anne's. He could neither read nor

write, nor had he ever married: being wounded in love more years back than he could recall, Robert Lambe was of the opinion that women were more trouble than they were worth as wives.

There was no reason why he should not see in his three score years and ten a hale and hearty man. Alas, however, it was not to be, for the uneventful tenor of his life had been cruelly interrupted by a moment's distraction which cost him not only his health and his peace of mind but his livelihood too.

The old fellow generally worked at Bostall's; but in early summer when his ox team were finished in the fields for a season, he might be hired out as general labour to some other employer. So it was that in 1889 he had come to be on the other side of Snow Hill at the old Linton farm, one of a gang threshing the last remaining stack in the yard before the new season's harvest was gathered in.

The accident had happened with brutal swiftness. His place was up on the thresher platform, feeding sheaves from the stack into the revolving drum of the machine. A too-hasty turn, a moment's unbalance, a stumble forward—and Robert Lambe's leg was trapped between the belt and the whirling drum and crushed as easily as if its flesh and bone had no more solid substance than the sheaves preceding it.

He had lost the leg; and with it his livelihood, since without two limbs a man cannot steer a team of oxen in the furrows. For a time he'd been put to stone-breaking, but that was no work for an old man and it had sapped the last of his strength. Not everything was taken from him, though. The parish Poor Law relief, meagre as it was, at least kept him from the workhouse; and John Linton, owner of the farm, accepting some liability for the accident, saw to it that he was not to be evicted from his tied cottage.

He could no longer tend his patch of garden, however, no longer keep his rooms in good repair, nor carry out the mundane tasks which had made up his existence until now. Though David Linton—John's cousin—provided without charge all the medical treatment required, and the labourer's wife from the next cottage came in whenever she'd time, the lack of activity and company gradually wore away at Robert Lambe's spirit, just as the constant pain in his body wore away at his endurance.

As the summer of 1891 waned slowly towards autumn, he lay on his bed watching the woods grow bare on Snow Hill and knew in his heart of hearts he would not be alive to see another year's leaves come into bud.

Now that he'd gone so far as to put into words the full measure of his love for Amy, it was as though David Linton had broken some seal to release a veritable daemon of emotion.

So long as his feelings were kept bottled up, so long as they were unexpressed, they had been no more than a dull ache at the back of his mind; but that moment of confession in Amy's drawing room at Lewes had given overwhelming substance to the shadow, and in the few weeks since he'd returned to Weatherfield the young doctor had felt like a man possessed.

The fact that Amy was encouraging the attentions of some other admirer caused him intolerable pain, exacerbated by his guilt as a married man for what he knew to be disloyalty. To assuage this guilt, he'd tried to show his wife greater affection; but Louisa, suspicious that this was for the purpose of renewing their former intimacy, reacted with a coolness which separated husband and wife yet further.

It was in this unhappy state, torn between duty and desire, between longing and hopelessness, that the doctor called to make his periodic examination of Robert Lambe.

Climbing the musty boxed-in staircase from the single room below, he found his patient, not propped as usual against the brass bedhead, but lying down; and was quick to note a pinched look about the bridge of the nose, a certain sign that death was not too far distant.

His examination completed, and satisfied there was nothing more to be done for the old fellow's physical comfort, he closed his black Gladstone bag and seated himself at the bedside.

The pallid sunken face was turned towards him on the pillow.

"Is there anything you'd like me to see to?" David asked

quietly. "Anything of a private nature? Don't be afraid to ask, Bob. I'll give it my personal attention."

The faded blue eyes looked back at him.

He waited.

Then—"Did you ever hear tell o' fairieses?" Robert Lambe asked hoarsely, giving the word the double-plural form common in Sussex dialect speech.

Despite his own melancholy frame of mind, the young doctor smiled a little. Like many another aged, lonely person living buried away in the past with their memories, his patient had a habit of re-telling the same few stories each time he came to see him. He had heard the tale of the "fairieses" more times than he could count; but knowing that he might well be hearing it now for the last time, he settled himself back in the creaking, lop-legged chair, and with a show of some interest answered, "Fairies, did you say?"

"Aye."

"D'you know, Bob, I'm not sure that I have."

"Ah. Well, now then. I'll tell you some'at, sir. Some'at to amaze you. I seen some of 'em, once on a time."

"Is that so? You actually saw some?"

"Aye. I did. 'Twere when I were a boy, mind, but it's a thing that's stayed clear wi' me ever since. Over at Tye Cross, it were, in a barn I seen 'em. Little things they were, an' all. Like a squirrel, mebbe, or a weasel. And d'you know what they were a-doing in that old barn, sir?"

David shook his head.

"I'll tell you. They mischieful creatures, they were a-thieving the grain from out the sacks."

"They were?"

"Oh, aye. I seen 'em at it wi' these very eyes. And d'you know what I heerd one o' they fairieses say? 'Jem,' he says, 'Jem, I sweat.' That's what he said. 'Jem, I sweat.' Now what d'you reckon to that, sir?"

"You've flummoxed me there, Bob."

The old man on the bed made a mirthful sound. "Aye, I remember it yet. 'Jem,' he says, 'Jem, I sweat.' As true as I lie here, sir, 'tis what I heerd that fairy creature say. Laugh? I couldn't hold meself. Whoever heerd o' fairieses a-sweating?"

"Who, indeed." David stood up and put his chair back against the wall.

"Well, you may be sure, soon as ever I burst out a-laughing, they fairieses made off out o' that old barn quick as ever they could. An' 'tis a fact, sir, I never seen hair nor hide of 'em again, in that place nor any other. Reckon I must've frighted 'em proper—Oh . . ." Robert Lambe's animation faded. "You're away now yourself, Mr Linton, sir?"

"I'm afraid I must." David bent to pick up his bag, looking down at his patient with a smile and a nod and pressing the fleshless, blue-veined hand in farewell.

"But you'll come again soon? Won't you, sir? It do get that wearisome wi'out company . . ."

Ducking his head to avoid the low lintel of the door below, the doctor put on his curly-brimmed bowler hat and stepped out into the garden. The woman from the neighbouring cottage, seeing him from her upper window, called down something; but he merely acknowledged her with a quick wave as he made his way along the weed-choked path to the gate into the lane, where his trap was standing.

In the act of untying the reins he paused, however; and after a moment's consideration turned back again with the intention of speaking to Robert Lambe's fellow-cottager about the old man's welfare. He had taken a few steps towards the gate and was about to lift the latch, when his attention was distracted by a movement at the side of the narrow, tree-lined lane.

A man and a woman were coming along together beneath the falling leaves, and to judge by appearance, greatly enjoying each other's company, for the young woman's hand was tucked into her companion's arm and both were laughing aloud at something she'd just said.

David Linton's heart gave a sudden wild leap as he recognised her. He had written, of course, to apologise for his gauche behaviour at their last meeting; but Amy had not replied to the letter, and he had no way of knowing when she'd be visiting Weatherfield with Ralph Herriot. To see her now, so unexpectedly, and with the man who to all intentions had replaced him in her affection, cut David to the very quick.

He was tempted to jump into the trap and drive away,

64

pretending he'd not seen them approaching. But then, what was the point of flight, since he would be bound to meet them sooner of later elsewhere in Weatherfield.

He waited, miserably.

"David!"

Already Amy had noticed him standing there at the gate. At least she did not seem in any way discomfited by their meeting, her smile as warm as ever as she released her companion's arm to run towards him, hands outstretched in greeting.

"David!" she said again; and then, turning—"Ralph, this is Doctor Linton. David—Ralph Herriot."

The two men moved to exchange handshakes. Had he not been so wretchedly sick at heart, David did not doubt that he would have taken to Herriot at once. As it was, he could only feel aggrieved that the other was a good inch taller than himself, the shoulders broader, the face strong, the grey eyes full of humour, and the tweed cap set back at a boyish angle on the curling chestnut hair.

With some effort of will, he went through the usual platitudes, forcing himself to smile, to be polite, to show interest; aching within to take Amy in his arms and hold her against him, if only for a moment to know the reassuring comfort of her nearness. She was standing a little apart, not looking at him as she talked brightly of the walk they'd just taken up to the mill, but giving her attention instead to the pony, whose gleaming dark neck was being patted and stroked as though it were the finest beast in all Sussex.

He learned that she and her companion had arrived yesterday in Weatherfield and taken rooms with Joel Adams and his wife at the alehouse. They were undecided as to when they'd be leaving, but certainly not later than the week's end since Mr Herriot had business in Dorchester the Tuesday following.

David listened, his face rigidly fixed in a smile; and as soon as courtesy allowed, made his apologies that he could stay no longer, being expected elsewhere, wished them both a pleasant holiday, expressed the hope of meeting them again before their departure; and somehow managed to keep his frozen features from crumpling into misery until he had driven a safe distance away down the lane.

Ralph Herriot watched the trap swing out of sight beyond a clump of elms in the dip. Then he turned, and leaning his elbow nonchalantly upon the cottage wall, regarded Amy in somewhat quizzical fashion.

"So that is your friend Doctor Linton? Obviously you must be acquainted with two different gentlemen of the same name."

She returned his look, puzzled; and after a moment's hesitation, asked, "What do you mean? What makes you say that?"

Ralph gestured with his head in the direction of the elms.

"I would never have recognised this gentleman as being one and the same as the Linton described to me in conversation. Unless memory plays me false, you represented him as an open, friendly sort of a fellow. Yet I find myself introduced to someone so far from being friendly as to exhibit every sign of wishing himself elsewhere but in my company. Tell me, Amy, is the good doctor always so distracted in manner?"

The young woman gave a shrug of the shoulder, pretending to make light of his words, and bent down to pluck a spray of ragged robin from beside the gate. Straightening herself, she answered indifferently, "Oh, I expect he is worried for one of his patients."

She had said nothing at all to Ralph about David's confession of being in love with her, mentioning only that he'd called at the house on his way through Lewes. His following letter, pathetic in its pleading for understanding and forgiveness, had served but to increase her distress, and she had not known how to respond without causing them both further hurt; nor did she think it right to reply on such a very personal matter in case by some mischance their correspondence should fall into the hands of Louisa or one of the servants.

If only that meeting had never been, those words never spoken . . .

"Let's go on, shall we?" Amy tossed the spray impatiently aside and smiled at Ralph in what seemed a sudden return to her former high spirits. "I'll show you the old track across the hill pasture to the holloway. Come on!"

Swinging her straw bonnet by its ribbons, she set off down

the lane, walking at such a pace through the drifts of leaves that her companion was forced almost into a half-run to catch up. Once they were clear of the dip, instead of continuing to the right towards Troy Town, she mounted nimbly over a stile-gate set in the thickness of the hedge and started away to the left along a gorse-dotted path which wound uphill to merge eventually with a sheep drove.

"This is one of the ways my Aunt Isabelle used to come as a girl to find scenes for her sketchbook."

Pausing at the top of the steep incline to get her breath, Amy pushed the windblown hair from her eyes and looked back.

"I told you, didn't I, that her work gets shown at exhibitions and suchlike? She sells it to raise money for the parish in Eastbourne."

Ralph Herriot, coming along behind with his hands thrust into the hip pockets of his tweed jacket, halted for a moment to answer, glancing around as he did so to take in the view.

"Yes, you did mention something of the family talent."

"There was a fallen tree hereabouts where she liked to sit," Amy went on, tidying the unruly hair away beneath her bonnet and fastening the ribbons into a bow. "My father carved his name in it, she told me. F.P.F. Francis Patrick Flynn. I expect it was chopped up and carted off for firewood a long time back. D'you see those sheep folds down there, beyond the dew pond?"

She indicated a huddle of lath-walled pens some distance away on the flank of the hill, where the ground levelled off towards a grove of holly. Near at hand, its glassy surface reflecting the pale clear autumn sky overhead, was a circular brickwork basin of the kind common to downland pastures.

"Aunt Belle made a sketch of that once on a time, before she left Weatherfield. I admired it so often that one year she copied the scene in watercolours and framed it as a birthday gift for me. I wish I knew what became of it. It was such a pretty picture. Harry Weldrake got hold of it, I suppose, and threw it out."

She cast her eyes once more over the tranquil setting below. Then, turning, added, "There was no love ever lost between those two," and began to walk on again, leaving Ralph to follow behind at a more leisurely pace, studying the

67

countryside with the observant eye of a man whose livelihood depends upon the goodness of the fields.

Their path now took the young couple over the crown of
the hill away from the sheep drove and on towards a further
stile-gate, leading down to the road to Weatherfield.

In days gone by, an ancient hawthorn had been a prominent
mark here on the parish boundary, and below it a sheltered
holloway which ran steeply between high banks to the bottom
of the hill to emerge opposite the alehouse. Some years
earlier, alas, the tree had been blasted by lightning and
all that now remained was the blackened heartwood of a
shrivelled, twisted skeleton.

The holloway survived still, as a narrow lane; but the open
fields which once stretched clear away to the skyline as far as
the eye could see were swallowed now by streets of terraced
redbrick houses, whose gardens had buried the slubby clay
of ridge and furrow beneath hen runs, vegetable plots, flower
beds and billowing lines of washing.

By the time Amy and Ralph had reached the foot of the
holloway, the grey softness of an autumn dusk was already
starting to fall. Gas lamps shone in the lower rooms of the
alehouse, their light framing the windows in rectangles of
yellow and spilling out over the steps into the empty road.

"Are you finished there, Joel?" a woman's voice called
from the back kitchen, hearing the passage door close. She
came out, wiping her hands on her apron, a plump red-
haired person with a trace still of bold Irish beauty in her
matronly features.

Seeing it was not her husband but her temporary guests,
she exclaimed, "Oh—have ye a moment, Amy, before ye're
away up to your room? Doctor Linton called by not ten
minutes past and left something to be given ye. Joseph—"
this to a tow-headed child sitting behind her at the kitchen
table, licking diligently at the inside of a mixing bowl—"be
sharp now, run and fetch me that note o' the doctor's from
off the bar counter."

The note, somewhat sticky from young Joseph's fingers,
was addressed in hurried fashion to Amy. Moving across to
the lamp on the passage wall she opened it, apprehensive of
the contents, and read it in silence.

"I am a fool. Forgive my incivility. You must both have

68

dinner with us tomorrow. Please, please don't refuse. Yrs ever, David."

"I hope 'tis nothing amiss," said Kate Adams, observing the flush of colour in Amy's cheeks. "Sure, but I've never in my life seen a man more sorrowed at heart than himself, the face he had on him."

"No—no, there's nothing wrong," Amy answered her quietly. "It's an invitation. To Mr Herriot and me. An invitation, that's all."

7

"What d'you mean—why am I here? You invited me, didn't you?" The engaging grin vanished, and Francis Bethway's face dropped back into its usual surly expression. "You said I could come and see you if I liked."

"I know that's what I said—"

"Then you might try looking better pleased about it."

Megwynn Evans bit her lip and cast a hurried glance behind her at the open door of the morning room. Her employer's elderly housekeeper, sending to the nursery with a message that a young gentleman was below to see the governess, had shown grim disapproval when she left them alone together just now, and Megwynn wouldn't put it past the old biddy to be out in the hall still, straining her ears to listen.

She moved away from the door towards the rain-smeared window and said in a low voice, "Look you, Mr Bates doesn't allow callers at the house. You'll have me dismissed, you will. I only said perhaps we could meet on one of my free days."

"So? This is your free day, isn't it?" Francis followed her across the room. "You told me it was always Tuesdays you were given."

"But I've had to change duties since we came back from Bonningale. Young Esmond's leg is that slow mending there's someone needs to stay with him all the time. And Florrie—she took your coat for you—she'd rather have the Tuesday, see, because her young man comes in to Lewes market that day of the week."

"You might've written and said as much," the youth responded sullenly. He was wearing a neatly-pressed suit and clean shirt with starched high collar, and his dark hair had been brushed sleekly into place with macassar oil. Only his boots, mud-spattered from the wet streets, marred the painstaking effort of his appearance. "I've come all the way here from Eastbourne just to see you."

Megwynn's brown eyes softened and a smile dimpled the corners of her mouth. Ever since their first meeting at Bonningale she had found her concentration frequently distracted by thoughts of Francis Bethway. He had been her partner at the harvest supper, and try as she might, she had not been able to put from her mind the warmth she'd felt at his strong young arms around her for the dancing, nor the tingle of her lips when he kissed her goodnight in the shadow of the stairwell.

She had been kissed before, but never as ardently as that; and the delicious sensation had quite robbed her of breath for several minutes after.

Turning from the dreary, rain-soaked vista beyond the window, she moved a little closer and said softly, "I'm glad to see you again, Francis. Indeed I am."

He scowled at her, then looked down at his feet.

With another hasty glance towards the door, she moved closer still. "I've missed your company."

The scowl lightened a fraction. "You have?"

A nod.

"You've been thinking of me?"

She nodded again, and smiled. "Often."

The scowl faded completely, and Megwynn found herself thinking that the change of expression revealed a most attractive handsomeness.

"I've thought about you, too," he said. "Thought about you all the time, every minute of the day and night. I've been right off my food, even. My mother thought I was ill. She thought it was some'at I'd eaten. Oh, Meggie—"

He reached forward and took her by the hand, pulling her towards him, his arms going tightly round her waist.

"Let me give you a kiss, won't you?"

And before she could say no, or perhaps yes, his mouth had found hers. It was only the briefest caress before he drew back, nervously looking into her face to see whether he'd trespassed too far. Then a sudden urgency seemed to possess him and he kissed her a second time, more force-fully, his warm lips fastening upon Megwynn's with even

71

greater ardour than she'd experienced that time with him at Bonningale.

For a moment her limbs felt quite boneless, as though they would have sunk beneath her were it not for the arms circling her waist. Then, remembering where she was, she gave him a little push and twisted her head aside, saying breathlessly, "No, *cariad*, not here—"

"Please, Meggie. Please let me."

"No! What if someone comes in?"

"They won't."

"They might."

His hands dropped reluctantly to his side.

"I want you," he mumbled. "Isn't there a place where we can be alone together?"

Megwynn's cheeks burned pink. Her heart seemed to have soared into her throat and it was as much as she could do to control the trembling of her legs. She had always been a careful girl, she reminded herself. In particular, careful about the company she kept. Apart from a nice young man in Ludlow who'd walked out with her several Sundays, she'd never cared to encourage familiarity.

Not until now.

What was it about Francis Bethway that made her usual good sense desert her entirely? They had nothing in common, either of them, and the fact alone that he was almost three years her junior should have counted against any intimacy. True, he was very handsome with his gipsy-dark hair and nutbrown eyes, and he was tall and well-built for his age. Yet so were a dozen other young men of her acquaintance.

The difference between them and Francis lay not in good looks or maturity, but in the sensations his closeness enkindled within her . . . the delicious warmth that throbbed through her veins at the touch of his hand on her skin . . . the lovely feeling of lassitude that made her want to close her eyes and have him cover her from head to toe with his kisses. No other man had ever made her feel so much a woman.

"There is a place," she whispered, breaking the awkward silence. "But we must take care, *cariad*, great care."

Francis's expression brightened, and eagerly came the

response, "Oh, we'll be careful. I'll see to that, don't you worry!"

He had no doubt that he was in love. He had known it was so the instant Ellis Bates's governess pressed herself against him in the darkness of the stairwell at Bonningale. For all his young years, he was no mere beginner in the ways of the world, having experienced his first taste of them at the age of fifteen when one of the older servants invited him into her bed.

She was dismissed, unfortunately, for extending the same invitation to several of the vicarage tradesmen; leaving Francis to look hungrily elsewhere, and perforce content himself with fumbling for backstairs kisses from his father's other, less accommodating, maids.

Until Megwynn, he'd almost despaired of meeting a female willing to show him the same kindness—or at least, one who would not repulse his familiarity with a slap or a threat of complaint. Now, to his great relief, Fate had found for him a comely and mature young woman who not only tolerated his attentions, but gave every sign of actually enjoying them.

Emboldened by her encouragement at the harvest supper, his feelings had been given free rein; and within an hour of that goodnight embrace, had grown to such a heat of passion as to leave the youth in no doubt that he'd fallen quite violently in love. Since then, every day that he did not see her, every mile that separated her from him, seemed almost too long to be borne; and his dreams and waking thoughts alike were occupied entirely by Megwynn's plump little body and warm soft lips.

It was in this heady state of infatuation with all its attendant excitement, impatience, nervousness, desire and uncertainty, that Francis Bethway had departed early that morning from Eastbourne, leaving behind a note for his mother that he was excusing himself from his studies for a day or so. He was going to Lewes, to pay a visit upon his cousin Amy.

"You've been such a long time away," young Esmond said plaintively. "Where were you, Miss Evans?"

"In the morning room." Megwynn seated herself in the

armchair beside the invalid's bed and took up the piece of embroidery laid aside earlier.

"What were you doing all that while in the morning room?"

"Oh, talking with someone."

"Who?"

"A caller."

"A caller for you?"

There was a slight lift of the eyebrow and a sideways glance at her interrogator. "What do you suppose?"

Esmond's pale pinched face took on a look of superiority.

"You are not meant to receive gentlemen callers, Miss Evans."

"How do you know it was a gentleman, then?"

"I can tell."

"Oh?"

A nod. "It must have been a gentleman by the silly way in which you were smiling to yourself when you came in just now. Ladies always put on silly smiles when they consort with gentlemen whom they admire."

"Is that a fact, indeed?"

Megwynn was in too good a humour to be vexed by this precocious observation. Reaching for the scissors from her work-basket, she snipped a strand of silk; then, re-threading her needle with a fresh colour, enquired, "Has Florrie been to sit with you whilst I was downstairs?"

Esmond nodded again.

"And did she read to you a story, as I asked?"

"I gave her my Mother Goose book," chimed in little Laura, who was playing quietly with her dolls in a corner of the nursery. "She looked at all of the pictures—"

"Florrie is not able to read as well as I, of course," interrupted her brother smugly. "She's stupid. She cannot understand long words."

"But there are no long words in Mother Goose, surely?"

"There are, too!" Esmond snatched up a Kate Greenaway book lying on his bed and opened it at a picture of quaintly-dressed children dancing in a circle at the foot of a windmill.

"Here's one—" He pointed.

Megwynn leaned forward to see. "Ring-a-ring-a-roses?"

"Yes."

74

"But that's not one word. It's five words, look you. Joined together by hyphens."

The smug expression vanished from Esmond's face and he tossed the book aside.

"Florrie couldn't read it, even so," he said peevishly. "She *is* stupid. She cannot tell the difference between a b and a d. Besides which, she smells of the kitchen."

"What a little prig it is, indeed to goodness!" Megwynn's good spirits did not prevent a sharp rebuke for this show of spite.

"But she *does* smell of the kitchen."

"And you, *fachgen*, smell of the sick-bed. But you cannot help it, no more than can Florrie help how it is that she smells."

Esmond's mouth turned down at the corners and he started to fidget with the fringe of the plaid rug thrown over the lower part of his body. The reprimand had discomfited him, and for several minutes he lay silent, smarting at the hurt to his young pride. Then, pretending his injured leg had begun to throb again, he gave a sudden loud groan, and at once succeeded in regaining sympathy and attention from both governess and small sister.

Screwing up his face and drawing in his breath between clenched teeth, he allowed Megwynn to ease him into a more comfortable position against the pillows.

"I shall be jolly glad when I'm allowed about downstairs," he said, and with some truth. "You cannot imagine what a tedious business it is, this having to rest up all the time."

"Never mind, 'Smond," lisped Laura, reaching out a small hand to stroke his cheek. The four-year-old was not finding her brother's convalescence in the least way boring, regarding him as a far more diverting patient than her collection of dolls, whose bland china faces and rosebud mouths never changed expression no matter how she might dose them with potions and paint them with pocks.

"How can I not mind, Laura," Esmond retorted, pushing the hand away. "I'm not allowed to ride my pony, even, and he is becoming so fat for the want of exercise, he'll be quite out of condition this winter."

Twisting himself about on the bed, the boy turned his face from them both and looked resentfully out through the nursery window. Between the wet naked branches of the garden trees it was possible to see as far as the paddock where Merry, a skittish piebald, shared pasture with Laura's pet donkey, the dairy cow kept to supply the household with milk, and Ellis Bates's hunter and pair of carriage greys.

"There is Merry now." The pony's young owner spoke again after a while. "Do you see him? Standing beside the gate? I dare say he is waiting for his treat, as he always does. Poor Merry, how he must miss me. Since Papa forbade his daily tit-bit he must wonder what it is he has done, to be deprived so."

"I hope your pony's want of comfort and company is a lesson to you," Megwynn said firmly. She had moved to the foot of the bed and was looking towards something in the field beyond the paddock. "I hope it will teach you not to go playing with scythes when you're told. If you'd paid me heed that day, instead of showing disobedience—"

"I would not be forced to keep to bed now," the boy finished morosely. "I know. And I regret my disobedience, truly I do, Miss Evans. But regret will not put sugar lumps into Merry's mouth, will it?"

"Now you know what your Papa has said. The pony must not be fed sugar while he is not being given his regular exercise."

Esmond hung his head and heaved a loud sigh.

"Poor Merry," he said again. "Poor old fellow."

The governess did not respond. She appeared suddenly to have become engrossed by whatever it was in the distance she was staring towards.

Then, without turning from the window, she said in a curious tone of excitement, "He does look sad, though, hanging his head over the gate. Why shouldn't he have his treat. There's no harm in it. I'll take him something myself, this evening after supper."

"Oh—will you? Will you, Miss Evans?"

"But it will be all dark after supper," observed Laura, interrupting her brother's exclamations. "How can you see Merry in the dark?"

"I'll have a lantern. Mind, though—it's me that is being the disobedient one now. We must keep this a secret between the three of us. A *big* secret."

"Upon my honour, we won't say a word!" Esmond assured her fervently. "Papa will not learn of it, we promise. We do promise, don't we, Laura? We won't breathe a word to a soul."

Megwynn could have hugged him.

The pastureland beyond the paddock belonged to a large old house called Spences, from which the lane fronting Ellis Bates's property had derived its name.

In the latter years of Victoria's reign, the place was owned by an elderly Quaker lady with an inordinate affection for horses. Despairing of the negligence and downright cruelty shown to these noble animals, she rescued those she could from the misery of being worked to death between the shafts, and brought them home to Spences to pass their old age, literally, in clover.

As each died, such was their benefactress's horror of the horsemeat trade, it was buried in its own plot in a field beside the house, and the grave marked with its name. One much loved favourite, called Charlie, had been given the distinction of a stone monument in the form of a conical mound whose summit, reached by a spiral path, was crowned with an inscribed slab of granite.

Charlie's Mound—a noted landmark in the Spences Lane area—stood close to the long, low building used as both winter stabling and hay store. It was here that Megwynn had arranged with Francis Bethway that they should meet that night.

The moon was at its fullest, and the cloud-rack blown in the fresh wind across its milk-white face sent ragged shadows scudding over the open field below. Watching from the concealment of the stable door, Francis did not see the figure in the dark cloak until a patch of moonlight cast Megwynn's silhouette against the paleness of the monument behind. He ran forward to meet her, dragging her into his arms, and she smelled a faint odour of hay and horses upon his coat. Then, with a hasty look over his shoulder, he took her by the hand and led her back to the shelter of the stable.

"You managed it, then? You got away from the house all right?" He kept his voice to a whisper, so as not to disturb

77

the animals stalled at the further end of the darkened building. "Nobody saw you leave?"

"Only the children. And they'll say nothing. They're in league with me, see." In a few words Megwynn told him about Esmond's pony.

He gave a low laugh. "That was lucky. I was wondering how you'd slip out o' the nursery without them knowing of it."

"It came to me in a flash when the boy was talking this morning. There's a good excuse now, I told myself. Handed to me on a platter, almost. Oh, Francis, Francis—" She pressed herself to him. "I don't know how I've got through this day for thinking of us both."

He kissed her clumsily on the mouth. "Nor me, Meggie. Nor me. I thought it was best I wasn't seen about the streets, so I've been sitting down by the river."

"In this weather?" She lifted his hands and pressed the open palms against her cheeks. "Ooh, there's cold you are, and damp still—"

"I know a way to get warmed, though." He grinned at her in the dimness.

"What way is that, now?"

"Don't you know?"

"I've an idea . . . perhaps."

"Only an idea? Nothing more?"

She gave a teasing little shrug of the shoulder.

Francis reached to fumble for the buttons securing her cloak. When he spoke again, there was the raw edge of excitement in his voice.

"Will you let me show you, then?"

"Show me what?"

"The way to warm us both."

Megwynn pretended to give this her consideration. "If you're careful, mind. I'm a good girl. I don't want you thinking I'm the kind who are no better than they should be—"

She was silenced by another kiss, less clumsy than the first, and then another; and when after several long minutes she was released, could only whisper breathlessly, "Oh *cariad*, oh . . . kiss me again . . ."

78

8

It had been a mistake, of course, to accept David Linton's impetuous invitation to dinner. Amy knew that, just as she knew it was a mistake to go on pretending that nothing between them had changed, that their relationship was still one of amiable cousinly affection.

There had been six at table that evening at the doctor's house in Church Lane: David and Louisa, herself and Ralph Herriot, and the Reverend John Wickenden and his wife. Mr Wickenden, recently appointed parish minister of Weatherfield on the death of the previous incumbent, Mr Everett Howard, whose curate he had been for some half-dozen years, was chairman of the local horticulture society, of which Louisa Linton was a founder member.

Conversation during the meal had been confined to polite social discussion, leavened as the evening wore on with personal topics ranging from Ralph's dairy herd and their hostess's Michaelmas daisies to the forthcoming Christmas bazaar at the church hall. David Linton spoke very little. Chided for this by his wife, he had apologised to the company pleading weariness after a long day, and made an effort to join in the table-talk with a few random remarks of his own before falling silent again.

Amy, seated opposite Ralph Herriot, observed the shrewd grey eyes of the young farmer fixed frequently upon their host with that watchful, thoughtful expression she'd noticed first at Bonningale; and she wished that David, weary or no, would pay a little more attention to his guests and rather less to his wine glass. She had never known him to be other than an abstemious drinker, but by the time they had finished the main course of stewed fillet of beef he'd already drunk the best part of a bottle of claret, and looked as though he now meant to ply himself further with the muscatel accompanying the compôte of fruit and stone cream.

It would have been unthinkable of Louisa to question her husband's orders in front of company, but her pink and white childish features took on an exasperated look when he requested they be served a second bottle of the sweet dessert wine, and she shot a glance across the table at Amy, as if to say, "I blame you for this. Why could you not stay away from us?"

Then, laying down the spoon beside her half-emptied dish, she had patted her napkin daintily to her lips.

"If you would excuse me? I thought I heard little Alice crying. David, will you assist me up, please?"

Her husband helped himself instead to some more of the stone cream.

"Lily will attend to her, my dear."

"Lily is already occupied." Louisa indicated the maid, neatly attired in black, with white collar and cuffs, and frilled cap with starched streamers, who was attending them at table. "She cannot be expected to be in two places at once."

"May I lend assistance, ma'am?" the Reverend Wickenden had offered, half-rising.

"No, no." The ringlets girlishly looped up with blue satin bows swayed from side to side as she shook her head. "Most kind of you, Mr Wickenden, but thank you, no. My husband is about to help me. David—?"

The doctor drained his glass and got up, thrusting back his chair with unnecessary impatience, and moved around the table to where his wife was seated.

Louisa seemed always to be ailing of something, Amy thought critically, watching her place her arms about her husband's neck so that he might lift her to her feet; but her condition—or rather, her helplessness—appeared to have worsened during the past half-year, for she was now apparently almost incapable of walking without assistance.

There had followed a somewhat embarrassed silence while the guests waited until their host had supported his wife from the dining room.

"Poor, dear lady." Mr Wickenden, clearing his throat, was the first to speak once Lily had closed the door behind

80

them. "How sad it is to see one so young afflicted in such fashion."

Mrs Wickenden, a little cottage-loaf of a woman in dark bombazine, echoed the sentiment. Neither Ralph nor Amy felt moved to add anything; and a further few minutes of silence ensued.

Then—"I trust you will have a good journey tomorrow, sir," and "What are your plans for the festive season, Miss Flynn?" the Wickendens asked both together, causing some slight confusion as to who should answer which question first.

Amy had been explaining that she intended to spend a quiet Christmas at home in Lewes, when David Linton returned alone to the table. She saw at once from his expression that something had occurred to vex him, and supposed that Louisa was the cause.

"My wife sends her apologies," he announced, re-seating himself. "She's sitting with Alice for a while. The child has a minor stomach upset which is making her fretful this evening."

He reached out for the decanter and offered it round the table.

"Then perhaps the gentlemen would care to join me in a glass of brandy?" he had suggested, since no one wished for more of the muscatel. "We'll adjourn to the drawing room, shall we? You ladies won't mind if we smoke, I'm sure."

Once settled in armchairs, and Louisa's arrangements of autumn flowers and dried foliage politely admired, Ralph's earlier mention of his acquaintance with Mr Thomas Hardy had been revived by the Reverend Wickenden and the two men, cigars alight, were soon earnestly discussing the merits of the author's work. Mrs Wickenden was content to sit comfortably back and enjoy the warmth of the fire, thankful that she had not laced her corsets too tightly when dressing for dinner, for the meal had been quite excellent and she had done full justice to each course.

It was not long before her head was nodding forward upon the ample bosom, and deprived of her conversation, David and Amy had been left to carry on a somewhat stilted exchange of their own.

"You were saying just now," the doctor began, making

great play of lighting his pipe and getting the tobacco to smoke to his satisfaction, "something about staying at Tea Garden Lane for Christmas this year."

"Yes. I am. There seems no point in going either to Eastbourne or Bonningale when there's still so much needs doing in the house. Now that the drawing room's finished—"

Amy paused awkwardly, the same memory rising unbidden in both their minds.

After a moment she continued, "I'm having a gas cooking range installed next month, which means the kitchen floor must come up for the pipes to be laid. When that's done, it seems as good a time as any to get on—with the kitchen and scullery, I mean."

"You're becoming quite the little home-maker, aren't you."

David had not meant to be sarcastic, but unhappiness, resentment and too much alcohol had together put him in a bitter frame of mind. He wished that Amy and the rest would get up and leave now, so that he might nurse his misery in peace; yet, such is the paradox of loving, he wished at the same time that she might stay and somehow redeem this awful evening with a word, a look, a gesture to assure him she cared far more for him than for this other.

Through a curling grey cloud of pipe smoke his narrowed glance went across the hearth to Ralph Herriot, seated at his ease, one leg resting on the knee of the other, flourishing his cigar as he held forth on some point made by Mr Wickenden.

In a low voice he went on, "I wonder you are not spending the season in Dorsetshire with your new friend. Repaying the compliment, as it were."

This petty display of jealousy irritated Amy, and her reaction had been a strong desire to take David Linton by his black satin lapels and shake some sense back into him.

With an effort of will, she succeeded in masking her annoyance with the light response, "I must await my turn. Henry's been invited instead. It wouldn't be fair of me to push myself forward in place of Maria's betrothed, not with the wedding so close as it is."

"What's that?" cried out Mrs Wickenden, waking from

her doze with a violent start. "What's that you say, John?" Then—"Lord a' mercy!" looking up at the moon-faced dial of the mantel clock. "Is that the time already? Come along, my dear, we must let good Doctor Linton take his rest."

Her husband stubbed the remains of his cigar into the ash-tray and heaved his bulk reluctantly up from the armchair.

His host was already on his feet before him, holding out a less than steady hand to take the minister's brandy glass; but if the Reverend Wickenden hoped it was about to be refilled, he hoped in vain.

"There are three things that rule and ruin a man," said Ralph Herriot, addressing himself to the pair of elongated shadows thrown along the pavement by the street lamp outside David Linton's gate. "Three things. Wine, women and wealth."

He adjusted his felt hat and glanced aside at Amy. "A favourite saying of my father's, that."

"Oh?"

The night air had an edge of frost to it, and she gave an involuntary shiver and paused to turn up the collar of her grey Ulster over-coat before falling into step with him.

He offered an arm. "Are you sure you wouldn't rather be driven back to our lodgings?"

She shook her head. Mr Wickenden had suggested at their leave-taking just now that he convey them both in his trap out to the alehouse, but Amy had declined.

"Yes, I'm sure. I prefer the walk. It's a clear night, and I could do with the fresh air after . . ." She was about to say, "after such a trying few hours," but not wanting to criticise David's aberrant behaviour, finished instead, "after sitting indoors all the evening."

They had gone a way further and were passing beside the wall of St Anne's churchyard when Ralph remarked suddenly, "I'm still waiting to meet him, you know."

"Meet who?"

"That hearty hail-fellow-well-met doctor. You remember, the one whose praises you've been singing? I presume it was Mr Hyde we dined with tonight."

"Mr Hyde? What are you on about? Who's Mr Hyde?"

83

He gave her arm a squeeze and said affectionately, "You *are* a dunce, Amy. I mean R. L. Stevenson's Mr Hyde. *Doctor Jekyll and Mr Hyde*. I suppose you'll say that's another work you haven't yet read—"

"I don't get the time for reading," Amy cut in rather sharply. Her failure to share Ralph's enthusiasm for poetry and prose had been the cause of some good-humoured banter between the two of them in the past, but she was not in a mood tonight for her companion's teasing.

"There are some folk," she went on, "who've nothing better to do all day than to part their hair in the middle—"

"Or sit with their nose in a book?"

"Yes, or sit with their nose in a book! The rest of us are too busy doing a hard day's work. If David seemed out of sorts, I dare say it's because he's bone-weary. He said as much himself at dinner. You heard him."

"Mmm." Ralph made a non-committal sound. "Though it was what I did *not* hear at dinner which interested me more."

"There you go again—talking in riddles!"

He laughed. "Don't scowl at me quite so fiercely, Amy. With a face as lovely as yours, it's a sin to spoil it. A woman's features should be trained to turn upwards. Without laughter, they lose their shape and sag into furrows, robbing maturity of its beauty."

Amy could not help but be a little amused by this piece of homespun philosophy.

"That's better," the young man exclaimed, seeing the shadow of a smile curve her lips.

He checked his step for a moment to swing her over a large puddle at the mouth of a side-street, then continued, "When I mentioned just now my father's old saying about wine, women and wealth, it was your Doctor Linton who'd brought it to mind. There, unless I'm much mistaken, is a man so mired to the neck with misery he's seeking to drown his sorrows in drink, in the hope they'll look smaller through the bottom of a glass."

There was no response to this, and Ralph cast a quick glance at his companion's face. The two of them were now walking past a row of small terraced cottages whose front doors opened directly on to the pavement, and in the light spilling from the lower windows he could see that the smile had disappeared and a tight little look taken its place.

"Well, you've chaffed me often enough about the way I like to watch people," he went on candidly. "There's more to be learned from reading folk's expressions than from listening to their words. Words can be lies. Expressions, especially the eyes, aren't so easily masked."

"And what did you manage to learn from them tonight, pray?" Amy challenged him.

"You told me Doctor Linton comes of yeoman farming stock."

"So he does. What of it?"

"It must have cost his people a pretty penny to support him through medical studies and meet all the other charges entailed. I know the price of a doctor's training. I have a cousin who's a general practitioner in Dorchester."

"You still haven't answered my question."

"Patience! What a hasty creature you are, to be sure." Again, the affectionate tone of voice belied the words. "You likewise informed me that Mrs Linton is the only child of wealthy parents."

"Was. I believe they're both dead."

"Ah. Like as not she's the sole beneficiary of the estate. Making her something by way of being an heiress."

Amy gave a little shrug of the shoulder.

"No doubt it was Mrs Linton's money," Ralph continued, "which paid for that expensive residence and furnished it so very handsomely."

"What if it was? It's hers to spend."

"Wine, women and wealth? There are some men, my dear, men of principle, who resent having to live on their wives' money. I suspect your friend is one of them."

"But David doesn't live on Louisa's money—"

"Has he said as much to you?"

"Well, no. Of course he hasn't."

"A country doctor's income is not as generous as you may suppose. My cousin's practice is a fairly large one, yet after deducting his one hundred pounds expenses, he earns little more than three hundred and fifty pounds a year on which to keep him and his family. Doctor Linton's household could hardly be managed on so low a figure as that, not without

85

some other source of income. And where would that come from, if not from his wife?"

"I can't see what business it is of ours."

"No. But it's interesting all the same."

The young man paused in his stride and made to lift Amy over another puddle. This time, however, instead of placing her hands on his shoulders as before, she pulled away and walked round on the other side of the gutter.

They continued together along the street in silence.

In one of the alleyways the neighbourhood cats were starting up a fight, their deep-throated wails magnified by the confines of the walls. Just as Amy and her companion passed the alley mouth, the wails rose to a sudden snarling, spitting fury, and a tabby shape shot out at their feet and vanished into the darkness of a row of allotments across the way.

"'Nature, red in tooth and claw'," Ralph quoted laconically. "There's something to be said for a cat-fight, I feel. The airing of mutual insults, the unsheathing of claws, the swift attack. And the quick retreat for a private licking of wounds. A pity in a way that civilised womanhood cannot behave in like fashion. So much more satisfying for all concerned than icy smiles and honeyed insincerities."

"If you want to see women fighting, there are plenty to watch on Saturday nights in Lewes outside the public houses," Amy retorted, still keeping her distance. "Lord knows, I saw enough as a child when I used to wait about in the streets for Uncle Harry—"

"No, no, you've misunderstood me entirely," the other came back hastily. "That wasn't what I meant at all. Oh, do take my arm again, Amy, and stop being quite so contrary."

She shook her head; then, seeing he was not to be dissuaded, relented with good grace and moved back to his side, to be rewarded with a warm squeeze of the hand.

"I was thinking of Louisa Linton when I spoke of cat-fights." Ralph returned to his theme. "From the glances she was giving you at the table this evening, it was obvious you were rather less than welcome company."

"Then it's just as well looks can't kill, isn't it. David said that she resents me. But I don't know why. I've never done anything to harm her."

"Except lead her husband into temptation."

"That's not true!" Amy at once tried to snatch her hand back again. "How dare you say such a thing. Leave go of me—"

She pulled away, but Ralph tightened his grip and held her hand firmly upon his arm, forcing her back into step beside him.

"It *is* true," he said quietly. "I don't say you've deliberately tempted David Linton. You're not capable of anything quite so deceitful. But one's only to look at the man's face to see what he feels for you. You should have told me, you know, Amy."

"Told you what?"

"The reason for your friend's marked alteration. You do know that he's in love with you, don't you?"

Amy averted her head and remained silent.

"His wife's not blind," the other continued. "Neither is she completely the giddy creature she seems. That little display of helplessness at dinner was all a charade. I'm not saying that Mrs Linton isn't genuinely of a delicate constitution, but watching her tonight, it seemed to me she rather tends to play on her ill-health to attract sympathy."

"You're very observant, aren't you," Amy turned on him cuttingly. "I suppose you're about to say next that I actually encourage David to pay me attention."

"No. I wouldn't go so far as to say that."

"I don't know why you should care anyway."

"Don't you?"

The two had by this time reached the top of the lane leading to the alehouse. Another couple walked in the opposite direction, calling out goodnight as they passed, the heels of the woman's boots click-clacking on the flinty surface.

Ralph stopped and looked back over his shoulder; and when the pair were out of earshot, asked again, "Don't you, Amy?"

The usual amused little half-smile had gone from his face and his expression, caught in the faint reflection of a street lamp, was one of total earnestness.

"David Linton isn't the only man whose wits have been led astray by your loveliness, you know. You must be aware, surely, of the very deep regard which I myself have for you—"

"Don't—please!" The cry held a note of alarm. "Don't say any more, Ralph. Please don't."

"You're frightened of being loved, aren't you. No, don't turn your face away. You *are* frightened. I can sense as much. You shy off from becoming too much involved in the emotions of others. You feel yourself threatened by them, perhaps."

Amy did not answer.

"It's because of your past. Because of what happened during your childhood and before," the young man went on. "The scars are still there, my dear, but you're too proud to let them show."

In a low voice she said, "I'd soonest not talk about such things."

"Why not? Scars can't heal cleanly unless they're kept bared for the air to get at them. They fester otherwise."

"Please—" Amy tried again to pull free of the grip upon her arm.

"No, listen to me. I know all about your background. About your father and what he did. And what became of him. Your mother, too."

"How can you know?" she demanded fearfully.

"Henry Bashford told me."

"He had no right!"

"His marriage to my sister gives him every right. I wanted to know all about you. And Henry obliged. He said . . ." Ralph hesitated.

"Well? What was it he said?"

"That you're the skeleton in the family closet."

There was a moment's silence; and then Amy gave an odd little laugh.

"The skeleton in the family closet," she repeated bitterly. "Yes, I suppose that's how they must see me. An outcast. A murderer for father. A lunatic for mother. Abandoned almost at birth, brought up in neglect and indifference, unwanted—"

"You see? You see how those scars of yours still fester? If you keep picking away at them in your mind, how are they ever to heal? Oh, Amy, Amy . . ."

He gave her a slight shake before drawing her closer into his arms.

"These things don't matter. It's you—the person you are—that's important. These things are behind you now, all part of the past, buried. You mustn't let them hurt you still. When people meet you for the first time, d'you think they stop to consider the circumstances of your childhood? No! They see a beautiful young woman whose grace and warmth and ease of manner they find immediately attracting. Heaven knows, I can't find it in me to blame David Linton for desiring you . . ."

Ralph paused again. Putting his hand beneath Amy's chin, he lifted her face to his. During their few days here together in Weatherfield, he had made no attempt at familiarity, beyond a touch of the hand or the occasional slight intimacy which courtesy and custom allowed. This was the first time he had so much as held her in his arms. He would very much have liked to kiss her at this moment; but somehow it would not have been quite in keeping with the mood of the evening.

Instead he said carefully, "What d'you intend doing about him, Amy?"

"About David? I don't know. I wish to God I did."

"You're going to have to choose, you realise that?"

"How d'you mean—choose?"

"Choose between us. David Linton and me. I want our friendship to continue. I want it to grow and deepen into something more. But I won't share you. Either you promise me never to see Doctor Linton again—or this evening will be the last time you and I spend together. The choice is yours, Amy. Which is it to be?"

9

The old labourer Robert Lambe died just as the first snow of winter began falling one bleak December morning. He was buried the week before Christmas in St Anne's churchyard, in the same grave as his long-dead father and mother.

There was no stone to mark the spot. Here, as elsewhere, the poor of the parish were interred without epitaph beneath the sheep-cropped greensward among the dignified memorials to their masters and betters, their resting places known only by a number and a name in the sexton's register.

Those coming to pay their respects to Robert Lambe would have little trouble in remembering where he lay, however, for his humble grave was over-shadowed by the churchyard's most imposing monument: an angel figure rising upon tiptoe, as though the widespread wings of stone were about to lift it into flight, the stern-visaged features tilted heavenward and one arm upraised with pointing finger to indicate that place upon which the beholder's thoughts ought firmly to be fixed.

The monument was of recent date, its livid appearance as yet unstained by time or nature, and on the day of the funeral the crust of frozen snow glistening upon its limbs in the pale winter sunlight had lent it a most unearthly aspect.

There had formerly been a plain headstone on the site, sacred to the memory of one Esmond Jezrahel Bates, sometime rector of Weatherfield; but Ellis Bates, considering his father deserving of a more impressive memorial, had had the stone replaced and the base of the angel mount inscribed in pious appreciation of the deceased's ministry.

Few parishioners still living were able to recall the Reverend Bates's brief incumbency almost half a century earlier, and questions had been asked at the parish council whether so undistinguished an individual ought rightly to be singled out for honour in this prominent fashion. Several of the more influential council members, however, including the present incumbent Mr Wickenden, were of the view that the figure greatly dignified St Anne's yard; and no more was said on the subject.

The day following Robert Lambe's burial, Ellis Bates came up from Lewes to visit his father's grave. It was raw, frosty weather and ice upon the roads had slowed his journey considerably so that the afternoon light was already beginning to fade by the time he drove his curricle and pair of greys into Weatherfield high street.

The delay was a vexatious circumstance and meant that his visit must of necessity be briefer than he wished, for he was expected to dine that evening in Tunbridge Wells at the house of a colleague, Frank Stone. Mr Stone, a partner with the firm of Stone, Simpson, Hanson, solicitors, was clerk to the Guardians and school attendance and assessment committees for Tonbridge Union, and Ellis's position as schools inspector brought the two men frequently into contact. There being several pressing matters for discussion, he had been invited to stay overnight in the Wells as Mr Stone's guest, and return to Lewes on the morrow in good time for the start of the Christmas festivities.

Leaving the horses to be watered and rested with the ostler of The Rising Sun tavern in the high street, Ellis Bates removed a wrapped box from the back of the curricle, and hoisting it beneath one arm, set off at a smart pace across the green to St Anne's. Arriving at the churchyard, he entered through the lychgate and took the left-hand path to reach his destination along by the west wall.

Yesterday's little funeral had left the crusted snow churned into dirty slush underfoot, and a deep frown etched Ellis's pale features as he examined the tumbled clods of earth heaped upon the new-dug mound beside his father's monument. Some of the clods had rolled down to rest against the base, soiling the bleached whiteness of the stone. He kicked them impatiently away with the side of his boot; then, bending a little awkwardly in the heavy Chesterfield over-coat he had worn for travelling, laid his bulky parcel on the ground and pulled away the paper wrapper.

The domed surface of a glass cover glinted in the last rays

of wintry sunlight as he drew the object carefully from its packing of wood shavings. Setting it to one side, he proceeded with even greater care to extract its partner, a round black base upon which was arranged a sheaf of arum lilies, wrought in wax and bound with purple velvet ribbon.

This decoration had been made to his order by a firm of funerary suppliers and was intended to stand in a niche sculpted for that purpose between the angel's up-rising foot and a fold of its garment hem. Upon fitting the base into position, however, Ellis discovered to his annoyance that there was not sufficient space to accommodate the glass cover, so that it was quite impossible to lock it correctly over the base.

For some minutes he struggled in an effort to get it right, cracking part of a waxen bloom in the process; and eventually, seeing that he would only damage the decoration further if he persisted, in some irritation set about replacing dome and base into the box, cursing beneath his breath at the ineptitude of whoever had misread his instructions and provided a cover which was patently inches too high for its purpose.

The sun had by now dwindled to a cherry-red globe behind the churchyard trees, its dying glow flushing the naked snow-rimmed branches crimson before it sank away into a veil of cloud and released the grey half-light of dusk from the shadows.

St Anne's tower clock chiming the half-hour reminded Ellis that time was getting short. Gathering up the box once more beneath his arm, he stood for a moment in dispirited contemplation, his eyes upon the lettering of his father's name, before turning abruptly to retrace his steps along the path.

As was his custom on these visits, he directed his way towards the church porch with the intention of going inside to spend a little while in prayer before leaving. The candles of the brass chandelier in the side chapel had already been lit, he noticed, and in the pool of light someone was moving about.

Removing his high-crowned bowler hat, he closed the church door behind him and walked quietly along the south aisle to his usual place, the pew nearest to a wall-board upon which was recorded a list of Weatherfield's parish ministers. Sitting down, the box beside him on the seat, he leaned forward and bowed his face into his hands.

Ellis Bates was not a particularly prayerful man, and his supplications to the Almighty were of habit brief and to the point. After a few minutes had passed he gave a heavy sigh; and lifting his head again, raised his eyes to the board above, conscious as ever of the tight little lump in the throat he invariably experienced on coming into this place.

It had been his father's church once. It had contained the living presence of a man Ellis had never known, but whose form and voice and character had moulded his own. This hushed little church, mustily redolent of great age and neglectful faith, seeming always, he thought, to be waiting for Evensong, was the only tangible thing he had of his father's memory.

Ellis's glance wandered past the darkening windows to the pulpit and down across the box pews to the communion rail. There had been a time when the Reverend Esmond Bates's eyes had surveyed this same scene, his feet had trodden the same floor, he had knelt before the same altar, his words had echoed in the same confines . . . sometimes it was almost as if he were here still, an invisible presence, no more than a breath's span away from the son he had created in the final hours of his unhappy life.

Footsteps sounded, coming hesitantly along the centre aisle. Ellis was no more than half-aware of them; and it was not until a voice addressed him in the stillness that he looked round to see who was there.

A young woman in a fur-edged cape stood silhouetted against the brightness of the chapel candles.

"Mr Bates?" she asked again, a trifle uncertain. "It is you, is it not?"

He rose to his feet and regarded her in almost cursory fashion before inclining his head in acknowledgement.

There followed an awkward pause; then she laughed faintly, embarrassed by the apparent lack of recognition.

"You remember me, I trust, sir? Doctor Linton's wife?"

"Yes. Yes, of course. Mrs Linton, to be sure." Ellis responded with a stiff little bow. "How d'you do, ma'am."

"I hope I am not intruding."

"Not at all." In the circumstances he could scarcely say otherwise.

"Then you will not mind if I am seated?"

Another pause; then another inclination of the head, this time betokening compliance, since inherent good breeding prevented the discourtesy of his promptly pleading an engagement elsewhere. He had met Louisa Linton here on several past occasions, and while finding her childish manner intensely cloying, had nonetheless appreciated the interest she evinced in his father's connection with Weatherfield.

As the doctor's young wife mounted the shallow step to take a seat in the pew in front, Ellis noted that she was using a malacca cane to support herself, and was moved to observe, "You have met with some accident, ma'am?"

In the reflected candlelight the large blue eyes were turned upon him with an expression that would have excited pity in one less deliberately self-inured against such sentiment.

"How kind of you to be concerned, Mr Bates. Alas, I fear it is my frailty which has brought me to such a poor state. My constitution has become yet more delicate since last we had the pleasure of meeting, so that now it has become quite impossible for me to stand without assistance for any length."

Ellis made a sound of polite regret.

"Why, I am not able even to walk from here so far as my own house," Louisa continued, and he would have sworn that the catch in her voice was intentional. "That is why I am so glad of your company. I have been arranging the ivy boughs in the chapel for Christmas Eve and must wait for our serving man to bring me home. I hope I do not seem to presume too far, Mr Bates, but would you remain with me until Albert comes? I am a little afraid to be alone now that daylight is failing, you see. I told him to fetch me before five o'clock and it is almost that now, I am sure."

The affected manner in which she spoke grated upon Ellis's nerves. Reaching inside the breast of his coat, he drew out his pocket watch and pressed the spring to release the lid. There was still some ten minutes needed to the hour, but he could hardly refuse Mrs Linton's request, not for the sake of so short a delay; and it was with something of an ill

94

grace that he snapped the time-piece shut and put it away again.

Louisa's features assumed a simpering expression. "You are intending to return to Lewes this evening?"

The answer came tersely. "No, ma'am. I am travelling on to Tunbridge Wells."

"How pleasant. Before my health became so indifferent, I used to visit the Wells almost every month. A very pretty town, do you not agree, sir?"

"Indeed."

"Is it to the Pantiles area you are going?"

Ellis raised his eyes and appeared to give his mind to the ministers' board on the wall above.

"Mount Sion, ma'am."

"But that is quite close to the Pantiles, is it not?"

A nod.

She followed the direction of his gaze. The board was of fairly recent date, an innovation of the previous incumbent of the parish; and though the twilight filtering through the stained glass windows was now almost too dim to see by, it was still possible to pick out the gold-leaf lettering of the final four names:

> John Yardley 1837–1852
> Esmond Jezrahel Bates 1852
> Everett Howard 1852–1889
> John Frederick Wickenden 1889–

"Of course, you have broken your journey to pay seasonal respects at your dear father's grave," Louisa began again after a moment.

A second nod.

Twisting herself round a little more, she craned her head forward, the better to see the box on the pew seat at his side. In his vexation, Ellis had paid no heed to securing it properly, and in carrying it into the church, the top had fallen open slightly to disclose the steely sheen of the glass cover.

For all her contrived veneer of childishness, Louisa had a sharply observant eye for small details, from which she was able often to draw the right conclusion. Mr Bates would not have brought the box with him unless it contained something pertinent to his errand; and a glass dome suggested the type of funerary decoration commonly seen on the better class of churchyard memorial.

"May I ask, sir, is that not an arrangement of wax flowers you have beside you?"

"It is." Ellis glanced at the offending object. "Unfortunately, I find it does not quite suit, and I am obliged to return it in exchange for another."

"Ah. My husband Doctor Linton ordered one such for his parents' grave at Shatterford, you know. A most delightful thing. Camellias and roses. And so life-like to look at, one would think the blooms were truly Nature's own work. It excited great admiration in the district and the manufacturer —an Italian figure-maker, of course, they are quite the best at the art—why, he told us he had never before known his order book to be so full."

"Indeed." Elllis drew in his breath in what sounded suspiciously like impatience, and stood up. "May I suggest, ma'am, it would be better if we were to wait in the porch. The light here is almost gone."

"Oh, but we can remove ourselves to the chapel—"

"The porch is more convenient for our purpose. Your manservant will doubtless be here in a few minutes more."

Louisa's lower lip jutted and her face took on a sulky expression. Without making any attempt to raise herself up, she said, "Then would you assist me, please?" and waited for him to leave the pew and help her to her feet.

As they proceeded at the slowest pace along the aisle to the porch door, it was politeness alone which prompted Ellis to enquire, "Doctor Linton is well, I trust, ma'am? And your child?"

"Yes, thank you. Both quite well. Little Alice has a weakness of the chest, you know, which is always worse during the winter months. But my husband says she will grow out of it. I wish it were possible to say the same of him."

"I beg your pardon?"

"I said, I wish it were possible to say the same of my husband." The voice had now acquired a petulant note.

"I'm sorry . . . I fail to understand you. Say what, precisely?"

"That he will grow out of it."

96

The irksome repetition of words tried Ellis sorely.

"Do I take it that Doctor Linton suffers from a weakness of the chest also?"

"Oh, no. Not a weakness of the chest. It is his heart, I think. Or his head. Or perhaps even both together, since the one appears to rule the other to the detriment of all sense."

This sounded too much as though she were about to launch into some tiresome complaint. Not wishing to encourage her, Ellis made no answer.

They went on through the shadowy gloom in silence, Louisa clinging to his arm with one hand and supporting herself with the malacca cane in the other. Then, as they reached the door and he was about to turn the large iron ring handle, she suddenly startled him by crying out, "No one seems to care. No one seems to understand. Oh, the humiliation of it all! The constant torment I am forced to suffer on that woman's account!"

The wild tones echoed through the quietness of the church in a most dramatic way, and as though excited by this effect, she continued loudly, "Oh, Mr Bates, if I could but tell you of the misery I endure because of her. She has turned my husband's love away from me, robbed my poor child of a father's attention. Would that I had never known that wicked creature's name, never welcomed her to my home!"

The fur-rimmed hood of Louisa's cape was tossed back, releasing a profusion of beribboned ringlets. Had she not been so self-aware of the attractive picture this created, she might have taken better note of her companion's frozen expression.

"You know who it is who has wronged me, sir . . . who it is who has brought me to this piteous condition?"

Wordlessly, Ellis reached forward and pulled open the heavy door, letting in the chill of nightfall. Outside, beyond the churchyard wall, a lamplighter could be seen making his way up the street, whistling tunelessly, his progress marked by the nimbus of gas-lamps threading the darkness behind him along Church Lane.

Were it not for Louisa Linton's hand clutched upon his sleeve, Ellis would have left her there and had no further part in this hysterical scene.

"You know who it is, do you not, Mr Bates?" she repeated in a high-pitched voice; and the lamplighter paused and shifted the ladder on his shoulder to see who it was creating a disturbance in the church porch.

The tower clock, striking the hour of five in sonorous chimes, spared Ellis the need of reply.

"I feel that we are fellow creatures in a shared adversity," she went on rather more calmly once the chimes had ceased. "You, sir, and my poor little Alice both have been robbed of a father because of the deeds of that woman's family. Oh, there is no justice in this life. If there were, God would not allow such wickedness to go unpunished. You must know, sir, the creature dared to show herself in Weatherfield again, in the company of some gullible young man she has snared with her falsity . . . pretending to all the world that he was the one for whom she cared, and no other. And all the while she was working to set a trap for my husband . . . using that Mr Herriot to blind us to her true purpose in returning here. She feared she was losing my husband's regard, you see, since he has tried to put an end to their acquaintance and have no futher connection with her. And now . . . oh, now he is like a man living some evil dream, Mr Bates. His health is suffering, and his work, and the welfare of his patients . . . all suffering on account of that Jezebel, that Amy Flynn."

She paused for a moment to draw her breath and to turn tear-filled eyes upon her companion. The tirade appeared to have left him oddly unmoved. Mistaking this stilly silence for sympathy, Louisa recovered herself and began once more in the same vein, embroidering upon her many grievances, repeatedly blaming Amy for her treachery and her husband for his weakness, while lamenting woefully upon the piteousness of her own situation as betrayed wife and mother.

Unmoved Ellis Bates might indeed appear—with not so much as the tic of a jaw muscle to betray his self-control— yet the frosty chill of the December air was hardly colder than the anger swelling slowly within him as he was forced to listen to this display of histrionics. He had believed the intimacy between Amy and David Linton had been checked by the girl's recent friendship with Ralph Herriot—"her very warm admirer" as his mother had been at pains to describe the fellow that day he'd been at Bonningale to learn the truth of his father's death. Now, from what he was hearing, the affair was as much alive as it had ever been.

Ellis's obsession with Amy and her background was of a most conflicting nature: emotional love warring constantly with intellectual loathing. Depending upon which course of events dictated the knife-edge balance of his mind, the scales of that obsession might be tipped sometimes one way, sometimes the other; and at present they were tipped towards a rancour which, needing some scapegoat, assumed the form of a totally irrational dislike of Louisa Linton.

This bitter mood was exacerbated by the numerous irritations of the day: the delayed journey, the frustration and disappointment, the prospect of a cold, dark drive ahead and a late arrival at his host's table, and not least, the way this silly creature had thrust herself upon him to bleat out the tawdry details of her marriage.

If David Linton still yearned after Amy, he told himself fiercely, then whose fault was it but Mrs Linton's alone. Had she managed her husband better, there would be no need for the man to look elsewhere for another woman's company. If, instead of behaving in the manner of a spoiled child, she learned to conduct herself as an intelligent wife, cease her simpering affectations and assume a little dignity, then perhaps her husband would be rather more inclined to pay his attentions at his own hearthside.

"Oh, Mr Bates, how well you comprehend my distress," Louisa was now exclaiming tearfully. "I can see in the sternness of your expression what pain you must feel at the injustice I am forced to suffer. Oh, unhappy creature that I am—"

Just as her lamentations threatened to dissolve into noisy sobs, the sound of a horse-drawn vehicle was heard emerging from the top of Church Lane.

"There—that will be Albert at last," she cried, visibly brightening. "Whatever can have kept him so late, I wonder."

She started forward a step, obviously expecting Ellis to assist her along the path to the lychgate; and turning up her face to his, prettily sniffed back her tears and with a sweet, sad smile declared, "How am I ever to express my gratitude

99

for all your kindness, sir? You cannot imagine how comforting it is to be able to pour out one's troubles to a sympathetic ear. Your tactful silence encourages me to believe that you have my well-being very much at heart. We are kindred spirits indeed. No—there is no need to speak of it—" as Ellis made an inarticulate noise—"I shall leave you, content in the knowledge that I have found the truest of friends to support me in my time of trial."

10

"If this Christmas goose had ha' been much bigger," Minnie Brocklebank declared, pausing to eye the plump-breasted bird lying to one side of the kitchen table ready for stuffing, "we'd never ha' got it in the blessed oven, let alone in the roasting pan."

She applied herself once more to the chopping board, vigorously working the blade of her knife fan-wise over a bunch of sage leaves.

"No, never got it in the blessed oven, we wouldn't."

Taking up the board, she scraped off the leaves into a bowl of crumbed bread and added several handfuls of chopped onion; then glanced across at her husband, down on his knees before the gas cooker.

"You not got that thing lit yet, our Ted?"

There was a grunt as Ted Brocklebank leaned forward and cautiously inserted a burning taper. Moments later the sudden loud pop! of the gas jets igniting made him jerk hurriedly away, catching himself a crack as he did so.

"Durned gas!" he exclaimed, rubbing furiously at his head so that the coarse ginger hair stood up in tufts. "Whyever Miss Amy wanted it laying on here, I'll never know. That old coal-range we had in this kitchen did well enough all the years Mr Harry was living."

He glared suspiciously at the shiny black apparatus standing on stubby legs against the kitchen wall. Along the skirting behind it ran a length of copper piping, one end rising up the side of the cooker to connect with four brass taps, the other end disappearing into a cupboard which housed the meter.

"Not safe, it ain't, exploding in your face like that. Gi' me a bit of honest coal in an open grate any day o' the week."

"Oh, stop your grumbling, do, and come and hold this fowl for me," his wife retorted good-humouredly. "I'll never

101

get the thing stuffed else. It's gone three already and we promised your Daisy we'd see her in The Grenadier come half-past."

Ted got from his knees, wiping his large red hands on the front of his waistcoat as he came to the table. One foot was twisted inwards, which caused him to walk with a limping gait, the result of a childhood accident when a carriage wheel had gone over the foot and crushed the bones. In spite of this deformity he was a well set-up man, with a thick bull neck upon brawny shoulders, his frame heavily muscled from years spent working as a coal-heaver on the wharves at the bottom end of Lewes.

"You haven't pushed that oven door shut," his wife reminded him, giving a brisk sideways jerk of the head.

"What's the point o' shutting the door afore there's some'at inside it to cook?"

"So's to get a good heat up, o' course. And there's no need to break the blessed thing off its hinges, neither! Now will you come round here and take hold o' this fowl's legs while I see to the stuffing."

In contrast to her husband, Minnie Brocklebank was so small and slight in build as to seem almost a child still, though she was well past thirty. Her mousy hair, worn fastened on top of her head with tortoiseshell combs, tended to hang down in whisps about the thin little face, accentuating the waif-like appearance. But what her features may have lacked in prettiness was more than compensated for by the lively expression of her eyes; and if there were lines about the mouth, they were formed not so much by hardship—though she had known much of that—as by laughter and good humour.

Minnie had first come to work here at the house in Tea Garden Lane as a young girl, when Amy's mother, Rosannah Weldrake, shared the place with her reprobate brother Harry. She could well remember Rosannah being wed to Frank Flynn, and Amy and her dead twin being born; and then, a short while later, the mother being taken away to a bedlam, and after that, Harry Weldrake's ill-starred marriage.

Her own marriage to Ted Brocklebank in 1879 had removed her from service for a time; but when the two of them failed to start a family she came back eventually to Tea Garden

Lane, and once Amy became mistress it seemed a practical step for her husband to join her there. The arrangement worked to the benefit of all, for the house required a general handyman-caretaker and Ted was only too pleased to give up the dirty, tiring work of coal-heaving, while Minnie happily assumed sole responsibility below stairs where she had spent so many years as a skivvy.

"There—that's about filled it nicely." She spooned the last of the stuffing into the goose. "I thought a quarter-pound o' crumbed bread would suffice wi' them four onions and a nice cooking apple."

Passing the tail rump through a slit in the skin, she picked up a length of thin twine from the table and dexterously trussed the bird ready for roasting. Then, stacking her used utensils together on the chopping board, carried the load across into the scullery to put to soak in the brownstone sink.

"Did you remember to put some more coppers in the meter, our Ted?" she called back above the splash of water from the pump.

"Aye." He had taken up his newspaper and was now reading a report of the association football match between Ardingly and North End Rangers.

"You'd best check it afore we go out," her voice came again after several minutes more.

No answer.

"Ted! You hear what I say?"

"What? Oh—aye. Aye, I'll check it."

Minnie came back into the kitchen, pulling off her long white pinafore to fold over the back of the Windsor chair.

Seeing her husband immersed in his reading, she cried, "Now then, look sharp! You can glance at your paper later. Put it aside and help me get this fowl into the oven. It'll never be cooked, else, and there's nothing tastes worse to my mind than an under-done bird. The roasting pan's there behind you on the dresser shelf. No, not that—that's the fish kettle. The one next it. Aye, that's it. Let's have it here on the table."

The goose was carefully transferred to the pan and carried over to the oven, which was now beginning to give off a solid warmth into the room.

"There—" Minnie declared with some satisfaction, closing the door firmly upon their Christmas dinner. "Now I've just got to swill my face and tidy my hair and I'm ready to go out. Oh, afore I forget—look in the tin on the mantelpiece, Ted, and make sure there's enough pennies for the meter in case I'll need to change a tanner at The Grenadier."

She threw a quick glance around the kitchen. The vegetables for the meal had been prepared earlier and were ready in their black enamel saucepans for her to cook as soon as she returned. The giblets to be stewed down for gravy—

Minnie snatched a hand to her mouth. "The giblets, Ted? What did you do wi' the blessed giblets?"

"Eh? Oh, I set 'em in the jug in the scullery."

"Best not leave 'em there. The cat'll have 'em for sure. Fetch the jug in, will you, and stand 'em inside the dresser. They won't hurt there for an hour or two till we come back. And when you've seen to that for me, go and change your collar—"

"Change my collar? What for? It were clean on yesterday morning."

"That's as may be, but I've starched you a fresh 'un for Christmas Eve. Now get a move on, do. You know your Daisy don't like having to mind the counter by herself, not wi' that daft Percy hanging about pestering her like he does."

"About time you pair got here!"

Daisy Brocklebank had to raise her voice to make herself heard above the noisy hubbub of conversation in the saloon bar of The Grenadier.

"I were beginning to think you'd stopped off for a couple o' quick 'uns in The Bricklayers Arms."

"I'd gi' you a couple o' quick 'uns in *my* arms, given half a chance, Daisy," called out a chubby moon-faced individual standing at the bar counter.

His invitation went ignored.

"It took me a sight longer than I thought, getting the Christmas goose in the oven," Minnie explained, settling herself down with a quick nod of thanks for the glass of port and lemon which her sister-in-law had already poured for her. "You never seen such a bird. Twice the size of anything

Coppard's got hanging outside his shop, eh Ted? It were delivered special all the way from Dorsetshire."

"What, that gentleman friend o' Miss Amy's sent it, did he?" the snubnosed young barmaid asked, handing her brother Ted his usual "sleeve" of Harvey's ale.

"Aye." Ted raised the glass and took a long swallow, wiping the froth from his moustache with the back of a hand. "Aye, sent it by the railway. I had to go down to the station last night to collect the durned thing."

Daisy eyed herself sideways in the reflection of one of the tall wall-mirrors set over the bench seats around the crowded room. Licking a finger to smooth down a stray hair or two in her frizzed ginger fringe, she said, "D'you reckon he's got a fancy for her, then, this gentleman of her'n?"

"Oh, aye. I reckon he's got that, all right—"

"I bet t'aint half the fancy I got for you, though, Daisy," the moon-faced customer interrupted again before Ted could finish answering his sister.

She turned angrily. "Why don't you go and cut your stick, Percy Parkes! I'm having a private conversation here."

She was about to add something more when a voice from along the counter started calling loudly for some service, and seeing the other barmaid already occupied, she went off to attend to the order herself.

"Can I treat you to a drink wi' me, Daisy?" her admirer asked, not in the least abashed, as soon as she returned.

She shook her head and turned her back on him; then, upon consideration, appeared to change her mind and said over her shoulder, "We're not supposed to drink wi' customers. But gi' me a florin, and I'll get myself some'at later on."

Accepting his coin with a small disdainful smile, she dropped it into her apron pocket and moved away down the counter to her sister-in-law.

"You ready for another port and lemon, Minnie?"indicating the glass in the other's hand. "Percy's paying. Ted? How about you?"

"Now that's what I call generous," Ted responded, grinning broadly and giving a wink.

"Will he marry her, though, d'you reckon?" Daisy took up the subject again as she refilled her brother's "sleeve" at the beer pump on the counter.

"If she'd have him."

"Oh? You think she won't?"

"Since they went off to Weatherfield together them few days last autumn, she's seen neither hair nor hide o' the chap."

"Belikes they had a falling-out?"

"It can't ha' been that," came in Minnie. "Why should he send her that fine goose, else? It's my opinion she can't make up her mind to have him. That's what it is. She's keeping him a-dangling at arm's reach."

"Would you marry *me* if I asked you, Daisy?" ventured the persistent Percy. "Would you take *me* for husband?"

The response was spirited. "Not you nor any man, Percy Parkes. Why in Lord's name should I? I've got a dog that snarls, a chimney that smokes, a parrot that swears, and a cat that stays out half the night. Whatever would I want wi' a husband?"

There was laughter from those around who had paused from their drinking to hear this piece of humour and some fun was poked at the expense of the amorous Mr Parkes, who responded by burying his face disconsolately in his tankard.

"You not having no company at the house this Christmas, you say, Minnie?" Daisy asked when she'd finished serving another customer.

"That's right. There'll be only the three of us. Me and Ted, and Miss Amy."

"A bit different from last year, eh?"

Minnie rolled her eyes by way of comment.

Last year, as she remembered, Harry Weldrake hadn't long installed his music hall moll Gertie Jukes at the house, and Gertie and her brother Fred had filled the place for a week with their cronies, drinking all the old man's liquor, picking his larder clean as a bone, and misusing the bedrooms in a manner that had made Minnie, for all that she was a wedded woman, blush to behold.

Since, however, Fred Jukes was now walking out with none other than Daisy herself, Minnie prudently kept these thoughts to herself and said only, "Aye. A bit different from last year." Then, changing the subject—"A quiet Christmas won't come amiss, though. She'll have had her fill o' company will Miss Amy, these past weeks in Eastbourne at her Aunt Isabelle's."

Daisy rather doubted whether a parsonage was the place for a girl to have a good time's enjoyment, and said so, adding, "She can't ha' seen much o' that cousin of her'n. That Francis Bethway. He's been back here in Lewes again. I seen him only the day afore yesterday, leaning on the wall by Cliffe bridge."

Ted Brocklebank set down his half-drained glass. "Aye, I seen him there myself. Looked to me like he'd been roughing it, an' all, he did."

"How d'you mean, Ted? Roughing it?" his wife wanted to know, somewhat concerned. "You never said ought o' this to me."

He shrugged.

"Belikes he's got a woman in the town," opined Daisy, smiling across at herself in the wall mirror opposite. "You know—a piece on the sly that he comes up to visit wi'out his mam and dad getting to know. I wonder who it is she can be? I wouldn't mind myself being in her shoes. He's a fine-looking fellow, is that Francis."

"You have a care for your tongue, Daisy," her brother said quickly, and there was a note of warning in his tone. "Whilst you're a-keeping company wi' Fred Jukes, you'd best not let him catch you throwing your eye about, you hear? You'll find yourself taking a tumble upon his fist, else."

"What, Fred? He wouldn't dare."

"You gi' him cause, my girl—"

"Oh, Lor'" Minnie suddenly clapped a hand to her head and threw herself back in her seat. "Oh, Lor', Ted—you know what you forgot to do afore we come away from the house? You forgot to check the blessed gas meter!"

"Blast it, so I did, an' all." He smacked his fist against the counter top in vexation. "That were you. Sending me off to change my collar. Put it clean out o' my head."

"You'd best go back directly and make sure there's sufficient to keep the oven burning."

"Why do I have to go? Why can't you go yourself? You'll walk faster."

"What, walk back all alone by myself through them dark streets?" His wife cast a nervous look over her shoulder towards the door and lowered her voice. "I'll go if you come

107

wi' me, but not otherwise. Who's to know but that Jack the Ripper ain't here in Lewes, a-lying low? They never caught him, did they, them London bobbies, for all their cleversome ways."

The last Ripper murder had been committed some three years earlier, in November 1888, but such was the morbid hysteria generated by lurid newspaper accounts of his atrocities that public alarm, especially among the womenfolk, had been slow to fade.

"He won't ha' come all this long way down here," Daisy cried. "More like he's taken hisself away up North well out o' the shires."

"Be that as it may, I'm not a-walking by myself to Tea Garden Lane," Minnie said adamantly.

Her husband uttered a loud sigh. Raising his glass he swallowed what remained of his ale and began buttoning up his jacket.

"There's no point in the both of us going, our Minnie. You bide here where you are."

She brightened at once. "There's tenpence worth o' coppers in the tin on the mantelpiece, you said? You did look to see?"

A nod.

"Good, then wrap your muffler well round you against the cold. And mind you come straight back, you hear?"

Ted's mouth beneath the bristly ginger moustache twisted in at the corner, and looking at his sister, he gave a quick jerk of the head and raised his eyes in wordless expression of long-suffering resignation. Tucking away the ends of his long woollen muffler, he turned and made his limping ungainly way across the saloon to the street door, letting in a knife-edge draught of chill air as he pulled it open and stood for a few moments talking to someone before finally going out into the thickening shadows of the December dusk.

Minnie dragged her shawl closer round her narrow shoulders.

"What's become o' that other gentleman friend o' Miss Amy's?" Daisy enquired casually, leaning her elbows forward on the bar counter. "That 'un from Weatherfield way?"

"Doctor Linton, you mean?"

"Aye. That's him."

There was a shrug.

"You not seen nothing of him, then?"

"Not lately, no."

"Strange, he were always coming over to visit at one time. And him a married man, an' all."

Minnie bridled up at this. "He's got every right to visit if he pleases. They're family, him and her. Cousins, or some'at."

"Aye. Kissing cousins."

"You mind what you're a-saying, Daisy Brocklebank. He who bespatters others generally rolls in the same mud hisself afore long. There's never been anything like that atween Miss Amy and the doctor. He's been mindful of her welfare, and that's all."

The young barmaid gave a disbelieving laugh. "His nose has been put out o' joint if you want my opinion. She's got herself this other now, this bachelor farmer from Dorsetshire. She don't want no old married man moithering her, not when there's a chance of another's ring for her finger. Married men, they're all grunt and no bacon. You hear that, Percy Parkes?" addressing herself to the moon-faced admirer who had been standing beside the counter silent all this time. "A man wi' a wife is as much use to a maid as a purse wi' a hole. Either or both, they bring her nothing but loss."

"That depends on how much she had in the first place to lose," Mr Parkes returned somewhat sullenly. He was the type of man who becomes morose in drink, and having imbibed several pints of Harvey's strong ale, had reached the stage of inebriation where he was beginning to feel thoroughly sorry for himself.

His remark caused Daisy to fly at once into a huff and demand to be told exactly what he'd meant by it; and her sharp tone attracted the attention of The Grenadier's licensee, coming through from the public bar next door to see to the dutch stove whose cheery glow warmed the room.

By the time the imagined affront to Daisy's honour was resolved and Mr Parkes had retreated with a hangdog expression to finish his drink elsewhere, Minnie had taken herself off for a gossip with an acquaintance; so it was some ten minutes or so before her conversation with her sister-in-law was resumed.

She was in the middle of saying that her mistress had gone for the afternoon to Spences Lane, to take Christmas gifts for little Esmond and Laura Bates, when Ted Brocklebank made a sudden reappearance through the saloon door.

"Land's sake, you were quick!" his wife greeted him in astonishment. "You grown wings, or some'at?"

"Bertie Ames gi' me a ride in his fly."

"What, there and back again?"

"Aye, there and back again."

Bertie Ames was what was known as a "fly proprietor", providing carriages and traps for those who needed them: a handy trade operated at some profit from stables at the back of The Grenadier, whose customers frequently and of necessity required his services to see them safely to their homes.

"How much he charge you for that, then?"

"Money and fair words, Minnie. It's Christmas, after all. Now what you doing a-nursing that empty glass? Hasn't our Daisy been looking after you? Daisy!"

He raised his voice above the noise of beer-hearty laughter from that end of the counter where she was serving; and when she moved down, smirking back at the younger and better-looking of her customers, said roughly, "Buck up, girl, and gi' Minnie another port and lemon. And when you've done that, pull me a fresh sleeve o' best ale."

"Did you look at the goose for me?" Minnie asked, handing her glass to be refilled.

Ted pulled off his muffler and gave a shake of the head. "I didn't have need to look. I could smell it cooking all the way up the scullery stairs."

Producing a handful of small change from his trouser pocket to pay his sister for the drinks, he went on. "A good thing I went back when I did, though. That durned gas meter was nigh empty, would you believe."

"There you are—what did I say!" came the vexed cry. "Didn't I ask you to check it betimes? We might ha' gone home to find the oven stone cold and us wi' no supper."

"Well, there's no harm done, so stop your fretting and sup your port," Ted answered carelessly. "I've put in a bob's worth o' coppers, to be on the safe side. We don't have to rush ourselves getting back now till turned six o'clock."

So saying, he raised his brimming glass, and with an

110

appreciative smack of the lips, sucked the creamy head of froth from his ale.

As things turned out, however, it was rather later than six o'clock when the Brocklebanks eventually departed from The Grenadier.

Minnie was preparing to leave in good time, settling her bonnet (the best one, with cherries) tidily on her head and pinning her shawl, when a crowd of Ted's mates from the coal wharf arrived in the public bar and insisted the couple should join them. Disliking the sawdust and spittle of the "public" she at first refused, but several port and lemons had put her in a merry mood and she was easily cajoled into changing her mind.

Being Christmas Eve, the customers might stay to celebrate the season however long they wished—always provided their credit was good and their merry-making not too festively spirited. So it was that by the time Minnie finally managed to get her husband out into the street, neither was capable of making a very steady progress home to Tea Garden Lane and they were obliged to call once more upon the services of Bertie Ames and his fly.

As the pair wended their way arm-in-arm across the darkened stable yard to the servants' entrance at the rear of the house, Minnie noticed to her relief that were were no lights showing anywhere, nor any curtains drawn.

"Thank the Lord for that," she said, pronouncing her words with the careful diction of one who has taken a drop more than she ought, "Miss Amy ain't back yet from Spences Lane. It won't matter if supper's a bit late on the table."

Ted grunted a reply. He was having some difficulty in finding the keyhole, but after fumbling about for a while, succeeded at last in getting the door unlocked and opened.

"Well, go on inside, then," his wife urged when he seemed to be hesitating. "It's cold a-standing here. What are you waiting for?"

A trifle indistinctly he said over his shoulder, "Can't you smell some'at, our Minnie?"

"Eh? What's that?"

"Can't you smell some'at?"

111

"Smell some'at?" She sniffed the air, the cherries on her bonnet bobbing. "Oh, aye. Aye, I can. It's that blessed goose, that's what it is. Burnt to a crisp, I shouldn't wonder."

"Smells more like gas to me," came the lugubrious response.

"Gas? Oh, Lor'!" Minnie pushed her way inside and sniffed again, louder. "The oven must ha' gone out, Ted."

"It can't ha' gone out. I fed the durned meter only a couple of hours back, didn't I?"

A terrible suspicion began to grow upon Minnie. Grabbing unsteadily for the box of vestas kept on the passage table beside the oil-lamp, she struck a light to the wick, crying, "The gas must already ha' gone out *afore* you fed the meter. You never looked to see, did you?"

In the flaring yellow of the flames Ted Brocklebank's faced turned the colour of wax. Snatching the lamp from his wife, he wheeled about and hobbled as fast as his lameness and Harvey's strong ale would allow along to the end of the passage and down the scullery stairs, his shadow thrown in crooked jumps behind him.

The low hiss of an unlit jet was faintly audible beyond the door into the kitchen, and the sickly sweet smell of coal gas, stronger here, started him coughing.

"Make haste and open the window, do!" Minnie cried, following behind. "Let's have some air in the place afore we're all poisoned."

Holding her shawl to her mouth, she scurried across the room and peered inside the oven door, reaching a hand to prod at the partly-cooked bird. To her chilled fingers the flesh felt quite warm still.

"Ah, well, we can but heat the blessed thing up again and hope for the best," she said dolefully. "Light us a taper, from the lamp, Ted, will you?"

"You mind out o' the way. I'll see to it."

He came to her side, seizing up his newspaper from the chair, and began waving it back and forth in front of the stove to clear away the fumes, already noticeably fainter as draughts from the open window sent currents of cold air into the room.

"Never mind that," his wife chided, bringing him the

112

taper. "There's gas escaping still. Hurry up and light it, for land's sake!"

Shielding the naked flame in his cupped hand, Ted knelt down clumsily in front of the oven's black mouth, and averting his face, shoved the taper towards the still-hissing jet.

The effect was immediate, and calamitous.

There was an almighty bang; and as if suddenly galvanised into life, the goose came flying out at him, followed by the roasting pan, which tipped on end and emptied itself in a pool of half-congealed fat upon the brown linoleum floor-cloth.

Minnie, startled out of her wits, took a jump backwards. Losing her balance, she made a grab for the table, missed, and slid awkwardly into a sitting position beneath it.

At the same moment, there came a cry from somewhere overhead and the sound of footsteps running along the passage.

"Minnie? Minnie, what is it? What's happened?"

Amy Flynn, returning home, had heard the explosion just as she was shutting the front porch door.

"What's happened?" she cried again, appearing at the foot of the scullery stairs and looking wildly about.

In the pallid glow of the lamp, the first thing she discerned was her handyman, on the floor with a trussed goose in his lap, his ginger hair standing up in tufts and the whites of his eyes shining in a blackened face. And then his wife, propped against the table leg, the cherries of her bonnet tipped forward over one ear.

"Durned gas!" swore Ted.

"Blessed goose!" echoed Minnie, both on the same breath.

Amy's lips began to quiver. The quivering persisted and spread slowly to a smile; and the smile broadened gradually and became a giggle, which, refusing to stop, turned into open laughter.

This was too much. The pair upon the floor looked at one another; and the next moment, struck that same instant by the comical absurdity of their situation, were themselves suddenly bursting out in mirth.

11

Amy's amusement at the Brocklebanks' misadventure was a timely catharsis. Since that last evening in Weatherfield with Ralph Herriot weeks before, she had begun to wonder whether she would ever be able to laugh at anything again, and it had needed something as ridiculous as a gassed goose to release her from her depression.

She had been very much unsettled by her companion's discerning insight into her character, the manner in which he had so casually probed the raw nerve of her past; and the more she reflected upon the conversation they'd had together that night as they walked back to the alehouse, the more troubled she felt that anyone should know the secret places of her mind so well.

She had come home to Lewes in a vexed state of mind; and vexation, aggravated by constant pin-pricks of resentment, had grown before very long to angry indignation.

How dare the Bashfords discuss her behind her back at Bonningale, as though she were one of the servants, she thought heatedly. How dare Ralph Herriot presume to dictate to her by laying down terms for their friendship, demanding she cease all acquaintance with David Linton. And how dare David Linton himself behave in such a boorish, silly fashion.

Well, she was done with the pair of them. She ought to have known better than trust herself to either. Men were the most insufferable creatures, lording their arrogant attitudes over those whom they condescendingly referred to as the weaker sex, weighing their own worth in the scales of their conceit with all the airs of the superior beings they plainly considered themselves to be.

"I'll wait to hear your decision," Ralph had said at their leave-taking. "Until I know your mind, I'll bide my time in silence."

Let him bide his time, then. What did she care? Let him go and kick his heels in Dorsetshire with his precious circle of pedigree poets and high society scribblers. If he thought that silence and absence would make her heart grow fonder, he was very much in error.

As for David Linton, doctor he might be, but he was no judge of a woman if he expected her to fall into his arms with gladsome cries the moment he announced himself in love. He, too, would do better to stay well away, out of sight and out of mind, and ponder the folly of souring an innocent friendship by seeking to drag it down to the level of some shameful hole-and-corner liaison.

Oh, why must men be so selfish, Amy had asked herself furiously. Why must they be for ever thinking of nothing but their own needs and pleasures? Could they not realise how much happiness they spoiled? She had been growing to like Ralph Herriot more and more, and enjoy herself in his company: he suited her high spirits, her sense of adventure, her humour. And David—well, David had always had her trust and respect. Yet what had she left of either man now but the rags and tatters of fellowship . . . so many empty words and meaningless assurances.

All her life, it seemed, she had been forced to contend with adversity of one kind or another, as though some black fairy had blighted her in the cradle with an ill-starred fate. Even her cousin, Francis Bethway, whom she regarded as a brother, almost, had now apparently forsaken her; and through no fault of her own.

Since the summer, Amy had seen her young cousin only once, though she was well aware he was using her as the excuse to his parents for the frequent visits he was making to Lewes. Isabelle Bethway's letters had revealed as much, thanking Amy for her kindness in having the youth so often to stay; and suspecting the truth of the matter, Amy had been loath to bring trouble upon Francis and worry to his parents by informing them otherwise.

She knew her cousin a trifle too well to believe he found Lewes more conducive to his studies than his father's Eastbourne parsonage—the impression Aunt Isabelle clearly appeared to have, for she'd written, "I am exceeding glad, dear Amy, to know my son applies himself with such tireless industry to his books. Eastbourne is a bustle, and so distracting. Who can wonder that he yearns for solitude? He has only six months more education. Far better, therefore, that he spend his time in pursuing his learning there upon the quiet banks of the Ouse, which he says gives him more pleasure than may be imagined."

In her present frame of mind, Amy could not but think that her aunt chose her words unwisely. If cousin Francis were finding pleasure on the banks of the River Ouse, it was more likely to be in the arms of some lusty female than in the pages of any text-book. All the same, his deceit had hurt her and she would have a few strong words to say the next time he deigned to show his face in Tea Garden Lane.

What a season of goodwill and cheer this was proving, she thought despondently as she had walked home that evening from Spences Lane through the dingy gas-lit streets. People were bustling along on every side, some to the shops before the shutters went up, others to church service; families calling on their neighbours, fathers hastening from work to their firesides, children shouting to one another, their young voices ringing with excitement in the frosty air at the prospect of tomorrow's holiday with its promise of oranges and nuts, new spinning-tops and hoops.

How nice it might have been, after all, had Ralph been able to visit, and the Bethways, and David and his family, all of them here together to share the celebrations with her. Instead, she must spend her first Christmas in her own house quite alone, with no company except Minnie and Ted; and much as she thought the world of both, it could not be the same.

Her thoughts had been thus joylessly preoccupied as she opened the porch door and heard almost in the same instant the sound of a dull explosion from the kitchen below . . . which was how it came about that she had cause to thank a goose, of all things, for bringing back the sparkle of laughter after so many gloomy weeks of ill-humour.

Later that night, lying abed and watching the shadow-play of firelight on the ceiling of her room, Amy found herself reflecting that nothing was ever as bad as worrying made it. After all, had not Ralph remembered her by the generous gift of a Christmas dinner, and David by sending her his compliments of the season in quite the prettiest card money could buy?

"I've never known a one for fretting so much as you, Meg Evans," Francis said, leaning to plant a kiss on his companion's round red cheek. "That bicycle 'ld carry me all the way from here to Land's End and back wi'out mishap. It's not one o' the old boneshakers, you know. It's the very latest machine, a 'safety' cycle, rear-driven, wi' pneumatic rubber tyres."

"Yes, but—"

"But nothing. You wanted me to see you tonight, didn't you? Well, here I am."

"But—"

"Now Meggie, have a little sense, do. You know there'll be trouble wi' my folks if I'm not back home by morning. My mother'll want me all spruced up in my Sunday best suit to take her to hear the governor preach his sermon. If I'm not there wi' them all in the family pew, there'll be a pretty set-out about it, I can tell you."

Megwynn bit her lip and cast her young sweetheart a look full of doubt. She had been given this evening off as a holiday, and had made Francis promise to take her to the music hall at the top of West Street, thinking he'd be able to spend Christmas Day itself with his cousin Amy Flynn on the other side of town.

Miss Flynn had been to take tea this afternoon in the nursery with Esmond and Laura; but she'd been so distant when Megwynn tried to make conversation that there was no way of learning whether Francis was invited to stay or not. Now, to the young Welsh governess's dismay, it appeared that as soon as he'd seen her safely back to Spences Lane at the end of their evening together, he was fully intent on setting straight off for Eastbourne—making the journey upon a bicycle he'd just acquired.

"Why on earth shouldn't I ride my 'cycle home?" Francis had demanded when reproved for such folly. "I rode it coming, didn't I?"

"It's so far, *cariad*!"

"It's less than twenty miles, and the road's a good 'un all the way."

"But it will be black night, look you. What if you run the wheel into a pot hole and pitch yourself down upon your head? You might lie there till morning, and freeze with the cold."

The argument, begun in their usual trysting place in the stables behind Spences, had continued all the way along to the theatre in West Street. Now, though, sitting on a hired cushion on one of the wooden bench-seats of the "gods" high above the stage, where the air was already a little stale and close from the press of bodies, Megwynn had been persuaded to forget her worries for a while.

The livid glare of the lime-lights burning along the stage foot shone out over the orchestra pit on to the first few rows of the crowded stalls, silhouetting the smoke-wreathed heads of a restless, noisy audience awaiting the start of the evening's main entertainment.

"There's a comedy turn on first," announced Francis, craning his neck for a look at the large programme boards on either side of the stage. "'Henery Baker, the Laughter Maker.' I saw him perform last month in Brighton, when I went to The Marine Palace wi' a crowd o' the fellows."

"Oh?"

"Aye. He brought the house down almost, some o' the jokes he fetched out."

"You never told me about going to any Marine Palace in Brighton."

"Maybe I'd no cause to. Anyhow, I'm telling you now, aren't I?"

Megwynn pursed her mouth and looked down.

"Oh, come on now, Meggie. Cheer up!" Francis urged, putting an arm about her plump waist and giving it a quick squeeze. "We've come out to enjoy ourselves, haven't we? Here—" he reached with his free hand into a pocket and drew out a paper cone filled with chocolate cream bonbons. "Look, I got you these as a treat. A whole six penn'orth. Best eat 'em before they all melt, eh?"

Releasing her, he reached into the cone with finger and thumb and produced a somewhat shapeless confection which he proffered to his companion.

"Open your mouth."

She did as she was bid, closing her lips over his sticky

118

fingers and pretending to bite them with her sharp little teeth. Francis gave a cry of mock anguish, then, laughing, bent over and kissed the lobe of her ear.

Down below them, the orchestra was striking up an introductory flourish and amid much applause, cheers and foot-stamping, a short stout individual in a loud check suit appeared on stage, acknowledging the house with a grandiose salute of his bowler hat.

"I say, I say, I say!" he began at once in a voice which carried all the way up to the back row of the "gods". "What d'you suppose it is that goes up a chimney down, yet can't go down a chimney up?"

There came an answering chorus of "Umbrella!" with one or two preferences for "Parasol!" but Mr Henery Baker stood shaking his large head in exaggerated fashion, and when the noise had abated, bellowed a riposte which so cleverly combined comicality with extraordinary coarseness that he had the auditorium roaring in delight.

Megwynn's cheeks blushed a little redder and she lowered her head, hiding her giggles behind a hand, while Francis rocked in mirthful whoops beside her.

The comedian had gauged his audience well. For the next ten minutes he paraded back and forth across the foot of the stage, lobbing his crudely witty jokes with the timing and skill of the true professional; and when he finally departed after two curtain calls, the applause went on and on for several minutes more and had not yet quite started to die away when the gold-fringed plush curtains drew back again for the commencement of the next turn, which was a troupe of dancers.

This act was billed as "Les Mam'selles de Joie", and proved to be some half-dozen young women in spangled costumes and flesh-pink tights whose cavortings revealed rather more leg than talent as they romped arm-in-arm up and down the stage to the enthusiastic accompaniment of the orchestra.

After a finale which threatened to bring down the house, they pranced away into the wings, the lime-lights glistening on the melted greasepaint moons of their smiling, sweating faces.

There then followed a solo performance by "our own,

our very own Gertie Jukes"; and at the appearance of her small, garishly-dressed figure against the backdrop of a flower-twined colonnade, a respectful hush fell upon the auditorium.

Francis stifled a snort of amusement and leaned to whisper to his companion, "You recall me telling you about Harry Weldrake, don't you?"

Megwynn nodded.

"Well, that piece o' laced mutton was the old devil's moll."

She digested this piece of information in silence. The chocolate cream bonbons she'd eaten were now making her feel a trifle queasy, and her discomfort was hardly helped by the stifling atmosphere and rank, greasy odours which permeated the tightly-packed benches all around.

"Francis—" She plucked at his sleeve. "Francis, I think I must step outside for a breath of fresh air."

The violinist had just risen in the pit to play the opening bars of Gertie's song, and she was forced to repeat herself a little louder. There was an immediate outbreak of hisses from those nearby, hushing her into silence as the wail of the violin rose in quivering echo of the singer's first words, giving Megwynn no choice but to stay where she was until the performance was over.

Down on stage, hands clasped in a gesture of supplication, eyes rolled upwards to the gallery, Gertie Jukes launched herself into a plaintive lament of heart-wrenching pathos:

"I am a little shoe-black, my mother she is dead,
My father is a drunkard and won't give me no bread.
Bluebells, cockle-shells, bury me by my mother,
Wi' six little angels round my grave,
Two to watch, and two to pray,
And two to carry my soul away."

When the last sad, throbbing note had faded off into silence one could have heard a pin drop in the house. Gertie's head, drooping upon her breast like a flower upon its stalk, was raised slowly up again, and as if this were the sign of release, the audience broke at once into rapturous applause. She held out her thin little arms to them all; then a quick nod to the conductor and the orchestra was surging into her next song, a lively ditty with plenty of action entitled "He wears a penny flower in his coat, La-di-da!" which had everyone joining in the chorus.

Towards the end of the fourth verse, Megwynn knew she could delay no longer or she would be fainting where she sat. Getting hurriedly to her feet, she pushed past her neighbours on the row of benches and made for the curtain which covered the exit. Behind it, a flight of wooden stairs descended steeply to the theatre's gallery corridor.

She was no more than half-way down when her head began to spin quite alarmingly and a blackness came over her sight, as though she'd been suddenly blinded. Gasping, she sank helplessly on to the bare step.

"Megwynn? Meggie!"

Francis came clattering down behind. Reaching the huddled figure, he crouched at her side and put out a hand.

"You not feeling well, or some'at?"

She shook her head.

"Shall I fetch you up a drink o' water?"

"I—I need some air . . . my head . . . it spins so."

He put an arm round her waist and raised her to her feet, where she stood swaying weakly from side to side and was only prevented from falling by clinging on to her sweetheart's coat front.

"*Duw . . . Duw*, I feel ill . . ."

"Hold up, Meggie—you'll have us both over!" Francis adjusted his grip, his other hand reaching for the rope which ran parallel to the wall as a safety rail. "Just you hang on to me, now. That's it. Take it steady, one foot at a time. Good. And the other. I've got you—you won't fall. That's right. Slowly does it. Now your left foot down."

He coaxed her step by step to the bottom of the stairs and out into the corridor; and was just turning away to fetch a chair when the chocolate cream bonbons made their reappearance.

"Oh, Lord!" The look on the youth's face turned to one of embarrassed concern. "Er . . . now, Meggie, best stay where you are a minute and I'll go and see if I can't find a woman to attend you."

121

Megwynn was in no state to make any reply.

He seemed to be gone for an age before he returned again, in company with a middle-aged person in black bonnet and shawl who had earlier taken their entrance money at the door below.

"Now then, ducks," this female said in not too kindly a fashion, advancing upon the sufferer. "Come over poorly, have we? Dear, dear, what's brought that on, d'you suppose?"

"It got a bit close for her in the gods," Francis apologised awkwardly. "What wi' that and eating chocolate creams—"

"Aye, and a few more than was good for her, by the look o' things." The bright button eyes slid from the girl's white face to her ringless fingers. "Still, can't be helped, can it? The damage's done."

"I—I am sorry," Megwynn responded weakly.

"Never mind. These things will happen. Upsadaisy now, ducks, let's have you down to the wash-place and cleanse you a bit, shall we? You can manage to walk your legs that far, I'm sure."

There was a sound of prolonged applause, muffled by the corridor walls, as Gertie Jukes took her final curtain call on stage.

"We've only missed the solo instrument turn," Francis announced hopefully when Megwynn, looking pale still, emerged alone a short while later to re-join him. "There's a lady acrobat on next. I wouldn't half mind seeing her performance. D'you reckon you're up to it?"

"Up to what?" Megwynn's voice sounded upset. "Going back upstairs?"

"Aye."

She shook her head miserably. "The way it is I'm feeling, I'd rather you be taking me home to Spences Lane."

"What? But we've hardly seen anything o' the bill yet, damn it, and I've paid for the whole evening."

"I am not well, Francis!"

"You'll be all right if we sit you near the exit where there's a bit of a draught."

"Oh . . ." Tears sprang to the young governess's eyes.

She was silent for a moment; then, turning her head away, said in a choked voice, "You will have to know the truth.

122

This . . . this is not the first time of late that I've been taken ill."

"Oh? Then mebbe you should see a doctor?"

From inside the auditorium there rose a sudden outburst of foot-stamping cries of "bravo!" as the lady acrobat made her entrance with a triple somersault across the stage.

"A doctor would only tell me what I know already," Megwynn answered forlornly.

Francis stared at the bowed head, and a frown of suspicion began to deepen the slight crease between his dark brows.

"And what's that supposed to mean?"

"It means I am carrying your child, *cariad*. It means that you must marry me."

"Bravo!" the audience cheered again. To Francis Bethway it sounded almost like derision.

12

"*Marry* her?"

The Reverend Alec Bethway's voice rose a pitch higher. He sat thrust forward in his chair, hands tensed upon the padded arms as though suddenly arrested in the act of rising, his normally mild expression frozen into disbelief.

"*Marry* her, Francis—?"

Words failed him. The news that his elder son had been engaged in some sort of clandestine affaire with a young woman who was now pregnant as a result, had dropped like a thunderbolt from heaven. Slowly, he sank back again in his seat, his gaze falling to the cluttered desk before him, eyes moving in unseeing, aimless manner from one object to the next as he tried to assimilate the gravity of what he'd just been told.

Francis's confession had been brief and to the point. Having made it, the youth now stood awkwardly in the middle of the parsonage study, his own gaze fixed upon the pattern of the Turkey carpet underfoot. At his side his mother, her lovely features aged with distress, plucked fretfully at the handkerchief which had wiped away her tears. In the background, just beyond the open doorway, the two younger children, Dinah and Kit, exchanged sideways looks of embarrassment.

For some minutes no one moved or spoke, giving the scene the appearance of a tableau; and in the tense silence the air seemed almost to throb with guilt and recrimination.

Finally Isabelle Bethway could bear it no longer. Turning with a half-gesture of appeal towards her husband, she cried, "Alec—Alec, what should we do?"

The appeal went unanswered. Without looking up, her husband gave a shake of the head. His mind was in no state for the moment to formulate convenient solutions as he tried

124

to marshal his thoughts into some kind of order, present himself with the bare facts: that his son had betrayed the code of honour to which he'd been bred; that he had gone behind his parents' backs and abused their trust; that he had wilfully indulged in promiscuous behaviour; and that he was now paying its price by bringing shame upon himself, his family, and the unfortunate creature who had been his partner in dissipation.

Alec Bethway sighed heavily, and passed a hand through his thick grey hair; then, looking once more across at Francis, asked quietly, "This young woman . . . may we know who she is?"

The reply was grudging. "Megwynn Evans."

"Megwynn? What manner of name is that?"

"It's Welsh."

"I see. Do I take it, then, that she's a native of that country?"

A nod.

"And she's in service, you say?"

"Aye. She's governess to Mr Bates."

The minister shot his wife a glance. Isabelle had known Ellis Bates since childhood, having spent a part of each year with the family at Bonningale; though there had never been any closeness between the two of them and they'd had little social contact since their marriages.

"Does Mr Bates know about your . . . friendship with his governess?" Isabelle asked her son.

There was a quick shake of the head. "I don't think so. He doesn't encourage callers. We've always met away from the house, Meggie and me. Well, apart from the first time, anyhow—and he wasn't at home that day, as I recall."

"And when exactly was the first time, Francis?" his father enquired.

"Beginning o' September, sir."

"Four months ago. It that all you've known this young woman—four months?"

Another nod.

"If she's employed as governess to Ellis Bates's children," Isabelle came in anxiously, "she must surely be older than you, mustn't she?"

Francis resumed his examination of the carpet.

125

"Answer your mother's question, if you please," his father admonished him sharply.

There was a reluctant shrug of the shoulders. "She's a bit older than me, aye."

"Well? How much older?"

"She'll be twenty-two at the end o' March."

Alec Bethway exchanged a further glance with his wife.

"Old enough to know better, in fact," he said. "Was it she who encouraged your relationship at the beginning?"

"Oh, no. It was me did all the chasing, sir. I doubt she'd have give me more'n a passing thought if I'd let well alone after we'd met at Bonningale, harvest-time."

His son's deliberately ill-bred manner of speaking grated on the minister's ears, but he let it pass without comment. There had already been more sharp exchanges in the past few years than he cared to recall over this uncouth, unmannered attitude, as though the youth were deliberately trying to provoke his parents' displeasure by behaving like some semi-illiterate boor.

"I remember Miss Evans, Papa," Kit Bethway came in importantly, anxious to justify his presence at this family inquest into his brother's fall from grace. "I remember her at the harvest supper. She and Francis danced together the entire evening and no one could find either of them anywhere when it was time to go indoors."

"How would you know that, pray?" his sister Dinah asked scornfully. "You told me you'd been with Georgie Bashford in the barn drinking cider and fell asleep the worse for it."

"I was not the worse for it!"

"You told me you were, too."

"That will be quite enough," their father interrupted them sharply. "I thought I had requested you both to leave the room?"

"Oh, but Papa!"

Dinah had her mother's sweet face and attractive auburn colouring, and as Alec Bethway's favourite child, knew better than any how to work upon his susceptibilities. On this occasion, however, her winsome smile had no effect. The outstretched hand remained pointing firmly towards the door.

"Do as Papa asks, now," her mother said a trifle abstractedly over her shoulder.

126

"Then may I take Titus for a walk?"

Titus was the King Charles spaniel which her parents, after much pleading by their daughter, had given her as a Christmas gift. She had not been allowed to take it outside herself since catching a slight chill on New Year's Day, and had tried everyone's patience as a result.

"If it will mean privacy and peace here, then very well, you may take the dog out, I suppose." Her father waved his hand in a motion of dismissal. "But wrap yourself warmly, Dinah. And you are not to venture upon the sands, do you hear? Kit, you will go with your sister, please, and see to it that she keeps to the promenade."

This diversion of attention to the younger Bethways gave Francis a brief respite after the unpalatable business of unburdening himself of his unwelcome fatherhood. He had deliberately withheld the news until the end of the Christmas festivities, not wanting to spoil the family's enjoyment; though there'd been scant pleasure for himself at the prospect of being forced into the shackles of matrimony before the best years of his life had even begun.

He loved Megwynn . . . of course he did, didn't he? At least, he was very fond of her still. Though perhaps not as fond as he'd been at the start . . . more sentimental, one might say, more fond in the way that close familiarity tended to make a man. If he were to be totally honest with himself, he'd have to admit that he didn't feel quite the same about her now as he had a month or two ago . . . there'd been other young women of late who had caught his eye. The only reason he'd gone so often to see her in Lewes was on account of her giving him such warm encouragement. Those times they'd spent together in the stable loft behind Spences . . . well, she'd always shown willing, whetting his appetite for more. What damnable bad luck that she'd had to go and get herself in the family way and spoil all the fun.

And now she was expecting him to marry her!

Francis fingered the moustache he had started to grow on his upper lip. In a way, though, he was rather proud of having proved his virility: none of his friends were able to boast the same achievement, and his reputation with them as being something of a lady-killer had increased no end as a result of Megwynn's inconveniently interesting condition.

127

"Would you be so kind as to close the door, Francis?" Alec Bethway rose to his feet and moved out from behind the desk. "Now that we are rid of curious young ears, perhaps we might discuss the more—er, personal aspects of this unhappy business?"

He held out a hand.

"Isabelle, dearest, won't you sit down? You would be far more comfortable, surely."

She gave a little start, as though her mind had been elsewhere; then complied with her husband's request, going to seat herself in a button-back chair at one side of the fireplace.

"What a miserable warmth this coal has," she remarked inconsequentially, reaching her small hands to the flames.

"Shall I ring for Jane to fetch you an extra wrap?"

"No, no. Thank you, Alec, but I'm not cold." She smiled up at him before turning her gaze once more upon her son.

"Francis—"

There followed a slight hesitation.

She tried again. "Francis, are you quite certain of this young woman's—Miss Evans, did you say the name was?—are you quite certain of her maternal condition? It seems a little odd that you should have known her only four months and already she claims to be with child. Does she know when she expects it to be born?"

Francis did not meet his mother's eye but looked instead out through the study window at the snow-patched garden.

"I think she said some'at about it being due to arrive in the summer. June or July."

She made a mental calculation. "Then the child must have been conceived either in September or October."

"Aye."

"But you said just now that you've only known Miss Evans since the beginning of September."

"I did, aye."

"Then, how—?"

Again, a hesitation.

"It seems to me," Isabelle began again, rather more slowly, "this young woman's virtue leaves much to be desired. The child *is* yours, I suppose? Not some other's?"

Francis considered this possibility; then shook his head.

128

"It's mine. She wouldn't play me false. She'd never been wi' a man before me."

"Then she was remarkably anxious to surrender her modesty," his father commented acidly.

"It happened she'd fallen in love—"

"Don't you toss love at me, my boy, as a reason or excuse for what's occurred! I was in love with your dear mother for many months before our marriage, but I'd sooner have died than take advantage of the affection she entrusted to me. Heaven knows how I deplore this altogether shameless attitude towards moral continence which you young people seem nowadays to hold, indulging yourselves in irresponsible sexual delinquency and calling it free love, or some such brazen term. It is not love to which you and your Miss Evans have fallen victim, Francis. It is lust. An emotion of a rather different colour."

Alec Bethway checked himself before anger should begin to distort the reasoning of his argument. He took a few paces up and down in front of his son; then after a moment or so went on more rationally, "What I would like to know is the part your cousin Amy played in this business. You've been a frequent guest beneath her roof. She must have a fair idea of what's been going on?"

"Amy knows nothing, sir." Having made a clean breast of things so far, Francis was not about to start lying now.

"Oh, come—your cousin may have turned a blind eye to your philandering, but—"

"She knows nothing," the other repeated emphatically. "When I told you and Mam I was staying wi' her in Lewes, it wasn't the truth. I haven't been near Tea Garden Lane once in all this time."

"Not been . . ." Isabelle grasped the arm of her chair, staring up at her son in consternation. "Not been near Tea Garden Lane?"

"No."

"Then . . . if you haven't been at Amy's, where on earth *have* you been? Surely not at Ellis Bates's house?"

There was a grunt of amusement. "Not there either."

"Where then, for goodness sake? You've sometimes been from home for nights at a stretch. There must have been somewhere or other you've gone to stay?"

129

"I've been making do wi' a stable loft. Oh, don't look so vexed, Mam. I didn't tell you, else you'd only have started fretting yourself. The place is dry, and clean enough for what it is. Nobody knew I was there. Except the horses, and they didn't mind me, I don't suppose."

Isabelle gave a soft sigh of exasperation. How like her ne'er-do-well brother Frank Flynn this son of hers could be. Too often was, in fact, as though by giving her firstborn the same name she had tempted Fate to give him the same nature. She had only to look at Francis, listen to him speak, and she could see and hear Frank all over again. Pray God he wasn't about to follow in the other's footsteps and become a second rotten apple in the family barrel.

Somewhat irritably she said, "I can't believe Amy's known nothing at all of what you've been up to. I've written to her several times to thank her for her hospitality. Why then hasn't she mentioned it when writing back?"

"Yes, what's your explanation for that?" Alec Bethway echoed.

Francis sketched a shrug. "Belikes she thought it best to leave well alone. Amy's a great 'un for minding her own business and letting others mind theirs. Anyhow, I reckon she's got her own fish to fry."

"And what am I to take that as meaning, pray?"

"Well—she's got her own life to lead."

"Then why not say so, instead of debasing the Queen's English with sloppy diction?" The minister's tone sharpened its edge again. "I must say, Francis, I find this attitude of yours something to be wondered at. Your gross misconduct has placed you in a most invidious position, and yet you persist in treating the whole thing with a levity which passes belief. Have you no feelings of contrition for the wrong you've committed? And you will kindly look at me when I address you! It makes me question my own wisdom in having you educated privately, when you'd have fared better as a boarder at some school where a regimen of discipline might have curbed your faults before they developed into habit. You make me ashamed to own you as my son—"

"Alec . . ." His wife made an effort to placate him. "Alec, don't let your anger make you say things you'll regret."

She was waved into silence.

130

"I'll offer you a word of advice, Francis," his father continued warmly. "It is this: all men are good, either for something or for nothing, and by their deeds the world judges which. You'd do well to ponder upon that."

Without speaking further, he swung upon his heel and walked back again to his desk by the window. Outside, a shadow passed like a small grey cloud across the even whiteness of the vicarage lawn as a flock of seagulls wheeled above it, the melancholy mockery of their cries muted by the wind.

Alec Bethway watched them for a moment, then re-seated himself and sat forward, elbows leaning on the desk top, hands clasped in outline against the black clerical stock.

After a while he spoke again.

"You were due to complete your studies this summer and offer yourself as a candidate for military training with the Sussex Artillery Militia at Southover depot. This was what you intended, was it not—to enlist in that regiment?"

"Yes, sir." In the face of his father's assertive displeasure, Francis had grown distinctly ill at ease and was careful how he responded.

"And you realise, of course, that those plans are now seriously in jeopardy?"

"Yes, sir. I do."

"Let us suppose that you act as honour dictates, that you shoulder your responsibility towards Miss Evans and marry her. How will you support a wife and child? Have you thought?"

A shake of the head. "No, sir."

"No. A difficult proposition. Her own people won't come to her assistance, I suppose?"

"She hasn't told 'em. Not yet. She said she'd wait till after . . . till after the wedding."

Francis re-commenced his examination of the carpet.

Then, suddenly, burst out wildly—"But there won't be no wedding. I don't want to marry her—I don't! Oh Mam, I won't have to marry her, will I? What do I know about setting up home? If she hadn't been so forward wi' me, none o' this would have happened. It was she put me up to it. She should've known better than go leading me on as she did. If she's wi' child, it's her fault, not mine. And if she

131

thinks I'll marry her all because I've been wi' her a time or two, then she's got another thought coming!"

He came to an abrupt stop, looking from one parent to another and back; then cast his eyes down again, his face clouded with sullen despondency.

"I won't marry her, I won't. And nobody can make me against my will, neither."

"Be quiet." His father's voice was heavy with contempt. "You flatter yourself if you suppose anyone expects you to behave like a gentleman and fulfil your obligations. Even if you could be persuaded to do so, in my opinion you are far too young and far too immature to marry yet awhile. Speaking as a minister of the church, it would be a mockery of God's holy sacrament were I to insist upon a ceremony of marriage in such circumstances. However—"

The clasped hands separated and fell palm-downward flat upon the desk.

"This does not mean that I am in any way suggesting you wriggle out of your responsibilities. There are certain claims of conscience. Miss Evans may even decide to bring a paternity order against you—"

"What, take me to court, you mean?" Obviously such a possibility had not occurred to the father-to-be.

"Oh, yes. She's quite within her rights, should you refuse support for the child. That surprises you, does it? You were beginning to think you might escape scot free? Unfortunately, Francis, you may yet succeed in doing so—unfortunately for me, as your father, that is. Since you have no income of your own other than the allowance I make you, it would appear that I must be the one to pay the cost of maintenance. A pretty how-d'you-do, I must say, for someone of my standing in the community, but out of Christian goodness I can do no less. I only hope your young woman may be trusted to show a little more prudence than she has hitherto."

"She'll have to leave her situation in Lewes, of course," Isabelle came in quietly. "Ellis Bates will hardly wish her to stay in his employment once her condition shows. No doubt she'll consider going back to her own folk in Wales."

"No she won't, Mam. I asked her . . . told her it'd be the best thing for her to do."

132

"And what was her answer?"

"She wouldn't hear o' such a thing. Said she'd be turned from the door. Said they'd treat her worse'n a beggar for bringing shame on the village."

"Oh, surely not?"

"Yes, I'm afraid it's very probably true, my dear," Alec Bethway said somewhat wearily. "These small communities . . . charity too often begins anywhere but at home. The most obvious solution would seem to be for Miss Evans to come to us here—"

"*Here?* Stay wi' us here at the vicarage?" Francis stared at his father, not sure he had heard him aright. The notion of having Megwynn share her pregnancy at such close quarters struck him as rather less than desirable.

"No, no." The other shook his head. "That would be bound to excite too much speculation in the parish. I mean, she should come here to Eastbourne. And soon, too, whilst she's still able to procure a reference from her employer—he'll hardly grant her one once her maternal condition necessitates her leaving. There are plenty of boarding houses behind the seafront. I'm sure we can find the young woman a comfortable lodging until her infant is born. Somewhere quiet, and discreet. Don't you think, my dear?"

The minister looked towards his wife. She had risen from her chair beside the fire and moved across the room to stand as before near her son.

"Don't you think that would be our best plan? Once we have Miss Evans settled in the town, it will be time enough then to decide what should be done with her and the child."

Isabelle turned her head. She did not return her husband's look however, but seemed to be watching something beyond the window; and when he moved to see what it was, noticed that the gulls had returned and it was their shadow-flight upon the snow that had distracted her.

"My dear?" he asked again, gently.

The response, when it came, was oddly disconcerting. In a voice that was no more than a breath above a whisper, Isabelle murmured, "We should never have named him Francis. We've called up a ghost . . . we shouldn't have named him that."

133

13

The first snows of 1892 had arrived with the New Year in a single heavy flurry that lay on the ground a day or so, and then melted into slush. A week later, the prevailing wind had shifted round to the north-east and the snow began again—not in scattered showers now, but as heavy falls that continued without respite well into the month.

There might be an occasional pause, an occasional wearying of the elements; but each time, just when it seemed the clouds must have emptied themselves at last, the northern horizon would darken again and the wind freshen in gusts that brought fresh snow swinging down into soft, pleated folds, billowing and swirling like a curtain being drawn across the skies.

After the snow came the rain, spears of it, a spiteful, sharp rain that fell for several days; and no sooner had that stopped than a hard frost set in, and then more snow, starching the ghost-pale countryside into a frozen winterland.

For all its harshness, it had a certain cruel loveliness about it: fields and woods and hills mantled into featureless forms of white upon uniform whiteness that at night sparkled like glass beneath the icy glitter of reflecting stars. Before long, though, villages were completely isolated, cut off from each other by impenetrable drifts blocking the lanes; and even in the towns, only the main thoroughfares were open to horse traffic. Straw had to be thrown down to give a grip on the iced-smooth cobbles, and wherever one looked there were doorways, steps and path slopes showing up amongst the banks of shovelled snow as dirty patches where hearth-ash had been scattered underfoot for safe passage.

Ted and Minnie Brocklebank were away from Lewes during this bleak, bitter period. First it had been Ted's father, dying of the "brown crisis" (otherwise bronchitis) at his home in Buckfield; and then Minnie's niece, over at Frant village on the edge of the Weald, about to be delivered of her first child while her husband, a cow-man, lay abed with frostbite blackening the toes of one foot.

Their absence did not greatly inconvenience Amy Flynn. Enjoying her own company as she did, she had not the least objection to being left alone all this time and was perfectly happy to stay at Tea Garden Lane and busy herself with this and that. Nor did the biting cold trouble her unduly: she made bedroom and kitchen her sole living quarters, with fires to warm each, and closed off those parts of the house not in use.

Every day, however inclement the weather, the young woman was to be found out of doors, sweeping the paths and the yard clear of snow, or else scrambling over the drifts along the lane to reach the copse of trees on the edge of the Downs. She came up here often, loving the clear, cold peace of the place, and would stand a while in its shelter beneath branches so cocooned in snow that the weight had bowed them into glistening arcades.

From this high vantage she could look out over Lewes as far as Juggs Road, where it snaked its way between the windmills on Cranedown at the far side of the valley. In between lay the whitened roofscape of the town, smudged with plumes of smoke that hung like a mist in the freezing air; and below her, the flat metallic gleam of the River Ouse, moving sluggishly past wharves and warehouses, ice-floes that made her think of broken panes of glass drifting upon its surface.

Twice a week or so Amy went down into the town for provisions and to visit the lending library where she now had a subscription. No one seemed inclined to stand long talking in the snow-blocked streets, and the place had a curious dream-like air about it, she thought, the sounds muffled, colours filmy, figures a soft blur of movement against the greyness of evening. She was always glad to be home again, tucked up with a blanket round her knees in the deep armchair before the fire, and a new book opened at the first page.

She had been thus contentedly engaged late one afternoon in mid-January, curtains drawn against the fading light, the cosy flicker of flames turning her room into a snug oasis of comfort and warmth against the elements outside, when there came a sudden urgent ringing of the front bell.

Taking up one of the oil lamps, Amy had descended through the silent, shadowed house to the entrance hall; and upon opening the door, had discovered a huddled figure wrapped in a snow-encrusted greatcoat, leaning weakly against the step rail and obviously in the final stages of exhaustion.

"Yes?"

She held the lamp a little higher.

"Yes? What do you want? Who is it?"

The light fell upon a gaunt, unshaven face, its eyes hollowed with fatigue; and at the sight of those features, the young woman's hand had flown to her mouth to stifle a cry.

It was David Linton.

There had been the most terrible scene with Louisa. Scenes were becoming almost an everyday occurrence at the house in Church Lane, and few members of their social circle in Weatherfield were not aware by now that the Lintons were a less than happy couple; but this latest scene was worse than any which had so far passed between them.

It had started innocently enough the previous morning, a Thursday. David had been away from home for almost thirty-six hours, his presence needed in the outlying hamlets which digging teams had finally broken through to reach, and where there were a number of cases of broken limbs, respiratory infections and sundry other ailments requiring medical attention.

Returning to Weatherfield dog-weary, the doctor had retired at once to bed and fallen almost unconscious into a sound sleep; and he might have remained there well into the following morning had it not been for his young daughter, Alice, creeping into the darkened room before breakfast and stumbling against the wash-stand.

Louisa, appearing on the scene, had begun reproaching the child for disturbing Papa as well as being disobedient and clumsy. Thus chastised, Alice began to wail, and the wailing, in turn, brought on a chesty attack of breathlessness. David, thoroughly woken, reproved Louisa for being too severe with the child. Louisa for her part, retaliated by complaining that he encouraged Alice's naughtiness; and so on and so forth. Words began to fly, growing more and more heated, while Alice meanwhile continued to wail and wheeze until finally removed to be held over a steaming bowl of camphor.

The hostile atmosphere had rumbled on into the afternoon, and it was Alice again who precipitated a second outburst. Told by her mother that she was not allowed to play in the garden but must keep to the nursery, she became resentful.

"I wish you were not my mama. Indeed I do. I wouldn't have to stay indoors if I were not poorly. And I wouldn't be poorly if I did not have a mama who was always poorly too."

"Alice!"

"I wish Amy could be my mama. *She's* never poorly. *She'd* let me play in the snow all day if I liked to. I know she would."

"Oh—you bad, wicked little girl! To wish that creature for your mother—"

"Amy is not a 'creature', Louisa." David Linton had entered the drawing room in time to overhear what had been said. "You are not to use that term when speaking of her to Alice."

"I shall use what term I see fit."

"I repeat, you will kindly not refer to Amy as a 'creature'."

Louisa gave a toss of the head. "That's right—defend her, as always. You have just this moment heard your daughter spurn me as mother because of my troublesome health, yet do you reprimand her? No! You reprimand *me* for daring to express my contempt for the female with whom she wishes me replaced."

"Nonsense. Alice meant no such thing. She was merely being pert, and for that she shall apologise."

The doctor looked down at his young daughter, who was standing awkwardly with one pantaletted leg wrapped around the other in the manner children adopt when made to feel uncomfortable in the presence of adults.

"Alice, you will please say sorry to Mama for answering her so."

The small rosebud mouth twisted itself to one side.

137

"Alice—?"

Plainly, Papa was in no mood to be humoured. Alice did as she was bid.

"I am sorry, Mama, for answering you so."

"Very well." Louisa gave her a cursory glance from the chaise longue. "Now go along and find Lily and ask her to bring you a glass of warmed milk in the nursery."

The child's eyes shifted sideways to look up at her father and the rounded chin began to tremble. It was so lonely always in the nursery, and warmed milk made her feel sick. There was no response, however, no secret wink to soothe the hurt; and the ringletted head, prettily adorned with satin ribbons like her mother's, was bowed in misery as Alice obediently departed from the drawing room, quietly closing the door behind her as she'd been taught to do.

David Linton picked up a copy of *The Lancet* from the mahogany canterbury, a partitioned stand placed to hold his journals and newspapers, and took it over to the armchair beside the fireplace. Seating himself in silence, he began to read.

After some two or three minutes had passed, Louisa gave an exaggerated sigh, but he took no notice. This piqued her, for she sighed again, louder, and commenced patting and pulling at the cushions behind her on the chaise longue.

Still she was ignored.

Finally, unable to contain her exasperation any longer, she demanded, "Well?"

"Well what?" David did not bother to raise his head.

"Have you nothing to say?"

He turned a page. "Ought I to have?"

"I think so, yes."

"Upon what subject?"

Louisa gestured impatiently. "Why, whatever you judge to be of greatest interest."

"At the present, I'm engaged in reading an article upon the dangers of artificial feeding of infants. Would you care that I give some statistics for discussion, perhaps? The greatest risk, of course, is from diarrhoea and vomiting, due to germ infection setting up gastro-enteritis. Figures show—and I quote—that out of every one hundred infants which die from diarrhoea and vomiting, ninety-two are

138

artificially fed, while of the remaining eight, four are breast-fed and four fed partly by breast and partly by hand."

The doctor lowered the page from which he'd been reading and looked across at his wife, his expression, like his tone, one of complete indifference.

"Do you have any observations of your own to add to those findings?"

Louisa's bottom lip jutted. "That was not what I meant, as you very well know."

"Oh? Then what did you mean?"

"Cannot we discourse upon something more sociable? The weather, perhaps?"

"I would have thought the feeding of infants has rather more to recommend it as a topic for discussion than the weather. What can one say of the weather? It is cold. But then one expects it to be cold at this season."

"The snow has been very much worse than usual. And there are still fresh falls to come, Lily thinks."

"No doubt Lily is right."

"She says that whenever the snow lies without a thaw, that is because it's waiting for more to join it."

"Ah."

David resumed his persual of *The Lancet*.

Silence again descended between them.

His wife sighed a few times more, watching his face with a little frown of vexation. Then her eyes began flickering about the room, alighting briefly on pictures, ornaments, needlework, while her fingers fidgeted with the tassled fringe of a cushion.

The only sounds were the rustle of flames in the hearth and the steady dull tick of the mantelpiece clock.

The passing minutes fretted her impatience. With a sudden thump of her fist, she burst out, "I suppose if I were Amy Flynn you would not be quite so dreadfully dull. If Amy Flynn were here in my place you'd not be sitting there with your nose thrust into a journal."

David took a deep breath. "Louisa—" he began warningly.

She paid no heed. "You'd be here at my side, gazing into my face with that frightfully silly expression you wear, like a dog yearning after its mistress—"

139

"Damn it, will you be silent!"

The words came out in a shout. *The Lancet* was tossed to the floor.

"Do we have to have this over and over again, day in and day out, the same ridiculous nonsense? Why is it, Louisa, that whenever you feel bored or neglected or in need of diversion, you must drag up Amy's name like a bone to be worried?"

The other's hands went to her ears. "Please, do not raise your voice so. The servants may hear."

"Let them hear. Dear God, they've heard it all often enough before. And so has half of Weatherfield, the way you've gone about airing your opinion of Amy to all and sundry. No wonder the poor girl chooses to keep away. And you can remove your hands and stop giving me that wounded-heart look. It's nothing but a sham. I've lived with you too long not to know when you're acting."

"Acting—!"

"Aye, acting . . . playing the part of the wronged, long-suffering wife wed to some philandering blackguard who doesn't give a tuppenny damn about her. Well, let me tell you something, Louisa. I've been a good and faithful husband to you these past years. I've put up with your sulks, your tantrums, your coldness, your childish demands. I've had to watch you deliberately turn yourself into a semi-invalid—"

"I have not deliberately turned myself into an invalid. Oh, how cruel! To blame me for the affliction I must bear—"

"Yes, I do blame you for it. Whatever physical debility you suffered from your miscarriage has long since been repaired. Your breakdown of health is nothing more than morbid hysteria, played upon to excite sympathy and attention. There, now—you see? I thought it wouldn't be long before we had a few tears. You weep most prettily, my dear. A sight to stir pity in the hardest breast. I don't suppose Ellen Terry herself could wring more pathos from the scene."

Louisa's distress increased, becoming rather more genuine. David had never spoken to her like this before and his harsh words as well as the savagery of his tone quite shook her. Throwing herself down upon the chaise longue, she buried her face in her hands, her tears giving way to a noisy sobbing, interspersed with tremulous cries of reproach.

"Oh, how I wish I were dead . . . to be abused so . . . what harm have I ever done you, that you should treat me thus . . . I have given you the best years of my youth, and now, to be thrust aside . . . spurned . . . slighted even by my own child . . . oh, that I should live to see the day . . ."

Her husband endured this threnody of woe for some minutes before he could stomach it no longer. Turning on his heel, he moved grim-faced towards the door.

"Where are you going?" Louisa cried, reluctant in spite of her genuine grief to lose his attention before she had made him feel sufficiently guilty.

"I am going to do some work in the study."

"Go to your study, then! Yes, go and bury yourself in your precious work and ignore the pain you leave behind you here. How heartless you are . . . any other husband would be down upon his knees begging forgiveness for such cruel, cruel wrong."

"Any other husband would not be so patiently tolerant of these self-indulgent displays of theatricality."

"Oh—you monster! You unfeeling brute!"

Louisa righted herself on the chaise longue and snatching up a cushion hurled it across the room. Unfortunately it struck one of her dried flower sprays on the pembroke table behind the sofa, causing the elegant vase to smash to the floor in a wreckage of broken pods and stalks and china fragments.

This immediately brought on an outburst of hysterical wailing.

David's self-command snapped. Striding to the hearth, he grasped his wife by the shoulder and delivered her a sharp slap to the side of the face.

Louisa's mouth fell open. For a moment it seemed she was screaming in silence; and then she fell forward against her husband, and began a desolate whimpering.

"I am sorry," he said tensely. "I am sorry . . . but you drive me to it. These constant scenes . . . don't you see how they wear me down?"

Pushing her from him, he went to stand before the fire,

141

rubbing the palm of his hand as though he would either salve its sting or wipe away the memory of the blow.

"I'm sorry," he repeated again after a time, when the whimpering had ceased. "I had no wish to hurt you. But how can I make you understand, Louisa? I have come to the end of my tether so far as this marriage is concerned. We live together under the same roof . . . and behave like strangers. When was the last time you allowed me into your bed? Can you remember? I'm sure I can't. When was the last time you showed me *any* affection? Can you remember that? You kiss me upon the cheek at breakfast and bedtime—and nothing more. I'm your husband, yet I'm expected to content myself with such grudging courtesy."

He paused. Louisa's head was still bowed and he noted dispassionately that the trickle of her tears upon the lap of her pale-grey grogram skirts had patched the material with dark stains.

When he spoke at length again, his tone was a little kinder. "Come now, we shall solve nothing by nursing our animosity. I have said that I'm sorry for striking you—"

"Oh, indeed, but you shall be sorry," his wife interrupted in a low, quivering voice. "I mean to see to it that you are sorry, David. The rector shall hear of your violence against me. Yes, and others, too."

"Don't you think that is being unnecessarily vindictive?" he asked carefully.

She ignored him. "We shall see how many there are who wish to continue as your patients when they learn what a vile bully you are, to raise your hand to a defenceless woman."

"Now you are being stupid." The doctor's tone immediately hardened again. "If I lose my patients, I lose money, and without income how am I to be expected to support this household?"

Louisa chose once more to ignore him. "And I shall write to Mr Bates in Lewes. Yes, I shall write to him this very day to inform him of your conduct."

The thought seemed to assuage her distress, for she recovered herself a little and straightening up, began dabbing at her wet cheeks with a handkerchief produced from her sleeve.

"What in God's name has Ellis Bates to do with us?"

demanded her husband. "Why should he become involved?"

The reddened eyes took on a look of spitefulness.

"Oh, did you not know? Perhaps not cared to know? Too busy eating out your heart for dear Amy?"

She gave a small, tight smile, as though savouring the coming words.

"Mr Bates is my admirer . . . my devoted admirer. Ah yes, I thought that would astonish you to hear. *There* is a gentleman who has not only openly expressed his deep concern for my well-being, but shown a sympathy which has strengthened me greatly during these past dreadful months."

"Has he, indeed."

"There is no need to sound so smug at my expense! You do not believe me?"

"What, that Ellis Bates yearns to be your lover?"

"Oh—!"

"I wish him better luck with you than I've had." David's tone was cuttingly contemptuous. "You're a very poor prospect in bed, Louisa. And you may write in your letter to say so."

Bending to pick up the copy of *The Lancet* from the floor where he'd earlier tossed it, he added, "It's time we concluded this farce of a scene. I have work to do, and patients to attend to this evening. I shall leave you to your correspondence, my dear."

Early the following morning, before first light, David Linton had risen from his sleepless bed and slipped away from the house. On his desk lay a note to Louisa that he intended being absent for a day or two in order to recollect himself.

Saddling up in the stable, he had wrapped his horse's hooves in sacking to give them purchase on the packed snow, and then walked the animal quietly out of Church Lane before rousing it into a trot along the darkened high street, towards the road leading south to the Downs.

It was a foolhardy venture to undertake in such perilous conditions, as he was very well aware; but he had to reach Amy, talk to her, be with her, and whatever the risks, he was a man desperate enough to face them.

14

"David . . . David, oh, David!"

Amy had to repeat his name several times, scarcely able to believe that the huddled figure swaying in front of her at the very limit of exhaustion was indeed David Linton, and not some wretched poor creature come begging at her door.

"Dear God in heaven . . . David! What a state you're in . . . what has happened?"

She put out a hand and grasped him by the sleeve, feeling the icy wetness of the snow-sodden material.

"Come in. Quickly. Inside with you."

Mutely he obeyed, shuffling forward like one of the bundles of tatters seen so often of late waiting at the makeshift soup kitchen by All Souls church.

Setting down the oil lamp, Amy pushed the door shut behind him, locking out the grey, chill bleakness of the winter dusk.

"Here . . . let's have this coat off at once before you catch your death."

He stood unresisting, making no move to help as she struggled to work the buttons of the greatcoat undone and drag it from his shoulders. Beneath, the brown tweed of jacket and waistcoat was discoloured with dark-rust patches where dampness had soaked through into the material, and the trousers were saturated almost to the thigh.

"I'll take you upstairs. There's a good fire burning in my room. We'll soon have you dry. Oh, how you're shaking . . . what on earth have you been at, David, to get yourself in such a sorry plight?"

Without waiting for any answer, she took up her lamp again and guided him across the hall to the stairs, assisting his clumsy, strengthless limbs to climb them step by step to reach the landing, and from there, the warm haven of her bedroom-cum-temporary abode.

Troubled by the violent spasms of shivering which came every few moments to wrack the doctor's ice-chill body, she tried to make him comfortable in the armchair before the fire, fetching a blanket to put round his shoulders; then, kneeling down, began removing the sodden footwear.

He made a sound and tried feebly to push her away.

"Be sensible now, you can hardly sit in a pair of soaking wet boots," she chided gently, continuing to pull at them. "You better than anyone ought to know that."

For the first time, David Linton made an effort to speak. In a voice that was hoarse and slurred with fatigue, he mumbled, "Don't want you . . . kneeling . . . not to me . . ."

Apart from giving him a quick look, the young woman disregarded him and carried on with what she was doing.

"There—" when the second boot, after a struggle, finally joined its partner by the hearth. "Now. I'll leave you to take off those other wet things yourself as best you can, while I find you something else to wear. What a good thing I decided to save Uncle Harry's best nightshirts. I confess, I've been making use of them myself this weather. I'll fetch one in, and then it's straight to bed with you while I make some hot beef tea to take the chill from your bones."

She was gone from the room before David could say a word.

When she returned, a little breathless, some ten minutes later, he was sitting before the fire swaddled in a blanket, his discarded outer clothing in a heap on the floor beside him.

Amy bent to pick them up. Despite the dramatically un-expected circumstances, and whatever the reason that lay behind, it gave her a curious feeling of gladness to be able to care for him like this, in her own home: almost as though she were making amends for her negligence of recent months, however much the cause for that negligence may have been of the other's own making.

"I'll take these things down to the kitchen and put them over the clothes-horse in front of the range. They'll be dry by morning. Here—" holding out a clean flannel night-shirt—"I've aired it ready for you, so see you get into it

145

while it's warm still. Now, is there anything else you need? The beef tea won't be long—it's on the hob."

She was answered by a shake of the head.

"Do say if there is, won't you? I'll heat a brick to put in the bed. We did have a warming-pan about the house somewhere, but Lord knows what's become of it."

She turned to go again; and as she did so, her busy glance fell upon the coal scuttle.

"Oh, I'd best fill that as well while I'm downstairs."

"Let . . . me." David was beginning to recover himself a little. "Let me . . . go for you."

"You'll stay where you are! You're as weak as a cat's kitten."

When the door had closed again after her, he struggled to clothe himself in the late Harry Weldrake's nightshirt, dragging the voluminous garment over his head with arms that felt as stiff as boards. If only this ridiculous shivering would stop . . . confound it, he was barely capable even of fastening a few buttons. He left them finally open; and wrapping himself once more in the blanket, re-seated himself clumsily and took stock of his surroundings.

It was a good-sized room, lit by several gas brackets whose mellow light showed him a large half-tester bed at the other side. Amy had obviously been pursuing her home-making abilities here, too, for the bed drapes were of the same dark-rose dimity material as the curtains drawn across the two windows, and the ornate Georgian plasterwork of the ceiling had been freshly rendered with white distemper.

David eased himself further back in the chair, grimacing a little at the discomfort in his limbs. Now that some sensation of feeling had started returning, it had brought on the biting pain of cramp, together with a disagreeable tingling in fingers and toes.

The door opened again behind him, introducing a savoury aroma into the room.

"Oh—now what were you told?" Clicking her tongue, Amy set down the beef tea. "Didn't I say you were to put yourself into bed?"

A ghost of a smile traced itself on the other's pale features. He said feebly, "You've missed your vocation . . . you should be a Nightingale at St Thomas's."

146

"I'm sure. I'd know then how to deal with patients who won't do as they're bid. Look at you, the way you're shivering still."

She knelt beside the chair, and taking David's hand, pressed it against her cheek. It trembled at her touch like that of a man in fever.

"Amy . . . oh, my Amy . . ." he whispered.

She did not respond, but gently withdrew herself and leaned aside to pick up the beverage she'd made for him.

"Here—" raising the steaming beaker carefully to his lips. "I see I must help you to drink this down. You'll only be spilling it everywhere."

Obediently, he drank in small slow sips, feeling the warm goodness thawing away the pit of ice within and putting fresh heart in his body. When he'd finished, he lay back in the chair, his eyes closed, and reached out to take Amy's hand again. It had been worth it—oh, how it had been worth it, that terrible, seemingly endless journey, that nightmare fight to survive against the gripping, numbing, killing winter cold.

"You're wondering, aren't you," he murmured at length, "how I came to be on your doorstep . . . and in such a way."

She smiled. "I must admit, I am curious. But the telling can wait a while till you're better recovered."

"No . . . I want you to hear it now."

"Then I think you should be abed before you begin."

He turned his head to look at her, and the mild brown eyes held such a strange, searching expression that for a moment it was as though he'd never seen her properly before; or perhaps had been blind for a time and needed to remember how truly lovely she was.

Amy rose to her feet, her hand still clasped in his, and gave a soft tug.

"David—please. To please me?"

"To please you, my dear . . . could any man refuse. Even though it were a matter of honour that he should."

"A matter of honour? Why, for pity's sake?" She gave a second, stronger tug at the clinging hand.

"It's for pity's sake that you've taken me in and cared for me. What right have I to expect more? It would be unmannerly of me to deprive you of your proper sleep and rest."

147

"What nonsense you're talking. I don't understand a word of it. Now come—get up, do."

She held out her other hand and assisted him out of the chair; and when he was unsteadily on his feet, put her strong young arms around him and led him from the hearth.

On reaching the bed, she threw back the patchwork counterpane; then, making to turn away again, said a little self-conciously, "I'll go and fetch the brick for your feet."

"No—" David restrained her. "I don't need it."

"Of course you do. You're as cold as ice still."

He shook his head, and once more there was that searching look in his face as he began pulling clumsily at the blanket covering his shoulders.

"Sit beside me and hold my hand as before . . . that will content me better than anything."

She hesitated; but seeing how haggard and weary he looked, and how he was trembling still in every limb despite her ministrations, she waited until he was settled comfortably against the pillows, and drawing the bed-clothes close about him, sat herself down at his side.

Were anyone to point out to her just now that her behaviour was quite beyond the bounds of convention, and not only indecorous but immodest in the extreme, Amy would have answered them forthrightly that David Linton was her friend, a friend in need; and convention could go hang if it said she must leave him to perish of cold for the sake of decorum and modesty.

"I have had a disagreement with Louisa," he began hesitantly, holding her hand in both his own. "It was my fault, that I must admit. I was tired out and irritable . . . not as tolerant as usual of her silliness. And oh, she can be so silly at times, so stupid . . ."

A pause. A fresh spasm of shivering.

"The fearful thing is, Amy . . . I don't think I love her now as before. May God forgive me, but I truly do not think I've any love left for her . . . none at all."

"You mustn't say such things, David. Louisa's your wife. It's your bounden duty to love her."

"Duty . . ." He savoured the word a moment, then discarded it. "Like a horse to water, you can urge a man to duty, but you cannot make him love. Love is a mirror, it

148

needs some reflection or it's empty. Louisa has no warmth for me. She makes not the least attempt to understand me, or show sympathy for the kind of man I am."

He paused again.

A gust of wind, caught in the chimney, sent the flames leaping upward in a sudden blazing flurry at the other side of the room; and a following gust brought with it the hiss of sleet against the windows behind the drawn curtains.

David drew Amy's hand closer, cradling it to his chest.

In a troubled voice he went on, "She is consumed, utterly consumed with her jealousy. It's become like a cancer, gnawing away at her day after day. If only she could be made to realise how destructive it's become to our marriage."

"Her jealousy of me?"

He nodded.

"Was that the cause of the disagreement between you?"

"Indirectly . . . yes, I suppose it was."

"What happened?"

"She became hysterical . . . I struck her. Oh, don't look at me like that, Amy. I'm ashamed enough as it is, God knows. I only meant to quieten her before she frightened little Alice with her noise."

He waited until another fit of uncontrollable shuddering had passed; then continued despondently, "After that, well, she turned vindictive . . . swearing she'd blacken my name and reputation . . . threatening even to write a letter of complaint to Ellis Bates."

"Ellis?" Amy gave a little laugh of astonishment. "But Louisa doesn't know Ellis, surely?"

"A slight acquaintance. They've met on occasion in Weatherfield at St Anne's."

"Too slight an acquaintance to be penning letters against one's husband, I would have thought."

"She claims the fellow has an admiration for her." David's tone held a note of indifference. "Would that it were true."

"I don't believe you mean that. How can you say such a thing, of your own wife?"

He made no reply. Instead, he reached out awkwardly with his free arm and rested it about Amy's waist.

After a time he began again, "I left the house early this morning, well before first light. It must have been five

149

o'clock when I set out on the road. Only a madman would have contemplated making such a journey . . . or a man in despair. And I don't think I'm mad, not yet."

"In despair, then. Why? Because of your wife?"

"Partly. But it wasn't for her that I was trying to reach Lewes."

Now it was the other's turn to make no answer.

"At first, conditions were not too hazardous," David went on a little wearily, leaning his head back against the pillows. "At least, so it seemed. My horse was fresh, and I was warmly clad and eager to press on as fast as the going allowed. I hadn't reckoned with the depth of the drifts in the darkness . . . dismounting time after time to pull the horse free, finding myself chest-high in snow . . . floundering off the road . . . losing all sense of direction."

His hand on Amy's tightened until the knuckles showed white, and she was forced to utter a soft cry before he realised how he was hurting her. Immediately, he raised her crushed fingers to his lips and kissed each one in turn.

"It was almost midday when I managed to reach Buckfield, and my horse was near enough foundered. I left him there at a hostelry . . . the Fordhouse . . . and tried to hire another. But there was none to be had. They were all out working with the digging teams. So I set out again on foot. I'd no other choice."

"You walked—all the way from Buckfield—in this weather? Dear God, no wonder you got here in the state you did. It's a miracle you got here at all."

"Despair can drive a man like nothing else on earth. I *had* to reach you, dearest, see you, be with you again. These past months I've been driven near mad with the ache of your absence . . . no one can have any idea what it's been like for me. Could you not have written, at least? Even a note, a few lines, would have sufficed. I sent you a greetings card at Christmas, in hope . . . but you never acknowledged it. Oh Amy, Amy, I have been in hell without you."

He shifted on the pillows to lay his head against her shoulder, an oddly forlorn little gesture which she found strangely moving. Stirred by an up-welling of emotion—whether it was affection, pity, nostalgia for the happiness of times past, or quite simply the need to be needed, she could

150

not say—she responded by enfolding David in her arms and gently stroking the thick, still-damp hair back from his forehead.

The soft, sly patter of sleet at the windows was more insistent now, as dark evening merged into darker night and the rising wind came scudding in sudden flurries along the swell of the Downs. Here in the still quietness Amy could hear its low whine among the overhanging eaves, and the rattle of one of the attic doors as the draught seeped up between the floorboards.

As she watched, the gas-jets dimmed momentarily on the wall brackets, blurring the edges of the room in shadow before flaring again inside their fluted glass hoods. For a few minutes they continued to burn brightly, then dipped and dimmed once more.

"The lights are burning low," she said quietly. "I shall have to go down and feed the meter."

There was no response.

"David?"

She lifted his head very gently from her shoulder. His eyes were closed and his breathing had grown slower. For a while longer she continued to stroke his hair; then, careful lest she waken him from this first, light sleep, eased away her arm and lowered him back against the pillows.

Treading quietly on tip-toe across the room, she took up her oil-lamp from the table beside the door and descended yet once again through the darkened house to the kitchen, where she attended to the gas meter and banked up the fire for the night in the range.

When she returned upstairs, David had rolled on to his side and was now quite soundly asleep.

Amy watched him for a little while; then, turning out the gas-jets, undressed herself on the hearth, and with the blanket wrapped about her, settled down in the armchair to find what rest she could.

It seemed she had barely slept more than a few hours when she awoke again suddenly. The wind must have died down, for the night was eerily silent. The room, too, felt strange: a waiting, watchful air about it.

She sat forward, surprised to discover how stiff and chilled

151

she was, and saw that the fire was almost out, only a few ruby-eyed sparks left still glowing among the embers. Surely it couldn't have burned down so soon, she thought. Perhaps she'd been asleep longer than it seemed. Yawning, she got to her knees, reaching across for the scuttle, and began feeding the moribund fire with pieces of paper and kindling, fanning them with her hand to make them catch alight. After several attempts, her efforts were rewarded with a flicker of flame, and once the kindling had started burning well, she sat back on her heels and cupped her cold hands towards the meagre warmth.

There—it *was* later than she thought: All Souls's clock was just chiming the hour. In a little while the first grey light of another day would be creeping into the eastern skies above Mount Caburn.

Bending forward to her task again, the young woman fed the strengthening flames with small pieces of coal, heaping larger lumps about them; then got up and turned to look towards the bed.

"Oh—" Startled, her hand flew to her breast. "I thought you were asleep still."

"No, I've been awake for some time." David Linton pushed himself with his elbows further up amongst the pillows.

"Then why didn't you speak?"

"I was watching you."

"You gave me a fright!" Taking up the blanket from the chair, Amy draped it round her shoulders and went across to the foot of the bed.

"Was that four or five o'clock chiming just now?" he asked her.

"Five. You should try and get some more sleep."

"I'm rested enough."

He looked at her, standing there against the bed-rail, the long loose waves of dark-gold hair outlined by the quickening firelight behind her.

After a moment he said quietly, "Oh, Amy . . . I love you so much . . . so very much. More than you'll ever know. You must believe that."

When she remained silent, he leaned forward and reached out a hand.

152

"Please . . . don't keep yourself apart from me. When day comes I'll leave, if you want me to go. And we'll never see each other again . . . if that's what you wish. But let me at least have something to remember you by, my dearest. Let me hold you once more, won't you . . . if only for a while?"

"David—oh, how difficult you make it for me."

But she did not refuse; though if he could have seen her face as she took the outstretched hand, he might have noticed the tears in her eyes, and how her mouth drooped a little in sadness that she could not love him more.

He drew her down against him, murmuring endearments that were muffled in her hair, his arms warm and strong now, wrapped about her pliant body; and when at last his mouth found hers she did not try to resist him, but yielded reluctantly to his kisses.

15

Ellis Bates's upper lip curled a little in distaste. He sat down at his desk, the pages of the letter he was reading held between finger and thumb as though their very contact was a contamination.

"Excuse—oh! excuse incoherence and impropriety in one whom you have honoured with the appellation of friend," ran the final line, and beneath it, looped in a violent spatter of ink—"Louisa A. Linton."

Irritably, he tossed the pages from him on to the desk. He had arrived home at Spences Lane a short while earlier in an already soured mood, having spent the morning at a borough meeting of board schools inspectors, fruitlessly endeavouring to drum up support for his arguments opposing the removal of certain regulations concerning corporal punishment. His views had been heard out in polite silence; and then blandly ignored.

This letter had been awaiting him on the tray in the entrance hall. Scanning it briefly while the maid removed his coat and hat, Ellis had been unable to make much sense of the thing at first reading, save that the overall tone was one of hysterical complaint larded throughout with self-pity.

"What the deuce—?" he'd muttered to himself, glancing at the signature as he closed the study door behind him. Turning again to the first page, he had begun a more deliberate perusal, and his reaction after the first few lines had quickly warmed from astonishment to disrelish and thence to incensed repugnance.

Adjuring him in the name of friendship and chivalry to come to her assistance, Louisa wrote that she was "almost overwhelmed with the extreme of affliction". Not so overwhelmed, however, that she could not put pen to paper, for "it unfortunately came into my mind that I might pour out the feelings of my heart to you, dear friend!—and believe me, this has a little soothed my grief and supported me under my painful lot".

The shrill refrain that her husband had misused her by deliberate neglect, unkindness and ill-treatment was emphasised almost to the point of exaggeration:

"The grossness of his conduct precludes all pardon, and has succeeded in eradicating from my bosom every vestige of sentiment. Oh! what species of diabolical pleasure could he promise himself in gaining the warmest affection of a wife, merely to leave her the victim of his cruelty? That man must be truly base who trifles with the peace of mind of a helpless invalid merely to render her the more wretched. He saw my agonies and plumed himself in wounding a heart too tenderly his own."

What excitable vapourings! And here—see—as expected, Amy Flynn's name dragged yet again through a mire of prejudice and execration, in tow to rancour-ridden accusations concerning her friendship with Doctor Linton.

"Alas, woman is the creature of disappointment, and her fairest prospects are frequently destroyed," Louisa continued in her childishly rounded hand. "I have not enjoyed one happy moment since I last had the compliment of your conversation, whilst the severity of my affliction has increased from the circumstances of my oh! so miserable situation. I am grieved to the very soul that a man on whom my warmest affections were placed should have acted so as to render me so wretched. His infidelity strikes as a dagger-blow to my devoted heart."

Had the woman no sense of her own ridiculous absurdity? To write such a farrago of nonsense—and to a near-stranger. Why, one could scarcely credit such presumption.

"Perhaps, dearest friend," the letter had concluded, "you will reject my outstretched hand, rather than be troubled with a poor, defenceless female. But no! no! pardon me, I beg, my sorrow clouds my reason. I am confident in your support. For pity's sake, write to me with some few words of comfort . . . I will value your advice the more highly for its plain candour."

Plain candour, indeed! Ellis Bates snorted aloud. Oh yes, yes, he would be writing to Mrs Linton plainly and candidly, though she would hardly find his words much to her comfort. Quite the opposite.

"Come!"

He gave the command sharply, his flow of indignation interrupted by a timid knocking at the study door. When it did not open immediately, he pushed back his chair with a muttered oath of anger and made to get to his feet.

"Come, I said!"

At that, the handle was turned and the door opened a short way to admit the plump figure of his children's governess.

"Miss Evans?" He re-seated himself, fixing the young woman with a look.

"Excuse me, Mr Bates," she addressed him, a little nervously. "I was wondering . . . if it is convenient, that is, sir . . . I was wondering whether I might have a word with you?"

"Very well." He motioned her abruptly to close the door. Then, consulting his gold watch-piece, replaced it in his waistcoat pocket and said, "If this concerns Esmond and Laura's visit to Heydon House—"

"Oh, no, sir." Megwynn shook her head. "At least—" hesitating a fraction— "at least, sir, I do not think it will affect it. I hope not, indeed, since they are looking forward, both of them, to seeing their Great-aunt Lovell again."

"A moment." Ellis held up a hand. "You are not making yourself clear, Miss Evans. *What* will not affect the visit?"

"It is what I have come about, look you, sir."

Another hesitation.

"Yes? Well?"

"I wish to give notice that I will be leaving your employment at the end of next month."

The words, in Megwynn's lilting Welsh accent, came out as rather too much of a gabble for the other to grasp precisely what it was she had said.

"What was that? Speak a little slower, if you please."

"My—my notice, sir. My contract of employment—" She swallowed, and tried again. "My contract of employment obliges me to give you fair and due warning that I wish to leave—"

"I am aware of the terms of your contract, since I drew

156

them up myself." Ellis Bates's voice was as coldly needle-sharp as the winter wind in the bare branches of the orchard trees beyond his window.

The governess looked down at her clasped hands. Her cheeks, normally so rosy-hued, were pale and the stippling of brown freckles across them gave her skin an oddly blemished appearance.

"So, you have decided to give up your position here?"

A nod of the bowed head.

"May I know why?"

"I've been offered another place, see . . . with a relative, sir." This was the pretext the Bethways had advised her to use. It was truth enough, under the circumstances.

"Ah." Ellis's fingers drummed impatiently on the surface of his desk. "You'll be returning to Wales, then?"

"Oh, no, sir. I'm going to Eastbourne."

"I thought you told me that you had no family outside your home village."

"Nor I haven't. This . . . this is a relative by marriage."

The drumming quickened. "And you will be employed by them as governess?"

This time the bowed head gave a small shake.

"No? What, then?"

Again, a hesitation. "Nursery-maid, sir."

"Nursery-maid? A poor exchange, I would have thought, Miss Evans. Your wage will be halved at a stroke."

No answer.

"Well, that is your business, I suppose," the other said briskly, "though I credited you with being a young woman of rather more sense. I must point out to you that your leaving creates great inconvenience to this household, not to mention the disturbance and distress caused to Laura and Esmond. They have grown not a little fond of you, I understand, in these past months. Indeed, I had hoped that in you they had found a person able to provide the discipline and stability which young children require in their formative years. I regret to learn that my judgement has been so misplaced. When I employed you first, Miss Evans, you gave me to believe that it was your wish to remain in service here for some considerable length of time. What have you to say now of that?"

The clasped hands were wrung agitatedly. "I—I am sorry, sir . . . indeed I am. But . . . well, my situation has changed, see."

"I do not see. A servant has a loyalty to those who provide their livelihood."

The drumming reached a crescendo. Then stopped abruptly.

"You wish to leave at the end of next month?"

"Yes, sir. If you please."

"Very well." Ellis referred to the almanac upon his desk. "February is increased by a day this year, being a leap year. However, I note that the twenty-eighth falls upon a Sunday, so I shall expect you to work up to and including that date, and we shall ignore the extra day."

"Yes, sir. Thank you, sir."

He waved his hand dismissively. "That is all. You may go."

Megwynn bobbed a curtsey, and was at the door before the words had hardly left her employer's mouth.

Once she had gone, the still-raised hand was brought down with great savagery upon the desk top, rattling the pens in their holder, followed by a forcibly uttered "Devil take it!" Then, snatching up Louisa Linton's letter, Ellis Bates gave vent to his feelings by tearing the pages through and through until there remained nothing but a pile of shredded fragments.

"That is the second time you have been taken ill today, Miss Evans," young Esmond observed in detached tones, swinging backward upon the paddock gate. "I trust it is not something you have eaten?"

Megwynn supported herself against the broad snow-marbled trunk of the oak behind which she had hoped to hide her sudden malaise from view.

She managed a weak shake of the head. "I think I must have a chill on the stomach, *cariad*."

"Then let us return to the house." The boy jumped from the gate, his injured leg now healed to leave no more than a slight stiffness beneath the purplish scar. "You would be far better sitting before a fire."

He proffered his arm.

"No, no, Esmond . . . I'm better where I am. The fresh air will do me more good than any fire."

"If you are sure."

"Quite sure. Thank you."

He resumed his swinging.

"I felt a trifle queasy myself after luncheon today," he remarked in his strange little adult manner after some further minutes had elapsed. "It was the sago pudding, no doubt. I have had an aversion to sago ever since Florrie told me how she was cured of the whooping cough."

"Oh? How was that, then?"

"Her grandmama made her to eat a bowl full of white slugs, sprinkled with sugar."

Megwynn felt her throat start to rise again. She took a deep breath of cold afternoon air and said distractedly, "Oh, wherever can Laura have gone to?"

"There, look—feeding Merry still." Her young charge indicated a thicket of holly bushes a short way away across the paddock. Just visible were the hindquarters and long white tail of the pony.

"Do you know, Miss Evans, it is a most curious thing. Merry seems actually to have grown thinner these last months, despite the quantity of sugar lumps you've been smuggling from the house. I cannot understand it. One would have thought he'd not had a tit-bit for simply ages, the way in which he falls upon those I bring now that I'm able to ride him again."

"He's the greediest beast I've ever known for sugar," the governess responded in what might have seemed unnecessary haste. "The only curiosity is where he puts it all."

"Mmm."

Esmond gave her a look out of the corner of his eye; then, wearied of his swinging, declared, "I think I shall make some snow-balls to throw at Laura."

"You will do no such thing, indeed! If you must play at snow-balls, aim them at something which cannot take harm."

There was a shrug of the shoulder. "Very well. Then I shall throw them . . . at your tree."

As he said these last words, the boy swooped to the

ground and seized a handful of snow, and before Megwynn could think to duck out of the way, he had hurled the ball past her head to smack against the trunk behind.

"Oh, you little tinker! That was my hat you took off almost, look you."

She stooped quickly herself and returned his fire, catching him on the shoulder of his thick navy-blue knitted jerkin. He shied back; and for some minutes the pair continued to lob missiles at one another, until they were both showered from head to foot with snow, and laughing too much to take proper aim.

"Pax!" cried Esmond. "Pax. You have an unfair advantage, Miss Evans."

"I have?"

"Yes—you are a lady."

"And is that an advantage, *fachgen*?"

"It is in a snow-ball fight."

Megwynn smiled. She was feeling so much better now that the temporary nausea had diminished, eased by the cold, sharp air and the exercise. Taking off her wide-brimmed hat she wiped the snow from it with her sleeve, and then bent forward to shake out her skirts.

"May I?" the boy volunteered politely. He came across to her and began brushing the back of her jacket. "I'm sorry, I seem to have scored a bull's-eye with my last shot."

There was something about the way he said that, and the open, candid expression on his young face when she turned to look at him, that affected Megwynn greatly. Putting her arms about the slender shoulders, she drew him to her and held him tightly for a moment.

"Oh, *Duw* . . . I wish I didn't need to leave you," she said in a low, anguished voice.

There was a responsive little hug. "You don't *have* to go yet. It won't be dark for another half-hour at least."

She smiled again, this time a sad, small smile for the boy's innocent lack of comprehension. Raising a gloved hand to caress the straight fair hair cut in a heavy fringe across his forehead, she answered, "That's true. I don't have to go yet. I think I'll sit over here for a while and watch you play with Laura."

"May we go to the other side of the paddock, please?

There's a robin's nest in the hedge there. Papa said I might take it for my nature collection."

"But if you take it, what then will the poor robin do for a home?"

Esmond laughed. Releasing himself from her arms, he pranced away, reciting in a sing-song voice, "The north wind doth blow, and we shall have snow, and what will the robin do then, poor thing? He'll sit in a barn to keep himself warm, and hide his head under his wing, poor thing."

Then, starting the rhyme again, he gave a jaunty wave and trotted off as fast as his stiff leg would allow across the paddock to the holly thicket where his small sister was amusing herself still with the pony.

Megwynn walked to the bench by the gate and sat down, watching her two charges move hand in hand between the frost-whitened tussocks of grass, their shadows stretching palely behind them in the strengthless winter sunlight.

They could be such difficult children at times, fractious, wilful, obstinate—and yet so endearingly charming. Now that she had gained their trust, they were beginning to be less afraid of openly expressing themselves, less wary of showing their affection. More than anything in the world they had needed a mother to love them; and being denied one, had perforce grown withdrawn and unresponsive under their father's inflexible regimen.

The pair of them had been like plants, Megwynn thought, looking back on her first weeks at Spences Lane: two small plants thirsting for attention, blossoming a little more with each kind word and act of tenderness. Only this last night, when she'd been hearing their prayers, Laura had turned and clung to her, asking in her quaint way, "Does Mama mind, d'you think, that I love you just as much as her?"

"She does not mind, I'm sure," the governess had answered. "Your mama knows how much I love you and Esmond on her behalf."

Yet now she was about to abandon them both, leave them once more to their loneliness, their tears and nightmare dreams, and all because she was to become a mother herself.

Tears welled suddenly in her eyes. It was true what she'd said to the boy just now: how she wished she didn't have to leave Spences Lane. *Duw*, how much she wished that! For

161

what was to become of her? Her love affair with Francis Bethway was finished. Oh, he hadn't said as much; but then, she had not seen him recently to hear him say anything. Nor had he written as much; but then again, she'd only had one letter from him since he learned of her pregnancy, and that was cool to the point of coldness and merely to inform her of his parents' reaction to the news.

What a fool she had been to believe all his promises, to allow herself to be so taken in by a handsome face and over-fond attentions. Handsomeness, after all, was no more than skin deep; and promises, like pie crusts, were made to be broken.

"*Nad yw y rhai a farchogant yn gyflym yn marchogaeth yn hir.*" She could hear her old granny in Bettws-y-Crwyn saying it even now. "They who ride fast never ride long." Well, she had let herself be taken for a ride, true enough, and now she must bear the pain of being thrown.

Francis's people meant well, offering to find "discreet" accommodation somewhere in Eastbourne where she might have the baby without fuss. They could hardly do less, being Church. There had been no mention of a wedding, though. Merely a line or two to the effect that their son was young and headstrong, but they trusted a career in the Army would temper his faults.

Sniffing miserably, Megwynn removed a snow-crusted glove to wipe away the tears from her cheeks. How could she have been so easily the dupe of infatuation—she who had always sworn to keep herself to herself before marriage? At times, it wellnigh drove her to distraction, thinking of what had been between them both.

Well, she had made her bed and she must lie upon it; but a hard and lonely bed it boded to be now that her faithless lover had deserted her, and left her stripped of position, prospects and any hope of respectability for the future.

16

"Go and see your mother?"

Minnie Brocklebank paused in her sweeping, her face a study of astonishment.

"Land's sake, Miss Amy, whatever for?"

"I feel I ought to. She *is* my mother, after all."

"Be warned by me, you'll be putting yourself to a wasted journey. Mebbe I say it as shouldn't, but she's doolally-tapped, is Miss Rosannah. She won't know you, and that's fact, no more'n she knew you when she were let out o' the bedlam for a bit all them years back."

Amy turned away from the drawing room window.

"I'm going to Heathbury to see her, Minnie," she said again, more emphatically. "It isn't right to pretend she doesn't exist. I've written to the overseer, Mr MacRae . . . he says I might visit by all means. So I shall go this Friday coming."

"Then you'll not go alone, Miss," the other declared, resuming work and applying her broom vigorously to the dried tea-leaves scattered on the carpet to catch the dust. "The very idea—as if I'd let you make such an expedition by yourself. You'll have me for company, whether you will or no."

"Now don't fly into one of your takings. I'd already decided to ask you."

"I should think so, an' all. Besides—" pausing again for a moment—"I'd like to see Miss Rosannah for myself after this long time. I was in service here when she was friendly wi' that Mr Adolphe de Retz—that 'un she fancies she's married to. Who knows but that it mightn't just jog her mind into some sense, having me wi' her to recall the olden days? You'd only make a worse boffle o' things, left to yourself, Miss Amy. Much better that I go along wi' you."

163

"I've already *said* you may—"

"Yes, well, no need to raise your voice."

"I was not raising my voice, Minnie," Amy rejoined, striving to control herself. "Now have you done with the sweeping? Oh, and don't scowl! I may ask a civil question, mayn't I? You're creating so much dust with that broom you might just as well not have bothered polishing in here yesterday."

There was a toss of the head. "Seeing as how I'll be polishing in here again tomorrow, I wouldn't ha' thought it'd make much difference. But I know when I'm not wanted, so I'll take myself off out o' the way—though why you should choose to spend so much time a-mooning through that blessed window, the Lord only knows."

"I'm not mooning through the window. I'm enjoying the sight of a patch of green again now the snow's starting to melt at last."

"So you say, Miss."

With an audible sniff and a final flourish of the broom to brush her sweepings out into the passage, Minnie departed, shutting the door very firmly in her wake.

Amy permitted herself a faint smile. None of this grumbling was to be taken seriously: the bustling assertiveness was only a way of showing fond attention, nothing more.

She turned again to gaze out through the window, the smile fading.

Minnie was right, though. She was spending far more time than she should looking at the view, instead of giving her attention to better things. It was David Linton who was the preoccupation, of course. The three weeks that had passed since that regrettably unwise night together seemed unreal, as though the only reality had been that moment when she'd reluctantly given herself to him and known for the first time what it was to lie in a man's arms.

Since then, she had been living in a troubled vacuum. Nothing was the same as before: her thoughts, her feelings, her values, all were coloured now by the realisation of knowing herself changed. Surely that change must be evident in her expression and her manner to those who knew her best? There were moments indeed when she felt that the bitter-sweet night with David had left its stamp upon her forehead, like the mark of Cain, for all to witness.

164

She gave a deep sigh, and leaned forward to rest her burning face against the cold windowpane. At least life was slowly returning to normal, now that the iron grip of the winter snows had been broken by a mild, damp start to February. Even that, though, had brought its problems, with swollen streams bursting their banks and flooding low-lying fields, and the Ouse running so high here in Lewes that riverside dwellings had been barricaded with bags of sand and the occupants, so Minnie reported, had removed themselves to the safety of their upper floors.

Amy wished that she were able to talk to Minnie about David Linton; but like so many decent women of her class, the housekeeper placed a high value upon propriety, and in her eyes no "nice" young woman would make herself unrespectable with another woman's husband. Nor could Amy be certain that Aunt Isabelle Bethway would prove any more tolerant, especially since relations between them both had been somewhat cool of late because of what the Bethways seemed to consider her tacit encouragement of Francis's misconduct.

Yet she desperately needed someone to turn to, someone who might simply listen without censure or reproach. Which was why she was going to Heathbury on Friday to see a stranger who, however unsound in mind, was still in heart her mother, her own flesh and blood.

"Ye'll have to speak a wee bit louder, ma'am, if ye're to make yeself heard," said the red-bearded overseer. "They're excitable today. It's the moon, ye ken."

"The moon?" Amy tore her gaze for a moment away from the rows of barred windows on either side of the corridor ahead.

"Aye. Aye, the moon. It has an effect upon them when it's at the full. That's why the poor creatures are called lunatics by some, d'ye follow."

"I—I'm afraid I don't."

Mr MacRae wagged his head. "Aye, well, it's a word taken from the Latin. *Luna*. Signifying the moon."

"Oh. Oh, I see."

She looked again along the corridor. Though it was broad day outside, the gas-lights were burning here, and the flicker

165

of shadows on the stone walls lent the place a dingy, sinister atmosphere. There was an overpowering smell of carbolic everywhere; but more than that, the thing which struck most forcefully was the sound: a strange, soft ululating moan which swelled and died again like the waves upon the shore and formed the background to a medley of individual cries, shrieks and frenzied bursts of laughter.

"I believe I wrote in my letter, did I not, that your mother's mental condition is quite stable," Mr MacRae went on, raising his voice a little.

Amy nodded.

"Her health, alas, is quite otherwise. Far from being as good as we'd wish. But then, she's—how old?"

"Forty-six. No . . . forty-seven, I think. I disremember."

"Aye, well, that's counted a good age in these institutions. Ye must understand, ma'am, the decay of the brain has a maleficent effect upon the body and its functions, causing premature physical deterioration in the mentally insane."

There was a slight pause before the hesitant question, "Does that mean, Mr MacRae, that my mother has not much longer left to live?"

He wagged his head again. "One should always be prepared to look a wee bit on the black side." Then, gesturing Amy forward—"Ye're wondering no doubt, the reason for my asking your companion to remain a while below. It's best that ye visit one at a time, d'ye follow, so that your mother is not too much stimulated by the company. There'll be a nurse in attendance, so ye've no need to fret for your safety. Mrs de Retz tends only to become violent when one tries to urge upon her that she's anything other than she wishes to believe."

"Mrs de Retz? I'm to call her by that name, am I? Not Mrs Flynn, or Mama?"

"Och, certainly not Mrs Flynn!" The red beard seemed almost to bristle in the gaslight. "Ye must bear well in mind, ma'am, that her dementia takes the form of a delusion. A very marked delusion. Your mother is convinced beyond all normal reason that she is married to a Mr Adolphe de Retz, that they have a daughter named Aimée, and that they live in France. The fact that she never actually sees her 'husband' nor her daughter, nor occupies a house abroad, is neither here nor there to her. It is a mental hallucination, d'ye follow."

"But then how am I to communicate with her, sir? If I address her in English, will she understand?"

"Aye, she'll understand well enough. She believes it's French she hears. Now—here we are."

Mr MacRae indicated the door they were approaching. Like all the rest in the corridor, it had a barred window to allow inspection of the room within.

"If ye'll bide here, a moment, Miss Flynn, I'll direct the nurse to attend ye."

He walked away towards the further end, to the section supervisor's office, and in a short time reappeared with a tall, stout female gowned in black, a white lace cap covering her hair. From the belt at her waist there hung a steel ring of keys.

The nurse approached Amy, treading with quiet, purposeful step, and acknowledging her presence with a tight smile before directing a glance in at the window; then, satisfied with what she saw, inserted one of the keys in the lock to open the door and went inside, beckoning the other to follow.

The room was of a medium size, sparsely furnished but comfortable enough for its purpose, and given a homely touch by the addition of several small pictures on the walls. Seated in a chair beside the bed, Rosannah Flynn *née* Weldrake raised her head from the book she was holding.

"Now then, madame," the nurse said briskly, "there's a visitor come to speak with you."

There was no response.

The last time she had seen her mother, Amy had been only a child, and Rosannah, for all her strange eccentric behaviour, had seemed to her a most wonderful creature, so tall and lovely in her fine sateen gown, like one of the ladies in Aunt Belle Bethway's fashion plates. The years between had taken their cruel toll, ageing the beauty, withering the fire, shrinking the body to an old woman's; hair that had once been the warm colour of honey was now an ugly cropped iron-grey; the eyes were blue still, but sunk in a mesh of lines.

Amy was not shocked by the alteration: that other image had long since grown faded in her memory. Instead, she felt curiously empty . . . disappointed almost that this meeting with a stranger had failed to produce any instant recognition of the bond between them both.

"Mama?" she said hesitantly, moving forward past the nurse. "Mama, it's Amy."

The blue eyes turned towards her.

"It's Amy," she said again, attempting a smile. "I—I've come to see how you are."

"Aimée? *Tu m'as dit* Aimée?" Rosannah's voice was hoarse and low. She put aside the book and made as if to stand up.

At once the nurse was at her side, a restraining hand on her arm.

"Now, madame, we're tired, remember? That long drive we took this morning? We'd best sit ourself down again, hadn't we, before we weary ourself out too much."

"Oh, is she allowed to go out for drives?"

"Indeed she is!" the other averred, winking heavily and at the same time screwing up one side of her mouth in a most exaggerated manner. "Every day. All the way round the Boose de Boo-loin and back again."

"Bois de Boulogne." Rosannah corrected the woman, giving the name its right pronunciation. She re-seated herself; then, ignoring Amy completely, spent some moments considering whether or not to take up her book again, putting out a hand and withdrawing it several times, before finally appearing to lose interest.

"May . . . may I see what it is you're reading?"

Her daughter indicated the leather-bound volume, at a loss to know what else to say. Obviously it was going to be quite impossible to unburden her conscience as she had hoped: even were the nurse not present, there would be little point, she realised now, in pouring out the details of her wretchedly tangled relationship with David Linton.

"Mama?" she asked again when her question went unanswered. "May I see your book?"

"*Le livre?*" Rosannah shrugged. "*Voici—*" She pushed it across the bed.

Amy picked it up, and after pretending to examine

168

the spine, opened it at the title page. The elegant black lettering read *Le Horla*, and beneath, Guy de Maupassant. Neither name meant anything to her.

"What is it about?" she asked. "Is it a story?"

Another shrug of the thin shoulders in the ill-fitting floral day gown. "*Oui. Un roman. Un roman de la folie.*"

"Folly?" Trying to make sense of her mother's unfamiliar words, the daughter repeated her.

"*Mais oui!*" Rosannah looked up sharply, and tapped a finger against her temple in an unmistakable gesture. "*La folie, tu sais. La folie.*"

She gave a strange smile; and suddenly, without warning, began to laugh, a shrill mirthless sound, throwing back her head and clapping her hands together. Then, as abruptly, she fell silent, and commenced rocking herself from side to side, arms clasped about her body.

Amy glanced anxiously at the nurse. Seeing the girl was about to speak, the other placed a finger to her lips and turned away to bend over the chair.

"Come now, madame," she addressed her patient in a wheedling tone, "this will never do. Your husband expected home at any minute, and you not ready for him? Whatever will he say to that when he comes in?"

Her words had the desired effect. At once, Rosannah ceased rocking, and an expression of excited anticipation lit the pale features.

"*La brosse?*" she cried, looking about her. "*Où est la brosse? Il faut que je fasse un brin de toilette.*"

"What's that she's saying?" questioned Amy. "What does she want?"

"She wants her hair-brush, ma'am." Again, the nurse winked with grotesque deliberation.

"Shall I fetch it for her? Where is it kept?"

"Here—" The other seemed to be miming something. Putting out a hand, she picked up an imaginary object and offered it to Rosannah, who accepted it with a graceful inclination of the head and began moving her arm as though she were indeed brushing her hair.

Amy felt tears of pity prick her eyes as she witnessed this dumb show, seeing the way her mother's madness deluded her, tricking her into believing she still had the waist-length hair of her youth and not the short grey bristles of her bedlam crop.

"There now," said the nurse, reaching out to take back the make-believe brush. "It'd never do to let your husband catch you looking a slummock, would it, madame? You know how particular he is. Which gown do you think he'd like you to wear for him today?" She made a movement as though opening a door. "Look, they're all hanging here ready in the wardrobe. I pressed them myself specially for you."

Rosannah put her head to one side, considering her choice. What must she be seeing, her daughter wondered compassionately: those clothes she wore twenty years ago at the house in Tea Garden Lane? Most of them had gone on the backs of Harry Weldrake's "ladies", that succession of hard-eyed, soft-bodied women he'd brought to live at the house during Amy's childhood.

"*Je préfère* . . ." Rosannah said softly, "*oui . . . je préfère la rose.*"

"The rose one? You mean this pink one here?" The nurse indicated thin air. "This is the one you want to wear?"

"*Oui. C'est ça.*"

There followed an elaborate pantomime of undressing and perfuming and re-robing, tying the strings of petticoats, hooking bodices, buttoning sleeves, fitting on shoes.

"Beautiful . . ." Amy said faintly, when all was finished and Rosannah was seated once more in her chair. "You look beautiful, Mama."

She turned to the nurse, trying to make herself sound natural for her mother's sake, though the lump in her throat was all but choking her.

"Before . . . before my father arrives . . . I'll go and call Minnie if I may. He'll be pleased to see her again . . . after all this time."

"What a good idea, ma'am." There was a nod and a little smile of understanding. Then, very quickly and quietly, "Don't say goodbye. Just leave."

The young woman looked back over her shoulder. Her mother held out a hand; not in a gesture of affection, but to grasp the imaginary mirror in which she was admiring herself.

170

"I'll tell you this much," said Lily Banks, lowering her voice and throwing a quick glance about her, "it would never surprise me one bit to find her a-laying dead in her bed one o' these mornings."

"Go on, you don't say!" Mary Jenner, parlour maid at Weatherfield rectory, rounded her eyes and leaned forward, head cocked to one side so that her good ear might not miss a word of Lily's gossip.

"As true as I stand here, Mary, it wouldn't surprise me to find her, no, not one bit. I were saying to our Albert only yesterday, the air in that house is so thick you might cut it wi' a knife, the way things be atween Doctor and Missus these days. And her so middling bad she can no more walk now, poor woman, than fly to the moon."

"Aye, I did hear some'at o' the same from Mrs Wickenden. In a fine ol' taking she were, an' all, when Rector says as how Mrs Linton is reduced to one o' they wheeled chairs for her locomotion. He should bring in a London man to gi' a second opinion, surely, said Mrs Wickenden. 'Tis contrary to Christian nature for a husband to watch his wife a-dwindle to the grave as that 'un's doing."

There were long faces and a shaking of heads and both women turned to look up the lane towards the Lintons' front gate.

"And yet I can't find it in me to mislike him," Lily Banks went on. "The Lord knows, he has his cross to bear wi' her, the tempersome vagaries she do throw. To hear her ill-speak him the way she does, 'tis a wonder Doctor's not quite done-over wi' her, yet to see him a-lifting and a-bathing her, you'd never think there were a misword spoke."

"He never did say, did he, where he took hisself off to that time?"

Lily shook her head again. "Mind you," she said darkly, "it were Buckfield way he'd gone. Albert were sent for to fetch back his horse from the Fordhouse t'other side the town. And Buckfield's close enough anigh Lewes if he were minded to take hisself a-visiting—" another cautious glance around—"a-visiting *her*."

Mary Jenner pursed her lips and a knowing expression crept into her face. "And Mrs Linton won't have her at all in the house, you said."

"No, nor she won't. To hear her squacketting on, you'd think Miss Amy and Doctor were like this—" Lily crossed her fingers tightly. "The names Missus ha' laid tongue to! She's eyed and limbed Miss Amy that many wearisome times, 'tis a marvel to me how Doctor can abide to suffer it."

"They do be very close, though, as I hear," the other said carefully, anxious not to stem the flow of confidences by seeming too eagerly curious.

"Oh, aye, they do be close, Miss Amy and Doctor. But I won't hold as to aught mischieful atween 'em, Mary, nohows I won't. There's some as 'ld say otherwise, mebbe, seeing as how Doctor's been mindful of her welfare these dunnamany years, having her into his home an' all, but I don't know as that argifies much, surely. 'Tis on account o' they being all family together, that."

"You never can tell wi' folk," Mary responded snidely. "Say what you will, she's a Flynn is Miss Amy, and they Flynns were ever a dubersome lot, what wi' Frank getting hisself hanged for murder and his father afore him being killed in his own blood along wi' that ol' Rector Bates."

She turned, and with a jerk of the head indicated the churchyard behind them, where the late Reverend Esmond Bates's monument stood out in pallid prominence, raising a cautionary finger towards the overcast February sky.

"Oh, there now—I knew there was some'at new as I'd to tell you!" Lily, suddenly animated, caught at the other's arm. "You'll never guess, but she's had another letter come, has Missus."

"*Another* 'un?"

"Aye. From him at Lewes. That Mr Bates."

"There's some'at a-going on there, d'you reckon?"

"Who's to say? She do bring his name into her talk more'n

is natural in a female. And you know the ol' saying, Mary—they who turns a morsel over and over in their mouth does so on account they likes the flavour."

There was some nodding in agreement of this adage.

"Another thing," continued Lily, warming to her gossip, "these letters o' Mr Bates's, why, she keeps 'em in a little box beside her. I seen it t'other day laid open on the bed when I took her up her bit o' breakfast. I says to our Albert, if she were a maid 'twould be nothing to remark on, but seeing as how she's a married woman an' all, 'tis a funny ol' business to behave in such a manner, a-hiding away his letters like he were her sweet-heart or some'at."

"A spark is fire, Lily. A spark is fire," Mary observed sagely. "Not that she can go much amiss, poor afflicted creature, but it do seem odd to be acting so secretsome."

"Aye, and when she writes her letters back, she most in general sends 'em down wi' Albert to the post office after Doctor's left for to make his rounds of a morning."

"'Tis a wonder how he can be so blind as to what's a-passing beneath his nose," rejoined the other. "Though I did hear Mrs Wickenden a-telling Rector the man's that dead-alive o' late she fears he's a deal too concerned in liquor, surely."

Lily answered this with a tut and a roll of the eyes, which Mary took as confirmation of her mistress's suspicions. Pulling her coarse woollen shawl closer about her shoulders, she went on, "And Rector, he says to Missus, why, he says, faults are always thick where love is thin."

"Aye, 'tis sadly true, that. Very true. Well—" Lily adjusted her own shawl and bent to pick up the basket at her feet. "I must be on my way, Mary, afore the butcher's out o' collops."

"I'll not keep you then, my dear. The wind's that bleat we'll fair be clemmed wi' cold a-standing here longer."

They parted, Lily Banks making her way towards the path across the green to the high street, Mary Jenner taking herself back to the rectory to pass on the tattle to Cook over a nice hot cup of tea.

Mrs Horatia Lovell, of Heydon House, would have looked perfectly well in place at a society soirée at the Marine

Pavilion in Brighton. Not now, at the present time—Queen Victoria, influenced as ever by her much lamented Prince Consort, had long since abandoned the seaside pleasure dome—but some sixty years or so earlier, in the raffish days of the Regency.

In appearance, the old lady was more than a trifle eccentric, for the whims and fads of fashion which had come and gone during the preceding decades, the vast gigot sleeves, swaying crinolines, panniers, bustles and trains, had affected her not at all here in her reclusive twilight world. She was like a ghost from the past, Megwynn Evans had thought on meeting her for the first time: the grey curls piled up under a muslin cap and decorated with feathers, the high-waisted day gown with wrap-over bodice and frilled chemisette, even the flat kid slippers tied with ribbon.

As for the house itself—*Duw*! what a gloomy old pile, miles away from anywhere high on the Downs, with the wind whistling in from the sea and the salt-stunted trees bent over like groups of crippled figures on the lonely landscape. The shutters on the windows gave the place a sly, shut-in appearance, as though it were peering through half-closed eyes to see who might be coming up its drive; and inside was even worse, a musty, fusty smell like dead mice under the floorboards, and high shadowy rooms full of the ghostly outlines of dust-wrappered furniture.

The Welsh governess had arrived with Laura and Esmond on the Friday afternoon to stay at Heydon House until the following Monday. The moment of their departure could not come soon enough: though she was sharing the same suite of rooms as her two charges, Megwynn had not been able to sleep a wink, but lay all night in her bed listening to the stealthy creaks and groans of the ancient fabric, the whimper of draughts in the chimney, the scurry and scratch of little claws behind the wainscot. She wished she might keep a lamp burning, but it might have disturbed the children, and besides, even the darkness was preferable to being watched by the eyes of long-dead Lovells whose portraits stared from gilded frames about the walls.

By Sunday afternoon, when she took Esmond and Laura downstairs for high tea, the young mother-to-be was feeling decidedly unwell, and in no mood to admire the grandeur of the large parlour, with its carved Adam mantel, rosewood furniture, starched white table napery and elegant Georgian silverware.

"Will you not take another slice of the seed cake, Miss Evans?" Mrs Lovell asked in her little fluting voice, graciously inclining a hand towards the cake-stand at the table side.

"Thank you, ma'am, no. One is quite enough."

"More tea, perhaps?" The other hand was inclined with equal grace towards the silver spirit kettle from the spout of which trickled a thin wisp of steam. "The water is sufficiently hot still to freshen up the leaves for a further pot. No? As you wish. Esmond? Another dish of tea for you?"

The old lady looked across the table at her great-nephew. This outmoded manner of referring to a cup as a dish amused the boy hugely, and he compressed his mouth on a smirk before answering politely, "No, thank you, ma'am."

"Well, then." She patted her thin, pale lips with her napkin and laid it aside. "If Laura is quite finished also, it is time to make our visit to the others to pay them our respects."

Laura's small chin began at once to tremble. She cast a look of mute appeal at her governess.

Already apprised of the ceremony which followed Sunday high tea at Heydon House, Megwynn did not fail her.

"Mr Bates said the children might be excused their . . . visit, ma'am. He did not think it necessary."

There was a long moment's silence, and Mrs Lovell's dusty cheeks took on a tinge of pink.

"I beg your pardon! Excused their visit? Excused their visit? Upon my honour, I have never heard of anything so disrespectful. He did not think it necessary? Fiddle-de-dee, the very idea!"

She was extremely indignant.

Megwynn tried again. "Indeed, ma'am, I am sorry, but Mr Bates—"

The old lady made a peremptory gesture and rose to her feet. "Not a word more. Mr Bates forgets himself. Come—"

She turned from the table and taking up her stick from the back of the chair, moved away with her strange little hobbling gait towards the parlour door.

The governess glanced again at Laura. The child's eyes were fixed upon her still, like those of a rabbit frozen in fear, and she had gone white about the mouth.

Esmond squared his shoulders. "Please-may-I-leave-the-table?" he intoned; and at the nod of permission, got down from his seat and leaned over to put an arm about his sister.

"Don't be such a baby bunting, Laura. It's only our mama we are going to see, after all. I should imagine it rather cheers her up to have us visit once in a while. I mean, it must be jolly boring, to be locked away in a stuffy old crypt with no other company than a lot of mouldering relatives."

The boy's show of casual bravado did nothing at all to ease the little girl's terror; and when Megwynn with some reluctance urged her to come along, she clung to the governess's skirts and begged tearfully to be carried.

It was this which led to the accident.

The east wing of the house contained a private chapel, reached by a door at one end of the cavernous entrance hall. Beyond this door lay a corridor, and a descent of steps leading into an arched vestibule. The way to the family crypt opened off to the left, at the head of a further flight of steep steps.

Mrs Lovell conducted the three of them down, lighting their path with an oil lamp; and in the poor light Megwynn had difficulty in seeing where to place her feet, encumbered as she was by the child in her arms.

Three steps from the bottom, she slipped. Trying to protect Laura, she twisted awkwardly and lost her balance, and though the distance to the ground was not great, the force of the blow winded her severely. She made to get up again; but no sooner had she moved than a sudden hot, sharp pain knifed agonisingly through her body.

"*Diw* . . ." The young woman gritted her teeth and kneeled forward, head bowed, arm clasping herself.

"Oh, Miss Evans—Miss Evans!" Esmond was beside her at once, his face full of anxious concern.

She raised herself cautiously. "It's nothing . . . I shall be all right in a moment, *cariad*. It shook me, that's all, falling like that." And to Mrs Lovell, who had come hobbling back to see what was amiss and was trying to quieten a sobbing

Laura—"I think, ma'am, it would be for the best . . . if we were to take her back again upstairs."

"Dear, dear, dear. Very well. *Most* unfortunate, however. *Most* unfortunate."

Somehow—how, she never knew—Megwynn managed to force her trembling legs to carry her to the privacy of her room. Somehow, she went through the motions of tending and soothing her charge, kissing away the hurt of a small lump beneath the glossy curls. Somehow, she endured the remainder of that evening until the moment when she might escape to her bed and spend the endlessly long hours until daybreak waiting for the jack-knife thrust of pain to pierce her, each time a little longer and a little stronger; praying for the strength to bear it if only for a dozen hours more, until she was away from Heydon House.

The journey back to Lewes by coach and train the following morning was a nightmare. As soon as they were arrived at Spences Lane, Megwynn excused herself, saying that she was exhausted and would lie down in her room for a while. Indeed, she looked so terribly pale and drawn that Mrs Lane the housekeeper advised her to remain there for the rest of the day.

It was advice the young governess was forced not to heed. Realising the commotion that would result if her predicament were discovered, she managed to steal unseen from the house and make her way, slowly, clumsily, to the stable block in the field beyond the paddock. There, in the straw in which it had been conceived, she miscarried of Francis Bethway's child.

"You have had a very fortunate escape, my boy. Let this be a lesson to you for the future."

The Reverend Alec Bethway laid Megwynn's letter aside and looked up at his elder son. Francis's face wore an expression of bored indifference.

"Well? Have you nothing to say? Not a word of regret for the miserable outcome of this sordid little episode?"

"Regret? No. Why should I feel any regret?" The youth smoothed his moustache with a forefinger, eyeing his reflection in the glass of a picture above the study mantelpiece. Yes, that moustache definitely suited him. Perhaps he ought to try waxing the tips. That should look rather fine with his uniform. Make him a regular military masher when he joined the artillery regiment.

Still admiring himself, he went on, "Good thing she's gone and lost it, I'd have thought. Nobody wanted the kid, after all, neither her nor me. It's the best that could've happened, getting rid of it the way she has."

His father regarded him with savage distaste. "That's the only thing which matters, isn't it, Francis. Saving your own hide. No doubt you think you've been extraordinarily clever, the way you've managed to dodge payment for the wrong you did that young woman—"

"The wrong *I* did her? It was *her* come after *me*."

The dark eyes removed themselves from their reflection and turned with a look of truculence towards the grey-haired clergyman. They were met and matched by a steady contemptuous gaze, and after a moment or two they switched to an examination of their owner's fingernails.

"I mean . . . it was only a bit o' fun. We neither of us thought anything about the consequences. I'm sorry if she's had a rough time of it."

"I am pleased to hear that much, at least," Alec Bethway said abrasively. "Contrition from you, however slight, is almost as acceptable as a full-length apology from a gentleman of honour."

Francis coloured up.

"However," continued the other, "one good thing at least has come out of this peck of troubles. Miss Evans has hopes of being able to keep her position as governess." He picked up Megwynn's letter again to refer to it. "Whether or not Mr Bates has been made aware of her—deliverance, I very much doubt. I see that she makes no mention of her employer here. She will not be coming to Eastbourne, though, that much is clear, so I need not proceed with the renting of rooms for her. Which rather ends my part in the affair."

"And mine," said Francis. "I'm done wi' her now, done wi' her for good. I've no wish to see the woman ever again."

His father shook his head in total disillusionment. He re-folded Megwynn's letter carefully.

"Would that I could wash my hands of you, as easily as you wash your hands of her. As it is, you are still my son

178

and while you remain under this roof, you remain under my authority. You will go into the church now, and you will fall down upon your knees and pray to God for forgiveness. You will also thank him, that in his infinite mercy he has seen fit to release you both from the shackles forged by your transgressions. And you will meditate upon these words: 'Sins are at first like cobwebs, at last like cables'."

Francis shrugged and turned away in leisurely fashion to saunter towards the door. Get down on his knees in church, be blowed. He had a girl to meet on the promenade in half-an-hour, a girl with warm, soft skin and cherry-ripe lips who quite rightly thought him the handsomest young devil in the world.

18

"You're looking tired," said Ralph Herriot considerately. "Was the journey too much for you?"

"No." Amy shook her head and returned his smile. "Not at all. I wish I could have seen more of the countryside, though, before the light faded."

"We must make the opportunity to go out together whilst you're here. Dorset in early spring is one of the loveliest places on earth. You'll let me show you something of it, I hope?"

"I doubt there'll be the time. Tomorrow's taken up with the wedding, and we leave again for home the day after."

She turned as someone went past her, moving aside to give them room in the passage. Together with the Bashford wedding party, she had travelled by railway that bright, sharp March day to attend the marriage of Henry Bashford to Maria Herriot, putting up here at a fine old medieval hostelry in the village of Winterbourne St Giles, a few miles beyond Dorchester. Ralph Herriot, who had made the arrangements for the party, had been at the station with his father to meet them with the family shooting brake and drive them through the darkened lanes to The George and Dragon.

"Mr Hardy will be a guest at the reception tomorrow," the young farmer told Amy now, taking her arm to lead her out of the way of a laden pot-boy.

"What—Mr Hardy the author?"

"The very same. I shall introduce you."

"But I won't know what to say."

"You don't need to say anything. He's very susceptible to a pretty face. Behave as naturally as you always do, Amy, and he'll be the one to do all the charming. Who knows, you may find yourself the model for one of his literary heroines."

"Me?" She started to laugh.

"Yes, you. You're Bathsheba Everdene to a 't'. The kind of young woman we Dorset men admire. Beautiful, proud and—"

Ralph paused.

"And?" she prompted.

"And vulnerable."

"Ah. Then I must disappoint you. I've a very thick skin as it happens."

"No, you haven't. Come along—" Still holding her by the arm, he directed her along the passage to the outer door.

"Where are you taking me?"

"For a short walk."

"Without so much as a by your leave?"

Ralph sketched a mock bow. "By your leave, ma'am."

"But the others will wonder where I am."

"Not for the sake of ten minutes they won't. And you are not due to dine until eight o'clock, which will allow ample time for changing."

"You appear to think of everything."

"Indeed I do. Especially of you. I've missed you, you know."

He said this lightly, as though it were nothing that mattered much, and went on in the next breath, "My mother hopes you'll stay as our guest at Sutton Bassett for a few days after the wedding. I've already accepted on your behalf. So you see, there'll be opportunity aplenty for excursions."

"You're very sure of yourself, aren't you," Amy replied a little coolly. Now that they were outside alone together, she was starting to feel ill at ease, almost as though it were wrong to be here with another man and feel the warmth of him beside her, after those few brief regrettable hours spent in the arms of David Linton.

"How do you know I would have accepted your mother's invitation?"

Ralph gave her arm a little squeeze. "I didn't. Which is why I decided to present you with it as an accomplished fact."

When there was no response to this, he went on blithely,

"She rather considers it a matter of family honour, you know."

"What, having me as guest?"

"Yes. That visit we made to Weatherfield together—well, I put you in something of a compromising position, it seems. Mother regards it as her duty to uncompromise you by receiving you at the Herriot hearth with all flags flying. Restore your good name in the public eye, and all that."

"My good name was never in any danger of being lost on your account, Ralph, you can assure her."

He pulled a droll face. "So much for my reputation as a lady-killing wolf in sheep's clothing."

They continued on along the side-path in silence for a few yards; then he said, rather more seriously, "You're quiet, Amy. Is there anything amiss?"

"Amiss? No. Should there be? I—I'm cold, that's all. Can we go back now?"

She made to pull away, but the young man merely slipped an arm about her slim waist and held her a little more firmly at his side.

"How is the good Doctor Linton these days?"

"David Linton?" The unexpectedness of that name startled Amy and threw her into momentary confusion; and before she could stop herself she had answered quickly, "I don't know. I've heard nothing of him for months."

"Oh? Is that so?"

"No. I—I mean, yes. That's to say . . . well . . . he did write. But I thought it best not to reply."

"Ah. So you've reached a parting of the ways with him?"

She was glad that the darkness hid the tell-tale flush of guilt in her face. Vexed at herself, she said sharply, "If I thought it was business of yours, Ralph, I'd tell you. Now please release me. I'll be late going in for dinner if I waste any more of my time here."

"Dear me, we still have little claws that scratch."

His tone was mildly reproving. Letting fall his arm, he stood aside and courteously indicated the way back along the path.

The Herriot family wealth had been founded on coprolite, a mineral substance whose discovery had created something of a boom amongst landowners in the second half of the century.

Found in underground seams along river valleys, the "coprolites" because of their nodule-like appearance were widely believed to be the fossilised droppings of prehistoric beasts, but were actually deposits of almost pure phosphate of calcium which, when treated with sulphuric acid, proved to be of immense value as an artificial fertiliser. At the peak of the boom the stuff was selling at £3 a ton; and with a single acre of land yielding as much as three hundred tons, the Herriots had found themselves quite literally standing on a fortune.

For a rent of £150 an acre they had let out their land on a three-year lease to a contractor, who had employed local labour to work the shallow-cast seams. This, it must be admitted, caused a deal of resentment among those farmers whose fields held no deposits, for they were hard pressed to compete with the wages of £2 a week being paid by the contractor, and were forced to raise their own labourers' pay if they did not want to watch their crops rot for want of harvesting.

Since the crest of the wave some eight years earlier, in 1884, the extraction of coprolite-fertiliser had started to decline as seams were worked out, and wages fell back to a more realistic fourteen shillings a week. Even so, the Herriots and other gentry farmers like them had made quite sufficient money to ensure a continuing prosperity for life.

It was, therefore, only to be expected that Maria Herriot's wedding should be the social event of the year for Sutton Bassett, a lavish affair costing more than a farmworker might hope to earn in half a lifetime. No expense had been spared: everything was the best that money could buy, from the enormous striped marquee accommodating the guests for the champagne wedding breakfast, to Maria's bridal gown of satin brocade whose many yards of frills and flounces were echoed on a lesser scale in the outfits of the three bride's maids. There was even a commercial photographer from Dorchester present outside the church to record the happy occasion on his "Instanto" taper bellows camera.

"Oh Lord, I do hope my hat's straight," Mary Bashford

murmured to Amy through clenched teeth, fixing her face in a rigor mortis smile and not daring to move for fear she should blur the picture.

"Our Phyllis ought to go and stand at the back," she went on rather more naturally once the photographer's head had reappeared from beneath the black cloth covering of his bulky apparatus. "The size she is, she's like the side of a house. Nobody'll be able to see round her."

Phyllis was Mary's married sister, expecting her first child in a month's time and swelled to such a girth as to strain the seams of her maternity gown. At her elbow stood her husband, Sidney, and beyond him the two elder Bashford sons, George and Richard, with their families. Flanking bride and groom at the centre of the group were Ralph, as principal groomsman, his parents, and Rachael Bashford.

"One more now, if you please, ladies and gentlemen," the photographer announced, sliding in a fresh plate and preparing to bury his head again. Movement in the group promptly ceased and all became as stiff at statues for the exposure, even the youngest child, Maria's train bearer, a small boy novelly dressed as Little Lord Fauntleroy in velvet and lace.

There was a pop and a flash, and everyone relaxed into laughter as Henry clutched at his heart and pretended to fall into the arms of his bride. Then, when the vicar had joined them from the vestry, the waiting carriages were summoned, appearing along the gravelled sweep of the walk with white ostrich plumes nodding, harness brass glinting in the bright spring sun, and the party took their seats to head the procession back to the Herriot residence for the wedding breakfast.

Mary settled herself down beside Amy and slipped a hand through the other's elbow.

"You'd think Ellis might have made the effort to be here with the rest of the family," she complained. "He is Henry's half-brother, after all, and I know he was sent an invitation. Maria told me so."

"He'd have been something of an unwelcome spectre at the feast," Amy said dryly. "No doubt he sent his apologies."

"Oh, I'm sure. I'll say this much for Ellis, he may be

as short of warmth as a hog is of wool, but his manners are beyond reproach. He'd as soon forget his own name as neglect his social proprieties. The children would have enjoyed themselves, though. Laura and Esmond. They don't see enough of their young cousins, Mama says. I wonder sometimes whether Ellis isn't rather too severe with them both."

Mary paused to adjust her errant hat with its pin, then went on, "Mama received a letter from him a week or two ago. She showed it to Phyllis, and Phyllis told me what was in it."

"Oh?"

"You'll never guess. It was all to do with your friend Louisa Linton."

"Fancy that." Amy adopted a casual tone and feigned complete indifference, gazing from the open carriage at the spreading country views on either side of the road.

"Well you might seem a little more interested," said Mary peevishly. "Ellis was in a most fearful taking against the poor woman, according to Phyllis. She's been pestering him for attention, can you imagine. Writing *billets-doux* to him. That kind of thing."

"Indeed?"

"Oh, really, Amy, you do disappoint me. Is that all you can say? Indeed? I was hoping you'd know all about it. I mean, Ellis of all people. He's the last man on earth I'd expect to receive *billets-doux*. And from a respectable married woman, too. Phyllis thought it the funniest thing ever."

"Then perhaps we should try to cultivate her sense of humour," Amy replied calmly.

Mary sighed; and was about to fall into a sulk when her companion gave her a nudge and pointed ahead, saying, "Look—look there," as the cavalcade rounded the bend of the road. "A band of musicians lining up to play for us. How very grand."

The two young women craned their necks to see the scarlet and gold figures as the jaunty sound of fife and drum struck up in front of the leading carriages. Some of the smaller Bashford children were already getting down and running along at the side of the road to join in.

185

"What excitement," Mary declared. "It's like the circus coming into town. And see, Ralph Herriot's there too." She turned with a knowing little look. "What a handsome figure he cuts. He marches very well, don't you think?"

"Well enough, I suppose."

"Oh, don't be such a pill, Amy. He marches divinely, and you know it. I can't think why you're so cool, admiring him as you do."

"I don't admire him."

"What a fib. I shall tell him."

There was a shrug of the shoulder. "Do so. I like him well enough. You may tell him that, too. But admiration has to be deserved before it's given."

"He's quite spoony about you, you know," Mary said mischievously. "Ah—I thought that would make you blush. But he is. I've seen the way he looks at you. I wish he'd look at *me* like that. You wouldn't find me playing Miss Touch-me-not, indeed you wouldn't. Has he asked you yet to marry him?"

"Certainly not! What a question."

"Supposing he did, what would you tell him?"

"He won't."

"But *if* he did?"

"Then I'd tell him . . ." It was on the tip of Amy's tongue to say no; but something made her hesitate, and with another shrug of the shoulder she went on reluctantly, "I'd tell him may be. Or then again, may be not."

"That's no answer."

"It's the only one either of you will be getting."

Ralph Herriot was not exactly certain, either. He had thought often of marriage, since it was expected of him to provide the estate with an heir. His courtships had hitherto been lacklustre affairs, though, pursued more from a sense of duty than any personal inclination; and not one of the young women had engaged his affections long enough to make him wish to know her better.

Amy Flynn, however, was a different concern altogether. He had at first meeting been attracted by her delicious beauty, a natural loveliness which needed no artifice to enhance it; and the poet in him had been inspired to reflect in private upon the rich, corn-gold hair, the summer-blue eyes, the creamy skin, the coral-pink lips, and slender, supple figure.

She was not, of course, the only charmer of his acquaintance: there had been others of almost equal beauty. But experience had taught him to look beyond the skin-deep fascination to the mind concealed, and too often he had found only shallowness, self-admiration, stupidity, all the hidden defects of character which the years would gradually reveal as the beauty faded.

He would not deny that Amy too had her defects: stubbornness, pride, ignorance even. But she was also totally unaffected, with a quality of forthright openness which brooked neither hypocrisy nor falsity in herself or in others. Her background was unusual to say the least; in fact, Ralph had often reflected that if one were to write it as fiction, no one would accept the events or participants as particularly credible. She was what she was, though, because of it all, because of that flawed pedigree of illegitimacy, neglect, violence and insanity. So easily might she have been the most wretchedly unlikable of creatures; but instead, a toss of the dice of Fate had created her otherwise.

He watched her now at the wedding breakfast, talking to Mr Thomas Hardy, her cheeks a little flushed from champagne and the attentions of her distinguished companion. When at last the great man was drawn away into another group of guests, Ralph walked across to her side.

"Well? And how are you enjoying yourself?"

"Oh, wonderfully! I can't remember when I last had such a good time."

"I'm pleased at least to find you in a more amenable mood than last night."

Amy laughed. The champagne had gone slightly to her head and she was feeling euphorically happy, the shadow of guilt hanging over her these past weeks evaporated.

"And did Mr Hardy admire you as I said he would?" Ralph continued, taking her empty glass and raising his hand to attract a tray-laden wine waiter at the other side of the marquee.

"He paid me some pretty compliments. Though I dare say he repeats the same thing to each and every other young female he meets." With a nod she indicated a stout, tight-faced woman standing a short way off. "And his wife seems to be of the same opinion."

"Poor Emma. Yes, I'm afraid she bears her sufferings heavily. So—your head has not been turned by Mr Hardy's blandishments?"

"Lord, no." Amy laughed again. "My Uncle Harry always used to maintain that woman's instincts are often truer than man's reason. I'll let my head be turned when my instincts tell me so, and not before."

Ralph's expression lost some of its amusement and a more sombre look crept into the deep-set grey eyes. His voice, however, lost none of its liveliness as he handed her a fresh glass, saying, "I'll give you a toast, my dear. To love—one of life's little ironies."

He raised his own glass and saluted her before drinking from it.

Amy hesitated a fraction; then responded to the gesture.

"What d'you think of that for a title?" her companion wanted to know, watching the delightful way in which the tip of her tongue licked the champagne from her moistened lips.

"What for a title?"

"Life's little ironies. I've suggested it to Mr Hardy for a collection of short stories he hopes to have completed for publication in a year or so."

"Ah. And what did *he* think of it?"

"It rather took his fancy."

"I've no doubt it'd take mine as well if I understood what it meant."

"Now you're making fun of me, Amy."

"Not at all." She smiled warmly, too content with life for the present to want anything but enjoyment from the day.

Taking another sip from her glass, she went on a trifle inconsequentially, "I'm glad you accepted your mother's invitation on my behalf, Ralph. I don't want to return to Lewes yet awhile. The place is very dull just now."

"I can imagine. Especially to a spirit like yours. I mean, what can provincial urbanity possibly offer? You should be living out here in the country where there's space and fresh-ness and the ever-changing landscape to satisfy that crying need of yours for freedom."

"I may have to do that. Live in the country."

"Oh?"

Amy nodded. "It's the house," she said lightly. "It gobbles up money at a most insatiable rate."

"I can imagine. So, you're thinking of selling it?"

Another nod.

"But where will you move to?"

"Oh, I expect I'll find somewhere. In the country, as you say."

"Not Weatherfield." Ralph's tone changed and became utterly serious.

"Why not Weatherfield? It's where my roots are, after all."

She turned her eyes to his, and read the tension there. The euphoria faded slightly.

"I've really no alternative," she went on after a pause. "Uncle Harry made very little financial provision in his Will with all the debts to pay. If it wasn't for Minnie and Ted . . ." She made a gesture and left the sentence unfinished.

"You are not going back to Weatherfield," Ralph said grimly. "Damn it, Amy, d'you think I'd let you? It would be tantamount to delivering you straight into the arms of David Linton. And I'd rather see the fellow dead before I'd let him so much as lay a finger on you."

A cloud seemed to pass across her heart, and of a sudden the day had lost all its sparkle.

She drained her glass and held it out. "Would you bring me another—please?"

189

19

"Miss Amy?" Minnie Brocklebank shook her head at the caller. "No, sir, I'm sorry."

"She's not at home?"

Another shake.

David Linton tried again. "When do you expect her? Within the hour, perhaps?"

"Lor' love you, no. Nor even within the day. Miss Amy's gone right away out o' the district."

"Away? Where?"

Minnie pursed her lips. "Well, seeing as how it's you, sir . . . She's gone to stay wi' Mr Herriot's family in Dorsetshire, and she won't be back afore the week's end."

The doctor's face fell. As Minnie remarked later to her husband Ted, it was as though all the wind had suddenly gone from his sails. His shoulders sagged, his head drooped, and his broad-chested frame seemed to crumple within the double-breasted frockcoat.

"Here—you all right, Doctor Linton?" she asked, concerned.

"Yes. Thank you, yes." He made an effort to straighten himself. "It's just that I seem to have had a wasted journey for nothing. I've ridden over from Weatherfield especially to call on your mistress."

As he began wearily to turn from the door, the housekeeper reached out a hand.

"Well, no need to take yourself straight off again, sir. Come inside, won't you, and let me make you a pot o' tea at least? Our Ted'll fetch your horse round to water it when he gets back home. It's a fair old ride, doing the both ways in one afternoon."

David hesitated. After the bitter-sweet anticipation of

seeing Amy once again, disappointment hung upon him like a dead weight.

"Thank you," he said finally with as much grace as he could muster. "A little refreshment would be most welcome." And as Minnie closed the door behind him and made as though to go ahead across the hall—"I can find my own way to the drawing room. There's no need to show me up."

"As you like, sir." She gave a bob. "Your tea won't be long a-coming. The kettle's only this minute come off the boil."

Upstairs, he put his curly-brimmed bowler hat down beside his gloves on the table and cast a long, slow glance around the room before seating himself. The only sign of Amy's absence was a lack of fresh flowers to bring life to the place; otherwise, he was able to sense her presence so strongly that for a moment he could almost convince himself she was here in the house still. The air held that faint scent of violets he had smelled on her warm skin that night—that haunting, poignantly beautiful night—when they had made love together.

He sat forward and thrust his face into his hands.

The memory of the tenderness they'd shared had stayed with him every aching minute of the lengthening hours of time which separated that moment from this. He had promised never to see her again, promised to put her from his mind, promised to do all he could to repair the breach with Louisa. Promises that were akin to being banished to the dark side of the moon, for he could no more forget the woman he loved than stop his heart from beating.

So he had broken his word, and come back. *Had* to come back . . . and only to find her gone away, leaving behind for him nothing but the echo of the past in the emptiness of the present.

There was a noise at the drawing room door, and he sat up sharply as Minnie came in backwards, elbowing her way with a laden tray of china.

"Here you are, sir—" placing it on the side table. "And I've brought you a bit o' plum cake and some soda biscuits. Tea tastes all the better to my way o' thinking when it's got some'at to wash down."

191

She picked up the rose-patterned tea pot.

"You'll take milk and sugar?"

David nodded, and when he had been handed cup and saucer, thanked her and said, "I'll ring, shall I, when I'm ready to leave?"

"If you would, sir. Soon as ever you wish—but no need to hasten yourself."

Left alone once more, he waited until the tea had cooled before gulping it down; then, taking a leather flask from his pocket, refilled the cup with a generous measure of neat Scotch whisky and raised it almost desperately again to his lips.

Below stairs, Minnie busied herself for a while preparing her husband a bite to eat for when he should return from his day's fishing along the Ouse. Ted's catch was always useful for eking out a meagre larder, as were the rabbits he caught with his ferrets out on the Downs.

She had just settled herself to some darning when the bell rang; and supposing it to be Doctor Linton preparing to leave already, she took off her pinafore and went out into the passage. There, glancing automatically at the board as she passed, she saw that the bell still quivering upon its metal spring was not the drawing room's as she'd thought, but that of the front door.

"Land's sake, it's like a tram junction here today," she told herself, hastening up the scullery stairs to the entrance hall. "Behopes that's not tradesmen again, a-wanting their blessed bills settled."

Upon opening the door and finding there instead a soberly-dressed, top-hatted individual, Minnie was inclined to be rather more garrulous than she might otherwise have been with this second caller.

"Why, bless me—Mr Bates! It's a long time since we last had the pleasure o' having you come a-visiting, sir. Indeed, to be sure, I was thinking to meself only t'other day—"

Her animation was short-lived.

"Your mistress—is she at home?" Ellis Bates demanded tersely. "If so, kindly inform her of my wish to see her."

"I'm sorry, sir, but Miss Amy's out o' town."

"Out of town?"

"Aye. And she's not expected back afore the week's end, as I told Doctor Linton just now."

Ellis's face tightened. "Linton? He's called too, has he?"

"Aye, sir. He's here now still, taking a cup o' tea in the drawing room."

"Is that so, indeed! Then I shall join him. He is the very purpose of my visit."

Before Minnie could say another word, the schools inspector had pushed brusquely past and was heading across the hall to the stairs.

"The drawing room, you said?" he barked over his shoulder. And at her flustered nod—"What I have to say to the gentleman is private. See to it that we are not disturbed."

If David was a trifle bemused to see who it was thrusting open the door, he was very soon left in no doubt as to the cause of this precipitate behaviour. Ellis Bates had that day received yet another letter from Louisa Linton; and one which had proved the final straw for his already threadbare patience. Determined to discover precisely why he should be so persecuted by this wretched woman's delusions of reciprocated passion, he had come here seeking an interview with Amy Flynn to get to the truth of her relationship with Linton. That he should find Linton himself at the house was a most paradoxical coincidence, but nevertheless one which he intended exploiting to the full.

Closing the drawing room door firmly behind him, and taking up a position which gave him immediate advantage over the still-seated doctor, Ellis began at once without preamble. "Sir, for some while now I have been the victim of an hysterical correspondence emanating from your household. Either it ceases forthwith, or I warn you, I shall take this matter to Law."

The sudden and totally unexpected assault caught David by surprise, robbing him of the wits to respond. One moment he had been sitting here enjoying in a somewhat miserable fashion the dulling effect of the whisky upon his mind—and the next, he was being verbally assailed by a furious individual with whom hitherto

193

he had scarcely exchanged more than a polite word of greeting.

He groped for something to say, but was not quick enough.

"I am not, I repeat, not enamoured of your wife," the other went on heatedly. "Let me tell you, sir, I have written upon numerous occasions to inform her in no uncertain terms that very far from being secretly enflamed by desire, as she mistakenly supposes, I find her approaches ridiculous, offensive and disgusting, and a cause for scandal in a woman of her position. I am nauseated, not to put too fine a point upon it, at being made an object of such sickly sentimental molestation, and I repeat my warning—either you bring your wife to heel, sir, or I shall see your reputation ruined and your name dragged through the mud of public litigation."

David's face had gone pale with anger under this tirade. Thrusting himself to his feet, he stood a few paces from his assailant, the alcohol he had taken fuelling the heat of his rousing temper.

"Damn you, sir, who the devil d'you think you are to threaten me!"

"I do not threaten. I am stating what shall be."

"And on what grounds? That Louisa has penned a few fanciful letters? Good God, if I were to take to court every husband whose wife has written naively to *me*, I'd be the laughing stock of my profession. Emotional women are an occupational hazard."

"That may well be. Though I would suggest, sir, that you are well on the way to becoming a laughing stock already. Your wife is not the only one to write 'fanciful' letters, since you yourself have composed a number which might be viewed as being in very questionable taste."

"What the deuce d'you mean by that?"

Ellis's expression contorted itself into a sneer. "I mean, Doctor Linton, the puerile expressions of adulterous sentiment received by Amy Flynn."

"Amy—? My God!"

"You may well sound dismayed," the other said smoothly. "During the short time she resided beneath my roof last year, some three or four letters were addressed to her which, as head of the household, it was my duty to read—"

194

"You *read* a private correspondence?" David's outrage almost choked him. "By what right, sir, did you think it fitting to pry into the personal business of a guest?"

"By my right as a guardian of the morals of those to whom the care of my children is entrusted. I have for some while suspected that your overtures of friendship towards Miss Flynn are not as platonic as you might wish them to appear. That on the contrary, they are very otherwise, and have resulted in a relationship which is suspect to say the least. I go further, sir. I suggest to you that you have formed some kind of clandestine attachment to this young woman which leaves you open to a charge of unprofessional conduct."

"The devil you do!" The doctor's features were stamped with a violence that should have warned his tormentor to take care how he provoked him. "Say one word more, you sanctimonious prig, and I shall have the greatest pleasure in teaching you a lesson you will not soon forget."

Ellis raised a sarcastic eyebrow. "Now you begin to show yourself in your true colours. Only a hobnail clod resorts to the antics of the gutter."

"And only a Peeping Tom seeks to satisfy his perverted tastes by ferreting through innocent correspondence in search of something to excite him."

Ellis began to laugh, a curious high-pitched whickering noise, the top lip curled back to show his strong teeth.

"Were that the case, my dear doctor, the indelicate impudicity of your wife's letters would have given more than sufficient gratification."

"I will not believe that! Louisa is a woman of great delicacy and refinement—"

"Indeed? Then how is it, do you suppose, that I am in possession of the fact that conjugal relations between you both ceased several years ago?"

David felt a flush of colour warm his cheeks.

"Well?" cried the other, seeing him fall silent. "Do you wish me to cite further details as example? I can assure you, sir, I have been force-fed upon the miseries of your marriage until I am full to here with them—"

He made a chopping motion at his throat.

"Then why encourage her all this while?" came the

response. "Why invite such confidences unless it is for the pleasure of being privy to them?"

"Encourage—? Invite—?" Ellis laughed again. "Have you ever read my correspondence to your wife, sir?"

There was a long pause; then a shrug and a shake of the head. "Until you thrust the matter so uncivilly upon my attention just now, I had no idea. I have never seen so much as an envelope."

"Then let me assure you, I have not minced words in expressing myself. Very far from encouraging this obsessive attachment she has formed for me, I have stated repeatedly—*repeatedly*—that I find it grossly distasteful and request that she desist forthwith from any further pursuance."

"Yet she has continued?"

"Yes! I marvel, Doctor Linton, that you should have remained so long in ignorance, seeing that it is your own neglect and inconsideration which appear to have driven her to such an extreme of self-delusion."

It was on the tip of David's tongue to make a heated defence against this accusation. But realising the folly of further anger, he checked himself and instead said in a terse, professional manner, "My wife is a sick woman, sir. Her illness is psychosomatic in nature—that is to say, it is an emotional disorder which manifests itself as a physical debility. She may appear to the untrained eye to be suffering from a wastage of the muscles, reducing her little by little to a helpless invalid who must needs be pushed about in a Bath chair and treated like an infant. Yet she is, in fact, a normal healthy young woman—and perfectly capable of leading a full and active life, were it not that in her mind she believes otherwise."

"You are saying, in effect, that she is unstable?" Ellis's expression echoed the scepticism of his tone.

"I would prefer to use the word disturbed, sir. She is the victim of a self-induced hysteria, and so perhaps more to be pitied than blamed for her questionable behaviour."

"That being so, why choose to exacerbate matters by continuing to pursue your relationship with Amy Flynn, since it is plainly this which is the root cause of your wife's distress?"

The muscles in David's jaw began to work again. Curtly

he answered, "My relationship with Amy—or with any other—is a personal affair, sir, and not one which I choose to discuss here."

"It may indeed be personal," countered the other, "but let me point out to you, insofar as it is the goad which spurs your wife to imagining a like relationship exists between herself and me, I am hardly a disinterested party in this business."

"I cannot accept that. You forget, Mr Bates, the seeds of Louisa's sickness were sown long before she ever made your acquaintance, and what we have now is but a further manifestation of her disorder."

Ellis made a contemptuous gesture of disbelief, and turning on his heel, took a few steps towards the window. He stood there in silence for several moments in apparent contemplation of the sun-capped stable roofline across the yard; then suddenly swung about again, and said harshly, "I came here today, sir, to thrash out this entire business with Miss Flynn herself, trusting that she might be brought to see the error of her ways, and by terminating her friendship, remove this temptation which clearly she represents for you. It would seem, however, that a little good sense has already prevailed, for she has taken herself out of town—no, have the courtesy to hear me, pray—" as David made to interrupt—"I am far from being finished. She has taken herself out of town, I say. And since you, sir, would hardly be present here otherwise, has apparently done so without informing you of her intention. That to me, is a sign that you are not so much in Miss Flynn's confidence as hitherto."

"Amy is a free woman," David got in. He was starting to weary of this senseless confrontation and badly wanted another drink. "She needs no permission from me or any other how she chooses to conduct her life. It may interest you to know, Mr Bates, since you feel yourself so embroiled in our affairs, she is staying in Dorset as the family guest of a Mr Ralph Herriot, a gentleman who appears to concern himself very warmly on her behalf."

It took the doctor some effort to say this without exposing the raw nerve of his own jealousy. Unless something were to happen in the near future—something unforeseen, some desperate action of his own, perhaps—he was all too well aware that Amy might be lost irretrievably to him through marriage to another; and the thought of that wellnigh drove him to such depths of black despair that many a time he sought refuge in the anaesthesia of alcohol.

Had he not been so intent upon masking his own feelings from Ellis Bates, he might have observed the curious alteration which had occurred in the other's expression at mention of Ralph Herriot's name. The pale features contorted themselves into what might almost have been a snarl and the eyes narrowed. The impression lasted no more than a moment before melting again into a sneer, and in the silken tones of sarcasm the schools inspector observed, "A gentleman, you say? How quaint. And how very far removed from the usual type of company she keeps."

David refused to rise to the barbed bait of this remark. Passing a hand through his dark hair, he said tersely, "It is high time I took leave of you, sir. There is nothing further to be gained by our conversation—"

"Not so hasty!" Ellis moved from the window. "I am not finished with my business yet, Doctor Linton. We have still to determine to my satisfaction what is to be done about your wife."

"Is there anything to be done? Can you not simply ignore these letters she sends?"

"Ha! More to the question, can *you* not prevent her from sending them?"

There was a shrug. "I will try. I will speak to her on the matter, certainly. Though to be frank, I very much doubt that anything I have to say will impress upon Louisa the senselessness of her behaviour. Rather the contrary."

"Come, sir, you have a husband's control over her actions, surely?"

"Only insofar as it is for the good of her well-being, and the peace of the household. Look, I will be perfectly honest with you, Mr Bates. My wife is passing through a stubborn and difficult phase just now, in that everything I say to her is twisted to represent the opposite. This may well explain her intransigence in refusing to believe that her attachment to you is not being reciprocated. In other words, she is deluding herself into reading your rebuff as some sort of dissemblement of your true feelings."

This observation was greeted with a snort of ridicule.

A little more warmly, the doctor went on, "You do not believe me? Then why not make a visit to call upon her yourself? Put it to her bluntly, face to face, how strongly you resent the continuance of this silly correspondence? She may well be brought to her senses by a personal rebuke from you."

"That is all you can suggest, sir?"

"It is."

"Very well. Let us suppose I were to make this visit. What guarantee have I that my actual appearance in the flesh will not excite the woman to some fresh manifestation of mania? God help us, she may imagine I have come to seduce her, or something equally extraordinary."

If David Linton could have known how his answer was to change the whole course and tenor of his life, he might well have thought twice before making it.

Moving over to the bell-pull beside the fireplace to advise Minnie of his departure, he said irritably, "I give you a free hand to deal with the situation as you see fit, Mr Bates. That is my guarantee. Only leave Amy out of the wretched business . . . and I will not stand in your way, you have my word on it."

20

"Megwynn . . . will you marry me? Please?"

A handful of daffodils, their half-opened trumpets some-what crushed from being hidden within a jacket breast, were thrust beneath the young governess's down-turned face as accompaniment to this proposal.

At the same time, the suitor continued in an earnest whisper, "I love you . . . truly I do. We get on frightfully well together, don't you think? So please promise you won't go marrying any other fellow."

A small smile curled the corners of Megwynn's lips. Taking the crumpled flowers, she said softly, "I promise. I won't go marrying any other fellow. Now sit you properly in the pew, *fachgen*, till your Grandmother Bashford is ready to leave."

Esmond Bates gave an exaggerated little sigh. Pushing himself back on the polished oak seat, he twisted his head to see over the top of the box pew; then, observing his grand-mother still at private devotion at one of the ornately-carved prie-dieu in the lady chapel, he hissed from the side of his mouth, "You haven't given an answer to my question."

"What question was that, now?"

"You know . . . about marriage and things."

"Ah. That."

There followed a short silence.

"Well?" the boy demanded finally, his voice beginning to rise with impatience.

"Oh, *hush*," came a sharp whisper from his sister Laura, kneeling at Megwynn's other side. "God can't hear me pray, 'Smond."

"Of course he can hear you, perfectly well—"

"That will do, Esmond," his governess reproved him quietly. "And as for your question, I will give you answer—

but on one condition, look you." There was another small smile. "That you ask it me again when you are twenty-one."

"Twenty-one? But that's years and years away. You'll be an old lady by that time, and I shall certainly not wish to marry you then."

"There's gallant!"

"Oh, I didn't mean . . ." Esmond bit his lip and cast a look of mortification upon the object of his juvenile affections. "Darnation, I *knew* I should spoil it all. I'm not much good at this sort of thing, am I."

"You haven't had the practice, *cariad*. And don't say darnation. It isn't polite in church." Megwynn touched a finger to the wilting flower heads. "Did you take these from your grandmam's garden?"

Before Esmond could make any answer, little Laura had scrambled from her knees and piped up, "*I* know where he got them, Miss Evans. *I* saw him. He picked them in the churchyard, so he did."

"You sneak!" hissed her brother. "You promised not to tell."

"No I didn't."

"Yes you did, too."

"Now stop it. Stop it, the pair of you," the governess admonished them in a sharp whisper. "That will be quite enough. Gather up your gloves and your prayer book, Laura. And Esmond—Esmond!" turning in time to catch him sticking out his tongue—"You will please not pull such faces at your sister. Indeed to goodness, but I have no wish at all to marry you if you cannot conduct yourself better. Now where is your cap? Look, your grandmam is coming back. We shall be sent home to Lewes in disgrace if she sees you misbehaving so."

These last words instantly had the required effect; both children sat up ram-rod straight on their seat, hands folded in their laps, faces suddenly wiped clear of expression by that curious magical alchemy of the young which transforms the worst little brat into the very picture of angelic innocence.

There had been some doubt whether their father would agree to allow them to spend Easter here at Bonningale; and it had taken repeated pleas from Megwynn that the country

201

air would benefit the children's health after the long winter in Lewes before Mr Bates was finally persuaded to let them come. That, and a letter from his mother whose conciliatory tone he was prepared to accept as apology for her recent negligent attitude.

The governess rose to her feet. "You may open the pew door now, Esmond, if you will."

When he had done so, she handed the daffodil bunch to him and bending her head, said quietly, "Go and put these among the flowers in the lady chapel. That will please your grandmam to see, as well as gladden me."

He did as he was asked, only pausing to stand aside for Rachael Bashford to pass him in the aisle and salute her politely with a little bow.

"What a good child that is." The black widow's cap on the beautifully neat grey hair dipped slightly towards Megwynn as Mrs Bashford drew abreast of the family pew. "He is becoming a credit to you, Miss Evans."

"Why, thank you, ma'am."

A net-gloved hand was held out to Laura. "My dear? Shall we go and look to see whether Uncle George has arrived with the carriage? Or you may wish to return on foot to the house, perhaps?"

"Oh, I should like better to ride with you, Grandmama, please."

"Then so you shall. Miss Evans?" There was a look of enquiry from the line-meshed eyes. "Will you ride with us in the carriage?"

"Thank you kindly, ma'am. But no, I will walk back with Esmond. I have to hear his recitation, see, and it will give me a chance to correct it before his cousins distract him from learning the lines by heart."

Rachael Bashford responded with a smile of acknowledgement; then, taking her granddaughter by the hand, moved away towards the porch, saying, "We shall see you both at luncheon, then."

"Why," Esmond asked diffidently, returning from his errand to the chapel, "why do you suppose it is that Grandmama dislikes my papa so?"

"Hush, *fachgen*!" Megwynn turned hurriedly to look over her shoulder.

"Oh, it's quite all right, Miss Evans. She can't possibly hear me. Not at this distance."

"*She* is the cat's mother. Where are your manners today?"

There was a shrug. "Why do you always answer my questions by going off into one of your Welsh huffs. I merely wondered why it is Grandmama seems to favour Papa least of all the family."

"I don't know that she does." The other took up her gloves and reticule from the ledge inside the pew. "What is it has given you that idea, now?"

"Well, whenever she—that is Grandmama—whenever she speaks of her other sons—Uncle George and Uncle Henry and Uncle Richard—it is always done . . . well, how can I put it . . . you know, the way people's voices become warm and kind when they mention someone they love? But I've noticed that whenever Grandmama must speak of my papa, she always calls him 'your father' or even 'Mr Bates' as though he were nothing to do with her at all. And her voice goes all thin and needly and cold."

"Does it indeed?" What was one to do with such a precociously observant child? "I cannot say I've heard it for myself."

"There is something in our closet, you know," the boy went on gravely, standing back to allow his governess to precede him through the porch door. "I mean, skeletons and things. I think Papa is one of them. At least, that's what I believe Aunt Phyllis meant when I chanced to hear her talking with Aunt Mary the other evening."

Megwynn paused on the church path to adjust the elastic securing her hat. Although the April day was cloudless and bright with sunlight, the breeze was quite fresh.

On a cautioning note she said, "I hope you did not deliberately chance to overhear your aunts' conversation, Esmond."

He responded with another shrug. "Well, they both have such silly, loud voices. And they were sitting at the drawing room window, which must have been left open, else how could I hear them so well from where I was?"

"And where were you, pray?"

"Oh . . . close by." He thrust his hands into his trouser pockets and began kicking a stone along the path.

"Esmond—?"

203

"Well . . . well, if you must know, Miss Evans, I was in the hysteria tree-thing, looking for a nest—"

"You mean the wistaria, do you?" The governess paused, and swung round upon her young charge.

There was a quick, guilty nod.

"You were forbidden to climb the wistaria." Her tone held an edge of annoyance. "There's your grandmam just now saying what a good child you've grown, and you straightway give her the lie with your naughty, wilful defiance. I shall take a strap to your hand, look you, if I catch you again at such disobedience!"

Snatching up the hem of her skirts to negotiate the steps, Megwynn moved briskly ahead through the church gate and out into the lane.

"But don't you wish to know what they were saying about my papa?" Esmond cried, hastening to catch up.

"No, I do not. Whatever it was, it was no business of any but their own." She threw the boy a sharp look. "Remember this, *fachgen*—silence seldom makes mischief, and a still tongue and stopped ears will spare you much hurt in life, for an eavesdropper rarely hears anything good of himself. Now, we have a long step ahead of us, so pick up your feet and don't dawdle. I shall attend to your recitation as we walk."

Whatever it was that Phyllis and her sister Mary Bashford had been saying about Ellis Bates, the young Welsh governess was quite sure it could be nothing good of the man. She had been in his service long enough to appreciate how little love there was lost between her employer and his Bonningale relations; and from talk in the Bashford household, had heard sufficient to gather that this family division stemmed from Mrs Bashford's first marriage, to Ellis Bates's father.

Megwynn acknowledged to herself that she had some feelings of sympathy for the man. He was a stern master, yes, and could be very harsh when he wished; yet she sensed a loneliness within him, a solitary friendlessness, as though he had never known what it was to belong anywhere. He had acquaintances by the dozen, but none one might call an intimate as such, and he rarely had any to dine at the house, preferring to do his entertaining in the more neutral atmosphere of his club.

Even his attitude towards his motherless children betrayed this inner isolation. Where other fathers joined in the fun of play and allowed their young a certain amount of liberty in nursery games, Mr Bates never so much as visited Esmond and Laura upstairs to read to them a goodnight story, and any affection he might feel for them both was restricted in expression to a single kiss upon the brow at breakfast and bedtime.

Despite all this—or even, perhaps, because of it—Megwynn had formed the greatest respect for her employer. Exacting he might be in the supervision of her duties, but he was just and he was upright; and if he kept himself severely to himself, why that was very much to be preferred to a master who was over-familiar and made himself a nuisance to his maidservants.

He was a fair man, too, she considered. He need not have taken her back again after she'd given her notice last winter. He had already advertised for another governess, and interviewed several applicants for the post. When she had approached him to ask that he reconsider the termination of her employment—giving as reason an alteration in the domestic arrangements made on her behalf by the "relatives" in Eastbourne (which was perfectly true) and her warm attachment to Laura and Esmond (equally true)—Ellis Bates had confined his annoyance to the remark that she had put him to a deal of trouble for nothing, but that he was agreeable to her remaining in his household; and he trusted there would be no second change of mind to inconvenience him further.

For which great mercy, Megwynn Evans had cause to be loyally grateful.

She paused now in the lane, and seeing young Esmond silent at her side, asked, "Well? Have you forgotten already the piece I set you to learn?"

There was a shake of the head.

"Then why do you not begin?"

"Oh, it is not for want of remembering the piece, Miss Evans," the boy assured her.

"Then what?"

"I would rather we talked together as we walked along. It would be so much more pleasant—"

"We shall have the recitation, if you please," she told him firmly. "You talk more than is good for you, sir."

"Now you are vexed with me. Are you displeased because I proposed to you in marriage?"

The young woman permitted herself a smile. "I would be better pleased if you agreed to *my* proposal, look you. That you let me hear your recitation."

"Oh—very well." Esmond blew out his cheeks. Fixing his blue eyes ahead on the tree-shadowed lane, he began at once in a gabbled reading-aloud voice, "Remembrances, by John Clare.

Summer's pleasures they are gone like to visions every one,
And the cloudy days of autumn and of winter cometh on.
I tried to call them back, but unbidden they are gone
Far away from heart and eye and forever far away—"

"Now stop. That is too fast," Megwynn interrupted. "*Think* the lines as you speak them, and take them at a slower pace."

A small sigh was heaved, and the boy set off again:

"Dear heart, and can it be that such raptures meet decay?
I thought them all eternal when by Langley Bush I lay,
I thought them joys eternal when I used to shout and play
On its banks at 'clink and bandy', 'chock' and 'taw' and 'ducking stone',
Where silence sitteth now on the wild heath as her own
Like a ruin of the past all alone."

"That was much better," she said encouragingly. "But do try to put a little expression into your voice, *cariad*. This is a sad poem, after all. Mr Clare is looking back upon his boyhood and remembering its pleasant hours, which now seem so far away and lost to him. Can you not feel the melancholy in his words?"

Esmond gave the question his consideration; then nodded.

"Very well. Now, continue with the next verse—'When I used to lie and sing—'"

Her young charge took up the opening line to the second of John Clare's eight stanzas, this time injecting a certain

206

amount of pathos into the recitation. As she walked beside
him listening, Megwyn's thought slipped away for a moment
or two to her own remembrances of time past, that recent
time of private anguish when she had lost her unborn child
and known herself to be abandoned by its faithless father.

"O I never dreamed of parting or that trouble had a sting,
Or that pleasures like a flock of birds would ever take to
    wing,
Leaving nothing but a little naked spring."

Naked indeed her spring had been for a short while—
naked of love, naked of hope, naked of self-respect. But she
had put that time behind her now, determined never to
repeat its mistake. Her only dread was that Francis Bethway
might turn up again in Lewes and through his idle bragging
manage to cast upon her reputation sufficient mud to stick.
It was to allay this fear that she'd written several times to
him, asking for the reassurance of his discretion and future
circumspect behaviour in the matter of their relationship.

"O words are poor receipts for what time hath stole
away . . ."

Receiving no acknowledgement, however, and growing
a little concerned that this silence might not betoken
something sinister, the young woman had taken one of her
days off to travel to Eastbourne, to see him in person at
his parents' house, and take the opportunity to thank the
Bethways properly for their offers of help and assistance.
  Francis had not been at home; and the interview with his
parents had proved a most uncomfortable business on both
sides, with the Bethways regarding her, Megwynn felt sure,
as being the guiltier of the pair, a flighty little piece who'd
led their son into bad ways and come a cropper for it. She
had taken her leave as soon as good manners permitted; and
before returning to the railway station, went for a walk along
the seafront to collect herself.
  It had been there, at the end of Grand Parade near the old
Martello tower known as the Wish Tower, that she'd caught
a sight of Francis among a group of young people over by the

railings of the promenade, indulging themselves in noisy horse-play. She noticed at once that he'd grown a moustache, and how much it suited him. Pressed close, arms encircling his waist beneath the striped blazer, was a pretty, dark-haired girl wearing his straw boater on the back of her head, and Francis kept leaning forward to cover her laughing, upturned face with kisses.

Megwynn had turned on her heel and hurried away, before she should be seen.

"O I never thought that joys would run away from boys,
Or that boys would change their minds and forsake such
    summer joys;
But alack I never dreamed that the world had other toys
To petrify first feelings like the fable into stone . . ."

Well, that was the end of that. He had plainly lost no time in replacing her with someone else in his affections; and as she travelled back to Lewes, the cast-off had wished her dark-haired successor much joy of him, for she too would no doubt be used for his pleasure and tossed aside once the novelty of intimacy began wearing thin.

"Miss Evans—?"

Megwynn's thoughts came quickly back to the present. Esmond's recitation had come to a halt without her noticing, and now the boy was standing behind her on the lane whilst she had gone walking blithely on ahead.

"Miss Evans, you are not paying me attention," he complained loudly. "Why, I may as well be saying my multiplication tables for all the interest you're showing!"

There was a look of apology. "Oh, I'm sorry, *cariad*. It was remiss of me to let my mind wander. But you are doing so well, see. Word perfect, you are, almost."

"Almost. I've forgotten a line." He caught up with her, a petulant expression on his old-young face.

"Which line is that, now?" Megwynn held out a hand, and side by side the two of them continued slowly on their way.

"The last verse. 'O had I known as then' . . . something, something."

"'O had I known as then joy had left the paths of men'."

"Ah yes, that's it." The carefully modulated boyish treble

took up the words from her, finishing some half-dozen lines later with a triumphant flourish—

"But love never heeded to treasure up the may,
So it went the common road to decay."

"That was lovely, Esmond. Well done!"

His governess bent to kiss his cheek, and he grinned back at her in quick pleasure, the breeze lifting the pale-gold hair from his forehead.

As always when he felt especially affectionate, he reverted to using her forename, an inoffensive little habit which she tended to overlook, recognising that it would do the boy more harm to forbid.

"If you wish, Megwynn, I'll recite the poem to Grandmama, shall I! I'm sure she would care to hear it. And it is bound to increase your good standing with her, that I should be such a scholar. My Bashford cousins are frightful dullards, you know. Farming is all they are fit for, every one. Poetry is quite beyond them. How gratified Grandmama will be to know that one of us at least shows promise of something loftier. Why, just think of it—she may write to declare as much to Papa. 'My dear Mr Bates,' she will say, 'you have a genius for son, and a gem for governess. Pray cherish them both in your bosom.' No, truly, Megwynn, don't laugh! I wish she would write that, indeed I do, for then you would never, ever leave us."

"Are you fearful still that I shall?"

The boy's face grew very grave, and he nodded. "Oh, I know you've promised not to, Megwynn dear. But all our other governesses, they've left. It would break my heart, and Laura's, if for any reason you should go away from us, like they."

She gave his hand a fond little squeeze. "Then I repeat my promise. I shall never leave you, Esmond, never. Nor Laura. Nor your dear papa."

"Cross your heart and swear it, for better or for worse!"

Obediently, Megwynn drew a cross upon her left breast with her thumb.

"*Er gwell ac er gwaeth, cariad,*" she said softly. "For better . . . or for worse."

21

The Reverend John Wickenden, of St Anne's at Weatherfield, had been especially apologetic in his prayers of late. Having been blessed with fine weather throughout the Easter season, it seemed almost something of an impertinence to petition the Almighty for sunshine and clear skies for the parish celebrations of May Day (which was, after all, a fertility festival of pagan origin, and still, albeit in a veiled way, highly symbolic in the manner of its observances).

Indeed, as a churchman he was well aware that there'd been a time when may-poles, or shafts, were prohibited by parliament as being lewd emblems of idolatry and ordered to be dismantled from the village greens and town meadows where they'd stood for as long as living memory could recall. Happily, no sooner had Merry England risen from the cold ashes of the Commonwealth than the poles likewise rose again throughout the land, together with all the rites and customs of yore; though Mr Wickenden, enthusiastic antiquarian as he might be, had cause to be thankful that the more vigorous aspects of those same customs had now fallen into abeyance.

Human nature being what it was, no doubt there were young people of his parish who still went a-maying among the early morning hedgerows for pleasures other than the gathering of hawthorn blossom; and no doubt there were a few—as the rector noted with a touch of humour—who, in due season, would bear their hedgerow fruit to prove it.

Such failings aside, however, May Day—or Garland Day, as it was generally known in Sussex—was in these modern times become a festival for children to celebrate for their elders' entertainment; and its purpose in Weatherfield was that it should be enjoyed as a parish occasion, with a May

Queen, Morris men, a may-pole dance, and a picnic tea for all upon the green to end the pleasant afternoon.

And for this, as Mr Wickenden humbly observed in his prayers, good weather was an essential requirement, for without its benison the numbers of spectators would be greatly reduced—as would be their valued contributions to church funds.

His supplications met with a favourable response. Sunday, the first of May 1892, dawned clear and fine, with a mildness in the air promising perfect conditions.

Roused from sleep as always by the six o'clock chimes of St Anne's, the rector looked from his bedroom window out across the broad slope of the green, and offered up thanks and praise as he watched the last of the dawn clouds disperse into rosy shreds upon the horizon. A little later, struggling to fasten the back stud of his collar band, he observed several groups of children gathering by the cricket pavilion at the far end, ready to make the short journey into the surrounding countryside to gather blossom for their garlands; and he commented to his wife, still abed, that last year, if she recalled, the Olivers from Snow Hill had decorated the May Queen's throne with swags of flowers and must needs let the whole thing down into their well for the night to keep the blooms fresh for the morrow.

The May Queen this year was to be young Alice Linton; and instead of the business of a flower-wreathed chair, the child's invalid mother had been prevailed upon to use her skills as a needlewoman to make an embroidered canopy and panels for the throne. Mr Wickenden was so sure this would prove a most attractive and original centrepiece to the proceedings that he'd arranged for one of the Queen's little attendants to stand with a collecting plate as a reminder to onlookers to offer some tangible proof of their appreciation.

By mid-morning, when church service was over and the first event of the festivity due to start, the groups of children had returned from their hedgerow forays, and as custom allowed on Garland Day, were now going about the neighbourhood bearing may-boughs plaited with cowslips, bluebells and primroses, cadging pennies from passers-by and shopkeepers with their shrill cries of "Please remember the garlands!"

211

Soon a fresh cry had gone up drawing the youngsters back to the green—"The Morris men! The Morris men!"—as a rhythmic jingle of bells heralded the team's approach along the high street, to the accompaniment of a barking dog and the protesting clamour of ducks on the lower pond.

The dancers made a brave sight in their black velveteen breeches with knee ties, light grey hose and pumps with small rosettes, the white shirts having ribbon streamers from the shoulders, and the hats bunches of ribbon from the crown, and each man carrying a large pocket handkerchief in his right hand.

Passing between the rows of bystanders, they halted near the may-pole at the centre of the green, and after time was allowed for the slaking of thirsts with ale, there followed a brief speech by the chairman of the Garland Day Committee. Then, without further ado, violin, tabor and pipe struck up a rousing tune and the Morris men drew themselves up into two facing lines and moved forward in a regular quick-step, at each turn of the tune throwing up their white handkerchiefs with a shout.

The Reverend John Wickenden, watching the proceedings with his wife, expressed great satisfaction. The day was living up to its early promise and drawing out the crowds, for already he could see a dozen or more brakes and other vehicles in the enclosure by the pond, and two horse-drawn omnibuses standing beyond in the high street.

Folding his hands upon his ample, black-waistcoated paunch, the rector began humming to himself, "Praise to the holiest in the height, and in the depth be praise . . ."

By two o'clock, when the crowning of the May Queen was due to take place, the numbers had increased considerably as farmworkers came in from the areas around. It being a Sunday as well as a fête day, the domestic servants of Weatherfield's more prosperous households had likewise been allowed the afternoon off to enjoy themselves; though the Lintons' Lily Banks had some misgivings about leaving her mistress alone at the house whilst she and Albert came out to see the sights.

"Oh, give over worritting, Lily, do," Albert told his wife, craning on tiptoe to watch his young niece Ruby twirl about

212

the may-pole with the rest of the white-frocked little dancers. "She wouldn't ha' said for us to come if she were afeared o' being left all by herself."

"It's not her being left by herself as worrits me," Lily fretted. "Lord knows, her own company don't bother her none, poor woman, the hours she do spend on her own. But supposing she were to catch some hurt, Albert? There's not a soul nearby to hear, and her in that Bath chair, an' all. We should never ha' left her a-sitting up the stairs, I know we shouldn't."

Albert's weather-creased face was furrowed in concentration. The may-pole dancers had reached the most intricate part of their display, weaving in and out to plait their coloured streamers in a regular pattern around the tall shaft, and he was more concerned that young Ruby should keep to her turn than that Mrs Linton should meet with some unlikely mishap.

"But Miss's did ask to be left a-sitting upstairs," he answered distractedly. "How's she to see little Alice being crowned, else? There's no window below to gi' any view o' the green, and she won't come outdoors, you know she won't, for fear o' folk squinneying at her."

"Whyever's the Doctor not here, I'd like to know." Finding fresh fuel for her concern, Lily's tone grew shriller. "Taking hisself off for the afternoon somewhere out o' the way . . . I never heard o' such a thing."

"Belikes he's got patients to visit. Oh! Look at our Ruby now! She did that turn a proper treat."

"Got patients to visit? What, of a Sunday? As if it couldn't ha' waited an hour while he stayed wi' his wife to see their daughter made Queen o' the May. A crying shame, I call it. I've a mind to tell him so, an' all—"

"What, and have us both put out o' work?" Now that the dancing was ending, Albert was free to give his wife his full attention. "You'll do no such thing, our Lily, d'you hear? Never you mind what the Miss's and Doctor be about, 'tis their own business and none of ourn. You're here wi' me to enjoy yourself, woman, and enjoy yourself you're darn' well a-going to."

So saying, he seized her by the arm; and was just about to add something further, when a sudden high drum-roll filled the air and a shout went up that the May Queen's procession was on its way.

Stretching their necks to see between the heads of those in front, the couple were able to catch a glimpse of the first of the attendants coming two by two across the green, each child dressed in white and crowned with a circlet of flowers, and holding posies in their hands. Behind them followed a pony-drawn cart decorated with boughs of may blossom, bearing little Alice Linton.

Lily shaded her eyes from the sun, the better to see the procession pass by.

"My, doesn't she look a picture?" she exclaimed, glancing proudly around to see who might be near to recognise her as the Lintons' housemaid. "She makes a prettier queen by far than ever did the Olivers' girl last year."

The cart drew to a stop at the far side of the may-pole, and there was another short drum-roll from the Morris men's tabor as Alice, hitching up the skirts of her showy satin gown and grinning from ear to ear with nervous excitement, came down from the cart and was led by the Reverend Mr Wickenden to take her seat upon the throne, placed a short distance off in the shade of a young oak tree.

A hush of expectation fell upon the onlookers.

At a nod from the rector, one of the attendants stepped forward with a cushion holding the crown, and making an awkward bow, presented it to the chairman of the Garland Day Committee.

"Ladies and gentlemen all," announced this individual in loud and self-important tones, raising aloft the flower-twined diadem, "pray acclaim your Queen of the May!"

With that, he set the crown upon Alice's golden ringlets, patted her cheek in avuncular fashion, and turned to give her attendants their cue to begin a stately perambulation of the throne, casting showers of may petals as they sang a song of salutation.

"Oh . . . that was done beautiful," Lily declared, when the ensuing cheers and clapping had died down. "Just beautiful. I disremember when I've seen it better performed."

"Aye, it's been a long year or more since we had such a handsome crowning as that."

Her husband nodded several times, looking about to see

what was happening next; and catching sight of movement over by the cricket pavilion, went on hastily, "Eh up, Lily, they're shifting the trestle tables out. Time for the tea and buns, I reckon. I'll go and gi' hand—"

"Just you hold on a minute." She stayed him firmly. "Afore you take yourself off anywhere, I want you to slip back to the house for me and see Mrs Linton's taken no harm. Go on—they'll not be setting out the food yet awhile."

There was a sound of exasperation; then, with a jerk of the head to indicate what he thought of his wife's harping concern for her mistress, Albert Banks turned away and began shouldering a path through the thick of bodies to reach the edge of the green.

Crossing from there over to the churchyard wall, he skirted along until he reached the junction with Church Lane; and was about to continue on down when he paused suddenly, and stood there squinting his eyes against the sun to see towards the Linton house.

A figure dressed in dark frockcoat and trousers and wearing a bowler hat was just at that moment going in at the gate.

"Now there's a good thing. Doctor's home betimes," said Albert to himself, and straightway turned on his heel to retrace his steps back to the green.

Observing Lily in animated conversation with her friend Mary Jenner, he took himself off to the pavilion to lend his help erecting the trestles for the picnic tea and setting out chairs and benches; so that it was rather more than a quarter of an hour later before he finally returned again to his wife.

"Well?" she raised her voice to ask, seeing him come towards her. "Everything's as it should be at the house, is it?"

Albert nodded. "Doctor's back. I saw him a-going in at the gate. Now p'raps you'll stop your chundering, woman, and gi' us all a chance to be merry for a change."

This was ignored. "Doctor's back, you say? Well there's some'at to be thankful for, at least. I was just this minute telling Mary here about him taking hisself off the way he did, leaving his poor wife to get what lonesome bit o' pleasure she might from the day."

Mary Jenner tossed her head in agreement, the wings of her cotton sun-bonnet flapping. "I saw her for myself, up at the window as I come by. Mebbe Doctor Linton'll fetch her here to the green now he's home."

"I much misdoubt it, my dear. He'll more'n likely sit wi' her upstairs till she drives him down again. Whatever he tries to do for the best, he's sure to make a boffle of it the way things be atween 'em."

As she spoke, Lily began moving off towards the line of tables to find herself a seat before they should all be taken. Mary Jenner followed; and Albert, looking around to see if he could catch sight of his niece Ruby, was left to bring up the rear.

The May Queen and her band of attendants had already taken their places at the table of honour, in the company of Mr Wickenden and his wife, the committee chairman, parish councillors, and several stalwart ladies responsible for overseeing the preparation of the food (donated by the shopkeepers of Weatherfield).

During the consumption which followed of innumerable platefuls of sandwiches, tarts, buns and jellies, washed down by innumerable cups of tea and glasses of barley water, a small orchestra from neighbouring Shatterford sat on the pavilion verandah to play popular excerpts from the operas of Gilbert and Sullivan. This was followed by a recitation of Tennyson's *May Queen* performed by pupils of St Anne's Church of England School, an ambitious entertainment which, alas, failed to rise to the occasion, several of the children being taken suddenly sick from eating too much jelly, and those left being drowned out by the hubbub of noise at the tables.

By the time the picnic tea was eventually finished and its detritus cleared away, the numbers of people had started dwindling considerably, and there were far fewer now in the lavender dusk of early evening to applaud little Alice Linton as she and her retinue made their departure from the scene. The final performance of the day came from the Morris men once more; and when they'd completed their dance and gone off across the green to their free pints of ale at The Rising Sun tavern in the high street, there remained even fewer left present to hear the Reverend John Wickenden make his speech of thanks to all who had contributed to the great success of the event.

Lily and Albert Banks had already started walking back to Church Lane, going a roundabout way to see young Ruby safely home to her widowed father. The two of them were approaching the Linton house from the other end of the lane when Lily remarked suddenly, "Can you hear some'at, Albert?" and paused, listening.

"Hear what?" he asked, stooping to knock a stone from his boot.

"That noise."

"What noise?"

"Like a wailing. There—there it goes again. Did you hear it that time?"

He straightened himself up and stood motionless, his wiry frame tensed in concentration and his head beneath the Sunday-best cap cocked a little to one side.

From somewhere up ahead a thin, high-pitched cry rose and fell on the warm, still air.

"Ah, 'tis only cats fighting," he said dismissively, "that's all it is. Belikes Mrs Martin's old ginger tom's got hisself into next door's garden again."

"That's no cats a-fighting, Albert. Sounds more like a child to me." Lily began walking on, quickening her step beneath the evening-shadowed branches of beech overhanging the lane.

The keening wail broke out again, louder now.

"That's no cats!" she cried a second time, throwing her husband a worried look over her shoulder.

Then—"Oh, Lor'—!"

"What? What is it, woman?"

She had snatched a hand to her mouth and stopped short once more, staring ahead. "Oh, Lor', Albert—behopes it's not our Miss Alice. What if it is? What if some'at's happened? Oh, come quick—we'd best hurry!"

Hoisting up her skirts, Lily took to her heels along the lane, the flowers on her bonnet nodding up and down as she ran. Raising his eyes to heaven, her husband began following at a slower gait, wondering to himself why it was that women must needs make such a fuss and palaver every time a child so much as bumped itself, and why the child's own father couldn't be tending to it instead of letting it kick up such a belvering racket out in the front garden.

217

"Albert! Albert—quick!" Lily was now inside the Lintons' gate, and leaning out to make violent motioning gestures to him.

Finishing the last few yards at a trot, he caught up.

"Will you look there—" She jabbed a finger.

Sprawled in the middle of the lawn, her May Queen's gown crumpled and stained and her flax-gold ringlets hanging in rats' tails about her tear-streaked face, little Alice Linton presented the very picture of frightened misery.

"Oh, pet . . . oh, there now, my pet . . ." Lily ran across and swooped upon her, and kneeling down, gathered her in her arms. "What is it, then? You tell Lily."

"Mama-mama-mama," gasped the child on a rising wail. "Mama-mama."

"Best I go and find Doctor, I reckon," Albert observed uncomfortably.

"Aye, and be quick. Some'at *has* happened. I know it." His wife's face had a strained look. "Whyever is he not out here already?" She turned her attention again to Alice, rocking the little girl against her breast and making soothing noises as the cries of "Mama-mama-mama" began once more.

Albert Banks took rapid stock of the situation. The front entrance door was closed; but in any case, he would not have dreamed of using it to gain access to the house. Moving from the lawn past the rose beds, he started walking along the gravelled driveway leading down the side towards the stables and the kitchen quarters.

"Now there's a rum thing," he said aloud to himself, checking his step as he reached the yard. "If Doctor's home, how come there's no trap a-standing out? No, nor no horse, neither?"

He took off his cap and scratched himself in perplexity; then, shaking his head, continued on round to the back of the house.

Here he found the kitchen door to be standing wide ajar. On the floor just within, a few wilted bluebells were lying scattered. Going inside, he noticed there were more of the flowers on the carpet across the room, and beyond them what looked like the white satin sash from Alice's gown. He went over and picked it up. The silky-fine tassle fringe at one

218

end was stained bright red, and when he touched it with a finger, he found the stain still wet.

Albert's sixth sense began sounding a warning note of alarm.

He sucked in a breath. "Doctor! Doctor Linton, sir!"

The shout sounded flat in the heavy shadowed silence of the house.

Moving quickly from the kitchen along the scullery passage to the entrance hall, he repeated his call several times, but without any response. The place seemed deserted.

"Miss's? Miss's Linton? You there, ma'am?"

Still, nothing but silence.

The doors of drawing room and study stood open, their dusk-darkened interiors empty. The warning sense of foreboding grew stronger.

As he turned towards the main staircase, a splash of blue on the lower step caught his eye: more of little Alice's flowers. She must have brought home her May posy to give to her mother.

Cautiously, he began climbing the stairs. Towards the top, when his head was on a level with the floor of the half-landing, he stopped. Mrs Linton's wheeled chair was lying tipped over on its side against the banister rail.

Albert took the last dozen steps at a run; and stopped again.

A few feet from the chair there was something lying in a crumpled heap in the shadows at the foot of the stairs leading to the upper floor. For several minutes he stood without moving, fearful of what he had found; then, hesitantly, his heart thumping with apprehension, went slowly across and looked down.

It was Louisa Linton herself. Her blue eyes were wide open and staring blindly towards the stairwell window where earlier she'd sat watching her daughter's crowning on the green. A darkening pool of blood had formed beneath one side of her face where it had run from her ears and nose; and from the grotesquely distorted angle of head to shoulders, it was clearly evident that her neck had been snapped like a twig.

22

"But I *did* see somebody, Mr Wickenden," a white-faced Albert Banks insisted. "He were just a-going in at the gate as I reached the head o' the lane."

The Reverend John Wickenden exchanged a glance with the police constable writing notes at David Linton's study desk.

"We don't dispute that you saw someone, Albert," the rector said patiently. "What we are trying to elucidate is the identity of this person."

"You say you thought it was your master the doctor," the constable came in, leaning back in the padded armchair and tucking his thumbs into the black leather belt of his tunic.

Albert nodded vigorously. "Aye, I did."

"On account of the clothes he had on."

"Aye." Another nod.

"But you couldn't see his face."

A shake this time. "He were a step too far on for that. And the sun were bright in my eyes."

"Didn't you think it strange he should be afoot, when he'd earlier set off by trap?"

"Aye, but you see, he might ha' brought the trap back afore I come along, and ha' taken hisself into the lane again for some other purpose. It never crossed my mind to wonder."

The constable levered himself upright and made a brief note in his book, sucking his thick brown moustaches thoughtfully.

"So this is all we have to go on, is it, Albert. That you got a glimpse of a gentleman at the Lintons' gate wearing a bowler hat together with dark frockcoat and trousers."

The other nodded again. "And I thought to meself, ah, good, here's Doctor home betimes," he added helpfully.

"Hmm."

"Supposing this figure were not Doctor Linton—then who else?" Mr Wickenden mused.

The constable sketched a shrug. "Whoever he was, sir, he seems to be the only witness we have who might have been in the vicinity at the time of Mrs Linton's unfortunate accident."

"Indeed." In the yellow flare of the gas mantle overhead, the rector's ruddy-hued complexion had a faintly sallow tinge. The sight of Louisa lying dead upstairs in her own blood had disquieted him considerably.

The first he had known of the tragedy was a breathless Albert running up to where he was standing talking with a parishioner on the green, and crying out for him to come as fast as he could "on account o' Miss's has met wi' a terrible accident."

Learning a few gasped details, Mr Wickenden had directed Albert to go at once to the police house for Constable Tate; and taking himself straightway to Church Lane, had discovered Lily Banks and little Alice Linton together in the garden in a state of great distress.

Both were now in the ministering hands of Mrs Wickenden; though it would be some good long while yet before the poor child could be comforted sufficiently to help her over the shock of finding her mother in such frightening and tragic circumstances.

Constable Tate cleared his throat. "When I questioned your wife up at the rectory earlier, Albert, she said you'd told her—" he consulted a page of his notebook—"yes, she said that so far as she could recall, you'd told her you'd seen Doctor Linton back here at the house."

"No, I never said that. Lily's mistook. I said 'Doctor's back. I just seen him at the gate', or some such words."

"You didn't say 'I've just seen him at the house'?"

Albert shook his head emphatically. "How could I. He were nowhere near the house. If he had ha' been, I couldn't ha' seen him from where I was a-standing, and I never went further down Church Lane than that old clump o' holly at the top."

"Fair enough." The constable made an additional note.

"May I make a suggestion?" put in Mr Wickenden. "Could

221

it not be that this gentleman—whoever he was—could it not be that he was not using the gate at all? We've had an unusually large number of visitors in Weatherfield today. Let us suppose for the sake of argument that this were merely some casual stroller passing along the lane.''

"He were a-going in at the gate, sir!" Albert asserted.

"Very well, then. Perhaps what you saw was our stroller pausing a while to admire the flower beds?"

The other shook his head again; and was about to repeat his assertion when of a sudden he checked himself, and turned with a sharp look towards the window. The curtains had not yet been drawn and the upper sash was still open a short way, letting in the sounds of the quiet evening.

An additional sound was now growing louder and closer: that of carriage wheels on the loose gravel of the driveway.

Hearing it for himself, Constable Tate glanced up at the rector, then shifted to look round over the back of the chair; and in a moment or two more, all three men saw the dark shape of horse and trap passing the window.

"Thank the good Lord for that," exclaimed Mr Wickenden fervently. "Here's Linton now. Perhaps this will make better sense of the situation."

Albert made to move towards the door. "I'd best get on and see to the horse—"

"No." The burly constable got to his feet. "No, you wait on here along with us."

"But hark, Master's a-shouting for me—" Even as he said this, David Linton's voice could be heard at the back of the house calling the manservant's name. "He'll be thinking there's some'at up, what wi' the place in darkness an' all."

"There *is* something up," the constable reminded him grimly. He came out from behind the desk.

"Let me—" Mr Wickenden forestalled him with a hand. "Let me be the one to break the ill news to him."

"Very well, sir."

They waited; and in a short time heard the bang of the passage door and the doctor's footsteps crossing the entrance hall.

Seeing the light burning in his study, he came over and looked in at the open doorway.

"What the deuce—?"

Mr Wickenden moved towards him. "David . . ." he said gently, "David, I'm sorry. I'm afraid you must prepare yourself to receive evil tidings. It is Louisa . . ."

"Louisa?" The other stared at him, then at the two men behind, his expression of initial astonishment darkening suddenly to fearful concern. "Why, what has happened?"

"She is dead," the rector answered him simply.

"Dead? *Dead*? But . . . in God's name, how? When?"

"This afternoon. She appears to have fallen from her chair down a flight of stairs. Believe me, I am most truly grieved—"

"Fallen?" David looked wildly about him. "Where is she now? And Alice—what of Alice?"

"Alice is in safe hands, never fear. She is with my wife at the rectory. But I'm afraid the child saw her mother . . . it was she who came first upon the body. She is very distraught, very shocked."

"God help us." The doctor passed a trembling hand across his face as though unable to grasp the truth of what had happened. "But where is Louisa? Where's my wife? What have you done with her?"

"The body is still where it was found, sir," Constable Tate informed him, stepping forward a few paces. "I'm sorry but it can't be moved until it's been properly examined by the police surgeon. He's on his way now from divisional head-quarters with the inspector."

"I see."

Observing how badly affected the younger man was, Mr Wickenden took him by the arm.

"Had you not better sit down, David? You've taken a grievous blow. And I think a stiff brandy would not come amiss. Albert will fetch you one."

"No . . . a moment." David held out a hand. "Not brandy. A whisky. A large whisky. Neat."

When it came, he gulped back almost half the tumbler at one go, then, grimacing at the fiery after-taste in his throat, went over and slumped down in his chair at the desk.

After a pause he asked more steadily, "How did she die, Mr Wickenden? A broken neck?"

"Yes."

"Then at least she suffered no pain." He raised the tumbler again. "That's something to be thankful for, I suppose."

Constable Tate watched him carefully. Judging his moment, he said, "This isn't the time for questions I know, sir. But I must ask you for the purpose of my enquiry, at what hour approximately did you leave the house today?"

"What hour?"

"That's right, sir. I'd like to fix the time, d'you see."

"Yes, of course. It was midday. A little after, perhaps."

"And did you call back at all for any reason?"

The doctor shook his head. "No."

"You're sure of that, sir? Nothing you'd forgotten, mebbe, and came by to collect?"

Another shake.

"I could ha' swore I seen you a-coming in at the gate—" Albert began, before being silenced by a sharp glance from the constable and a terse, "That will do."

David finished his whisky. "A mistake of identity. I left Weatherfield shortly after noon, and I wasn't in the neighbourhood again until after dusk."

"It might be helpful if you'd tell me where it is you've been all these hours, sir," Constable Tate said steadily.

The other put down his empty glass. There was a pause.

"I am not at liberty to say where I've been. But you may be certain of one thing—it was not here in this house contriving the death of my wife."

What was it he had said to Amy earlier, out on the Downs? "Supposing there were no Louisa. Supposing something happened to her, and I was free again. Would you think more kindly of me then, my sweet? Would you marry me, if only it were possible?"

If only it were possible . . . How Fate liked to work its small sly twists! When he had spoken those words in the bright clear air above Lewes, the sun warm on his face and the only sound the carol of larksong, it had been no more than a clutching at straws, a cry in the face of reality, a wish-induced flight of fancy's dreams. He had never imagined—how could he?—that even as he was saying them,

224

like the working of some arcane spell they were already being brought to pass.

If only it were possible, he had said. And now it was.

David had driven the trap down to Lewes that afternoon; not in another of his despairing attempts to break the months-long exile imposed upon him by Amy, but in response to a note she had sent.

"I understand you and Ellis Bates had a meeting together at my house during my recent absence. This has very much vexed me. I suppose I was your topic of conversation?"

The rebuke, sharp as it was, had then been softened a little by her final sentence—"Hoping all is well with you . . ." above the bold, firm loop of her signature.

It was all the excuse David Linton had needed.

This time, chance fortune seemed to favour him, for he arrived at Tea Garden Lane to find Amy standing at her open front door, about to set off on a walk across the Downs. She looked mightily put out to see who it was reining in his horse at the foot of her steps; but after a brief, stilted exchange of conversation, she agreed with some reluctance that he might accompany her on the walk and say whatever it was he'd come for.

Seeing her again, after so long, was to the doctor's starved emotions like food at the end of a bitter fast. She was wearing a very modish day dress of light checked wool, the long skirts flared at the back with pleats and the short fitted jacket gathered at the shoulders; and this, with her beautiful hair piled up beneath a straw sailor hat, lent her appearance a lovely maturity and elegance.

Without waiting for him to return from taking his horse and trap round to the stables, she began walking away up the lane, forcing him to run after her to catch up.

"I wish I'd never written that wretched note," she said irritably, not looking round. "I might have known you'd use it as a pretext."

"A drowning man will grasp at anything," he answered, holding out his arm for her to take.

It was ignored.

"You've broken your word, David. You promised me you'd keep away."

"I have tried. Believe me, dearest, I've tried so very hard—"

"Then why do you persist in wanting to see me again?"

She quickened her pace along the lane, swinging her arms in a purposeful manner.

"You know why," David said mournfully, catching up once more. "Dear God, Amy, I've been driven near to breaking point these past months. Don't be angry with me . . . please."

"I'm not angry with you. I just wish you'd have the sense to see there's no use in hoping things might change. They won't."

"Not even after what happened between us?"

"Don't—!" The young woman snatched her hands to her ears. "I don't want to talk about that."

"But why not, for pity's sake?"

She let her hands fall again and threw her companion a look of vexed reproach. "It'd be too much like holding a post-mortem in the chance of finding life still left."

"There are some things which simply will not die, sweet heart, and my love for you is one of them. You'll never kill it. Never. No matter how hard you try."

There was no answer to this, beyond a quick tightening of the generous mouth and a slight shake of the head. Without bothering to see whether or not he would follow, she turned off the narrowing lane along a track leading away towards the open sunlit slopes of the Lewes Downs.

Ahead was a small belt of trees, and it was not until she'd gone past them that Amy broke her silence again and said in a curiously diffident tone, "I can't forget you, David . . . I can't put that night from my mind and say it never happened. But I don't encourage memories by harking back. I try and think of it as something belonging to a different time . . . different people, if you like."

Had she been looking at him as she spoke, she would have seen a terrible hurt show for a moment in the doctor's face.

"I wish we'd never done what we did," she went on heedlessly. "It was wrong . . . we both know that. It's gone and spoiled everything between us."

"It's spoiled nothing!" he cried miserably, feeling his world begin to fall apart to hear her saying these things. "Oh God,

226

Amy, how can I make you understand? All we did was share our love, prove how tenderly and dearly we cared for one another.''

Irritation sharpened her tone again. "The love we shared, David, was as friends and no more. The affection of kinship. It had precious little to do with the kind of love you wanted from me that night—and still want from me.''

"Did it mean nothing to you, then? Nothing at all?''

She paused and swung round upon him, her blue eyes darkening with emotion in the shadow of the sailor hat.

"Nothing? Oh—how can you ask such a thing! You were the first man I'd ever let touch me . . . d'you think it meant nothing to give myself to you? D'you think it meant nothing to fly in the face of conscience and loyalty and do something I knew in my heart I'd regret?''

"But why? Why?'' He seized her by the arms and grasped her tightly. "Why regret it, Amy?''

"It was wrong, I've told you.''

"Again, why?''

"I only did it to please you, David . . . because of our situation together that night, because it was what you wanted. I hadn't the will to say no.''

"I don't believe that!'' In his frustration and pain he shook her violently. "I don't believe it was only what *I* wanted. You took as much pleasure from our loving as I did. You were totally mine. Oh—Amy, Amy, the nights I've burned to hold you in my arms again. No one knows the hell I've suffered these past months, shut off from you, denied the sight of your face, the sound of your voice . . . I've been like a man possessed, craving for you day after empty day, needing you so. God forgive me, but there've been times when I've wanted to destroy myself, rather than go on living this torment. Oh, Amy . . . Amy, my love, my sweetest darling—''

He pulled her against him, and would have pressed his avid mouth to her lips had she not twisted her head to one side and pushed him away, wresting herself from his grip.

"Don't! David, don't—please. Go away. Go away, like you promised, and leave me alone. You're only making things worse, behaving like this.''

Tugging her hat into place, she turned back along the track, half-running to leave him behind.

227

"No, I won't go away," he cried after her. "You're my life, Amy. What is there left for me now if I lose you?"

She made no response, but continued on her determined, hurried course, head down, shoulders hunched, arms hugged about herself as though in self-defence.

David went after her.

"Answer me! What am I to do?"

"Leave me alone. Please. Do as I ask. Go away and leave me be."

Again he took hold of her, forcing her to stop and swing back to face him.

"There's someone else, isn't there. Some other man. No— don't struggle. I'll have the truth. It's that chap Herriot, isn't it. He's the one. You loved me well enough until he came along, damn him."

"Stop it—stop it! You must be mad, David—"

"Aye, mad with despair. Everything was fine between us both before you let your head be turned by a lot of smart talk."

"Leave go of my arm. You're hurting me." Amy's temper was starting to rise.

Heedless of the tell-tale high, bright spots on her cheeks, the doctor rushed on jealously, "Yes, I've been cast aside for that Bobby Dazzler, haven't I. It's he who's enjoying your favours now, I suppose—"

Amy's free hand came up and slapped him hard across one side of the face.

He stared at her; and in the sudden silence her breathing sounded unnaturally rapid, as though she were panting. Then she broke free, but instead of moving off, stood where she was, the bright spots gradually paling.

David bowed his head. "I'm sorry," he said humbly. "Forgive me. I shouldn't have said that. I didn't mean it."

"It doesn't matter."

There was another silence. Beyond the inner numbing anguish, he was aware of a number of disjointed sensations: the warmth of the sunlight on his skin, the green smell of the Downland turf, birdsong from the trees behind punctuating the warbling notes of larks in the cloudless sky.

"Will you marry him, do you think?"

She shook her head. "I don't know."

228

"Has he asked you?"

Another shake.

Desperately, he began, "If I were a free man . . . if I were to set Louisa aside . . ." Then stopped; and after a time started again more calmly, "Supposing there were no Louisa. Supposing something happened to her, and I was free again. Would you think more kindly of me then, my sweet? Would you marry *me*, if only it were possible?"

Amy's forehead was marked by a small frown between the dark straight brows. For several moments she looked into his face, as though seeking something there. Then, glancing away with a shrug, repeated her words.

"I don't know."

"If only it were possible . . ." he had said that afternoon.

Now, hunched at his desk in the Church Lane study, clutching another tumbler of whisky to dull the shock of seeing Louisa's crumpled, broken body, David turned the import of the day's tragedy over and over in his swimming mind.

The whole thing had taken on an aspect of bizarre distortion. Were it not that he'd knelt just now on the landing and touched the clammy flesh to close those staring, empty eyes, he would have been only half-convinced that his wife wasn't playing another of her silly childish tricks to deceive him.

How in the name of heaven had it happened? Did she fall from her Bath chair at the head of the stairs, tip forward somehow while reaching for the rail? Or was there some other, far more sinister explanation? And if the latter, then how much significance should be attached to the figure whom Albert said he saw at the gate?

David gulped another mouthful of whisky. It might have been anyone: the area round Weatherfield green had been swarming with strange faces this afternoon. But why had Albert been so emphatically convinced it was himself, unless the man were the same height and wearing the same type of clothing.

And why did his mind keep going back to one name—Ellis Bates?

229

23

"But surely," Isabelle Bethway exclaimed, "surely you never thought Linton himself might have had some hand in his wife's death?"

Amy made a little gesture of uncertainty. "I didn't know what to think, Aunt Belle. The suspicion did cross my mind, yes. I mean, it all seemed too much of a coincidence."

"What, that the poor woman should be found with a broken neck the very same day there'd been all this wild talk about putting her aside?"

Amy nodded.

"But her husband was in Lewes with you when the accident happened," her aunt pointed out.

"Oh, I know that now. But when I heard about it first, when that constable turned up on my doorstep to ask all those questions, I thought they were holding David to blame . . . that in the state he was in that day, *he* was somehow responsible."

"The front wheel of the Bath chair had worked itself loose," Isabelle reminded her practically. "No one could have foreseen that the wretched thing would give way and pitch Mrs Linton headlong downstairs. It was just one of those unfortunate things. The inquest verdict was quite specific, my dear."

"Accidental death. Yes."

Amy turned her head beneath the fringed parasol and looked out across the sunlit lawn where she and her aunt were sitting together. The slight coolness which had arisen between them over cousin Francis and his misconduct with Ellis Bates's governess, was done with and forgotten now, and she was here to spend a fortnight's holiday with the Bethways beside the sea at the vicarage at Eastbourne.

She needed the change of air. The inquest on Louisa

Linton had been held a week previously; and though Amy was not called to give evidence, her name had been mentioned at the hearing as a witness who would, if required, testify to the whereabouts of the deceased's husband at the time the body was discovered.

It had all been very distressing—and not a little embarrassing; and the fact that David Linton had been in her company that day instead of attending his wife to see their daughter crowned Queen of the May had fuelled the murmurs of gossip in Weatherfield. There had even been a letter addressed to Amy at Tea Garden Lane, a nasty vindictive thing which she'd ripped up in disgust, accusing her and David of conniving together to bring about Louisa's sad end.

"Come—cheer up, do," Isabelle Bethway urged, seeing the despondency in her niece's lovely face. "Brooding upon the past won't bring it back to alter anything. I know. We've been through all this before, remember, when Frank . . . when your father got himself involved with the Law."

There was no resentment in her tone. That earlier inquest had been held in the year of Amy's birth, 1871, and as a result of its verdict Frank Flynn had been sent for trial at Lewes on a charge of the manslaughter of his mistress's husband. But these intervening years of happy marriage to Alec Bethway had soothed away the pain of memory, and Isabelle was able now to look back with nothing more than a sister's deep regret for a brother's wasted life.

This time, there had been a less sensational outcome. Though questions had been raised about the identity of some stranger seen in the vicinity of the Linton house at the supposed time of Louisa's fall, the Coroner had not hesitated to return his verdict of death being due to accidental causes.

"I'm sorry the family have had to be dragged into this awful business, Aunt Belle," Amy said quietly, reaching out to clasp the other's hand where it rested on the open sketchpad. "You and Uncle Alec have been so very kind about it all, letting me come here to stay."

She had unburdened herself to them both of David Linton's difficult demands upon her relationship with him, and the tone those demands had taken in recent months; but prudently said nothing of the night spent together at Tea

231

Garden Lane, judging it wiser to practise discretion on that count.

Isabelle gave a warm smile. "We're glad you agreed to come, my dear. This has always been your home, after all, and we hope you'll continue to regard it as such." She moved aside the pad on which she'd been making a pencil drawing of her niece in profile, and went on, "You *will* reconsider Alec's invitation, won't you?"

"To return to live here when I sell the house in Lewes?"

"Indeed. It would give such pleasure to have you with us again."

Withdrawing her hand, Amy sat back in the garden chair and began twirling her parasol in a manner which betrayed a certain agitation. When she had mentioned at dinner last night her intention of moving from Tea Garden Lane, she had not expected her relatives to be so demonstratively solicitous for her future welfare. She had tried to explain her position clearly, saying that it would be difficult, after being mistress of her own house, to become a dependent again, and that she did not wish to forfeit her freedom and be once more beholden to their charity; but all this had merely sounded selfish and petty and the Bethways had refused to accept such argument, pressing her to accept their roof as her own.

Speaking hesitantly and choosing her words with care, she tried again to explain herself.

"Aunt Belle . . . it really isn't possible for me to come back to live with you and Uncle Alec. You see, I've already made plans for the future. I hope to find a smaller place . . . a cottage, may be . . . to share as a home with my mother."

"Amy! Oh, my dear, what are you talking about?" Her aunt's expression was at once one of horrified astonishment. "Share a place with your mother? Why, Rosannah's in no fit state for any such thing! What in heaven has put that preposterous notion into your head?"

"The visit I made to Heathbury . . . it upset me so. I've been haunted ever since by the idea of doing something for her. You've been to that asylum, Aunt Belle. You've seen for yourself the condition she lives in, the way she's expected to pass the rest of her life."

"But it's the only way she knows. Oh, child, you may

232

think you'd be acting for the best, to take her away from there, but it would be a cruelty—believe me, a great cruelty. Your mother is far, far happier left where she is than brought back into a world she's forgotten even exists."

Amy gave the parasol a few more sharp little twirls.

"Besides," the older woman went on earnestly, "how on earth would you ever manage to care for her? You know how she is, likely at any time to fly into one of her frenzied rages."

"I thought . . . well, Minnie and Ted would be with us, of course."

"Oh? You've already suggested it to them?"

"To Minnie, yes."

"And what was her answer?"

Amy sketched a faint shrug. "She told me she'd have to give it some thinking over."

"I should say so! You and the Brocklebanks in one small cottage with poor, crazy Rosannah lifting the roof with her screams—" Isabelle Bethway let out a disbelieving laugh. "Oh, Amy, no. No, my dear, it would never, never do. Please, listen to sense and put this ludicrous notion from you."

"But I wouldn't keep a dog in a place like that at Heathbury."

"Of course not. And it does credit to your compassion that you should want to help someone, mother or no, who's almost a stranger to you. But you must see, Rosannah is insane. Quite insane. And has been these many years. In her own deluded imaginings, she's living a life of perfect contentment as the wife of Dolly de Retz, and mistress of a gracious country estate somewhere in France. Would you take that away from her, that illusion of happiness, and give her instead the plain, harsh truth of her pitiable madness?"

Amy bowed her head. For a time she made no answer. In her mind's eye she saw again that gaunt, fantastic figure who played out her life in some private world of make-believe, dressed in the threads of self-created fantasy, beguiling herself with a foreign tongue and waiting, always waiting, for a lover who'd been dead for as many long years as this delusion had persisted, flawing all sense of reality.

Slowly, the young woman's head was raised again.

"No. You're right, Aunt Belle. It's best to leave things as they are."

The other heaved an audible sigh of relief. There were times when this headstrong niece of hers provoked quite as much concern as did her son Francis. Thank the good Lord he at least was off their hands now that he'd got his commission as an officer cadet and was discovering for himself the rough, tough discipline and duty of a soldier's life stationed at the regimental depot at Southover.

A soft breeze blowing in from the sea fluttered the pages of the pad, recalling Isabelle Bethway's thoughts to more pleasant occupation.

"Come," she said lightly, "let me finish this sketch. It's a pity to leave off just when I've caught a good likeness of you."

Amy folded her parasol and placed it on the grass at her feet. "May I have it when it's done?"

"Of course."

Taking her pencil, her aunt began sketching with deft, smooth strokes, looking up at quick intervals to catch the curve and contour of the sitter's profile. For a while neither spoke, and in the stillness there came clearly the sounds of horse traffic on the sea road beyond the garden, and the plaintive mew of gulls soaring and dipping above in the cloud-flecked sky.

Thinking aloud, Isabelle remarked after a while, "Your gentleman friend from Dorset—he knew Mrs Linton, didn't he?"

"Ralph Herriot? Yes, slightly. Why?"

"Oh, no reason in particular. I was wondering whether you'd written to tell him the news."

"He'll have read it for himself in the papers, I dare say." Amy's tone sounded suddenly flat. "They made such a nine-days-wonder of the whole thing."

"Mm."

Another busy silence followed.

Then—"Have you made any plans to see him this summer? I was saying to Alec only the other day, you enjoyed yourself so much as his parents' guest after the Bashford wedding, perhaps you were hoping they'd invite you again."

"I don't think that's likely. Not now."

"Oh? Why not?"

"Well . . . Ralph gave me a choice. Between him and David Linton. He said I must decide which friendship of the two I preferred."

"That was being a bit churlish, surely?"

Amy shook her head. "He knew David was in love with me . . . and like a fool, I wouldn't believe him. I thought Ralph was simply being awkward."

"But why should this make any difference to whether or not you meet again this summer?" Isabelle held the sketch-pad at arm's length and squinted at her work.

"After he's read about David spending that afternoon with me in Lewes?" Her niece made a little gesture of hopelessness. "I've broken my side of the bargain, Aunt Belle. In more ways than one. Do you think he'd want me now?"

As though in answer, from above on the vicarage gable there came the strident cries of a gull, like raucous laughter.

Had Ellis Bates been a man to excite sympathy amongst his associates, it may have been possible that one at least would have been conscious that Her Majesty's Inspector of Schools appeared to be wrestling with some greatly burdensome anxiety. As it was, however, the aloofness of his personal nature precluded the close attention of his fellows, and if his high, pale brow seemed more heavily marked of late by the crease of a frown, and his manner more brusque and unsmiling than hitherto, there was no one to remark upon this fact other than the servants of his own household.

He was not a man to pass the time of day in idle conversation; and unless there happened to be something quite specific which he wished to discuss, he had never been known to make any of the observations customary to normal courtesy, beyond the brief civility of a "good morning" or "goodnight".

It was, therefore, all the more astonishing that Megwynn Evans should be asked by her employer if he might accompany her with Laura and Esmond that afternoon to the paddock; and not only that, but to hear him enquire after her health and that of her family for all the world as though this concern were a casual everyday observance.

235

The two children were markedly subdued by their father's presence on the walk, and instead of running about at play, stayed close beside Megwynn's skirts, answering her in monosyllables and casting her companion little nervous darting glances.

Upon reaching the gate of the paddock, she had almost to cajole them both into feeding Esmond's pony—a treat which was normally the highlight of the afternoon.

"Do I make my children nervous, do you suppose, Miss Evans?" Ellis Bates asked, with an unwonted candour which startled the young governess considerably.

"What's that? Nervous, sir?"

"Yes. I watch the two of them occasionally from my study window. It seems to me that they are usually far more animated when in your company alone, and I must therefore presume that it is my presence here today which is to blame for their lack of spirits. Would you not agree?"

Megwynn skirted carefully around this question, confining her answer to a tactful, "Well, sir, all children are a little strange, look you, when something occurs to disturb what they're used to."

"Ah. So it is the interruption to their routine which has quietened them both?"

"It is, sir."

Ellis nodded; and after further consideration, permitted himself a thin smile.

Now that Laura and Esmond had removed themselves away from their father's immediate proximity, their natural liveliness was starting to return to give life and a little laughter to the game they were playing together at the edge of the paddock.

Watching them, the schools inspector observed after a while, "I must confess, Miss Evans, I have never known my children to be as content with a governess as they are with you. Your care of them reflects greatly to your credit."

A blush deepened the rosy hue of Megwynn's plump cheeks as she ducked her head in pleasure at this compliment. "It's very kind of you to say so, sir."

"Not at all. Would you care to walk a way further along?" Her employer made a motion of the hand to indicate the grassy path running beside the paddock fence. "The sun really has a deal of heat in it for the time of year. It will be cooler under the trees."

When they had gone a short distance and still had the children well in view, he went on in what for him was almost jolly fashion, "So you have had no more thoughts of leaving us, eh?"

"No, sir. No more thoughts." There was a vehement shake of the head beneath the calico sun bonnet.

"Good. It would have been such a great pity had you deserted us for Eastbourne."

"Yes, sir."

"The children are grown so very attached to you."

"Yes, sir."

"You might not have found your new position at all as congenial."

"No, sir."

"Come—is this all you have to say for yourself, Miss Evans? Yes sir, no sir?" Ellis turned to look at her and essayed another of his thin little smiles. "May I not at least know that you are happy in your service here?"

"Oh, indeed, Mr Bates. I am very happy, thank you, sir. My employment gives me great satisfaction."

"Excellent. That is as it should be. And you are sure, now, quite sure, that you will not allow yourself to be tempted elsewhere?"

"I am quite sure, sir. I know I'd never find a better situation and—and . . ." The young governess paused awkwardly, not certain whether she'd be wise to say what she was about to.

Her employer pounced upon the hesitation. "And what, Miss Evans?"

"Well, sir, it's like this, see. You took me back when you needn't, gave me another chance. Perhaps I shouldn't be telling you so, but that's made me feel I owe you a great loyalty . . . you and Esmond, and little Laura, sir."

She looked up doubtfully, wondering whether she'd spoken out of turn; but Ellis Bates appeared quite extraordinarily elated by her timid declaration, and stood rubbing his long, white hands and nodding his head and smiling his tight-lipped smile at her.

"I am pleased to hear you say that, Miss Evans. Very

237

pleased! It is right and proper that you should offer your service in a spirit of loyalty. Of faithfulness, also—and trust-worthiness." He leaned forward, fixing her keenly with his gaze. "You would agree that you were to be trusted, would you not?"

"Oh yes, indeed, sir. Upon my honour."

"As I thought. 'The servant is worthy of her hire.' I am a good judge of character, Miss Evans, and believe me, you would not have lasted above a month in my employ had I found you fallen one jot below the high standard which I set for the goodly conduct of my household. I deplore all grace-less, false and weak-minded behaviour, and you may be sure, I would not tolerate such among those in my service."

Megwynn responded with a nervous little nod of the head, and covered any tell-tale look of guilt by glancing over her shoulder to where her two young charges were engaged in walking Merry the pony about the field.

"As a mark of my satisfaction," her employer continued in the same curiously animated tone, "I propose to make an increase in your pay as from the end of this month."

"An increase, sir?" She turned quickly back again, her expression at once one of mingled pleasure and astonishment.

"I had thought an additional two shillings a week a fair reward for your constancy and devotion."

"Two shillings—!" This was a generous sum indeed. It meant almost five pounds more a year, at a time when an under-housemaid working a sixteen-hour day earned a living wage of barely more than nine pounds.

"Oh, Mr Bates, sir—oh, there's kind you are—" she began warmly; then, at a loss to know how to thank him sufficiently, fell silent, shaking her head and smiling in dis-belief.

Ellis Bates's gaze was fixed upon her still in careful scru-tiny.

After a few moments she managed to collect herself enough to ask him, "Oh sir, how am I ever to repay you for your goodness?"

"If you wish to show some tangible proof of your gratitude, my dear . . . why, then perhaps you would do something in return." A pause. "You see, I have a favour to ask of you."

238

"A favour?"

"Yes. You will grant it me, I hope?"

Megwynn returned the gaze, and saw in the ice-blue eyes something which might almost have been entreaty.

She smiled again.

"I would do anything for you, Mr Bates. Anything."

24

That fateful May Day, the young governess had asked permission to take Laura and Esmond out for the afternoon to hear the band of the Sussex Rifle Volunteers play on the castle green above Lewes high street. The other house servants having been granted a holiday, this seemed to Ellis Bates an ideal opportunity to drive across to Weatherfield, as David Linton had suggested to him, and take Mrs Linton firmly to task over the woman's ridiculously deluded behaviour.

As it happened, her letters had grown fewer in recent weeks, but there had started creeping into them a spiteful self-pitying tone which hinted at threats to inform others— "those best placed in the community"—of the schools inspector's cold neglect "of the love you did once so warmly encourage."

The whole tedious business obviously required drastic action to bring it to an end.

Setting out from Lewes after an early luncheon, he had arrived at his destination in good time to find a place for his horse and trap at the top of the high street, away from the hurly-burly of activity on the village green; and after giving a boy a penny to water the horse, had taken the short cut along a cobbled twitten which ran at the back of a row of cottages to bring him into the bottom end of Church Lane.

It was much quieter here, the noise of crowds and music deadened by trees, and the air was full of the sun-warmed scents of mock orange and lilac and stocks from bordering gardens.

The Linton house was easily to be identified by a brass plate inset into the gate post:
DAVID W. LINTON ESQ., M.R.C.S., L.R.C.P.

Ellis paused for several moments before pushing open the wicket at the side of the double carriage gates. Was he perhaps not being a trifle over-hasty to come here on such an errand, he asked himself? Might it not after all be more prudent to ignore the woman's silly threats, and, instead, continue on his way to the top of the lane, pay his respects at his father's grave, and return at once to Lewes? At least the day's journey would not have been wasted.

The frown deepened between his brows.

Then, with a resolute shake of the head, he put out a gloved hand and lifted the wicket latch.

The driveway to the house was deserted, with nothing to disturb the stillness except the dart and flutter of birds in the neatly-clipped shrubberies and a few early butterflies curvetting among purple clumps of dwarf iris. Approaching the front entrance porch, he rang the bell-pull; and when there was no response, rang it a second time, hearing its distant jangle reverberate somewhere at the back of the house.

After several minutes had passed, he stepped out from the porch and walked a short way back along the drive. Pausing here, he turned for a brief examination of the upper storey; and was about to conclude that there was no one at home, when a sudden movement at one of the net-draped windows caught his eye.

As he watched, the movement resolved itself into a woman's arms and hands struggling to raise the sash.

"Hello?" he said loudly. "Hello?"

A face now appeared at the opening; and a moment later a voice which he recognised as Louisa Linton's called down, "Who is it there?"

Ellis walked back a little further, so that he could be more clearly seen.

She now evidently recognised her caller at once, for she cried out, "Oh, will you come in, please? The scullery door at the back is open. I'm sorry you must find your own way up. I'm here on the second floor landing."

With that, she lowered the sash and retreated from view.

The schools inspector looked about him in an uncertain fashion; then, growing resolute once more, took himself along the drive past the stables and round to the back of the house. Entering by the rear door, he found his way through the servants' area to the scullery passage, and from there into the dim-lit coolness of the entrance hall.

"Mr Bates?" He heard Louisa Linton's voice from somewhere overhead.

"Yes. I'm here."

There was a trundling noise, and he recalled from one of her maddening letters that she now had to rely upon a wheeled Bath chair to get herself about.

Grasping the carved mahogany balustrade, he was about to ascend the main flight of stairs when his progress was dramatically arrested by a sudden cry of alarm. It was repeated almost immediately, followed by a clattering crash as of something heavy falling; and then a shrill wailing scream—cut off abruptly as the crash ended in a sickeningly loud thud on the landing above.

"Mrs Linton?"

Silence.

Ellis hesitated. "Mrs Linton?" he called again, tentatively.

No answer. Nothing but a curious spinning sound which gradually slowed and then finally ceased altogether.

He stood biting his lip at the foot of the stairs; then with a muttered exclamation went running up, taking two steps at a time.

"God in heaven . . ."

For a moment he hung back at what he found there on the landing, shocked by the sight. A sudden feeling of nausea threatened to part him from his half-digested luncheon; but after a few seconds it passed, leaving small beads of sweat standing out on his brow.

Faint-heartedly, he went over to kneel beside the sprawled, motionless body and stretched out a hand, vexed to see how much it trembled as he held it to the half-open mouth to feel for any warmth of breath.

There was none.

He passed his fingers up and down in front of the staring eyes. They remained fixed, gazing sightlessly upward with a faintly surprised expression. The only movement was a stream of blood flowing crookedly across one cheek to form a widening pool matching the scarlet pattern of the carpet.

"God in heaven . . ." Ellis said again quietly.

He got to his feet and backed away towards the head of

the stairs. An accident. It had been an accident. Of course it had. But—yes, but suppose someone were to come into the house at this moment and find him here? How the deuce was he to explain?

His mind began to race. What infernal ill luck, that this should happen at the very time he was alone with the woman! Supposing her husband were to hold him somehow to blame? Supposing the police were to question him about his reason for being here? What was he to say? That Mrs Linton had been pestering him for attention and he'd come to put a stop to it? That would be damning himself out of his own mouth.

And what if the matter were to reach the newspapers? Think of the notoriety! He had been seriously considering marrying again, to the niece of his colleague Frank Stone, of Tunbridge Wells. Dorothy was an agreeable, quiet young woman. She would make an ideal second wife, and a good mother to Esmond and Laura. What chance though would he ever stand of winning her if his name were to be publicly mentioned in connection with Louisa Linton?

Ellis wiped a trickle of sweat from his temple, and backed further away.

Wait, though—no one knew he was here in the house, did they? His visit had been unplanned. He'd made no mention of it to anyone in Lewes. And so far as he was aware, he had not been seen in Church Lane.

His lips set in a thin, bloodless line. Replacing his black bowler hat, he took a few hesitant steps down the stairs. Then, with one final fleeting backward look towards the landing, scrambled down the rest of the flight and was through the hall and out at the rear door as fast as his legs would take him.

The house drive was deserted still as he hastened along in the concealment of the shrubberies, eyes moving this way and that, alert for any sound, any movement; and on reaching the gate, he leaned warily out to glance up and down the lane before opening the wicket to cross over into the shade of the trees.

Towards the bottom of Church Lane, his hurrying figure was passed by several couples walking up to the green for the May Day tea, and he had to force himself to slow to a more leisurely pace so as not to attract attention, keeping his head averted and pretending to mop his brow so that his face would be hidden by the large white handkerchief.

In less than five minutes he had reached his horse and trap; and in another five, was driving like Jehu on the road out of Weatherfield.

"I was, of course, extremely sorry to learn of the death of your wife," Ellis Bates said calmly. "A great tragedy. May I express my condolences, Doctor Linton."

David Linton gestured an acknowledgement.

"Will you not be seated, sir?" his host went on, indicating a chair at one side of the empty fireplace.

"Thank you."

"May I offer some refreshment? A glass of port, perhaps?"

A glass of whisky would have been more to the doctor's preference, to add to those he'd drunk just a short time ago in the public bar at Lewes railway station; but it would have been discourteous to say so, especially since he was here at Ellis's house without invitation.

"A glass of port would be acceptable."

He looked around the room. It was austerely furnished, one wall entirely hidden by a massive library bookcase whose shelves behind the glass doors were filled from end to end with leather-bound volumes, and a large desk occupying the centre of the floor, with a table beside it to take the overflow of neat piles of papers. Apart from a few chairs, that was all; except for a large portrait in oils above the marble fireplace.

David gave it a cursory glance before moving to seat himself. It showed a fair-haired, melancholy-featured gentleman in sombre clerical dress, standing with one hand holding an opened book and the other resting upon the back of a prie-dieu. From the similarity of appearance, he judged that this must be some close relative of his host.

Accepting the glass of port, he motioned towards the portrait, and was about to make some polite comment on it when he was forestalled by Ellis Bates saying affably, "A pleasing work, would you not agree, sir? I had it made from a copy of a studio photograph."

"From a photograph? Is that so? Remarkable." The doctor went up to make a closer examination. "Impossible to say it was not painted directly from life."

"Indeed, would that it had been. But the photograph was the only likeness I had of my late father. It was taken before his marriage, when he was curate of All Souls here in Lewes."

David nodded, a trifle bemused by the unexpected civility of this conversation.

"He was afterwards rector of Weatherfield," the other continued, seating himself in the opposite chair. "No doubt you may have seen his name among the list of incumbents upon the wall of St Anne's church."

"No doubt."

"It was purely by a fortuitous circumstance that the photograph passed into my possession. Not many years ago, it came to light in a bundle of old sermon notes at All Souls vicarage, and would have been disposed of as waste for the fire had not my father's name been found upon it."

"Indeed?"

"Indeed." Ellis crossed one leg over the other and leaned back to take a sip from his own glass.

"As you say, sir. A fortuitous circumstance." His guest took a drink himself; then, clearing his throat unnecessarily, went on, "You are interested to know, I'm sure, why it is I've called upon you this evening."

"It had occurred to me to wonder, yes."

"I will not mince words, sir. Your name was not mentioned in the evidence given at the inquest into my wife's death."

The other raised an eyebrow a fraction. "And ought it to have been?"

"I think perhaps yes."

"For what reason, sir?" Still, the friendly, conversational tone of voice.

"It would have suited you very well to have my wife—shall we say, silenced? The attitude you expressed toward her at our last meeting was sufficiently emphasised to leave no doubt of your ill-will."

"I agree. I do agree. At the time I felt a great deal of ill-will, occasioned, you may remember, by the irritation of Mrs Linton's persistent soliciting of my attention."

"Of which you are now free."

"Indeed."

David's manner grew more agitated. Leaning forward in his chair, he said, "I must be frank with you, Mr Bates. I cannot put from my mind the idea that you may have had some hand in causing Louisa's tragic accident."

Ellis smiled slightly; though a careful study of his expression might have revealed a certain wariness.

"Come, sir, you do not enter a man's house and drink his wine, and then accuse him to his face of criminal misconduct. What proof have you for this supposition?"

"Someone was seen at my house gate that afternoon."

"Someone was seen at your gate?"

"Someone resembling your description, Mr Bates."

The other smiled again. Beneath the facade of polite amusement, he was frantically racking his brain to think who might possibly have recognised him in Church Lane. Apart from the group he'd passed at the end, there had not been a soul in sight.

Lightly he said, "My dear Doctor Linton, I could take you into Lewes high street at this moment and show you a dozen men resembling me in description. It is my misfortune to have an unremarkable appearance and a conservative taste in attire."

He paused, and made a little gesture of the hand.

"You'll join me in another glass of port?"

Automatically, almost, David held out his empty glass. This interview was not going at all as he'd envisaged. He had intended to come and put his case bluntly without any equivocation, tackle the schools inspector in a confrontation which might confirm his suspicions. Yet here he was, striving to present his argument and allowing himself to be totally unmanned by the other's bland, imperturbable hospitality.

"You have been frank with me, sir," went on Ellis Bates once he had re-seated himself. "And I shall now be equally frank with you. I will confess, beyond my first shock on learning of your wife's sudden death, I cannot in all honesty say that I was greatly affected by it. Relieved, rather. You see, it is my intention to marry again—ah, that surprises you? But yes, it is so. I mean to take a second wife, and Mrs Linton's obsessional behaviour had it continued, might

246

easily have placed me in a most awkward position. More especially in view of her threats to make our non-existent *'grand amour'* a matter of public knowledge by exposing it to my immediate superiors as well as to my parish minister."

"Louisa threatened that?" David seemed sincerely non-plussed by this revelation.

"She did indeed. You do not believe me? Well, I have the proof here to hand."

As he spoke, the schools inspector indicated his desk; and getting again to his feet, went across to it. Selecting a key from several small ones attached to his heavy Prince Albert watch chain, he bent to unlock a side drawer.

"Instead of destroying them as I did all the rest, I pre-served this later correspondence as evidence of blackmail should I ever be called upon to defend my reputation in this wretched business."

He took out a bundle of some three or four letters and passed them to the doctor.

"Read for yourself, sir!"

For several long moments the other examined in silence the oblong manilla envelopes with their large, looping script dashed across the paper in Louisa's untidy scrawl. Then, with a shake of the head, he handed them back.

"I have no need to read anything, Mr Bates. I've already had sight of a number of your replies to my wife, found hidden in her room, and you could not have made yourself more expressly clear."

A pause; then, in a firmer voice, "I must say, however, and quite candidly, that looking through them, my suspicion of your involvement in her death has been all the more strongly aroused."

Ellis tossed the letters down into the drawer, and closed and locked it again.

In a manner that was close to being amiable, he responded, "You cannot have heard me clearly, Doctor Linton. I am to take another wife. A most advantageous alliance with a family of influence which will not only bring personal happiness but should add greatly to my professional standing. Do you think I would be fool enough to jeopardise all this by soiling my hands with the taint of violence, and putting at risk my good name in the community—not to mention the future security of my children?"

"But you had the motive for violence. And someone closely resembling you *was* seen near my house that afternoon," David came back doggedly.

"And if I were able to prove to you beyond all doubt that it could not possibly have been I, would you believe me then?"

There was a brooding hesitation; then, reluctantly a nod.

"Very well." Ellis moved to the side of the fireplace and pulled the bell-rope.

When after a few minutes his ring was answered by the maid, he said, "Oh, Florrie, would you ask Miss Evans to come down?"

His guest finished his port and rose to place the glass beside the lead-cut crystal tantalus on the side-table. Neither man spoke.

In a little while more there was another knock at the study door.

"Come."

David turned as a plump young woman with a pleasant freckled face and brown hair worn plaited about her head entered the room.

"Doctor Linton, this is my children's governess, Miss Megwynn Evans."

Polite inclinations of acknowledgement.

"My dear, would you be so good," Ellis continued calmly, "as to inform the doctor of my whereabouts on the afternoon of May the first. The May Day holiday."

"The May Day holiday, sir?" Not by a single flicker of the eye did Megwynn betray herself. She had not the faintest notion why her employer should have primed her to make a specific answer in the event of this question being asked. He had his reasons, and doubtless they were good ones. That was enough for her.

"Why, sir," she said easily, "that was the afternoon you spent with the children and me on the castle green, listening to the band of the Rifle Volunteers."

25

Beyond the high, forbidding red brick walls of Heathbury's
Bethlehem Hospital for the Insane, the world basked in
one of those gloriously warm early July days of which childhood memories are made, with a sky that reflected the
colour of cornflowers amid the ripening field-gold of the
countryside.

Inside, it was as though the dead grey hand of winter still
held an iron grip upon the place. No warmth seemed to
penetrate the stone walls, and what light there was in the
vaulted corridors came from the dingy mustard flicker of
gas-lamps. Even here, in the chapel, the sunshine was reluctant to shed its rays, creeping palely in through narrow
lancets in the roof to cast a subdued reflection upon the
stone paved floor far below.

Dressed as she was in light summer cotton, Amy Flynn
could not stop shivering. It was not merely the cold in this
place seeping into her bones after the heat of the golden day
outside: equally it was an inner bleakness caused by the
numbing effect of personal desolation.

Rosannah Weldrake Flynn died here in the asylum two
days before, at the age of forty-eight. Her death was not
entirely unexpected; but at the last she had seemed to grow
strangely happy, saying several times in English to her nurse,
"I can go now. Dolly is here. He's come to take me home to
him."

The only sound in the chapel came from little Minnie
Brocklebank, sitting behind Amy, a handkerchief pressed to
her mouth to stifle her grief. Beside her, Isabelle Bethway's
head was bent forward above clasped hands. Belle's husband Alec had been here for a while to pray with the three of
them at the open coffin, but had left a short time ago to see
the overseer, Mr MacRae, in his office.

Amy hugged her arms about herself, against grief as much as against the dank chill in this sombre place. If only Ralph were here, she thought bleakly, to dispel this cheerless atmosphere with the warmth of his presence; to lift her spirits with a few quiet words of humour. She had not heard from him in weeks now, and her headstrong wilfulness in thinking she had no need of him was being gradually crushed as much by bitter self-knowledge as by the pain of his rejection.

What cruel irony, that pride should have made her scorn to take his love when it was offered . . . and now it was pride again which held her back from confessing how much he'd come to mean to her.

She gave a tremulous sigh, and rising from her seat, went forward to look one last time upon her dead mother. The body had been laid out in a shroud, but no one had thought to colour the shrunken cheeks as was generally done, so that the face resembled an empty mask, its once-generous lips like a bloodless scar in the livid grey of the features. There was no trace now of the imperious beauty which had once mocked the tittle-tattling tongues of Lewes with its flaunted sensuality; nothing but a shell sucked dry by Death.

"Amy . . . Amy, dear."

There was a light touch on her arm.

"Come away now, do. It's time to take our leave."

She nodded dumbly; and after a few moments allowed her aunt to lead her away from the coffin along the aisle to the double doors of the chapel. Minnie, still sniffing noisily, got up to follow behind them, her lace-up boots scraping on the cold floor.

Once beyond the doors, Isabelle Bethway spoke again. "Mr MacRae will wish to see you . . . your mother's effects, the disposal of her body—"

"She's to be buried in Lewes," Amy answered at once, quietly. "In the family vault at All Souls. I'm not leaving her here, to lie among strangers."

"Of course. Your Uncle Alec will see to all the arrangements."

They began to walk along the corridor towards the overseer's office, and now that they were free of the stony silence of the chapel the air all about was filled again with sound, the constant muted wash of sound of a bedlam swelling and receding beyond the shadows of gaslight.

How can the sane stay in a place like this and not be driven mad themselves, Amy wondered, accepting the overseer's invitation to be seated when the office door had closed behind them upon that dreadful dirge. She looked at him doubtfully; and found herself reassured by the calmness of his manner and the steady, kindly smile he gave.

The outside world of summer had managed to intrude a little here, and not even the iron bars at the window could keep the sunlight from pouring in and patterning the floor with dusty squares of gold. She sat back, feeling the chapel chill easing from her, and returned his smile with something more like confidence.

Indicating the Reverend Alec Bethway sitting to one side in close perusal of a document, Mr MacRae explained, "Acting on behalf of the Board of Guardians, I've arranged with Mr Bethway for the handing over of the body for burial. Since I understand from him that ye're of age now, Miss Flynn, I have to ask ye to sign for its receipt, upon the authorisation I have here."

He held up a paper.

"It's a mere formality, d'ye follow. But we have to have a record."

Amy nodded. "Of course."

She looked across at her aunt's husband. With a motion of the hand he invited her to proceed, saying, "It's for you to do, my dear, as next of kin. The rest of the paperwork I myself will deal with on your behalf."

She nodded again.

"There is one other business still needing discussion," Mr MacRae observed carefully when the young woman had re-seated herself. "As it relates to a private matter, I wonder if I should ask you, ma'am—" directing a look at Minnie Brocklebank——"if ye'd be so good as to step outside the door a wee while?"

"No—Minnie shall stay," Amy said at once, putting out a hand. "She's one of the family. She has my full trust. Anything there is to discuss, sir, may safely be said in front of her, believe me."

"Very well. As ye wish."

Taking up a pair of steel-framed spectacles, the other set them upon his nose; and after referring briefly to a second paper on the desk in front of him, began without further preamble, "You and your late mother lived as no better than strangers, Miss Flynn, so I presume to suppose ye have scant knowledge of matters pertaining to the deceased's financial position. I must explain, therefore, that at the time she was first admitted to this institution in—" he consulted the paper—"in 1871, Mrs Flynn was in receipt of a private income from her father's estate."

"That would be your grandfather, Norris Weldrake," put in Alec.Bethway. "I see from these documents here that he made a settlement upon your mother which was to remain hers and hers alone for life, even in the event of her marriage . . . or incapacity through illness, which he seems to have foreseen."

"Just so." The overseer lowered his spectacles to glance across the top of them. "It was the income from this settlement which has been paying all these years for your mother to be kept under safe supervision here. Now that she is dead, as the sole heir of her estate it passes to you, Miss Flynn. D'ye follow?"

The blunt, prosaic manner in which this information was given robbed it of any immediate impact, and for several moments Amy sat in uncomprehending silence, unable to marshal her thoughts. She had supposed there must be money coming from somewhere to pay for Rosannah's board and nursing, but had never bothered her head to enquire its source. And Grandfather Norris Weldrake was but a shadowy figure from the long-ago past; a name she'd heard mentioned once or twice as a child by her Uncle Harry Weldrake, and only then in cursing reference to money.

Money . . .

"Does this—does this mean I'm an heiress?" she asked, wonderingly. "Does it mean the Weldrake money comes to me now?"

"Aye. But I wouldna' say it makes you an heiress exactly, ma'am. Comfortably off—if ye're careful."

"Oh, my dear, just think!" Isabelle Bethway leaned forward to clasp her niece's hand. "Now you may not need to sell the house after all."

It was as though the sun had transferred itself to shine from Amy's face. Her expression lit up, her eyes widened, and her parted lips curved into a disbelieving smile.

Then, almost beside herself, she leapt to her feet and turning, cried, "Did you hear that, Minnie? I don't have to sell the house. Oh, I don't have to sell the house! We can go on living there just as before, you and me and Ted. Everything will be all right now. I'll be able to afford to give you proper wages. And we can settle the tradesmen's bills at last . . . and stock up the larder . . . and open accounts like respectable folk. Oh, Minnie, Minnie—can you imagine what this will mean for us!"

There was a watery grin and a nod in answer.

"But I tell you some'at," the housekeeper observed, sniffing back her tears, "our Ted's a-going to miss catching rabbits on the Downs wi' his blessed ferrets."

David Linton flung himself round, hands outstretched in desperate appeal.

"But *why* won't you say you'll marry me? *Why*?"

Again the young woman shook her head, this time more vehemently, and the expression in her eyes should have warned him not to press his demands any further. Without looking at him, she swung on her heel and walked past him to the drawing room door.

"Where are you going?" he cried after her.

"I'm going nowhere, David. It's you who are leaving."

She opened the door, and stood there, her back to him, hand on the polished brass knob, waiting.

"Will you please take yourself from my house?"

"No. Not until I get the answer I want."

"You've already had my answer."

"It's not the one I came for."

"It's the only one you're getting. Now will you go please."

The doctor sat down again on the chesterfield sofa, and buried his face in his hands.

"Why won't you understand," he said bleakly. "I love you, Amy. I love you more than heaven and earth together. I'm nothing without you, nothing. My life is meaningless."

"I've heard all this already," she responded tonelessly.

"Then hear it again." He raised his head and looked at the

253

slim, taut back turned resolutely against him. "I want you to be my wife. I want you to marry me."

"No!"

"Yes! Oh God, why won't you say yes?"

"Because I don't want to marry you, David. Can't you understand that?" Now she turned back to face him, impatiently beating a tattoo on the doorknob with her fingers. "We've had this conversation so many times before—"

"Twice before."

"Well, it seems like a dozen times to me—always the same thing, over and over again. I accept that you love me. I wish that you didn't. And that's all there is to be said. Now will you go?"

He gave a shake of the head and stayed where he was, looking miserably down at his clasped hands.

"David—" she began again, a last-straw note of exasperation in her voice. Oh, why wouldn't he give up this pestering? Why couldn't time be turned back to last summer when they'd still been as brother and sister together, enjoying the trust of a loving friendship—and nothing more. What was it about her life that it attracted complication? Just when one batch of problems had been solved at last, here was another presenting itself to vex her.

"David—"

"Is it because of Louisa? Because of the way she died?" He turned to look towards her over his shoulder. "Is that why you're refusing me?"

"I don't wish to talk about that. I just want you to leave."

"There have been letters, you know. Unsigned. Spiteful, malevolent letters, accusing me of murdering her . . . arranging her death to make it seem an accident." It was as though he were suddenly speaking to himself now. "I thought they'd cease once the inquest finding was made known. But I'm still getting them . . . saying I killed her, saying I wanted her out of the way."

Amy remembered the one similar letter she'd received here at Tea Garden Lane, and felt a momentary twinge of conscience at the doubts she, too, had entertained about the cleanness of David's hands in the business.

As though sensing what was passing through her mind, he said loudly, "I swear before God, I had nothing to do with it.

I was here in Lewes with you, my sweet. I was here with you when it happened."

Before she could stop herself, she was answering, "That's as may be. But I seem to recall you spoke very wildly about putting her away—"

"But I only meant divorce! To put her away by divorce. That was all I intended. In heaven's name say you believe me!"

"So that was it? A separation? Nothing more?"

"No, nothing. Oh, I'd wished Louisa dead a hundred times, I admit it. But I'd never have harmed her. In all the years of our marriage, I struck her only once—and I confess it to my shame—when she'd driven me near mad with her constant jealous harping about you."

"I don't doubt she had good reason." This was said in an oddly self-depreciating tone, as though prompted by some residue of guilt.

Noting it, he said quickly, "You mustn't blame yourself, my love. You were never at fault—"

"Except once. I shouldn't have let you stay that night— just as I shouldn't be letting you stay again now. Better I'd shut the door in your face. I'd have been spared all this."

"Spared what? The trouble of having to see me again?"

"The trouble of having you in love with me, David! If I hadn't given you shelter and comfort the night we spent together here, we'd be having none of this now."

"None of what?" He was being deliberately obtuse.

"None of this ridiculous talk of marriage."

"For one so lovely, you can be very cruel when you wish, Amy."

"I'm being cruel to be kind. Now for the last time, will you please go?"

She held the door wider, one hand on her hip in an attitude of open impatience.

From down in the lower part of the house, there could be heard a faint cheerful singing as Minnie went about her work. She had been singing a lot in the few days since they'd returned from Heathbury and her repertoire was becoming repetitive.

Slowly, David got up from the sofa.

255

"I'm not leaving until you've promised me something."

"And what's that?"

He hesitated before making an answer, looking at her with a kind of mistrustful appeal, as though fearing the response might but give him further hurt.

"Perhaps it's a little too soon," he said at length, heavily. "Perhaps I've been too hasty with you, dearest. In such a short while so much has happened. Yes, perhaps that's it . . . I've been too hasty, expecting more than you're ready yet to give."

The tattoo began again upon the doorknob. "David, whatever it is you have to say—"

"Oh, won't you give me time?"

There was something so piteous in his sudden cry that Amy's fingers were stilled and a small frown crept between the straight, dark brows.

"Only a little time, my darling? I would give you all the time there is in the world, should you but ask for it."

Against her better judgement she acquiesced, abruptly pushing the door shut behind her and moving away to face him. The morning sunlight from the window spilled across the room on to her features, burnishing the corn-gold hair and gilding the creamy lustre of her skin. But there was no corresponding warmth in the eyes that regarded him, only resignation and perhaps a touch of regret.

"Well?"

The doctor reached out a hand. "Won't you come here and sit beside me?"

"No. Whatever you have to say, I can hear perfectly well where I am."

"Oh, why are you being so hard, my sweet? And don't look at me in such a manner—as though you utterly disliked me. Where has all that love gone which not so long ago we shared together?"

Amy closed her eyes and drew in a breath; then released it again on a heavy sigh. This was a conversation which could chase itself around in circles all day, and still resolve nothing between them.

Looking at him again, she made an effort to soften her expression and asked quietly, "What was the promise you wanted?"

256

He essayed a bleak smile in response. "That you'll think over my proposal. Give it consideration. Please?"

"David, there's no point. My mind's made up. Won't you accept that?"

"Change your mind!"

"I can't."

"Why not?"

A shrug.

He pressed her again. "Damn it, why not?"

She half-turned away, to look out across the stable roof-line to the green spires of trees etched against the paint-box blue of the sky.

"I owe you nothing," she said flatly. "The debt of friend-ship has been paid, I think. I'm sorry I can't make the promise you want from me. My answer will still be the same, whether you ask me again tomorrow, or next year. I *don't* want to marry you, David. I *don't* want to be your wife. And that's all there is to it."

"No! There's more than that. Far more. I have loved you with a greater devotion than you could ever dream of, and I shall always love you so. I deserve better of you than this, Amy—to be tossed aside upon the scrapheap of your past to make way for some arrogant Johnny-come-lately like Ralph Herriot."

A truculent note was starting to make itself heard in the doctor's words as his voice rose jealously.

"If you cannot find it in you to promise you'll be mine, then at least let me have the satisfaction of knowing you'll never betray my love in the arms of a man like that."

"Now you're being absurd."

"Oh, absurd, am I? Absurd to want you so much that it's breaking my heart just to be here together in the same room and not hold you against me? Absurd to consider I'd be better off dead than living only half a life without you?"

"Don't raise your voice—"

"Oh, I'll raise more than my voice, sweet heart, if I lose you now. I'll raise all hell itself, you'll see."

She swung back to face him. "What do you mean?"

"I mean this." David seemed to be deliberately working himself up into a frenzy of bitter frustration. "If *I* cannot be the one to have you, Herriot certainly won't be. I'll make sure of that. Think now, he'd hardly want to handle tarnished second-hand goods, would he?"

Amy's cheeks paled as she realised the threat these words implied.

"You wouldn't . . . no—you wouldn't dare!"

"Try me. Either you'll marry me. Or I'll make certain that gentleman learns every last intimate detail of the night you allowed me into your bed. The choice is entirely yours, my darling. But either way, you'll never be Ralph Herriot's wife. Never."

26

It had been on a cold, raw morning in November over twenty years before that Rosannah Weldrake had married Frank Flynn here in the church of All Souls, Lewes. Isabelle Bethway remembered it well; and in part with a special affection, for that was the day she had first met the young curate who was to become her beloved husband, Alec.

The weather was going to be kinder to Rosannah on this occasion, she thought, looking about her from her pew while waiting for the funeral service to start. The balmy summer morning brought scents of briar rose and woodbine drifting in through the open doors from the churchyard beyond, and shafts of sunlight streaming through the stained glass panels of the high windows spilled pools of jewel-rich colours across the aisles.

Casting her mind back to Rosannah's wedding day, Isabelle recalled what a disagreeable service that had proved: people crowding the pews merely to stare their fill at a bride who was flouting convention and class to marry her brother's young groom. Well, there would be no crowds here today to see the poor woman buried. In the fickle fashion of notoriety, no one remembered her now, or if they did, it was only as a name from the blurred memory of days long past.

Amy had wanted a simple, private funeral for her mother. Nothing gloomy, she insisted; and to that end, the church was free of the sombre effect of black crêpe drapes, and instead decorated freshly with sprays of white roses whose sweet perfume hung lightly about the oakwood bier before the altar. Amy herself was seated to one side, alone as she had wished. Not in prayer, her aunt noted, but in an attitude of reflection, eyes cast down as though her mind were far away elsewhere.

Not for the first time, Isabelle Bethway wondered whether she had done the right thing to interfere in her niece's private life by writing that letter to Bonningale. But *something* had to be done, as she'd said to Alec. It was all very well to mind her own business and keep out of the matter, but there were times when Fate required a helpful hand to steer it on to the right course; and this decidedly had been one of those times.

She leaned forward to see past her children Dinah and Kit along the neighbouring rows of pews. Then, not finding what she sought, turned to glance behind. Ah, yes, good, Henry Bashford and his wife Maria had arrived and were just seating themselves at the back of the church.

Isabelle smiled to herself, and with a little nod of the head settled contentedly to a few prayers of her own, thanking God that of his great goodness he'd granted a favourable answer to her request.

The service was over, the last faint vibrations of the organ now faded upon the quiet air, and her mother's body taken away to be interred in the family vault below.

The rest of the small funeral party had left the church to return to Tea Garden Lane; but Amy remained where she was. They could manage without her, she told her Aunt Belle; Minnie would look after them and ensure they had ample refreshment before their departure from Lewes.

"But won't you come with us?" Isabelle had urged her quietly. "As chief mourner you ought—"

"No!" The response had been quite definite. "No one is in mourning, Aunt Belle. Why, on a day like this it's a crime to be downcast and sad. I'm sure my mother would have wanted us to see her off in style. So, no long faces, please. Wherever she is, she's happier now than she ever was alive."

"Doubtless she is, my dear, as you say."

Isabelle placed a gloved hand on the slender shoulder and pressed it gently. At the same time, she had glanced along the aisle towards the porch and given a quick nod of indication to someone standing there, someone tall and broad-shouldered silhouetted darkly against the sunlight outside.

"Well, we shall see you again soon, hopefully," she had added. "You must come down to us for the harvest thanksgiving."

And then was gone.

Amy was hardly conscious of the receding footsteps. The warm soothing stillness of the church wrapped itself around her once more and she sank back into her thoughts.

Choose, David Linton had told her. But it was no real choice he offered: marry him or not, whichever course she took she was still the loser. She'd told him to go to the devil that day he'd called, so incensed by his selfish threat it was as much as she could do to keep her temper in check; and wisely he'd taken himself off home to Weatherfield and troubled her no more. Nor would do for the next four weeks, which was all the time she was allowed in which to consider her answer: yes or no.

The young woman bowed her head and closed her eyes. Strange how this place had affected her today. She'd never had much patience with religion, considering it fell between the stools of hypocrisy and superstition and—apart from those like her Bethway relations—seemed to attract the kind of folk who were all prunes and prisms, as Minnie would say. But there was something here, something indefinable, which had touched upon a deeply-buried nerve; and in her need, Amy had prayed she might somehow find the means to be delivered from her present difficulty.

The scent of roses seemed to grow stronger. Distractedly she wondered whether it might be the warmth inside the church; then realised that it was not roses but eau de cologne she could smell, and that there was someone behind in the aisle close to her.

She sat up and turned to look over her shoulder; and at once started visibly, her hand going to her breast, as she recognised the young man standing there.

"Oh! Oh . . . you!"

Ralph Herriot smiled, and said quietly, "Hello, Amy. How are you?"

She nodded. "I—I'm well, thank you. And you?" Then, without waiting for an answer, rushed on in a flustered whisper, "What are you doing here? I wasn't expecting to see you. I'd no idea you were in Lewes, even."

"I came with Maria and Henry. Look, shall we go out-side?" This was said with another smile, his hand reaching out in invitation. "It's deuced awkward, trying to hold a conversation in an empty church. Like talking in a public library."

Amy picked up her gloves and parasol and rose hurriedly to her feet, the pulse of her heartbeat drumming so loudly in her ears that it seemed to fill the silence with its sound. To see him again like this, so unexpectedly . . . she hadn't realised how much she had been missing him these past months; nor how fearful she was of liking him too well, since all the worse would be her hurt in losing him.

As they went along the aisle together, Ralph commiser-ated gently, "I was sorry to learn of your mother's death. Maria wrote from Bonningale to tell me of it."

"That was kind of her."

"Well, she knew I would wish to know."

He stood aside to let Amy pass in front of him through the porch door, adding as he did so, "My parents heard the news with regret, and ask to have their condolences conveyed."

"Thank you."

After the cool dim quietness of the church, the brilliance of the sunlit day outside was almost blinding, and the air seemed suddenly to be filled with a muted babble of noise from the streets of the town beyond.

Ralph took her by the elbow.

"Shall we walk a little way along?" he suggested, indicat-ing a side path leading by the wall of the clock tower into the old part of All Souls churchyard. "It will be as peaceful there as anywhere, I dare say."

She acquiesced, putting up her silk-fringed parasol and hoping that he would take the colour in her cheeks to be no more than a flush from the morning's warmth.

Closing the wicket-gate behind them, her companion pro-ferred his arm and when she had placed a hand upon it, began strolling with her at an easy pace between the clumps of sweetbriar and self-sown willowherb on either side the path. There was a tangible calm in this place, uninterrupted by the bustle of the world outside, even the pipe of birdsong in the leafy trees subduing the distant cries of market traders and the rumble of iron cart-tyres in the cobbled lanes.

For a while, neither spoke.

Then Ralph Herriot said lightly, "I saw your name mentioned recently."

"Oh—oh, did you?" Amy cast him a nervous glance from beneath the parasol.

"Mm. It appeared in a report of the inquest into Mrs Linton's death, in the *County Advertiser*."

"Yes. Yes, I thought you'd probably read of it in the newspapers."

"Is that why I've not received a letter these past few months? Because you were fearful of what my reaction might be?"

She gave a quick, guilty nod.

"I suppose you thought you'd rather queered the pitch with me, as the saying goes?"

There was a hint of humour in the young man's voice as he put this question; and emboldened by it, she responded, "To be honest, I did believe you'd think the worst . . . and, well, that it would mean the end of our friendship."

"I'm made of sterner stuff than that, I hope." He gave the hand on his arm a little squeeze, and went on, "Let us sit down, shall we?" nodding his head towards a bench off the path, harboured in the shade of an old table-top tomb whose railings were festooned with scented swags of wild woodbine.

"You weren't vexed to see my name linked with David Linton's?" Amy asked cautiously, seating herself at his side. Then, without giving time for an answer, heard herself hurrying on, her tongue tripping on the words in her haste, "I hadn't invited him to call on me that day, you know—truly I hadn't. I was just setting out from the house as he arrived. He insisted that he must speak to me. What was I to do? When I asked him to leave me be and go away, he began following and—"

"Amy . . ." Ralph moved her parasol aside so that he might see her face. "Amy, there's no need to explain. I know all this already."

She turned to look at him, lips parted in astonishment. Then, finding her voice again, repeated incredulously, "You *know*?"

He nodded. "Everything. So no apology, please. You

263

don't have any cause to defend yourself. You see, your aunt Mrs Bethway wrote to me recently—"

"Aunt Belle? Aunt Belle wrote to you?"

"Yes. Don't look so dumbfounded! She thought I should know how very grieved you'd been to think I might misunderstand your position."

"And what else?" The question was almost a cry. "What else did she write?"

"Well, she told me candidly of Doctor Linton's demands upon your friendship, and of your steadfast refusal to be drawn into further meeting with him until he should see the folly of his behaviour."

There was a pause; then—"I must admit, Amy dear, that letter removed a weighty load from my heart. So when I learned that my sister and her husband were attending your mother's funeral here today, I resolved to come with them, to see you again and ask your pardon for the jealous doubts I had of you."

"*You* ask *my* pardon—"

Suddenly she was very near to tears, and had to avert her head while she fought to control them, chiding herself bitterly for a moment's foolish hope that her secret had already been uncovered and was now forgiven, releasing her from the burden of its guilt. Ralph had claimed that he knew everything; but that could not possibly be, since there was one thing which she and David Linton shared alone, and neither had betrayed . . . at least, not yet.

Oh, why not admit the whole thing now and be rid of it, she asked herself miserably. At best, Ralph might react by showing pity for someone who had fallen by the wayside of respectability; and at worst, could but treat her with honest scornful contempt and sever all further connection.

"Amy?"

The young man beside her reached out a hand and turned her chin towards him, about to pass some light remark upon her silence; but seeing the distress in her lovely face, checked himself and instead said quietly, "Oh, what a boor I am. Forgive me. I shouldn't have come here to trouble you, not today while your grief is still so fresh."

She bit her trembling lip and took a deep breath, then shook her head, not trusting herself to answer.

"I'm sorry," he said again. "You must think me a most insensitive clod. The fact is, my dear, I was so impatient to see you . . . there's such a lot I want to say. Listen, can we not meet again, soon? I am staying at Bonningale until Saturday—no, better still, I shall be in Heathbury on Friday. There's some business I have there at the Corn Exchange. Why not come with me? Do say you will. We can have luncheon together, and I'll tell you all the news of Sutton Bassett—oh, and yes, I almost forgot—I've brought for you the signed copy of Mr Hardy's *Tess* which I promised."

All this was said in such a warm and genuinely considerate fashion that Amy felt the tears closer than ever. She ducked her head, pretending to brush an imaginary thread of cotton from her dark skirts. Why not accept—why not go with him to Heathbury, she told herself despairingly. At least it would be a little chance of happiness, a final chance . . . something to remember in the lonely times to come.

Heathbury's Corn Exchange occupied one side of the town square and provided an elegant vista from the top of the high street, a large stone building in the style of a Doric temple whose cornice was surmounted by the figure of Ceres, goddess of agriculture.

Ralph Herriot raised his cap to wipe the sweat from his brow, and nodded towards it.

"Handsome, isn't it? I've always admired the way they built in the good old days. Honest plainness. None of the frilly trimmings you see on these endless rows of terraces they've cluttered the towns with of late."

Dodging behind the wheels of a hansom cab, he steered Amy across the wide cobbled square, crowded with vehicles lined side by side at the horse rails, and through the massively-pillared portico of the 'Change into the cool interior.

Here the young farmer paused a moment to get his bearings; then began looking about him, craning his head to see along the busy aisles.

"Ah, there's the fellow I want." He took his companion by the elbow, raising his voice to make himself heard above the hubbub of trading. "This way. Come on—"

The further end of the main hall had been partitioned off to make a refreshment area for the dealers' wives and families, and children were running up and down between the trestle tables shrieking noisily, in total disregard of their mothers' cries of reproval. Several dogs added their own activity to the scene, scattering in a flurry of feathers a few bold chickens which had found their way in to peck beneath the tables.

In the roof overhead, iron girders provided perches for innumerable pigeons whose lime and moulted feathers lay mixed with the spilled grain and sawdust on the stone slabs far below. By chance design, this perch-pattern was repeated in the rows of wooden stands dividing the floor of the 'Change into alleys where each chandler had his individual pitch, with a selection of corn or horse fodder or whatever grain was his speciality, before him in pound sample-bags from which prospective buyers might scoop a handful to gauge its quality and "nose".

While Ralph was occupied in business, Amy distracted herself by wandering about the aisles, her attention caught here and there by pairs of men engaged in the time-honoured custom of slapping each other on the backs of the hands, the traditional sign of good faith used by country dealers to seal their bargains.

Ralph Herriot likewise observed this ritual at the conclusion of trade, having argued down the other's price to a mutually agreeable figure; and well pleased with the transaction, came over to where Amy was now waiting and told her cheerfully, "D'you know, my dear, you remind me of Bathsheba Everdene at Casterbridge cornmarket."

"Do I?" It took her a moment or so to realise that the reference was to one of Mr Thomas Hardy's heroines.

"Mm. I can't quite recall the quotation exactly, but it was something to the effect that she walked as a queen among the gods of the fallow."

The young man cast a hand about him to indicate the dealers at their pitches; then turning back to his companion, held out his arm, and with a glance at the moon-faced clock set in the far wall of the 'Change, said, "I hope you've an appetite. I'm told they provide an excellent luncheon at The Swan just across the square."

Without waiting for an answer, he conducted her back again out through the portico into the blinding brightness

266

of the sun-burnished day, and keeping within the shade of the buildings, strolled leisurely at her side towards their destination, talking with great enthusiasm of his plans for the new season's farming at Sutton Bassett.

Amy was grateful that she was not expected to add much to the conversation. All morning, since Ralph had been at the station to meet her from the Lewes train, she'd felt very much on edge; and try as she might to feign an appearance of ease, the hidden stresses of a fretful conscience made this a brittle facade which threatened to crack apart before the day was ended.

During luncheon she managed a determined effort to respond to her companion's good humour, and for a while even succeeded in raising her spirits enough to seem something like her usual confident lively self. But by the time they'd finished their meal and left The Swan, that earlier sense of hopelessness was waiting to steal upon her once more.

Ralph had previously suggested he drive her back to Lewes himself in the buggy he'd borrowed from Henry Bashford.

"Trouble? It's no trouble," he insisted now, in response to Amy's reluctance to put him to such a journey. "The horse is a good one, and fresh. And I can rest him again in Lewes before starting away to Bonningale."

"But—"

"No buts!" He held up a hand. "It's high time someone took you in charge, Amy Flynn, and put an end to this confounded stubbornness of yours. I'll convey you home to Lewes against your will if I must—and that's all to be said on the matter."

She had not the strength of mind to argue.

They had driven perhaps six miles out of Heathbury and had started climbing up into the cooler air of the Downs, when the smooth trotting rhythm of their horse altered pace and began to falter.

"Whoa, there. Whoa."

Ralph Herriot halted the buggy at the side of the deserted road, and handing the reins to Amy, jumped down to see what was amiss with the animal.

"Probably picked up a stone," he said. "There were a lot of flint chippings scattered back there on the hill."

He bent to examine each hoof in turn, gripping the fetlock between his knees to keep it steady; and after a minute or two announced, "Ah, here it is. Here's the culprit. Reach into my pocket, would you—" indicating the tweed jacket lying behind the driver's seat—"and pass me my jack-knife?"

She complied, watching him roll up his shirt sleeves before bending again to prise the flint free of its lodging.

"There—"

Flinging the stone aside, the young man re-folded his knife with a firm click and handed it up to her again; then stood back to watch the way the horse placed its weight on the hoof.

"Walk him forward a few steps."

A pause.

"Hmm. Still a touch tender. Best rest him for a bit before we go on. Give the discomfort chance to wear off."

He rolled down his sleeves once more and buttoned the cuffs, then held out a hand to his passenger.

"Would you care to stretch your legs, may be? Here—give me the reins. I'll hook them over the dashboard."

He caught her by the arm as she got down from the buggy step, and without releasing his grasp pulled her gently against him and put the other arm about her shoulder to lead her off the road a short way to the low knapped-flint wall edging its winding course towards the distant heat-shimmer of the horizon.

Turning, he rested his back against the stones and held her by the waist in front of him.

For a little while neither said anything. In the silence between them, the soft soughing of the upland breeze could be heard whispering among the clumps of whin and heather, and the clear, sweet song of larks sounded all about in a glissade of notes falling from the cloudless curve of heaven.

Amy closed her eyes, yearning for the peace and beauty of this stolen moment to last for ever; and the dark eyelashes trembling against the creamy warmth of her skin gave her such an innocent vulnerability that before he could stop himself, Ralph Herriot had leaned forward and kissed her

268

lightly upon the lips. It was only the merest touch before he drew back, a quizzical look on his face as he waited to observe her reaction.

She opened her eyes again; and there was nothing of displeasure or vexation there, just a terrible sadness, as though she had lost something more precious to her than life itself.

He put a finger beneath her chin and tilted her face to his.

"What is it, Amy? What are you afraid of? Don't you wish me to kiss you?"

There was no answer, though he had the strongest feeling that she wanted to say something. He kissed her gently again; and this time the warm lips quivered a little and parted, before she thrust him suddenly away from her, crying, "No, Ralph! No! Don't!"

"But why not? Where's the harm in it? I love you, Amy. There, damn it—now I've confessed to it. I love you. And I want you for my wife."

There was an instant's glimpse of something joyous in her face before it was replaced by the most distraught expression he had ever witnessed in a woman.

"Did you not hear me?" he repeated, reaching out to hold her again. "I want you for my wife. And don't push me off like that! What, have I now become offensive to you? If so, how am I at fault?"

"No—no—the fault isn't yours, Ralph. It's mine—mine—mine—" In a sudden burst of despair, Amy began beating herself upon the breast, repeating the word over and over again.

He caught at her hands and tried to calm her.

"Hush, now, hush. What is it? You must tell me."

"I cannot!"

"But why?"

"You would only hate me for it."

"Hate you? Sweet heart, what's this you're saying? How could I ever hate you, when I love you so?"

"Oh, if you knew the truth, you wouldn't love me . . . You wouldn't want to take such as me to soil your marriage bed . . ."

Her voice faltered and broke, and there were tears welling in her eyes as she raised her head to look at him.

"Do I have to say it aloud, Ralph . . . must I add further to my shame?"

For long moments he stared back at her, reading the confession in those anguished features; and a look of unutterable sorrow passed across his face.

Then the bitter-cold anger of disappointment possessed him, and he said harshly, "Which man was it—Linton, I suppose?"

Amy nodded dumbly.

"When?"

"January . . . only once . . ."

"Only once? And were you willing?"

She shook her head.

"What, you mean he took advantage of you?"

Another silent nod.

The young man wheeled away to stare sightlessly out across the deserted miles of downland. Damn David Linton! Damn him! God, if he could but get his hands on him at this moment—!

He leaned forward and rested his fists on the flinty wall, bowing his head between his shoulders.

Then, for some inexplicable reason, he found the name Angel Clare intruding suddenly into the burning turmoil of his anger, and it took him a while to realise that it was *Tess of the D'Urbervilles* he was thinking of: the poignant scene in which Tess confesses her wretched past to her husband Angel—a fallen angel himself, as Hardy inferred by the name—but instead of forgiveness, finds only the age-old message "it is the woman who pays".

Ralph Herriot thrust his fingers through a heavy strand of curling chestnut hair that had fallen forward over his forehead. He straightened himself up with a deep breath.

After a few moments he turned slowly round again, and making an effort to keep the bitterness from his voice, said, "What happened? Tell me. I must know."

"Everything?"

"Everything!"

Nervously, Amy began to speak; awkwardly at first, with many hesitations, then gradually with more determination, feeling a kind of dull relief that she was able to purge herself of this burden at last.

270

When she had finished, there was a long pause before Ralph said tensely, "Why could you not have told me all this before? Why? I would have made him pay for what he did to you. As God is my witness, I would have made him pay for such an act of desecration—"

"It wasn't desecration!" she cried out, hating the brutal image conjured by that word. "David needed me . . . and I was weak . . . too weak to turn him from my door . . . too weak to refuse what he begged of me. Believe me—oh, believe me, please, what took place that night had no rhyme or reason to it. It was a senseless folly. I acted out of pity, nothing more. And this is my punishment . . . to have you Ralph, you, the man I care for most, spurn me with the heel of his contempt."

"I am not spurning you!"

He pulled her roughly against him.

Then, in a kind of desperate self-anger, he went on, "Oh, Amy, Amy, are we such hypocrites, all of us, that we must needs take up the stones of middle-class hypocrisy to fling at those who stumble because of the mote in their eye—and we so blinded by the beam in our own we can scarcely see to aim? Who am *I* to judge *you*, for God's sake? Look at me—look! Twenty-six years old, a healthy, normal man with a healthy, normal appetite. D'you suppose I've lived like a monk all my life? D'you suppose curiosity has never tempted me into an affair or two of my own? You talk of being spurned as a punishment for what you did. But it was not your fault! It is seldom any woman's fault—I know that from my own experience. Oh Amy, what's past is over and done with, so where's the use in recrimination and bitterness? It'll profit us nothing to keep looking back over our shoulder for the rest of our lives."

Her tears brimmed over and ran in glinting streams down her cheeks.

"Do you mean all this?" she asked brokenly. "Do you truly mean you aren't holding me to blame . . . that I'm forgiven—"

Ralph silenced the words with a kiss, harder this time than the first, tasting the saltness on her lips and the lingering fragrance of strawberries in her mouth. As his arms tightened strongly about her to press her closer against him, he felt her respond, quickening in answer to his passion with an eagerness that thrilled him.

Like a butterfly in a clumsy hand, she had struggled against David Linton and escaped again to freedom; and in spite of everything, Ralph could almost find it in him at this moment to pity the man for losing so precious and lovely a creature.

"Will you marry me, Amy my darling?" he whispered again after a time. "Will you be my wife?"

There was no need for words. Her kisses told him everything.